ANSTEY HARRIS

WHERE WE BELONG

**SIMON &
SCHUSTER**

London · New York · Sydney · Toronto · New Delhi

First published in Great Britain by Simon & Schuster UK Ltd, 2020
This paperback edition published 2021

1 3 5 7 9 10 8 6 4 2

Simon & Schuster UK Ltd
1st Floor
222 Gray's Inn Road
London WC1X 8HB

Simon & Schuster Australia, Sydney
Simon & Schuster India, New Delhi

www.simonandschuster.co.uk
www.simonandschuster.com.au
www.simonandschuster.co.in

A CIP catalogue record for this book
is available from the British Library

Paperback ISBN: 978-1-4711-7386-8
eBook ISBN: 978-1-4711-7385-1
Audio ISBN: 978-1-4711-7519-0

Typeset in the UK by M Rules
Printed and bound in Great Britain by CPI Group (UK) Ltd, Croydon, CR0 4YY

MIX
Paper from
responsible sources
FSC® C020471

'An incredibly moving and atmospheric novel, as beautiful and complex and curious as the museum in which it is set' **Beth O'Leary**

'Absorbing, powerful and lovely. This book swept me away and then brought me home' **Milly Johnson**

'A perfectly crafted novel: beautifully written, insightful and tender – it's simply stunning' **Fionnuala Kearney**

'I was completely swept along by the wonderful storytelling. This is an emotional story, heartbreaking in places, but joyful and uplifting' **Susan Elliot Wright**

'This beautifully written novel is not only absorbing and original, it will challenge preconceptions in the very best way' **Katie Fforde**

'A book as rare and exquisite as the objects in Hatters museum . . . I could not look away for a moment' **Kate Furnivall**

'Such a beautifully written and engrossing novel' **Jacqueline Ward**

'Original and atmospheric . . . an enchanting tale of families, secrets and lies with an exquisite love story running through it' ***Daily Express***

'A beautifully warm-hearted story for these times' ***Heat***

'Gorgeous storytelling . . . I loved this joyful book about friendship, happiness and finding your passion in life' ***Good Housekeeping***

'Anstey Harris doesn't flinch from shining a light on some of the most difficult situations anyone can face, but she does it with warmth and compassion' ***Woman & Home***

'Harris, with her crew of colourfully offbeat characters, navigates beautifully through the choppy waters of guilt, heartbreak and redemption' ***Daily Mail***

'Moving and carefully crafted, this is a novel with true hope at its heart' ***Woman's Own***

Anstey Harris teaches creative writing in the community with her own company, Writing Matters. She has been featured in various literary magazines and anthologies, been shortlisted for many prizes, and won the HG Wells Short Story award. Anstey lives in Kent, UK, and is the mother of the singer-songwriter Lucy Spraggan. Her debut novel *The Truths and Triumphs of Grace Atherton* was a Richard and Judy Book Club pick for 2019 and won the Romantic Novelists' Association Sapere Books Popular Romantic Fiction Award.

Also by Anstey Harris

The Truths and Triumphs of Grace Atherton

For Wilfred, who was ready at the same time as this book, and for Gordon, Charlie and Tom who inspire us every day with their courage and strength

Note on the Powell–Cotton Museum

I first fell in love with the Powell–Cotton Museum, in Birchington, Kent, when I was three years old. Back then it was a magical zoo, one where the animals never duck out of sight or hide in the back of their cages. I accepted Major Percy Powell-Cotton's Victorian ideas of conservation in the spirit with which they were meant and, much as he'd intended, I learnt about Africa and Asia, about wild animals, and about other lifestyles and cultures from his exhibits. Percy Powell-Cotton put his collection together with an, albeit misguided by modern standards, ecological intention. He wanted the people of Kent to see these animals in their natural habitat and to understand the importance – and the potential – of the wider world.

In 2012 I moved back to Kent, where I grew up, and my love affair with the house, museum, and gardens rekindled. I was lucky enough to meet Susan Johnson, Percy's great-granddaughter, who told me so much more of the incredible stories behind her family and their legacy and it was that deeper knowledge that made me determined to write about a fictional version of the Powell–Cotton Museum, its grounds, and its collections.

Percy Horace Gordon Powell-Cotton was born in 1866 and established his museum in 1896, adding the animal specimens and cultural objects to collections his family had begun a century before. Consequently, the collection is one of the most diverse and interesting in Europe: from Napoleon's childhood drawings, to a canon from the Mary Rose.

Percy met his wife, Hannah, when she was appointed to help him with his papers and journals. They embarked on a trip – part African expedition, part honeymoon and married in Nairobi Cathedral. There is a theory (and one I very much favour) that Edgar Rice-Burroughs first got the idea for Tarzan and Jane from a newspaper story about Percy and Hannah and their life in the wilds. As Andrew Joynes writes in his biography *Tracking the Major*, 'there are a number of themes common to Hannah's tabloid account of her real-life jungle honeymoon and the setting of the Tarzan story. It is a startling coincidence that Tarzan, the jungle child, was the heir of the Greystoke family: Hannah's husband, the Major, had been the heir of Quex.' and that Hannah herself had collaborated on an article headed 'Keeping House in the Boundless Wilds' for the British Press.

There are so many wild and wonderful stories in the Powell-Cotton Museum: of Percy narrowly escaping death from a lion attack because of a rolled-up copy of *Punch* in his pocket; of his daughters – as a doctor and a nurse – accompanying him on many trips at a time when women

did nothing of the kind; or the soldiers who came to conva-
lesce at Quex, following injuries in the First World War. As
Joynes reports in his biography: 'The next morning Diana
and Mary found some fifty wounded Belgian soldiers laid
out in rows in front of the wildlife dioramas in the African
galleries. Mute with morphine, traumatised by battle, the
men gazed at the elephant, and the aardvark, the rhinoceros
and the forest pig.'

Please do try and visit the Powell-Cotton Museum in its
home on the Quex Estate in Birchington-on-Sea. Although
you might not find Cate and Leo, a chapel or a domed
library, you will find boundless magic and wonder.

Tracking the Major, Andrew Joynes, 2016, is published by
Mickle Print (Canterbury) Limited.

WHERE
WE
BELONG

Chapter One

A house absorbs happiness, it blooms into the wallpaper, the wood of the window frames, the bricks: that's how it becomes a home. The people in it are movable, exchangeable: one set of hugs and shouts and words of love easily swapped for another. I am packing up our lives into cardboard boxes, folding away that happiness, those memories. It makes me want to turn to someone, anyone, and talk about Leo's paintings, old gig tickets of Richard's, postcards sent to me by friends, but it's just me – all alone with the shriek of the tape gun as it zips up the boxes.

Everything is changing: the school term ended yesterday – my last term as a teacher, at least in the job I've been in for over twenty years. I am 'redundant': I don't know yet how far into my life that word will stretch, how many parts it will cover. I am also – much more concerning as it involves my son every bit as much as it does me – homeless.

Leo has gone swimming with our neighbour and her

daughter. The boxes and the bubble wrap have been making him feel unsettled. He'd be far worse if he'd seen the emails and the letters, but they're my responsibility – and mine alone. There is a special anger that comes with impotence; with the basic failure to provide for your family. It is worse when that failure is caused by someone else, someone who had promised to be there and to help and to share the burden, someone who hasn't upheld their side of that bargain.

Instead, I think, I'm supposed to be grateful that Richard's family have offered us a place to go.

The offer is grudging. There have been letters backwards and forwards from solicitors. There have been emails of questions that are never answered, at least, not in any straightforward way: no promises, no reassurance. I have googled and searched, I have looked on maps and at faded postcards, but there's very little information to be found about 'Hatters Museum of the Wide Wide World'. Today is the day that I finally get to speak to the 'old family retainer', to inform her that we'll be joining her at the museum – or at least in the apartments above it – for the whole of this summer: until I find a new job and a new home for my son and me.

I've said I'll ring at noon. Leo and I had a late breakfast – now that my schedule isn't a daily drama of juggling school and home, and trying to get us both out of the door on time, I can do that – so I'm not hungry yet. Instead, I've made a coffee and set it down on a packing box marked 'dining room, unnecessary'. Already I've forgotten what's in that box or why I've kept it if it's 'unnecessary'. I found some biscuits at the back of a kitchen cupboard earlier: they're out of date but unopened. I test one on my teeth and they're fine so I'll have a couple with my coffee. That'll see me through till teatime when Leo gets home and I have to cook for both of us.

I arranged to call today because the landline is disconnected at midnight and then I'll only have my mobile. It's strange that I won't have the same number that I've put down on forms and contact sheets for the last ten years. As I understand it, I won't have a number of my own at all – apart from the mobile. It makes me feel unsettled: I'm not from the generation that exists solely through cell phones. What if I can't get a signal?

I have no way of knowing whether there's a signal in the house or not, or how isolated it is: Richard mostly refused to discuss his family home and I certainly can't ask him now. He hated the place and so we've never even visited: he said it's cold and draughty and miserable.

I've been curious over the years – and especially since Richard went – but one thing and another, and real life, and work and responsibility have conspired to keep me away. Almost every weekend for the last few years, I've intended to throw Leo in the car and go and look at this place, at Richard's childhood and Leo's inheritance, but it's never worked out that way. In London, we have had too many friends to see, too many things to do, too many full and happy weekends. In my mind's eye, in a sketch drawn from his very limited descriptions, it is gothic and decrepit, overgrown and covered in clinging spidery ivy; dotted with grey panes of glass that stare like blind eyes onto rusted iron gates at the end of the drive. Where we live now, in the heart of a London that is steadily being gentrified, there are lots of strange old buildings – hospitals, schools, fire stations, that have been converted into flats – and they're all gorgeous. How bad can it be?

I sit on the sofa and take a sip of my coffee while the phone rings through. I bite the first half of one of the biscuits and the rhythmic tone at the end of the line continues. I dip the second half into my coffee, shake the drips over the cup and eat the biscuit. Still no answer. I wonder if there is a limit to how long a phone line will ring for and picture a tiny old lady, slightly confused and wearing pink slippers, scurrying through passageways to answer it.

I put most of the second biscuit in my mouth and bite through it. A crumb dislodges and goes the wrong way down my throat. By the time the phone is answered, my eyes are streaming and my voice sounds like something that runs on cogs.

'Hatters Museum of the Wide Wide World.' The voice does not sound elderly, or like it might wear the slippers I'd imagined the old lady hobbling through the corridors in.

'Hello.' I clear my throat. Twice. 'This is Cate Morris.'

'Cate Morris?'

This call has been booked, via communication with the

4

solicitor. She knows I'm due to ring at noon, and it's exactly that now. I grit my teeth. 'Richard's wife, Cate.'

'Richard Lyons-Morris?'

'We dropped the Lyons.' I say it quietly, as if I shouldn't be saying it at all, as if she's going to tell me off.

I'd known Richard for two years before I found out his surname was Lyons-Morris, not just plain old Morris. 'I hate it,' he'd said. 'Everyone says "lions" like the animal and it's "Lyons" like the city. I don't bother with it.' We compromised by calling our son Leo – Leo Morris instead of Lyons-Morris. She doesn't need to know this and I don't tell her.

'That's a great shame.' She sighs down the phone to make it clear that I've disappointed her already.

I make an effort to take back some ground. 'Is this Ms Buchan?'

'Yes.' She is utterly unapologetic.

'Ah, good. Only ... you didn't say.' As soon as I say it, I feel pathetic. My game of one-upmanship is obvious and crude. The biscuit crumbs start to tickle my throat again and I stifle a cough.

'We had arranged this call, therefore I assumed you would expect me to answer the telephone. I am, at present, the only person here.' She has taken the high ground and pauses in triumphant silence. 'Do you need to call back later? Are you quite well?' Her voice is clipped and curt: she isn't responding to my bout of coughing out of kindness – it's just annoying her.

'I'm sorry,' I say when I can speak. 'We seem to have got off on the wrong foot. Leo and I are very much looking forward to arriving at the museum tomorrow.'

'I'm sure,' she says. 'And I wish I could say that we'll put out a spectacular welcome for you ...' She pauses and I choose not to second-guess what she's going to say next: it is clearly a sentence that hinges around 'but'. 'But ...'

I roll my eyes although there is no one in the room to see me. This is like dealing with a difficult pupil – or worse, a difficult pupil's difficult parent. It always gets my back up. I wish people would say what they mean without resorting to excuses.

'I am almost the only person left here. Aside from a handful of volunteers in the house and garden, I am the last person working at Hatters. We are on our knees, I'm afraid.' She clears her throat. 'As a museum, at any rate.'

'To be honest, Mrs Buchan ...'

'It's Miss,' she says and her voice is sharp again.

'Sorry. To be honest, we're not really anything to do with the museum. We're merely making use of Leo's right to reside in the house. Because of his father. Because of Richard.'

Sometimes I find it hard to say Richard's name. Sometimes it chokes up my throat with such anger and blind injustice. Other times, it's bare self-pity and loneliness that brings the same, pointless, tears to my eyes. This time it's a mix of both: a frustrated longing to tell Richard what he's putting us through, what he's caused here in this boxed-up flat.

'That wasn't what I meant, unfortunately. My point was rather that it's the Museum Trust that keeps the entire building going. And that, I'm afraid, is at the point of collapse.'

The fear inside me is a physical pain – a stab of uncertainty. It is the pain caused by the barely stifled threat that has lived inside me every day for four years: the inability of a teacher to raise a family, without support, in the centre of a big city that is being swallowed up day-by-day by investors. Our rent has stayed almost stationary for nine years, ever since we first came here, since a friend of a friend first took pity on Richard and me and let us move in without the usual credit checks or deposits. Now, the value of the flat has escalated to a point where our landlord is doing his own family a disservice by continuing to prop up mine. He has to sell – and we have to move.

'The trustees have agreed that we can live there for the foreseeable future. I have it in writing.'

'I'm sure that is so.' Her speech is punctuated by deliberate pauses: it makes it difficult to work up to any vehement response. 'The trustees have granted you temporary residency – they have no choice but to do that – but they have neglected to inform you that they are also engaged in a committed campaign to close the whole museum and sell off the contents. Having you and Leo here will ...' The pause again. I wonder if she is licking her lips. 'Having you and Leo here will tip the delicate balance of managing on a shoestring over into complete liquidation.'

'I'm sure you can't simply sell museums. It belongs to

Richard's great-grandfather and he's dead.' There is an ache at the side of my temple and the first flashing lights of a migraine dance into the edge of my eye. 'The family have rights.'

'They do.' This is the longest pause. 'And you have the right to live here – with Leo – until such time as the museum closes, but it is not an exaggeration to suggest that that will be within the next six weeks.'

I have applied for twenty-five jobs since my redundancy was announced. Twenty-five teaching posts, all over London and even into the Home Counties, but I've been in the business for almost thirty years: my pay-scale is much higher than someone just out of college, newly qualified. I haven't had a single interview.

I'm not about to start discussing the paralysing terror of my financial situation, of four years of single parenthood and its consequences, with this cold old woman: I am shocked into saying my goodbyes and telling her that we'll see her tomorrow. And then what?

The cardboard boxes, with their anonymous brown sides, tower around me, and the walls of the flat I have loved close in on me with a similar pressure: a low bitter wind starts to gust around the guttering glimmers of hope in mine and Leo's future.

Richard and I met at university. I was almost nineteen and halfway through my first year. He was twenty-four; a worldly and debonair PhD student, far more interesting than I was.

My boyfriend, Simon, was Richard's best friend. Simon and I had only been together a few weeks: we'd been to a couple of gigs together, spent a few evenings in the pub down by my halls and I liked him – I really did. Simon was tall, funny, and incredibly kind. I really thought that he and I would work, that we had potential. But then I met Richard.

The pub was hazy and dark. People still smoked indoors then and it gave everything an ethereal glow, at least until we smelled our hair and clothes in the morning. Simon and I were at a corner table. The jukebox was playing something old, country music from decades before: the pub was too London, too achingly cool, for pop music. We were deep in conversation, hands wrapped round our pint glasses, our feet touching under the table.

'Rich!' Simon half-stood and shouted across the bar. 'All right?'

The man he'd shouted to came over. I knew straightaway. I knew before he sat down, before he spoke. It was something utterly primal.

Richard had straight dark hair, and the deepest brownest eyes I'd ever seen. I see those same eyes every day now, and the same perfect white teeth in an enormous and constant smile. Leo's hair is as poker straight, as charcoal-black.

I remember moving my foot away from Simon's: an unconscious gesture. I wasn't that girl. I was young – new to this city, to being a grown-up. What I knew I was about to do was so out of character, so unlike me.

'Rich, this is Cate, my girlfriend.'

Rich put his hand out and shook mine. I looked into his eyes and knew that he felt exactly the same way.

I've always believed in honesty – there are a few, unusual and unfortunate, exceptions but I've lived most of my life by the principle that it's easier to tell the truth than lie – whatever the situation. I told Simon that night, as soon as we got in. I told him gently, and I told him long before Rich and I ever kissed, ever spoke about spending the rest of our lives together, about bringing another, much-wanted, tiny human into the world.

Simon and Richard stayed best friends: they widened their closeness to include me, and Simon has been an amazing godfather to Leo – going far beyond the reach of duty, especially in the final, traumatic, years with Richard, years I couldn't have navigated without him.

All of that is four years behind us now. Simon is in New Zealand, doing research. Leo and I are headed out into the Great Unknown, whatever that might bring.

I don't know where Richard is. And that, more than anything, is the hardest part.

My thoughts of Richard are so complicated, so impossible to separate out from one another. I try not to be bitter – my mother used to say that bitterness is like drinking poison and waiting for your enemy to die – and I try not to dwell between the twin despairs of 'why me?' and 'it's not fair'. No one set out for any of this to happen: not me; not Richard; and most of all, not Leo. And Leo has to stay the most important thing. I'm strict about wallowing and I'm strict about remaining positive – but sometimes I struggle.

All through our marriage, Richard was my best friend, and an amazing father. He knocked himself out trying to provide for us, trying to make us the perfect family: but so much of the time, he just couldn't make that work.

I was overwhelmed by the shuddering loneliness of living with someone with chronic depression. It's hard to stay sympathetic and sad and angry all at the same time, torn between meeting the needs of both the people you love. I held my breath for so long trying not to let Richard's illness impact on Leo, trying not to let Leo's day-to-day demands take too much of a strain on Richard. I once imagined there was nothing worse than being in charge all the time, the press-ganged pilot who navigated Richard's anxieties and worries and got him back onto even ground.

But then Richard killed himself and the sheer joy of being with him, the summer warmth of caring for someone, the human softness of his body, it all came flooding back. A spotlight of pain projected my loss in vivid relief: still does. I live with a Richard-sized hole in my life: almost a physical thing in the room we slept in; in the places we took Leo to; in the kitchen every day when I finish work. He isn't here and I don't know where he is.

All I know is how much I loved him.

Chapter Two

The gravel drive crunches a song of despair under the wheels of my car, each pop a painful reminder that we're inching towards this life we didn't ask for, and away from everything we ever had.

In the passenger seat, Leo has kept up a steady stream of 'Are we there yet?' punctuated only by a dirge of his friends' names repeated over and over to the tune of a horrible television advert. I'm trying not to shout at him, trying not to be an even worse parent than I already am. The strain of keeping quiet shows in my knuckles, wrapped tight white around the wheel.

'Are we there yet?' asks Leo, one more time.

This time, with my heart in my mouth, I have to answer, 'Yes.'

'Eric? And Sadie? And Ollie? And Dean?' He's being deliberately obnoxious, believing that he can winkle a promise out of me if he's sufficiently irritating; a chafing grain of sand that could grow, if Leo tries long enough, into, 'Yes, all your friends are here, they're going to jump out and shout surprise and we'll both go back to our real lives.' Lives we both, in most ways, loved. And that's the most bitter thing about love; you can't understand it, measure it – not all its edges and intricacies – until it's gone and the clear print of its negative self is left behind.

Evidence of the house is everywhere, though the house itself is still out of sight: a faded sign on the main road pointed us down a lane that became a gated tunnel of green leaves – hopeful spatters of lime-coloured light landing on the bonnet of the car. There were stone pillars either side of what must have once been a magnificent gateway, bridges in the classical Greek style that have long since lost the fountains that played over them or the ponds they led into. A quarter of a mile or so down the lane, it peters out into this long tree-lined drive, the sound of gravel, and the uneasy feeling of regret.

Each side of the drive, aspen trees wave us on. They are so overgrown that their tops mingle with each other, forming a hedge high in the air. Their trunks are straight and bleak.

'Are we there yet?' says Leo.

'I said we are.' I want to stop the car – delay the inevitable – but the removal men in the van behind us are paid by the hour.

'There's no house.' Leo is sinking further down in his seat, scrunching his shoulders up and his head down, working up to full a meltdown.

I know how he feels. We've been driving for seven hours,

13

stuck in traffic for five of those, inching south down the M25 and grudgingly moving forward on the M20. I'm a Londoner. I belong in a place full of chattering people, of smells, sounds and tastes of multiculture, of dozens of nosy, self-absorbed villages strung together into one huge city. Leo had everything he needed in London. A club for every afternoon of the week while I finished work, sports teams and music lessons, art group and dancing. I had neighbours to step in and take him swimming if I was stuck, friends who could watch him at the drop of a hat if I wanted to go to the pictures or lie in a park and watch the clouds overhead by myself.

When people move, they say they're swapping something for something else: the bustle of the city for the bucolic countryside, the chill winter breezes of the seaside for the shores of southern Spain. Leo and I don't have the luxury of a swap. What we had has gone.

'I want to see Dean.'

'Dean's in London. Can you see the house yet?'

'I want to see Dean.'

There is nothing I can say. Leo doesn't like change, and he doesn't have the life experience to know that people move around, float by, stay sometimes or are gone: that there will be more people. I have that experience but my faith in it has disappeared.

There is a flash in the road, an amber streak across my peripheral vision at the bottom right-hand edge of the windscreen. The bump, when it comes, is more a noise than a feeling.

I stop the car and get out. I know I have hit something, I know it is an animal: a small soft creature versus the metal of my car bumper. Behind me, the removal van pulls over too.

The fox is lying by the side of the drive. It looks perfect except for the one angry gash on its pointed head, almost hidden by the way its tail curls around the small body, for all the world as if it is sleeping.

'Did the fox get run over, Mummy?' Leo has got out of the car. He is looking at the sad little corpse.

'It ran straight out in front of me,' I say and my voice cracks slightly. 'Poor thing.'

The fox doesn't look like foxes did in London. The foxes we're used to are coloured by the grey landscape, infected by the soot and the brick and the car fumes. This one is vivid orange, glossy and plump. We are used to mangy foxes with scratched-up fur, living out of bins: this one has had an altogether more organic diet.

'Oh, dear.' The oldest of the three removal men has climbed down from his van. 'Poor little bugger. Let's move him to the hedge.' He grabs a piece of old fabric from the cab of the van and uses it to protect his hands from the fur. 'There you go.'

I feel like I should say some words, stroke the still small ribs. I have never killed anything before.

'We do need to get on, Cate.' The removal man taps his watch. 'I've got to get that lot home for tonight.' He gestures towards his colleagues.

'Sorry, little fox,' I whisper. I am near to tears. I look in

15

the rear-view mirror as I drive away but his body is hidden by the green hedgerow.

One last curve in this dilapidated drive and the left-hand edge of the house breaks out of the trees. And then it keeps going. Across and across, window after window.

'Where's our house?' asks Leo.

This place looks like a hospital, or a boarding school, or – exactly what it is – a museum. 'This is our house,' I tell Leo.

'Daddy's house?' This is as much as Leo has grasped of where we are going – and to some extent it's true.

Richard's family have owned this house for two hundred years, since they built it. My blood runs cold when I think what might have happened if it wasn't here, if there wasn't a trust still running it. I knew all along that the heir to the estate is entitled to live on the premises, although I never imagined a scenario where that might need to happen. Now, with every other avenue closed, we are here at the door.

I reach in my handbag for the solicitor's letter and the keys. The letter explains that Leo and I will have our own apartment but we will share the building and garden with the museum and its visitors. It's not ideal, but none of this is. We're supposed to be greeted by Mrs Buchan – although greeted seems unlikely to be the right word – but we're five hours late and she's probably gone home.

I dig into my bag a bit deeper. The keys aren't there. I'm not the sort of person to lose things, unless you count jobs, husbands, and homes. I don't lose keys or letters or small, ineffectual everyday details. I get out of the car so that I can tip my handbag onto the seat, but I know they're not there. Tissues and envelopes, Leo's asthma pump, my purse, the keys aren't there. They really aren't. And I checked at least ten times before we left, I checked once we were in the actual car.

'Leo?'

He's got out too, he's standing on the drive looking up at his ancestors' achievement.

'Leo, where are the keys? Did you take them out of my bag?'

Leo looks at his feet. 'Nope.'

And then I remember the new keyring, the shiny silver abacus that one of my work colleagues gave me as a leaving present and the way its tiny perfect beads slid from one end of the frame to the other. I remember how much Leo wanted to play with it and how I said he couldn't. And that's when I know that the keyring, and the keys, are in a lavatory stall at the M20 services.

It's one of those parenting moments, one where every fibre of you wants to shout, scream, even run away. But another part of you — almost always the dominant one — remembers that you can't. You're the grown-up. You can do this the easy way or the hard way. You can suck it up and deal with what you have or you can waste hours of your life on an exercise that will simply result in two of you crying instead of one. An inner part of me, one I ban and hide and silence, asks me whether Richard's version of parenting was the same and, it whispers in a voice I hate admitting to, 'Isn't that why we are where we are now?'

'Very impressive, Cate.' The oldest of the three removal men walks towards my car. 'Your furniture's going to rattle a bit in there.' Behind him, the others have pushed up the back of the van and are standing around – stretching out tense muscles, rolling cigarettes, waiting to unpack.

'It's a flat, two bedrooms. The rest is mostly empty. And I've lost the keys.' My angry inner voice adds, *I haven't lost the keys, Leo has*, but that's not going to help us right now. I smile at him, trying to disarm the fact that he thinks I'm an idiot.

'Are they in your bag?'

I'm still smiling, my face rigid with tension. 'I looked.'

'The car?'

Leo stops me from explicitly outlining my frustrations by throwing up on the gravel drive. Spatters of vomit moisten the dust on the removal man's boots.

When I've cleaned Leo up – and apologised profusely – things seem to have reached a new entente cordiale. The removal men are prepared to excuse my stupidity in the light of Leo's car sickness and the entire plaintive horror of the situation. They have started stacking boxes near the front door while I sink myself in the task of opening it.

The traffic jam has meant that the solicitor's office closed long before we got here. All the numbers I have for the museum and the estate office ring out and there don't appear to be any neighbours.

Leo is being entertained by the removal men – they are lovely with him. He's been allowed to sit in the cab although, since he confided in the youngest one, Frank, that it was him who lost the keys, they've turned the radio off and taken the keys out of the ignition. 'Just in case, mate,' they told him when he said he'd like to work the windscreen wipers a bit more.

'I reckon I can get in there.' Frank points to an upstairs window that's slightly ajar. The front door of the house is porticoed, two sandstone pillars flank the wide door, and a tumble of tangled vegetation grows round them. Here and there a wide purple flower turns its face to the sinking sun.

'Are you sure?' It's a long way up and seeing Frank break his neck would really finish the day off. 'And I don't know which window is which; you might end up in the actual museum.'

'We haven't got that much choice,' Philip, the oldest removal man says. 'It wouldn't be the first time we've had to take an alternative route in.'

'And there's an alarm,' I add, 'because of the museum. The instructions are here but the keypad is inside the front door. I doubt you'd get there in time.'

'The only certain thing,' Philip says, 'is that we can't stay here all night.'

'My tent is in one of the boxes,' Leo offers, both helpfully and hopefully.

'We won't get all these boxes in your tent, mate,' says Frank. 'Even if we could find it.'

The wide grounds in front of the house are edged with

railings rusted with age and weather. Once upon a time, they would have been painted an elegant white, now they are bent brown rails running around the edge of an overgrown field. I try to imagine the field full of carriage horses, resting their soft muzzles over the top rail, keeping the grass neat and clipped with their slow snuffled chewing. It's a million miles away from the reality. I don't know what I was thinking of, coming here, how I thought this could possibly be the answer to our homelessness, me losing my job. And now we are here, we can't even get in.

'Well?' says Frank, looking up at the window, two floors above us.

'I don't think you ought to.' I don't know what my alternative suggestion is. 'What about Health and Safety?' Years of school-teaching have left their mark on me.

'Beauty of working for yourself,' says Phil. 'And no witnesses.' He nods towards Frank, who starts to climb onto the wide green windowsill.

Leo spins round and round on the spot, his arms above his head. 'Frank's a superhero,' he shouts. 'Can I go up too?'

I can see Leo won't even be able to heave himself up to the windowsill that Frank now stands on, body flat against the window, arms splayed like a tightrope walker, so at least that's not one of my worries.

Frank reaches above him. There is a wisteria clinging to the front of the house, its twisted trunks long-dead and past flowering; twigs and wizened leaves drop down as Frank tries to get purchase over the window frame. The noise he

makes as he heaves himself from the windowsill to the flat
porch roof of the portico is loud in the silence of the drive.
This really is the countryside; the absence of cars, people,
sirens, all remarkable on the still air.

'Go on!' shouts Leo as Frank bicycles his legs for momen-
tum, his top half lying flat on the portico.

'You're nearly there, lad,' Phil says, and we both will
Frank's upper body to weigh more than his legs or he's going
to crash back down onto the drive in a way that he'd be
lucky to survive in one piece.

Below, Frank's white trainers waving in mid-air, the door
opens. It doesn't open wide, like someone is welcoming us
with expansive gestures or enthusiasm. It opens slightly,
with suspicion and unease.

'Can I help you?' The welcome isn't gracious but I'm
overwhelmed with relief that there's someone here.

'Miss Buchan?'

The sunshine is thrown onto her face in the gap of the
doorway. Her eyes wrinkle up against it. Her hair is short
and steel grey, her face unlined and powder soft. She is
small, thin, and angular.

'How nice to meet you properly,' I say, recognising one of
the moments when one must tell slight untruths.

'How do you do, Mrs Lyons-Morris?' She has the tone of
someone who is being inconvenienced.

Above her, Frank's legs have stopped flapping, his trainers
are peaceful, side by side, to the left of her head. It is not a
good start.

I'm sure Frank and Phil are hoping as hard as me that she hasn't noticed the legs, or the man on the porch roof.

'We dropped the Lyons,' I remind her. 'And this is Leo, Leo Morris.'

'Hello, Leo,' says Miss Buchan and steps out of the doorway. 'You look just like your daddy.'

I try to put an exact age on her but it's difficult: her clothes are tight and tweed, a short necklace of pearls sits neatly on her neck. She holds her slim hand out towards me, ready to shake my hand. She is somewhere between forty-five and seventy-five but then, so am I.

Her hand looks tiny in mine. My fingers wrap round hers and I feel like an oaf. I compensate by shaking her hand vigorously and she looks at me as if she'd rather I let go.

'You may call me Araminta,' she says in a cold flat voice and nods her head to show that she means both of us. 'I take care of the house and museum.' She says that mainly to Leo.

'I live here,' shouts Leo. 'And Frank. And Phil.'

As he says it, Frank lets go of the porch roof and half-slithers, half-falls into the drive next to Araminta.

'We couldn't get in,' Phil and I say at the same time, leaving a gaping void of silence afterwards.

'I lost the . . .'

'We were unloading . . .'

We sound like children and both stop trying to explain.

'Well, you're here now,' says Araminta, in a voice that shows how much that displeases her. 'Shall I show you to the apartment?'

'Are we going in my house?' asks Leo, and Araminta breaks the straight line of her grimace for the first time.

'Yes. This is your house. And it was your daddy's house too. He lived here when he was a little boy.'

I open my mouth to argue, to say that, no, Richard never lived here. His grandparents lived here but he hated the place and seldom came near it, but something in her face makes me stop. There's a sudden softness – directed at Leo, definitely, but more than that, beyond that. I wonder if she is old enough for it to be a memory of Richard.

I look at Leo standing by the door and imagine Richard on the same steps, his hair sticking up in the summer breeze, like Leo's does. I picture a boy-Richard running through the paddock opposite, climbing the iron-railed fences, swinging up the huge oak tree that spreads its green branches wide over the field. And, if he did come here often, will he have left any of himself behind?

Chapter Three

Inside, the house is grand. A staircase leads the eye away from the front door and breaks into two galleries running away from each other and around the top of the hallway. Hallway isn't really the right word – our whole flat in London would have fitted in this space, upstairs and downstairs – perhaps it won't be so bad after all. Maybe it has improved since Richard last came here.

The galleries that run out from the stairs like twin branches are – Araminta says as she rushes us through – open to the public. She didn't have to tell me: you couldn't possibly mistake this for a home, there are 'exit' and 'fire door' signs everywhere, red rope cordons hang on bronze pillars either side of the stair carpet. Nothing about it is homely but it's certainly grand. I can see portraits and antique furniture, display cases and statues. This is the worst of all environments for Leo: Leo who dances with his headphones on; Leo who runs headlong everywhere; Leo who loves football.

A door on the landing is marked 'private', it leads into a far narrower corridor. We pass door after door, but Araminta does not pause until we see a smaller staircase going up to the next floor. I can only assume this would have been the servants' quarters, once upon a time. The first two floors, or what I've seen of them so far at any rate, have oak-panelling along the lower halves of the walls and patterned paper above that. These walls are dark, mostly painted and, here and there, sections of some sort of hessian or sacking stuck up instead of wallpaper. Phil, following with the first box, whistles through his teeth.

Araminta doesn't turn to look back at me once as we go up to the rooms, just leads the way with an irritated energy and assumes we are following.

And they are 'rooms', like something you'd expect to find if you took an academic residency in the oldest university in the country, or the matron's job at an expensive, but ancient, private school. It's a long way from the 'apartment' described by the solicitor. 'Apartment' implies modern and well-proportioned, airy and clean. This place hasn't been lived in for years, unless you count spiders and woodlice and earwigs. The solicitor failed to say that the wallpaper was peeling in the corners and the windows grey with years of winter rain and summer dust. She didn't mention the bathroom: a chipped enamel bath with taps white with limescale and – next door to that – a loo with a cistern up above it and a long rusty chain to pull to flush it. The solicitor forgot to say that the only thing that marks our rooms out as separate to the rest of the building is a green baize door that doesn't quite shut. Most of all, she kept the absence of a kitchen right out of every single piece of correspondence.

'There isn't a kitchen, Mrs Buchan,' I say as Araminta goes to leave, her whirlwind tour completed.

'It's "Miss",' she says. 'But, as I said, you may call me Araminta. And we do have a kitchen, it's downstairs. Do you need it tonight?'

I thought about the burger we'd had at the Services when Leo felt sick, remembered the crisps, apples, and chocolate biscuits in the car. 'I'm sure we'll be all right for tonight.'

'You might, Cate,' Phil says, 'but we won't. We've got at least ten boxes marked "kitchen".'

'The kitchen is fully stocked. There will be very little you could need that you won't find down there already.' Araminta stands in the hallway. 'And there is no spare cupboard space.'

I realise that we can't stay here, this was a mistake and this place isn't for us. A second later, I remember that we have absolutely nowhere else to go.

It is late by the time Frank, Phil, and the removal man whose name I could never quite catch have carried all the boxes upstairs.

They put Leo's room together first to try and bring some semblance of order. Now they've finished, I'm relieved that we have this oasis of our past to hide in. Leo's room looks much as it always did. Frank even helped him get some posters on the wall until Phil and the other man realised he wasn't helping them carry boxes up three flights of stairs.

I've convinced Leo that a bedroom picnic is exciting and we're sitting on his bed with apples and chocolate biscuits pretending, like we did when he was little, that the bed is a boat and all around us is water. He still thinks this will be an adventure.

I lie back on his pillows and listen to the empty house. I imagine that I'm in London, that I can hear the Pearsons next door – their television always too loud for us but not quite high enough for them to hear. Or Delores and Alfie upstairs, art students that Leo has counted amongst his best friends for the last couple of years. Instead, there's us: Leo and me.

I don't know where Araminta went. She said a very firm goodnight and told me that she'd be back at 9 a.m. to show me how things work and where the kitchen is. I sip warm water from a plastic bottle we had in the car and think about when I lived in a city, when I could get a mocha chai latte with almond milk at midnight if I ever felt like it; I never did, but that doesn't stop me adding the rural isolation to my list of woes.

Leo is scrolling through music on his iPad, displaying an impressive line in choices for someone whose literacy skills aren't that hot. He puts his big headphones on and lies back on the pillow. Every now and then he bursts into song. Leo inherited his father's voice. If he'd had mine he might have been able to roughly carry a tune, maybe even do a reasonable karaoke. Instead he sings like Richard, like a cinder under a door, but that doesn't harm his love of singing loudly and often.

The music makes Leo smile, his fingers tap out a rhythm on the duvet and his feet jiggle. I envy him his ease and his confidence. Leo feels like this because he has me, because he has every trust in me. I don't have anyone to lean on right now, unless you count Simon – inexorably linked to us by shared history and by the fact that he's Leo's godfather – but he's 12,000 miles away researching fish that walk along the bottom of the sea.

I leave Leo to it and go into my own room, before he can see the tears that are welling up in my eyes. I lie back on the bed and breathe deeply. The mattress is solid and lumpy: we are not going to get on well. With each breath I take in more of the musty smell, the creased old curtains, I become more and more aware of the utter hopelessness of our surroundings. I think I had visions of moulded ceilings, patterns of white plaster edging every room. Instead, this low ceiling is cracked at the edges, with a tiny gap all the way round for insects to come and go through. A spider clings to a dusty web in the off-white corner as if to prove to me that he was here first.

I pick up my phone – I just want to share my wretchedness, my deflating hopes as they ebb into the threadbare old rug. I scroll through my recent calls, through my friend list. The trouble with being a teacher for so long is that all my friends are teachers too. They have escaped to warmer climes, as I used to, on the first day of the holidays and – apart from texts and postcards – none of them will really be in touch again until the grind of the September term starts anew. It's going to be a long summer.

Simon and I signed up for an online grieving course, after the first months of incredulity had worn off – when it had been long enough for me to realise I'd never love anyone as much as I'd loved Richard, and for Simon to learn that you only have one lifelong best friend. Some of our other old friends find it hard to talk about suicide: they're embarrassed and sorry for me in equal measure. Others can't deal with my anger. Simon knows exactly what I'm going through: the sadness, the regret, the pulsing guilt that has pounded in my ears every day for the last four years. And the utter negativity of helpless powerless fury. Simon knows first-hand that people are able to support you in sadness, but not so comfortable with despair.

There was never a moment where Simon wasn't Richard's best friend, wasn't utterly devoted to him – even when things became so complicated, when those relationships were blurred and stretched and hard to focus on.

My first problem when I met Richard wasn't how to finish with Simon but how to tell Richard why I'd done it. I let Simon down gently and without too much anguish, then spent two nights tossing and turning, wide awake: nights that would have been far less troubled had Richard and I had mobile phones or emails.

On the third day, I slunk into work for an afternoon shift,

exhausted and tense. I was working in the uni bar: the floor was sticky with spilt beer and the customers were mostly a nightmare, but it was near my halls and it fitted round my course.

I'd had my back to the bar when Richard approached and I heard his voice before I saw him.

'Si said I'd find you here.'

I blushed to the roots of my hair. Warm lager splashed onto my hand as I turned. My hand was shaking so much I had to put the plastic cup down on the bar. My throat was dry and all my words lost somewhere deep in my belly.

'Can you talk? Do you have a break any time soon?' His fringe was slightly spiky at the front; it made him look vulnerable and it quivered nervously when he spoke.

'I finished with Simon,' I told him, instead of answering his question.

Even at twenty-four his boyishness caught up with him. 'I know,' he whispered, and his voice trembled.

I made my excuses to the other bar staff and led him outside to a bench in the university plaza. Students wandered past us like safari animals ranging the plains: they were all a blur, all background. The sun was low in the sky and the afternoon still warm, still brightly lit.

'I have to know that you feel the same.' He just said it, no preamble, no explanation. 'I need to talk to Si about him and me and you, and I need to know that – that you feel the same – before I do it.'

'I do,' I said, for the first time.

'He'll be very upset, betrayed.'

I nodded, looked at the floor, the detritus of sweet wrappers, leaves, and cigarette ends.

'But there's no point in not telling him, in not doing it.' He reached out for my hand and his skin against mine was like fire. 'I'm going to tell him today.'

'Thanks.' I dared look up at him, at his earnest face, his worried eyes. 'It's the right thing.'

'This is it, you know.' He leaned in towards me. In the distance someone played a radio through a window, people called out to one another across the quad. Our world was just the tiny space between the two of us. 'I mean this is really it,' he said – before we had so much as kissed for the first time. 'Till death do us part.'

Now, as part of our therapy, Simon and I are supposed to email each other every day with memories of Richard – things that touch us and make the past a warm day or a Christmas morning, or things that are less happy, even painful. Over time we've got lazy, we either don't write for days or we send one line at best. More often than not, it ends up being a brief history of what we've had to eat.

Tonight, I wait until Leo is engrossed in his music, dancing around his new bedroom without a care in the world and go into my own room. I close the curtains, although there's nothing and no one outside: an overhanging roof or something obscures my view and I can't see the stars. It is truly dark in a way I doubt Leo has ever seen. I sit down on my bed and write an email on my phone; at least now I have something to write about.

From: Cate Morris

To: Simon Henderson

Subject: We've arrived

Mail: It's so much worse than I ever thought it could be: I don't know what I was actually expecting. Not this, anyway. At work we've all been telling ourselves that these things are new beginnings, that when one door closes etc, we've said it so much we've all started believing it. Not that anyone else who took the redundancy is in a cartoon spooky castle in the middle of nowhere.

Not even any food to report today, your godson and I mainly lived on burgers and chocolate biscuits.

Seriously though, I wish you were here. Or Richard. One of you. Anyone really (if that doesn't make you feel unimportant).

C xxx

PS Did Richard ever mention living here to you?

If there was a time when Simon resented Richard and me, he has never said so. He has been charm and elegance itself from the first time Richard and I met him as a couple.

It didn't take him long to meet someone new: a succession

of someone-news as it turned out. Simon was always the more handsome one, the more outgoing: he'd always found it easier to charm the girls than Richard had.

The three of us got on and pretended it hadn't happened; that I had never known Simon before Richard and that they were, equally, my two best friends. Girlfriends of mine queued up for years to have a go at being the fourth wheel of our strange little friendship but it never quite-worked out.

One of my best friends tried harder than most. It suited me and I encouraged it at every opportunity. It was going well: we had some good laughs together. And then, one day, we were on the way home from a seaside funfair. We went together in Richard's car: he drove and I rode shotgun – Simon and Emily were in the back. The boys had won huge teddy bears in displays of uncharacteristic machismo at the sideshows and Emily and I were still laughing at how easily they'd turned into totally different sorts of men once they'd started competing.

The light was fading into dusk, the scent of wheat fields and wild flowers was drifting through the car windows on the warm breeze. It was a balmy dream end to a beautiful day.

Simon saw it at the same time as Richard and me – I don't know how. The tiny baby rabbit lolloping on soft grey paws across the road.

The moment of brakes and shouts lasted only a second and then we saw the oyster-coloured ball of fur bounce away behind us before lying still in the middle of the lane.

Richard ran from the car, leaving the door open in the road. He crouched by the tiny rabbit, his head in his hands. 'No, no,' he kept repeating. I put my hand on his shoulder.

'Rich, mate, it's a rabbit. It's only a rabbit.' Simon was standing over the two of us and the little dead body. He picked it up by its ears and swung it into the field beside the road. 'At least another animal can take it.'

'I killed it.' Richard was whispering, still squatting in the road. 'I killed it.'

'Are you all right, Richard?' I got him to his feet.

He shook his head, his face was wet with tears.

'Do you want me to drive?' I asked. I'd never driven his car before and it seemed intimate somehow.

He nodded and we all got back in the car. Behind us a red Mini beeped to get us to move.

Richard didn't speak again until we got back to the flat he shared with Simon. 'Can you stay?' he asked me. 'I don't want to be on my own.'

I didn't say, 'It's just a rabbit.' Not then or when he woke up screaming in the night. Instead I held him tight, my arms around his muscular back, and murmured, 'It's okay, Richard,' until he went back to sleep.

I think of today's little fox, a bigger mammal than the rabbit and on a more sensitive day. Not for the first time I am thankful that I have never felt the weight of world as heavily as Richard did. Not for the first time, a diamond dust of resentment grinds in my silent inner self; in the part that always copes, in the part that bears the whole weight of the boy who was once Richard's world.

It takes a second to remember where I am when I wake up. Some things are normal. The duvet cover is mine and instantly recognisable, but the view at the end of its straight blue stripes is completely new. The furniture isn't mine. The heavy old oak drawers were too solid to move when we tried yesterday; it wasn't even worth trying the wardrobe. The wardrobe is antique and enormous; it would easily hold any number of children looking for adventures and it will easily hold far more clothes than I have ever owned. The wardrobe smelled the same as the rest of the room when I looked inside – a strange smell, not mothballs and not damp, but a smell of neglect and emptiness, nonetheless. Leo wakes early.

'And we can go in the garden.' He is excited and I haven't been listening or, for that matter, awake. 'It's a really big garden. Look.' Leo pulls the dark velvet curtain away from the window.

The sunlight streams in uninvited; the day insistent upon me, demanding my attention. In the morning light, I can see that the overhanging roof that obscured my view of the sky last night is so much more than that. Wooden panels, as intricate as lace, line the guttering of the roof above my window. They drip down like icicles, roughened by peeling paint that would be impossible to reach to redo. At the top of each eave, I can see the underbelly and chin of a gargoyle, both with their tongues poking out in front of them. 'Gog and Magog,' Richard used to say every time he met a pair of anythings – puppies, infants, artwork – that could be described as ugly. I wonder if these two stone monsters are the reason why.

We are three storeys up and the view of the garden is breathtaking. Then I realise that's the wrong phrase. This isn't a garden, these are 'gardens': wild and sprawling, over- grown and unkempt, but 'gardens', in the same way that this apartment is 'rooms'. I wonder if every aspect of this place will require new vocabulary. The lawn spreads away from the house – it isn't as overgrown as I would have expected. Someone mows this vast expanse of grass, clipping the edges where the trees have been so carefully planted around it, ancient enormous trees with trunks you could never fit your arms round.

Beyond the lawns – they are large enough to be plural too – I can see what I assume is the outside edge of a walled garden. There are shrubs and vines growing over the red brick wall and back towards the house. I can only imagine what else might be in there.

To the left of the walled garden and gesturing up to the back of the house, two gold statues gleam. They are so incongruous in all the disorder, as if they have a daily maintenance routine that involves scrubbing and brushing and polishing. The two life-sized figures look like skaters, moving across the surface of a large pond but stuck, for now, in the middle. Each balan- ces on one leg, the opposite arm outstretched and their heads turned slightly to look at one another.

'Who are they?' asks Leo and something in his voice says that he's not sure whether they're real people or not.

'They're statues,' I say. 'But I don't know who of. Aren't they beautiful?'

'Are we allowed to touch them?'

'Probably. I would have thought so. But we can't because of the pond. The pond's too big.'

'I can swim.' Leo has a twinkle in his eye.

'I know you can but that pond is probably heaving with slime and diseases. Seriously, you must be very careful near the water. Really.' I pat the bed beside me so he can hop on. 'What time is it?'

We're not in any rush so we spend the next few minutes figuring out the time on the big face of Leo's watch. It's not quite 7 a.m. At home we would be listening to a familiar soundtrack now. There would be movement from the flat upstairs – nothing from the Pearsons next door yet – it would be far too early for them. Below us, cars would be starting to choke the main road by our block, a popular rat-run for commuters. There would be shouts, and buses, and the wail of sirens.

I expected this place to be as silent as it was last night but it isn't. Birds fly in and out of the eaves above my window, screeching like insistent and unanswered phones. They're a blur but I don't think I'd know what sort they were even if they sat still long enough. I know a pigeon from a chicken, and a sparrow from a starling, but I'm very much a city girl. There are other noises too, the trees rustle gently in the wind and bird song pours in from every angle. On the warm air, the burr of a tractor engine reaches the window, someone out and at work early. Someone with work to go to.

Leo and I are going to have to fill the days of this long still summer. Before I was made redundant, the six-week break was an urgent rush of everything we needed to get done ahead of the new term. This autumn will be different but I have no idea how, or where. I had thought that perhaps they'd need some help in the museum – I could see myself as a tour guide, knowledgeable and bossy, a bit funny – but according to Araminta there will be no museum.

'I'm hungry.' Leo always wakes up hungry.

'Shall we go and find the kitchen? Then you can make some cereal.' I had the foresight to bring a carton of UHT milk – I knew we were coming beyond civilisation. Leo won't notice the difference if I let him have a special occasion cereal, drenched in sugar coating. The kitchen boxes are stacked up in my bedroom, the one with the bowls, cereal and spoons in is clearly marked.

'Is the kitchen in the house?' Leo asks.

'I bloody hope so.' I swing my feet out of bed.

I pull on the same clothes as yesterday, jeans and a T-shirt. Leo has already dressed himself with one of the flamboyant outfits he packed in his overnight bag. His shirt is orange and floral, underneath a waistcoat with a plaid silk front.

'Nice Thursday kind of clothes,' I say.

'Thank you.' Leo has lovely manners; everyone says so. And a complete disregard for sarcasm.

I let Leo lead the way along the corridor. He's excited and slaps his palms on his thighs in anticipation: I wish I felt the same.

We find our way out of the flat easily enough and we're back in the long corridor that leads to our little set of rooms. If claustrophobia had a smell, the unstirred damp of this passage-way is the one it would choose.

'It's down here.' Leo starts off down the corridor at a pace and I might as well trust him – he's got as much idea of where the kitchen is as I have.

'Hold on,' I say. I put the breakfast things down on the floor while I check my jeans pockets. 'I need to find the number for the alarm. We might set it off.' The scrap of paper is still there and I chant the numbers under my breath in case I need them in a hurry. There were times in my life when remembering a four-digit code wouldn't have been a challenge: this isn't one of them.

'I could dive under the alarm.' Leo waves his arms about, an adventurer warding off any dangers. 'I can stop it.'

'And you'll knock the paintings off the wall if you carry on like that. You've got to be careful. We can go mad when we get outside.' I give him the cereal box and the milk carton to keep his hands busy and close to his body. 'You take these and I'll carry the cups and bowls.'

'It's a long way.' Leo doesn't want to carry anything.

'It is, but when we get there you can have breakfast. I hope we haven't missed it.' We go down the same staircases we came up last night and back into the hallway. There must have been plenty of balls and weddings in this room once upon a time, with brides and debutantes coming down these stairs in cascades of satin and silk. Leo and I make a rather poor apology, although he's done his best to dress for an occasion.

Several doors lead from the hall. There is the huge heavy door we came in through last night, even more impressive from the back with its iron bolts and long black hinges. The key is noticeably missing and the idea of being locked in makes me uncomfortable.

'Let's see if we can find another door and get into the garden.' I keep my voice light but it is trapped in this huge hall, stifled by the fact we couldn't get out if we wanted to. The door I pick opens on to another little corridor. At the end I can see the outside world clearly visible and still real on the other side of the back door. It is the ordinary half-glazed back door of any house, a three-bed suburban semi somewhere. It looks as out of place as we are.

We creep down the half-lit corridor; Leo is silent now and I feel like a burglar.

The door on my right is ajar and I peer in. It's a kitchen of sorts but I think it might be part of the museum. The room is enormous and work surfaces run all the way round apart from under the window where a gleaming white porcelain sink straddles two scrubbed wooden draining boards, and in the middle of the far wall where an impressive old range squats, immovable and ancient.

40

I gesture for Leo to follow me in. Whether it's part of the museum or not, there's a big kitchen table in the middle and we can sit there to eat our cereal.

The work surfaces are all white enamel, scratched with age and the elbow grease that years of cooks must have used to clean it. The edges are blue where they curl over onto the wooden cupboards below. It must be the best part of a hundred years old – I've never seen anything like it. I knock lightly on the surface to check it's really made of metal. It is.

Pots and pans hang on the wall and from the clothes airer on the ceiling: there are jelly moulds and vast copper tureens, shined and buffed ready to feed a hundred hungry dinner guests. Huge spoons and ladles hang from a row of hooks by the cooker like something from a fairy tale. These are the very tools you'd use to cook Hansel and Gretel.

'Can I help you?'

'Oh, Araminta, good morning. I didn't expect to see you this early.'

She looks at the cereal box I've just taken from Leo; the very worst of pink marshmallow and tooth rot, and I swear her lip curls. 'So I see.'

'I'm making the breakfast.' Leo beams at her with his disarming smile. 'This is birthday cereal.'

'He usually has to have a healthy breakfast unless it's his birthday.' I'm talking too fast because Araminta makes me nervous. It's like I'm back at school, being reprimanded by the headmistress.

'It looks very . . .' She swallows. '. . . tasty.'

'Have you got a bowl, Mrs Minta? Would you like some? There is nearly a whole boxful.' Leo offers her the box and I want the kitchen to open up and swallow me.

'I've had my breakfast, thank you, Leo.'

I attempt to lighten the mood. 'This kitchen is amazing. How old is it?'

'It was all completely refurbished in 1918,' says Araminta. 'When Colonel Hugo married.'

'So it's part of the museum?' It starts to make sense. I run my fingers along the work surface. The whole thing is in incredible condition. The nicks of knife cuts and the odd missing flake of enamel are testament to the work that must have gone on in here back in its heyday.

'Not at all, it's the kitchen. The public have no access.' She gives me a look which shows that she thinks 'public' ought to include me. 'All Colonel and Lady Lyons-Morris's meals were made in here right up until they passed away.'

'I'm sorry,' I say, though I didn't know Richard's grand-parents and have no idea how Araminta may have felt about them.

'The range was replaced in the 1950s.' Araminta says it as casually as if she were telling me that the wallpaper was done last week. That still makes it seventy years old.

'Does it work?' I ask.

'Perfectly.' She walks across the room and opens the door of the tall fridge. 'The fridge didn't arrive until the 1970s. They used the larder and the garden ice house until then.'

Araminta clearly knows a lot about the place. She's also definitely in charge.

'Can I have more?' Leo has finished his first bowl of cereal. He's managed to keep the milk in the bowl and any extra bits that have fallen on the table have been scooped up and into his mouth.

'Half a one,' I say. 'Is this the kitchen Leo and I will use?'

'Yes,' says Araminta, and I'm sure she and I are both aware that she doesn't bother to add, 'Make yourself at home.'

I wonder how on earth I'm ever going to work the cooker but, for now, I'm not going to show any fear. 'Smashing. Is there some cupboard space for our things?'

'I've cleared this one for you.' She bends down and opens one small cupboard on the side of a wooden dresser. It will just about fit four tins of beans and a packet of pasta.

I nod. 'And our plates? Cups and stuff?'

'Everything you will need is here.' 'Here' is a dresser full of exquisite china. Every plate faces forward with a little bowl, saucer and teacup arrangement in front of it. The pattern is pale green and intricate. 'This service was made for your husband's great grandfather.'

'It's lovely.' I feel like laughing at the absurdity of it. 'It's lovely but it's not really suitable for us to use.' By 'us', I mean Leo.

'Every generation of Lyons-Morris has used it since then.' Araminta bows her head at the gravity of it. The gravity I imagine when I think of Leo and her precious plates is a different sort.

43

Araminta has been arranging dainty pieces of cheese and ham on one of the china side plates. She takes it out into the corridor and opens the back door. I can hear her calling a cat or something.

'You feed your cat cheese?' I try to make light conversation, talk about something that might make her happy.

Even before she answers, I know. I think of the shiny red fur, the healthy plump softness with the life knocked out of it.

'I feed a little fox.'

I scramble to change the subject before Leo loses interest in the cereal. I feel physically sick. 'Do you have far to come to the museum?' I ask her, praying that the answer will be yes.

'I live here,' Araminta says and smiles without moving her cheeks. 'My apartment is down the hall from yours. Now, if you will excuse me, I have a museum to open.'

We have navigated away from the fox, from the accident, from what – effectively – is a lie.

Leo, clearly sensing that I'm distracted, pours himself another bowl of cereal.

Chapter Four

From: Simon Henderson

To: Cate Morris

Subject: More things in heaven and earth, Horatio

Mail: Well done. It must have been so hard packing up your old life and arriving in such a very strange land. There's so much to love about Hatters but I admit it's an unusual place. I first went there when I was about 18, when I first met Rich, and I fell head over heels in love with it. It's probably responsible for the fact that I spend most of my life underwater sucking microscopic bugs into high-tech pooters. There are some crazy things in the collection.

Secondly, I'm glad you've arrived – even if you're not (yet). Hatters was very much a part of Rich – as hard as he kicked against it – very much a part of who he was. I miss him a lot this evening, thinking about you guys, so I'm having a beer, watching the sunset, and wishing we were all at Hatters together. No one knew the secrets of that place like Rich, although you did have to winkle the information out of him with a stick. I learnt a lot about Rich by being there – I think you will too.

Kisses to Leo, hugs to you, you'll be grand.

Sx

I only see Simon's email because my phone is in my hand as I scroll through correspondence looking for the solicitor's direct line. Her PA fudges for a while but I don't give in. I can hear the steel in my voice that warns I'll call all day if necessary.

'So, do forgive me if I sound a little bit hysterical, Susan, but we discussed the ins and outs of this place right down to the phone bill and you neglected to mention that it was a shared house.'

'It's not a shared house, per se.' Susan is on the back foot. 'But there are aspects of the accommodation that are shared with Ms Buchan.'

'Aspects?' I keep my voice low and, I hope, threatening. Beside me Leo is lining up his DVDs in the bookcase. 'Not that shelf, Leo, that's where the books go.' I try to whisper away from the phone so that Susan doesn't hear me being nice.

'Glad to hear you settling in,' she says cheerfully.

'Settling in is over-generous.'

'It's early days.'

Leo drops a whole box of DVDs and they shoot across the rug. It's enough to put him off the task completely and he stomps out of the sitting room. I can only hope he stays in the apartment while I sort this all out.

'So you knew Ms Buchan lives here: Araminta lives here. Who is she?'

'As far as I can see from the details of the Trust, she's a former employee turned family friend. She looked after Richard's grandfather and then, after his death, she stayed on to take care of the place.'

'Have we been suddenly transported to the eighteenth century? Hold on a moment, please. Leo?' I can hear him moving around in the bedroom. We have to be careful, he could be lost for hours in this warren of a place.

'I haven't met Ms Buchan personally,' the solicitor continues, 'but I'm sure she's very nice. She's been with the family for decades and Colonel Hugo's will was very firm about her keeping her place there until she no longer requires it.'

'Until she retires?' I try to keep the triumph out of my voice. Araminta must be past retirement age now.

'Until she, not to put too fine a point on it, dies. She has a right to remain in perpetuity. Although it doesn't pass on to her descendants.'

'Does she have descendants?'

'I don't believe so, no.'

*

47

When I catch up with Leo he's lying on his bed looking miserable. Everyone from his old school gave him cards when he left. He's covered in them like a blanket, an eiderdown of memories.

'Shall we work out whose is whose? Do you remember who they're from?'

'This is from Dean.' Dean's card, on floppy white paper, has two complicated gaming characters on it. The yellow one has a big 'L' on his front, the other – head to toe in red – has a 'D'. 'I can't play TimeQuake properly now. Not without Dean.'

'You can play online. And you're going to make new friends soon.'

'You always tell me to get off the computer, always, and I don't want new friends. I want old friends. And my old house.'

Leo has been with his friends since nursery, most of them. And we've lived in the flat for as long as he can remember. After Richard died, when we were completely lost, we still had all that. I want that too. I had thought about day trips back to London, liaisons with friends – we could easily drive there – but we need to get used to our new lives first.

Leo starts to cry.

'Come on, mate.' I put my arm round him. 'What about finding the way to the garden? We were going to do that earlier.' Even as I say it, I'm wondering how I will move him all over again in a month's time. I am going to have to tackle the subject, to speak to Araminta about it. There is a horrible feeling in the pit of my stomach.

Leo jumps up and grabs his trainers. His misery is

forgotten, the world is brimming with opportunity. I so often wish I was Leo.

We retrace our steps to the kitchen. I bring down the perishables that we had upstairs and I put them on one of the empty shelves in the fridge. For all Araminta's territorial attitude to the kitchen, there isn't much in here. The bright yellow bulb shows up milk, a loaf of white bread in a sweaty plastic wrapper, the cheese and ham the fox won't be eating any more, and clean white wire shelves: there's plenty of room for us to stake a claim. I'll use the same tactics with the dresser cupboard later on too.

We go back through the door we saw first thing this morning, green shoots and curling flowers framing the sunshine glowing in through its window. I allow myself a tiny uplifting of my spirits. The sunshine is beckoning, the garden looks bright against the cool shade of the corridor. This is the summer I had imagined for us.

The grounds are magnificent. The statues I could see from my window when I woke up are straight ahead of us on the wide sloping lawn. From upstairs, I couldn't see the slope of the garden and that the lawns roll down towards the small lake, that the trees are carefully planted, architectural against the perfect carpet of grass. I look around at the trees I know from London parks or children's books: oak, monkey puzzle, sycamore, aspen, a few more and then I run out – it would need a trained eye. Richard knew his trees, and birds – sometimes birdsong too. In time, he might have passed their names on to Leo.

'Is this a park?' Leo asks. 'Are there swings?'

'It's our garden.' My voice is wide with wonder, and more than a little doubt. 'Shall we go and see if there are swings?'

The house is behind us. The back is less ornate than the front and, somehow, seems bigger and more real for that. The facade has balconies and pillars. This is different; vast and utilitarian. There are so many windows, all set squarely in the brickwork, all of them identical except some are larger than others. The sun catches on the roof and, for a moment, I'm dazzled. When I take my hand from my eyes, I see it – a glass dome rising from the centre of this, otherwise traditional, country house. I walk backwards to get away from it and fit more of the dome in my eyeline. It rises up from the house like a bubble.

'In Xanadu did Kubla Khan . . .' I whisper.

'Is all of this our garden, Mum? Right down to there? And over there?' Leo asks me with his arms outstretched. I stop staring at the glass structure and look where he's pointing.

'We'll have to go and find out. I tell you what, why don't we walk all round the house first and see if we can find the entrance to the museum?'

'I love museums. Is there a museum?'

I almost ask him what he thinks that kitchen was. 'I told you fifty times. It's Daddy's grandfather's museum.'

Leo takes up a chant of, 'You told me, you told me,' meaning that he knows I'm right and can remember the fifty times that I explained it. Singing makes him walk faster and

I join in his song, although that's hard when he changes key every other line.

When we turn the corner of the house, hedging starts to line the path; to our right is woodland, dark and tangled. The gap between the trees and the house is under shadow and it's momentarily cold. There are inviting tracks through the wood but we stick to the gravel path around the edge of the house. 'It's going to take us all summer to explore all this,' I say, more to myself than Leo.

Leo gasps and I look up. A peacock struts across the path in front of us. 'Make him put his tail up,' Leo shouts, 'Like Daddy did.' He starts searching the edge of the path for a suitable blade of grass.

This was one of Richard's party tricks, every time we visited a zoo or a country house. He would take a broad piece of grass, hold his hands together – palms facing and fingers knitted – and stretch the grass between the tops and bottoms of his thumbs, pressing them tight against each other. Then he would put his mouth against the heel of his hands and blow. The rude squeak it made would almost always, after a few dud goes, result in the peacock looking indignantly at him and fanning its spectacular tail in annoyance.

Leo finds the right piece of grass. 'This one. Come on, Mummy, before he walks off. Hurry.'

This isn't going to go well. It's another of those moments, ones I'm used to, where Leo remembers that I'm not Richard and that those wonderful things that went with Richard are gone forever. It breaks his heart every time.

I stretch the piece of grass taut between my thumbs and blow.

The sound is hideous: loud, rude and perfectly peacock. His tail goes first time and he shakes his bottom as he circles, the eyes on the end of each feather quiver and sparkle in the sun.

I could cry.

Leo cannot contain his excitement and chases after the peacock with a fresh piece of grass. He is the image of Richard when he's laughing. I imagine a younger Richard, with other peacocks, perfecting the trick. Why did I never ask him where he learnt to do it? Was it here? It's an unusual skill to have, but Richard was an unusual person.

We keep going, anti-clockwise, round the building and there – on the front side of the house but at the other end to where we went in last night, is the ticket office. It's a real museum. You can't see the dome from here and, for a second, I wonder what else hides behind the grey-painted turnstile, the misty window of the kiosk.

I pat my jeans' pockets, I've got money. I wouldn't put it past Araminta to make us pay. And maybe we should pay. That wasn't in any of the discussions about gas bills or broadband: there wasn't a set number of museum passes for the year. Would Richard have paid? That's a simple answer – Richard wouldn't have come here. I cajoled and encouraged him: after we had Leo I'd go as far as to say I begged him. But the answer was always a flat – immovable – no.

'Well, we're here now,' I say to the stubborn ghost of Richard, 'Come what may.'

There's an old man behind the desk at the entrance. He sits in what could loosely be called a 'gift shop', a collection of dusty toys and 1950s postcards and a brightly coloured ice cream freezer. I grimace at the idea of Leo living so close to an ice cream shop, and anticipate months of push-me-pull-you rows.

'Two please.' I smile at the man.

'One concession?' he asks.

'Yes, one student please. And one adult.'

He tears pink paper tickets from a roll, more slowly than I would have thought was possible. 'Have you been before?'

I want to tell him that we were here all night, that we've seen the ancient kitchen and had our first disagreement with Araminta, but that's not going to help. 'We haven't,' I say and play nice.

'Down this corridor is Gallery One, start in there – most people do – and then go on to Gallery Two after that. Then Three and Four. They're numbered, you see.'

It's not the most sparkling museum tour I've ever had.

'Do you have a map?' Ghost Richard laughs beside me: he thinks I'm funny.

'We don't. But they're all numbered, you see.'

Leo and I set off down the corridor. There are a few boards explaining the nature of the collection, but I can't really stop and read too much of them without losing Leo's attention. And then, right in front of us, is a picture of Leo's great-grandfather.

The genes are strong. The photograph is monochrome but Richard's dark hooded eyes – and Leo's – are there. The thick hair, almost black and poker straight, is the same. His face is narrower than Leo's and his cheeks more chiselled than Richard's but the likeness is unmistakable. 'This is a picture of Daddy's grandfather.'

'Why is he wearing that hat?'

'He was an explorer. This is his camp. See his tent behind him?'

'Is that a real gun? I would be great with a gun.' Leo starts to spin round, his imaginary gun held up to his shoulder but, for the sake of the painting, I touch him lightly on the arm and he stops.

In the painting, Colonel Hugo is sitting in a fold-up chair outside a canvas tent. He wears a pith helmet and desert fatigues. His legs are stretched out in front of him, gaitered up to his knees, and a rifle lies along the length of his legs, down to his crossed ankles.

'It is definitely a real gun,' I say.

'What did he do with it?'

And this bit I do know. I know that Richard's grandfather was a Victorian conservationist, and that meant that he shot, stuffed, and brought to England thousands of animals from all over the world. He believed he was preserving them for posterity and education and, in that, Richard supported him 100 per cent. The one beef that Richard could have had with this museum – Richard the committed vegetarian who couldn't bear the death of so much as an insect, Richard the lifelong green campaigner – he didn't have at all. Whatever kept Richard from this place, it wasn't the stuffed animals: I always felt that it was something far more human.

Leo is bored with waiting and has answered his, pretty fatuous, question for himself. He is walking off down the corridor.

There is an archway on the left-hand side. The sign the man in the booth promised looms up in front of us: Gallery One. Leo, fractionally ahead of me, slips round the corner into the room and gasps.

I stifle a scream.

The animals are stuffed, just as Richard told me. And they're mainly displayed in twos, exactly as he said: an 'ark of death' he called it. What is so incredible, what made Leo gasp and me scream, is the scale of it. The humans stand in a relatively small spot in the middle and the animals take up the rest of the space: virtual reality designers of the present day would have trouble making anything so amazing. The gallery is huge, a lantern of glass in the ceiling lets in enough light to cast eerie shadows around the room.

Every animal is posed, mostly with another of its species, as if it is mid-breath, so lifelike it feels that they are about to place one hoof or claw or foot in front of the other and walk right towards us. Their glass eyes twinkle with the reflected sunlight and I prepare for the inevitability of seeing one blink.

Okapi bend to drink from a pond as a hippo roars up at

them, its peg teeth snarling. Giraffes splay their elegant legs to reach leaves from the small trees growing – although they can't be real – here and there through the scene. At the back, walking between the scene on our left and the scene in front of us, no bars to contain the animals except for the glass that keeps them from the centre of the room, the biggest elephant I've ever imagined strolls – benign – above the other animals. The sheer height of him throws my gaze to the floor of the display and I'm amazed to see snakes, mid-slither, and tiny rodents – frozen in terror – looking up at the snakes' pointed tongues. I've never seen anything more real in all my life and yet, at the same time, it is the stuff of nightmares.

'Are they alive, Mummy?' Leo's voice is unsteady. His hands flutter on his thighs.

I reach out and take his hand, stilling the nervous movement. His fingers weave between mine and I squeeze hard. 'They're dead. Stuffed.'

'They're not stuffed,' says a cold voice behind me and I remember that, as this house gives, it instantly takes away: a seesaw of expectation and emotion. 'They're mounted. The skins are stretched over frames of wood, and then posed in lifelike positions. It's infinitely superior to stuffing.' Behind her, a zebra looks at me with contempt. I move my head slightly to one side and, as I suspected, every pair of black glass eyes follows me.

'Mrs Minta,' says Leo, turning to face her. 'Are these your animals?'

'They're not my animals.' She is softer when she speaks directly to Leo. 'They are your great-grandfather's animals.'

'Why did he put them in here?'

'He was a collector. He loved animals and travelling, and he wanted all the people who lived here – who didn't have television or the internet – to see them too.' She sounds almost human.

'It's . . . I can't . . .' I'm almost lost for words. 'It's barbaric.'

'Really?' Her question is rhetorical, a way of letting her breath freeze the room, of spreading ice across the parquet floors and up through my feet. 'I'm sorry that you think so.' A mouse looks up at me in support of her: I swear its whiskers are jiggling in disgust, its little brown nose twitching towards the bad smell.

'What's "barbaric" mean?' Leo walks up to the glass. It runs from the floor to the ceiling and he bumps his face against it when he leans forward to look in. 'Ow.'

'Watch out, Leo,' Araminta chips in before I can. 'The glass has to stay very clean so you can see in.'

It's making me feel light-headed, my palms are sweating. 'All those poor dead animals.'

Leo turns round to look at me. Behind him a tiger lies on its side, bathing in the shafts of sunlight, its orange stripes as vivid as when muscle rippled beneath them. 'But they're dead, Mum. Like the fox.' He looks thoughtful, sad.

The animals stare at me: judge and jury. They wait, in silence, for me to speak. Araminta stands in front of them, as if she is about to command the vast army to attack. I imagine

57

the teeth and claws and wings and hoofs: the noise they would make, the squawking, the bellowing, the accusing.

'The fox?' Araminta's head swivels: for a moment I think it will rotate a full 360 but her owl eyes settle on me, burn into my conscience.

'Mummy killed a fox. Poor fox.'

'It ran in front of my car. I didn't see it till it was too late. I'm so sorry.'

She does not blink. 'But you decided not to say, not to tell me. Even when I was looking for her.'

'Her?'

'She had cubs. She has been teaching them to hunt out on the lawn in the evenings.'

'I . . . I didn't know it, she, was your fox.' I am burning with guilt, with embarrassment. I inhale deeply to keep myself from crying. It is bad enough to be responsible for that little death, without this inquisition.

'We have a tradition of foxes being safe here.' She speaks to Leo but, simultaneously, glares at me. 'Colonel Hugo refused to let the local Hunt onto the land. He thought hunting with hounds was inhumane, barbarous.'

I resist the urge to gesture around me, at these hundreds of animals, dead as door nails. A vulture hovers, wings outstretched to the width of my arms, behind Araminta, literally backing her up.

'We could get the fox and put him in here.' Leo is trying to be helpful.

Araminta shakes her head. 'We can't get into these

cases – we would accidentally take little bugs in, mites, and they would eat the animals.'

'How did the animals get in?' Leo asks. It's a good question.

My mind sees the animals, two-by-two, coming down a wide plank in the drive, descending from the mouth of a huge wooden ship and walking, trotting, flapping, their way into this room. I can hear the noise they made as they settled into position, the snorting, growling, trumpeting.

Araminta points at the back of the case in front of us. 'There, do you see?' she asks Leo. 'There are two big doors hidden in the landscape.'

We lean forward and I can just make out the top edges of the doors in the painted background behind the animals.

'But you mustn't ever open them.' Araminta says and looks at us very seriously. 'It would be catastrophic.'

'The animals are very beautiful,' says Leo. He strokes the glass.

'They were beautiful. Before someone shot them.' I mutter it, mostly to myself. Araminta is angry enough already: I don't want to get into a debate with her but I can't keep my mouth shut either.

Araminta stands beside Leo. She peers into the case. Doleful fawns gaze back at her, their dead brown eyes convincingly wet. 'The Victorians didn't know that some animals would become extinct one day,' she says. 'Do you know what extinct means?'

Leo nods his head.

'This is a West African Black Rhino. There aren't any left alive. Not one.' She points at the rhino, at his wide shoulders, his thick wrinkled skin. 'Should we put him in a cupboard where no one can see him?' She looks at me when she says this, the set of her shoulders challenging me to respond. She's made this argument before.

'Or should he be in here so people can learn? So we can talk about the fact that the rhino's family are all dead and that we need to take care of the planet, even species we don't see or know about?' She exhales loudly, showing that she's done, the lecture is over.

Leo presses his face too close to the case. His lips leave a moist kiss on the glass.

'Yuck, Leo,' I say. 'Wipe that off.'

He stands up straight, running the glass with the edge of his shirt sleeve. 'I think the animals are very beautiful. I like them.' Team Araminta.

She looks at me for a moment, victory held tight behind her thin lips, then leaves as quietly as she came in.

To: Simon Henderson

From: Cate Morris

Subject: Not Even About Food

Mail: We looked around the museum – not in any detail but as much as Leo could take in/enjoy – I can't say I felt the same way – and then we had to give up and go to the supermarket. I needed to know that there was still a real world out there, still normal people who do dull shit like shopping or spitting. I bought pizza and bottles of water and washing powder. I bought wine.

I was coping, I was, until I saw the emperor penguin. Have you seen it? It's not much shorter than me and it's in a wooden case – still in its original packaging. Next to it, in a glass display panel, is a letter from Ernest Shackleton offering the penguin as a gift to Colonel Hugo. And that's not the weird bit. The weird bit is the second letter, the answer from Colonel H, from Richard's very own grandfather – that never got sent. He explains, in terribly polite terms – not wanting to cause offence – why he can't possibly accept the gift of an emperor penguin. AND IT'S BECAUSE IT DOESN'T MATCH. Because Hugo's exhibits are from non-Antarctic environments and it DOESN'T MATCH. A penguin. Not wallpaper, not kitchen chairs, a penguin – a penguin almost as tall as me. Is that what I'm here to learn, Simon? That it wasn't only Richard who was bonkers? That it was his grandfather, and his grandfather's father: the whole bloody lot of them. That they were all utterly utterly mad. For generations and generations.

Is this when I become truly grateful for Leo's extra chromosome? Is that the only thing that might save him?

C xxx

Chapter Five

The making of Leo Morris turned out to be far harder than Richard or I had thought it would be. We were young and fit, we assumed we would have as much sex as possible and then a tiny Richard or a miniature me would appear. The first part was easy enough but the second proved almost impossible.

All around us our friends were hatching in droves – except Simon; every time he met a suitable girl she'd turn out to be too high maintenance or unwilling to wait while he went off on yet another expedition.

One by one, our couples friends – and even a few single ones – dropped out of the restaurant meals and the theatre evenings and stayed in with their new wonder – or wonders as it turned out for a couple of them.

But for Richard and me, nothing. We didn't worry about it: time was on our side and we knew these things aren't always as easy as people would like, but it was still hard every time I shopped for another baby present or wrote out the message – the one we longed to hear – on a congratulations card.

And then, out of nowhere and with no intervention other than our silent pleading with the universe, we got Leo. It was a perfect pregnancy, marked out at first by summer strolls through London parks and, later, by Christmas shopping trips around the traditional stores, breathless with excitement at how different our shopping would be for the next Christmas and all the ones after that, how much our priorities would have changed by then.

There were a few raised markers in some of the tests, but none of them claimed to be definite, just that they might indicate a higher risk of Down's syndrome. We concentrated on the words 'might' and 'risk' rather than worrying unnecessarily. And then, in the last scan of my pregnancy, they found that Leo had a tiny hole in his heart, tiny but still a significant danger for his minuscule body. That was far more of a worry than any chromosome condition might or might not be.

Richard was in robust health back then, a strong and emotionally intelligent man. I know he was as frightened as me, but he covered my hand with his, meshing a finger between each of mine. 'Down's syndrome isn't going to kill him,' he said, 'so let's not worry about that.' The unspoken part of the sentence was, 'But a tiny anomaly, measured in micromillimetres, could.'

Leo has spent nineteen years proving what an extraordinary man he is but his first fight, the one he and Richard did by themselves in the early hours of that cold February morning was his hardest. Leo was taken into surgery for his first heart repair when he weighed less than two bags of sugar. I was spared the worst of it by a general anaesthetic and three blood transfusions.

Richard, who thought he might lose both of us, sat in the waiting room, looking anxiously up and down the corridor for anyone wearing surgeon's scrubs; hoping for one who'd saved his wife and one who'd salvaged his son.

By the time we were all reunited, Leo's eyes were open. We knew by then that the 'maybe' diagnosis was a real one, but we also knew our baby was out of danger for the time being. Tiny beads of water glistened like crystals between his long eyelashes, and his black pupils searched round the shapes of us for focus.

'He's absolutely perfect,' Richard whispered. 'We've hit the bloody jackpot.'

I've sat in my bedroom since lunchtime, and Leo in his. We can't sustain that for the rest of our lives. Leo is grumbling to himself, mostly about me, and occasionally throws his arms up in despair. I've tried to settle him to read, to draw, but he's too agitated by all the recent change, and too bored without anything properly organised to do. The only people who can improve our lot are us.

'Come on.' My jolly let's-do-this face is only skin deep but it's better than moping in here all day. 'I invoke the Nice Day Rule.'

'It's not a nice day,' Leo says. 'It is – in fact – a very boring day. A bad day.'

'Let's change that then.' I pull on my trainers. 'Come on, we'll check out the gardens, then we'll go and do some shopping. What would you like for supper?'

Leo runs through a list of options as he puts his shoes on. 'Anchovies, tomatoes, peppers. And linguine.'

I wonder, without much faith, whether the village shop has anchovies or linguine. 'Great choice. Come on.'

We head right at the bottom of our stairs and into the long corridor that leads to the library – there must be doors somewhere along here that lead to the garden. We could go through the tiny one at the end of the kitchen passageway, but I'm trying to avoid Araminta.

Leo has bucked up a little and is ahead of me, his commentary lighter now – some of it is even sung.

We follow the arrow-shaped signs that direct us to 'the library' – we both enjoy books. Suddenly, about twenty feet or so away from me, Leo stops. He is bathed in light, haloed amber and glittering. I see him raise his head, look upwards towards the sky. He spins – slowly – on the spot as I walk towards him.

This is the huge glass dome. We are standing underneath metre after metre of glass, curving up and away from us into a perfect bubble above our heads. All around its circumference, from the ground up to what must be midway up the first floor of the house, are shelves and shelves of

Anstey Harris

leather-bound books, perfectly arranged and squeezed in next to each other in matching sizes.

Ladders scale the cliffs of books, reaching up over shelf after shelf and, every now and again, a banner flies like an injured bird, dramatic colours hanging limply. There is an air of dust about the place, the upper reaches can't have been cleaned for years and the brass poles that the banners hang from are tarnished and dull.

Leo shouts out. 'Woo hoo, woo hoo.' And the sound doubles back to us in the huge space. It's another Richard thing, something he always did in tunnels or underpasses or, with enough booze inside him, Tube stations. Did he learn that here too? Leo's sounds bounce back to us, growing fainter, and I imagine that I hear Richard's voice in harmony with it.

The afternoon sun is settling and it casts a line of coral light around the point where the shelves meet the glass, almost as if the whole library is on fire, lit from the tips of these delicate pages.

Around the edges of the library there are carved wooden booths, each one containing a desk and one or two chairs. Twenty people could easily sit and work in this room and I can only assume they must have done once. Each booth has an animal head mounted onto a shield above the desk, caribou, elk, a moose stretches its huge antlers over one of them.

Exactly as I assumed, two wide French windows open from the library on to the lawn and, when I push them, they swing open. When we step down the four stone steps

66

we are directly opposite, although still a fair way away from, the golden statues in the lake. They could be skating right at us and they both make direct eye contact with me. It is unnerving.

Outside the sun is still warm on the wide lawns. We zigzag across between light and shade. The majestic trees that I saw from my bedroom window are much more impressive at close quarters and very old. Some are traditional English trees that might, apart from the even spacing and elegant angles, have found their way here by nature – oak, beech, a chestnut that spreads its wide branches over a dappled circle of grass. Others are evidence of Hugo's travel or maybe those of the generations before him: the vast Chinese monkey puzzle I saw from upstairs, its crooked branches rambling out and upwards, and a fig, prehistoric knobbled leaves bent over to the ground, its tangled branches heavy with unripe figs.

One tree, which I don't recognise, has strange hairy fruits hanging from it. It isn't until I reach up and hold one in my hand that I realise they are kiwi fruit – Chinese gooseberries – a plant that I had no idea could grow in the UK, let alone outdoors. Perhaps they only can in this enchanted place.

Up close, the statues are breathtaking. They stop just short of life-size, everything about them perfect but reduced by, perhaps, 20 per cent. They are a boy and a girl, or a man and a woman – but from their fine features and their lithe limbs, I'd say they're in their late teens or early twenties: Leo's age.

They each wear a version of a toga: short and gathered at the waist, with – for her – a knotted rope, and – for him – a belt with a short dagger hanging from it. The detail is incredible. Their gold skin stretches around their features, clearly alarmed, clearly running. Their hands are fastened tight together, whoever they're running from or to, they are doing it as one.

The water they skate across is less elegant. There are a few ragged waterlily leaves trying their best to dominate the surface, but the pond is dark and green with slime.

'Don't like it.' Leo stands with his trainers at the very edge of the pond.

'Be careful, it's slippery.'

He gives me a withering look. 'These are my best trainers. I'm not getting them wet.'

I don't want to go back to the mood we were both in upstairs. The sensible option is to find something else to look at, something away from the water. From upstairs, I could see a long red-brick wall with a pale green door in it: presumably the old kitchen garden. The same wall is ahead of us, only a couple of hundred yards away. In front of it, the female peacock turns to look at us, as if beckoning us in.

Maybe, I hope, as we cross the lawns towards it, we might finally find our refuge behind that gate.

Up close, the gate is an old blue door, eaten away at the bottom by some hungry rodent, and flaking with curled leaves of ancient paint. The catch is peeling and rusted but clicks open easily enough. The door itself sticks at the top but yields to a light 'thump' from the heel of my hand.

If I were a member of the public or a museum visitor, I would take its reluctance as a sign that I shouldn't go in, and that adds to the idea that this might be our sanctuary.

Inside, the plants are extraordinary. Huge ferns droop over the paths and green bananas hang in upside-down bunches from the tall palm trees. Grasses as high as my head swish and sway in the afternoon breeze and enormous green leaves, the size of tabletops, stick up from the flowerbeds. Everything is savage and wild and yet, at the same time, tamed and kept away from the flagged path we are walking on. The smells are those of a hothouse, exotic and fragrant; flashes of colour catch at the edge of my line of vision and a parakeet circles, screaming, overhead.

'This looks like dinosaur land,' Leo says, a slight nervousness in his voice.

'No dinosaurs, I promise. It's amazing though, isn't it? Look – those are real bananas.'

'Why are they green? Bananas are yellow. Or horrible and black.'

'It's not sunny enough for them to finish growing, to ripen. That's why all the bananas we eat are grown abroad.' We are still walking along the path, it takes a sharp right-hand turn and we follow it.

This side must have been the hothouses. There are brick-built greenhouses, bigger than most people's houses, all missing panes of glass here and there. The plants inside have taken over but I can see edible fruit hanging from the tangled vines – tomatoes, peppers, cucumbers. They look like coloured birds peeking through the foliage and I think of the still displays inside the museum.

'Look at that.' I point them out to Leo. 'We could come here in the evenings to get stuff for our tea.'

There is another smell on the evening breeze: a smell I know from London – not one I expect to smell here. On a bench at the end of the hothouses, his back against the wall and his eyes closed, is a young man. In his hand is an enormous spliff and he blows out puffs of cannabis smoke like a long slow dragon. His legs are stretched out in front of him and his face turned up towards the fading sun, the back of his head is entirely hidden by the hood of his jumper.

'Excuse me?' I say in my best teacher voice. 'Do you have permission to be in here?'

He jumps up, flings the joint to the floor and grinds it with his trainer. 'Sorry, I thought I was on my own.'

He isn't very old, a little younger than Leo probably. He has a round silver ring through his lip and as he moves his head, I notice a smudged blue tattoo on his neck.

Behind him, a blackbird hops onto a garden fork to watch us.

'Should you be in here? This is private property.'

'I'm Leo,' Leo says in his best friendly voice: I shoot him a death stare.

'I'm Curtis,' says the boy. 'I'm a volunteer here. I dig the garden.'

'I don't care who you are: you can't sit in this garden taking drugs.' All sorts of thoughts fly through my mind: the priceless animal skins, the statues. I wonder whether Araminta stops to vet her helpers at all.

'Is that drugs?' Leo asks, pointing to the dog end on the ground.

'It's ... it's stupid, mate. Forget it.' Curtis at least has the good grace to backtrack.

'I have come to live here,' Leo says.

'For a short time ...' I want us all to be clear on this.

'And I need to make some friends ...' Leo continues.

Curtis rubs his nose with the sleeve of his hoodie. The jumper is a dusty dark blue and has frayed string hanging down from the collar. 'Araminta told me you were coming. There aren't many people our age round here. Are you on TimeQuakeTwo?'

Leo nods and an exchange I can't understand follows.

'LeoLion123.'

'HogBoy2004. You on tonight?'

'Yes.' Leo looks at me, his face set in a frown of determination. 'What time?' he asks Curtis.

'I'll be on as soon as I get home. I only live in the village.' Curtis nods at Leo, ignores me completely, and walks out through the pale blue garden door.

Chapter Six

Leo can't wait to get back. His plans to cook linguini are abandoned in favour of an evening playing online video games with Curtis and a pasta sauce from a box in the cupboard. I'm furious on every level and so, unfortunately, is Leo. I have had to cajole and bargain even to get him to eat supper with one hand while he plays his computer game.

I sit beside him on the sofa to look at my emails on my phone.

To: Cate Morris

From: Simon Henderson

Subject: You're in then . . .

Mail: You've seen it now so you'll kind of get why I didn't warn you. To be honest, there wasn't much I could say. I gave it serious thought and decided Rich would want

you to see the legacy of his family exactly as it is, see
who they are first-hand. And now you have. You could
call it bonkers, or you could call it a glorious investment
in the wonders that our planet has to give and a record
of a life none of us can begin to imagine. When I went
there, all those years ago, there were researchers from
every corner of the globe beetling about in the attics,
uncovering packing case after packing case of skeletons,
measuring the bones and sampling the genes. I met a
guy recently who'd been there, who was one of those
scurrying researchers. Did you know that only one in
ten humans is left-handed, but half the chimpanzee
population are – 50 per cent. Why would that be? They're
our closest relative. His research took him to Rich's
grandfather's collection: that's amazing. What a legacy.

Sadly, none of us have got the money they had back
then (or I'd pack up my fish data and be on the next plane
over to help you guys settle in). At least now you can see
what they spent it on. Amazing, eh? That's some vision
Rich's grandfather had, and I think Rich would be glad
that Leo's part of it now.

I never knew what went on between Rich and his
grandfather. One day they were best friends and Rich
went down to Hatters all the time, the next it was history.
Your guess is as good as mine and I don't suppose
there's anyone still there who would know.

Keep smiling, mate. All three of you are in my thoughts.

Xxx

PS. Rich didn't live there as far as I know but he knew everything there was to know about it.

It's time Leo did something else instead of gaming. 'You'll get square eyes,' I say, sounding painfully like my parents, back in the day.

'Curtis and Mrs Minta are my only friends from here. All of them. I don't have any others.' He smacks his hands down onto his thighs in protest. 'And I want to play my game with Curtis.'

'You're not exactly "with him",' I say as part of my losing battle.

'You said playing games with Dean was the same as being with him. You did.'

My frustration is boiling over. The trip to the village shop wasn't going to change the world but it would have been nice to see another human being. There is no way to shift Leo from this machine.

'Look.' Leo points to the screen. A man swings through a jungle not unlike the kitchen garden where we met Curtis. Underneath him, a second man crouches low in the undergrowth, watchfully. A tribal drum beat bangs out as a tinny sound from Leo's headphones. 'That's me, in the trees, and Curtis is watching, being very, very careful of me.'

The figure in the undergrowth raises a warning hand, his camouflage jacket no more colourful than Curtis's real clothes. Leo bangs the pause button and leans forward. I can see him holding his breath.

From the next tree, the one Leo was about to swing into, a huge dinosaur head appears, teeth wide and dripping with something awful. I can hear its roar leak out of the headphones.

'Phew!' shouts Leo at the top of his voice. And then, more quietly and into his microphone, 'You saved me.'

I can't hear what Curtis replies, except that it ends in 'Bruv'.

I write a quick reply to Simon in an effort to feel listened to.

From: Cate Morris

To: Simon Henderson

Subject: FFS

Mail: Do you want to know what my favourite part of the museum is right now? The first glimpse of civilisation when you turn the last corner of the drive.
   Xxx

I sigh as the message leaves and take the plates downstairs.

Araminta is in the kitchen, of course she is. I swear she listens to my every movement in order to appear, ghostlike and silent, beside me wherever I am.

'Am I in your way?' I gather up the plates I'd put down on the side ready to wash.

'No, I'm only getting a drink.' She glides past me to the

fridge, where she takes out a milk bottle, the old-fashioned sort, glass and delivered by a milkman.

'You still have a milkman here?' I ask. I haven't seen one of these bottles in a decade.

'A lot of the old ways are better for the environment.' She glares at my four-litre plastic carton in the fridge door.

'While Leo isn't here . . .'

'Where is Leo?' she asks: there is accusation in her voice.

'He's playing on his games consol. He's playing an online game with one of your volunteers – Curtis?'

She nods. 'That's good, Curtis is a nice boy.'

'I'm not sure about that. Do you normally let your volunteers smoke cannabis in the gardens?'

She glares at me. 'Firstly, no – obviously we do not – and I will have words with Curtis. Secondly, he's not a volunteer – he's on Community Service.'

I am speechless. I have moved my son from inner-city London to hang out with a drug-taking convicted criminal.

'And he does it very well. He's a hard worker.' Araminta turns her back to me and pours milk – from her recyclable glass bottle – into a pan.

I don't want this boy to be Leo's only friend. It makes all my failures that much louder, brings all my mistakes crashing and banging into my head. This wouldn't happen in our old lives, it really wouldn't. In London all sorts of people appear – briefly – on one's horizon before going off at a tangent. Leo and I managed his environment at the centre of a huge community and he had options: he could make his own, safe, choices. Here, there are so few people, such a small pool, that that isn't the case anymore.

The claustrophobia of the situation overwhelms me. I need to get outside. I need to think. 'Could you keep an ear out for Leo if I go for a walk? He won't budge from his console and, of course, there's no door between our flat and yours.' I don't want to be in her debt but if I don't get outside and breathe my head is going to explode.

'It would be a pleasure.' She smiles a charmless smile, like one of the predators in the cases, white teeth and dead eyes.

It takes a good twenty minutes to find the chapel but the walk gives me a good idea of the gardens and how far they stretch. It also reminds me how static I've been, how much my limbs long for some exercise, almost as much as my mind longs for some quiet. Maybe once we are settled and I'm less worried about Leo, I can run around here in the mornings, wake my body up.

When I finally find it, I wonder if I've accidentally walked past the edge of the property and into the town itself. I had expected a tiny, humble, building but this is in a similar vein to everything else at Hatters: ridiculously grand and inappropriately huge. The chapel is, to all intents and purposes, a church. The arched doorway is protected by a stone porch with a metal gate across its front. I push the catch of the rusty gate, expecting it to be firmly shut, but it moves easily under my fingers and lets me in without so much as a creak. I'm surprised Araminta doesn't keep more doors locked. And then I realise, with a feeling that makes my stomach lurch, that I don't know what Curtis was convicted of or how long ago.

Inside, there is a cool quiet breeze I hadn't expected. The same flat damp scent of ancient paper, tinged with the visceral smell of aged leather, that floats around the circular library makes me sniff deeply, once, twice.

The peace in the tiny chapel is overwhelming. I feel as if part of the house has accepted me, as if this place could be my ally.

I slide, sideways, into one of the old oak pews. Faint cobwebs string between the hymnal rest in front and the pew, a trap to keep out unwanted visitors or at least to warn the residents of their presence. I wave my hand through the gossamer and it vanishes.

The wooden seat is clean. There must be some visitors to the little chapel or it would be far more run-down, far less welcoming. I rest my head on the empty shelf in front of me, my forehead cool against the smooth wood. It has been a long time since I have had a moment to think, a second to myself.

I thought I would cry if I stopped moving, if I stood still. I imagined I'd be swallowed by the jaw-clenching anxiety that has been nibbling at the corners of my mind and the muscles of my face since we got here. Maybe if I were in another place I might, but this chapel, I don't know why, gives me the first sanctuary I've had since we arrived.

I'm as far from spiritual as it's possible to be – 'deeply

irreligious', Richard once called me – but here in the silence I can feel history everywhere, coating my skin, asking no questions. It's a new departure for me. I resist spirituality where I can, preferring instead to give to charity or work behind the counter of a thrift store for a few hours. It was Richard who insisted Leo have a godfather. I thought the idea was preposterous, although a tiny – silent – part of me wanted to recognise Simon's part in this story.

'Traditionally,' Richard said, 'a godfather steps in and marries the widowed wife – the mother of his godchildren – should the father cark it.' We were lying in bed, one each side of a sparkling baby Leo who was wrapped in a baby sleeping bag like a giant cocoon. Leo was plump and robust, so different to the stringy chicken he'd been at birth. At six months, he'd already defied so many of the doom-laden prophecies we'd been warned of when he was born. The feeding problems we'd been almost guaranteed had never materialised and Leo fed as if every meal was his last – a miniature of Richard.

'And that's why you've got to choose someone utterly reliable. Someone who will focus on a challenge. Like Simon.'

'I'm not marrying Simon. Not even if you're dead.' I touched Leo's forehead to check he wasn't too hot. Our draughty Victorian terrace was just about warm enough to risk peeling his chubby thighs out of the sleeping bag. He kicked his feet in relief.

'My godfather was called Valentine.' Richard raised his eyebrows at me. 'My father moved with some pretty dodgy sorts, and Valentine was some kind of flash millionaire my parents met in Cannes.'

I kept very quiet, Richard so rarely talked about his father. His mother, long-divorced and living on a remote stretch of coast in Wales, was emotionally, as well as physically, distant. She and Richard had never been close.

'If you look at my birth certificate – the long one – the one you've never seen ...' Richard grinned, 'you will see that that pair of numpties made "Valentine" my second middle name in the hope that the playboy millions would make their way to me when he died.'

'No!'

Richard nods, his dark eyes wide.

'You let me marry you, and bear your son, and you never told me your middle name was Valentine. Richard Valentine Hugo Lyons-Morris.' I laid back on the pillow, laughing.

'Richard Hugo Valentine, actually.' He caught one of Leo's little feet in his hand and bent his head down to kiss the toes. 'Which is why I am plain old Richard Morris on my passport.'

'And what happened to Valentine?'

'They never saw him again. And I never got so much as a Christmas present.'

I blew a raspberry on Leo's arm and he chuckled. 'Weren't Daddy's parents silly?' I asked him and he beamed back at me. 'You should look him up, Richard. He might have left you money. Us money. I wouldn't have to go back to school after my mat leave. No more Year Four: Heaven.'

'Shall I do a search on the internet? Sixties playboy, Valentine, Europe.'

'You could try.' I knew Richard wouldn't, but I did. Of course, there was nothing there. I called Richard 'Valentine' for as long as I could until it got on his nerves. That was back when Richard still laughed, back when he could still take a joke. Fabulous days.

I get up and walk down the aisle of the chapel towards the altar. I wonder if people were allowed to marry here: there must have been funerals – the floor is studded with memorial stones. There are long names and Latin inscriptions, there are wives and daughters, husbands and sons. Some of the dates reach far further back than the chapel possibly can, perhaps the result of some Victorian genealogy. There are Morris family members buried everywhere in here: I step carefully over their stones set in the floor of the aisle. Just in front of the altar there is a huge white marble plaque. It says, in perfect lettering "Loveday Charles Stapleton Morris" and I presume, from his position in the church, that he paid for all the rest of it.

There is a small step up to the altar area of the church – I'm sure it has a name but I'm not familiar enough with churches to know what that might be. To the right of the step is a lectern with a large leather-bound book on it. I open the book, half-afraid that its ancient pages will crumble under my fingers. The paper is thick and heavy. It is a ledger and records the births and deaths of the Lyons-Morris family.

I turn to the end first, at least, the end of the entries – which are far from the end of the book. There is a certain self-assurance, or is that arrogance, in believing that your dynasty will continue long enough to fill the pages of a ledger this big.

There he is, my tiny baby written huge on the page in curling letters:

Lyons-Morris, Leo Richard Charles. Born, Islington, London, 2001.

I'm annoyed – but not surprised – that whoever wrote this put the 'Lyons' back in. And then another thought blows in like a draught through the silent chapel: it is that legacy, this certainty, that has rescued Leo and me from homelessness. It is being part of this dynasty that shapes him, makes his ancestry as special as he is. Here, in the peace, that legacy feels more of a safety net than a burden and I wonder if Richard might have thought differently of it all if it wasn't for his illness.

I trace back.

Lyons-Morris, Richard Hugo Valentine. Born, London, 1961. Died, London, 2016. Missed always by his loving family.

My Richard Hugo Valentine, with his death date there to remind everyone of the terrible tragedy it was. I don't know who would have written the words after it: Richard's grand-father died decades before he did.

I feel a hot anger that someone made that assumption: that no one asked me about the anger or the sadness or the guilt or the confusion. That no one asked me what verb I would use to describe our loss. Richard is missed always, of course he is, but whoever wrote those words did not know the story – they cannot know what happened.

The book is a litany of sadness: I suppose such things always are over time. Two lines above Richard's name is his grandfather's:

Lyons-Morris, Hugo John Loveday. Born 30th September 1895 at Hatters. Died, Hatters, 1990. He did his duty to his king, his country, and his family. Fidelis servus.

Even my schoolgirl Latin knows that fidelus means faithful. A faithful servant. I suppose that's a good thing to be. It makes the entry for Geoffrey seem spiky.

Lyons-Morris, Geoffrey Hugo John. Born 23rd July 1930 at Hatters. Died, France, 30th October 1975. To God's judgement we commit him.

I know that Richard's father died in a car crash: one that Richard described as 'inevitable'. And that's pretty much all I know, apart from that he went off when Richard was young and rarely, if ever, made an appearance in Richard's life. The six words of his obituary do little to enlighten me any further.

It's a strange idea that, however disparate the three men were in life, they are reduced to these lines, to covering two pages with four generations of their family. A family tree that has Leo on the end of its newest, and I hope strongest, branch.

I'm glad he doesn't know how much rests on his shoulders.

At each side of the altar are choir stalls and, in the absence of any other living humans, I sit in the one on the left, looking back down the church as choir boys must have done on hundreds of Sundays over the centuries. My only companions are the quiet, still, dead, the strange male line that skirts around the issue of wives and mothers, that presumably had no daughters. At least – no matter what their differences – they are all peaceful now.

I close my eyes and rest my head on the chalky white paint behind me. My sigh is long and heartfelt and rustles through the stillness. It ripples with the echo of all the other sighs that have brought us here.

Richard's illness arrived quietly. We were on holiday. We were the handsome couple on the promenade, laughing: him, taller than average and immediately appealing; bright white teeth in a broad smile and brooding dark features that offset his instant likeability; her, carefree, loving the early years of parenting, the daily magic; they walk together, her happiness evident on the outside, her short brown hair expensively cut and chic and between them a sturdy little boy swings on their hands. The little boy is precious in a miniature yellow oilskin and striped leggings.

Back then, Richard and I – and little Leo, beautiful Leo – looked like the family everyone would want to be. Most importantly we were the family we wanted to be.

'Did you see that man?' Richard asked me. His smile had disappeared. He looked, and I struggled to find the word at first, bewildered.

'What man?' We were fighting our way down a busy

French seafront, trying to keep together and still swing Leo up in the air without damaging any of the multitudinous passers-by.

'The guy in the hat. There.' Richard pointed at a man strolling away from us, deep in conversation with the women beside him. 'He was talking about me.'

'You don't speak French.' I laughed at him, trying to turn it into a joke. The words themselves made a joke but something in Richard, some light that should have been twinkling, had gone out. His face was pale. 'He wasn't, Richard – he didn't even look at us.'

'I want to go back to the hotel.' He was adamant.

Luckily it was before Leo had much in the way of speech and if he wanted an ice cream he was too little to tell me, so we got away with all going back to the hotel. In the room, Richard lay on the bed pretending to be asleep.

'What about dinner?'

'You go. Take Leo. I'm not hungry.'

I tried a few times to persuade him to come but he clearly wasn't going to move. I ate goat cheese salad that night, walnuts sticky with honey, my jaw tense with anger. Leo ploughed his way through a baby portion of mussels and chips, juice up to his elbows. In the morning, Richard was his normal self – except that he refused to talk about the beach incident.

I told Simon about it when we were home. The three of us were in the pub and Richard had gone to the loo.

'And he wouldn't talk about it again, that was it. But

I swear nothing happened. The man didn't so much as look at him.'

'Rich was probably hungover,' Simon said. 'Beer fear.'

I shook my head. I knew something was wrong, even then, even when it was a fleeting glimpse of what he would become. It was a premonition to the hospital stays that tormented him, the medication that blunted him. That moment the illness entered our lives was only that, a moment, but it had wriggled its way in and it had started to burrow. Most of Richard's illness was background, quiet but always there: a nervousness watching him standing on a train platform; a slight unpredictability when faced with change; the flicker of a shadow walking past our lives. That day was different: the day the ball started rolling, faster and faster, towards the end.

I open my eyes, aware that time has passed and yet stood still while I've been in here. In front of me, scratched into the back of the choir stall are the letters RHVL-M. Richard sat here. The ghost of the boy Richard sat here long enough to scratch his name into the wood with a penknife. I trace the smooth letters with my fingers and my heart.

Chapter Seven

My sleep is fitful and interrupted. For almost every minute between 3 and 5 a.m., I was composing single lines about my life: the kind someone — generation after generation — has seen fit to attribute to each man in Richard's family. Who will write Leo's? It kept me awake for a long time.

From: Simon Henderson

To: Cate Morris

Subject: Oh . . .

Mail: That Good, eh?

You can do this, my friend. You have been through so much worse: kept body and soul together in the darkest days. You survived before by putting Leo first – as I'm sure you're doing now. Don't write it off – give it

a chance. Don't forget to be kind to yourself as well – I
wish I could help.
  Sx

The chapel has stirred something in me. In the dark – and
most lonely – hours, apart from Simon's message from the
other side of the planet, I thought about those letters carved
in the wood: wondered how many pieces of Richard,
how many tiny ghosts, I will find here if I look. There is
more to this place than animals and books, than scientific
instruments and old cannons. I commented on the cannons
outside the front door when I came in last night.

'The plural of "cannon" is "cannon".' Araminta smiled at
me in sympathy: as if I had committed a terrible faux pas.

'Every day's a school day,' I said and gave her a smile with
all the depth in it that she reserves for me. 'The cannon are
quite remarkable.'

I walked back the long way and came along the front
side of the house, from the museum door to the front door
that Leo and I used on the first day: a row of cannon –
straight from the deck of a ship and dulled to a mottled
verdigris – point out across the gravel to the wide paddock.
They looked particularly incongruous when I saw them this
morning, with two pints of milk delivered to the step they
are guarding.

'Do you want cereal?' I ask Leo as he comes out of his
bedroom. He is up very late for him and I can see from his
puffy eyes that he's still tired.

'Don't want breakfast. I'm busy.' He is pulling on his trainers in what passes for a hallway. His backside knocks the green baize curtain as he does up his shoes. Leo has dressed in a hurry: mustard-coloured T-shirt with red trousers and a green waistcoat – he looks like a traffic light.

'That's good to hear. Busy doing what?'

'I'm going to see Curtis. In the garden.'

'I'm not sure that's a good idea.' I think of the cloud of foul-smelling smoke around Curtis, of the smudged blue tattoo on his neck. 'Not today. We're going to the shops today. Whatever you think.'

Leo bangs the sitting room door as he comes in to illustrate his unhappiness. 'I want to help Curtis in the garden.'

'I was wondering if the local shop does comics. I mean, you are going to get behind on your stories if . . .' I trail off and pretend to be absorbed by the view outside. I'm surprised to find it genuinely is absorbing if you give it a moment or two: the planting – now that I'm staring at it with the soft focus I reserve for when I'm ignoring Leo – is far more planned than I'd realised. The trees have been meticulously measured, pruned and lopped in the past so that they look effortless, elegant, against the setting of the long green lawns – despite the neglect they suffer from now.

Leo taps his hands on his thighs, but it's a thoughtful tap, not an angry one. His frustration at my parenting abilities is ebbing now that he's remembered he's a fortnight out on his superhero stories.

'It might be a good idea to go to the shops.' He nods his

head, but the dialogue doesn't include me, yet. 'Curtis will like comics too.' He looks up at me. 'Okay. But I want to get breakfast first. I need my cereal.'

Sometimes it's worth pointing out the things that were my idea in the first place, but other times – like this – it really isn't.

The shop isn't dissimilar to ones I went to as a child with my mother. There is a smell that I remember, the earth of the potatoes, the cold of the chiller, another – floral – scent that might be the sweet-williams in a bucket by the door but is more likely floor cleaner.

The lady behind the meat counter wears a chequered blue-and-white coat and a white hairnet. She smiles at us warmly. 'Can I help you?'

'Do you have chicken sausages?' Leo asks.

'Not on this counter.' She takes off her apron. 'But I can come and show you where they are.'

I look around but there are no other customers to serve, she might as well come with us.

She keeps up a chatter of geography as we walk the few metres to the cabinet. 'There we are: anything else?'

'I want to do anchovy pasta tonight,' Leo says.

'Smashing,' she says. 'We've got two kinds of anchovies. Fresh or tinned?'

This is one step too far for Leo. He taps his hands on his thighs while he thinks.

'Tinned please,' I say. 'I'm sure we can find them.'

She's a little older than me, probably late fifties, and she clearly hasn't got anything else to do. The sun shines in through the bright stickers on the shop window, bathing the empty aisles with a kaleidoscope of light. 'No, no, I'll show you.' And she leads us round the aisles like a tour guide. 'Are you on holiday?' she asks Leo. 'In Crouch-on-Sea, I mean.'

'I live here.' Leo doesn't look at her when he answers, he is scanning the shelves of tins, running his finger along the coloured labels.

'We're only here for the summer,' I say, 'from London.'

'Are you the artist? The one who's moved into Pear Tree Cottage?'

'Oh, I wish.' I smile at her. 'I'm a teacher – was a teacher. But we've moved into Hatters Hall.'

She stands upright and stares at me. 'How lovely. Are you related to Araminta?' She goes on without pausing, absent-mindedly straightening the front of a row of baked bean cans. 'She's wonderful, isn't she? Absolutely tireless.'

I want to say that no, she's nasty and – as far as I can tell – only relentless in making sure I have a miserable time, but instead, I smile. 'She does very well.'

'She tries so hard to keep that old place going. Goodness knows how – all on her own in that enormous building. Must be very creepy at night.'

'It's not creepy.' Leo's brow is furrowed. 'It's my daddy's house.'

'Colonel Hugo was my husband's grandfather,' I say, feeling a lot less grand than that sounds.

The shop assistant puts her hands on her hips. 'Well, I never. How exciting. Lyons-Morrises back at the house.' The 'lions' makes me flinch. 'You must be so grateful to Araminta for keeping it all going for you.'

I try to distract the woman by pretending to search for something on the bread shelf. It makes no difference at all.

'She's absolutely devoted to that place: it'll be so nice for her to have someone to help her.'

Leo saves the day. 'Do you stock XD comics?' he asks in the voice he keeps for when he is determined to get what he wants.

'The one with the man shaped like a boulder?'

'Rockman.' Leo says it to her first, then a few times under his breath to mark his disapproval that she doesn't know her products better.

She leads us to the front of the shop where there are banks of magazines. Leo spots it immediately.

'Got it.' He pulls the comic out and dances from foot to foot in excitement. He is singing a tuneless little song about the fight scenes and explosions he's looking forward to inside.

'It's so lovely to have the Lyons-Morris family back ...' she says as we wait at the till.

I can't bear the pronunciation any longer. 'I'm Cate,' I say, 'and this is Leo – Colonel Hugo's great-grandson.'

'Jess.' She points to her name badge. 'Colonel Hugo built most of this village – as I'm sure you know. And he paid for the library and the swimming pool from the money he left when he died. We're very much indebted to him. To your family.' She beams at me as I try to stack the wire basket into the pile by the till.

'I didn't know.' I feel a little ashamed, and hide my embarrassment by concentrating on packing the shopping.

'The Colonel's very well thought of in Crouch-on-Sea, and often remembered. Araminta too. It's taken its toll on her over the last few years. It'll be lovely for her to have a bit of help.' She looks up and smiles. 'We're all very fond of her round here.'

Leo's magazine doesn't occupy him for that long.

'I'm going to go and find Curtis now. He said I can help him in the garden.'

I need to have a bit of a chat with Curtis before anything like that can happen. 'Maybe we need to get to know him a bit better before you do that?' Maybe I need to threaten him with exactly what will happen to him if I smell cannabis on my son's clothes. I have a duty of care to Leo that has to come before offending strangers or making assumptions: I will wear my suspicion of Curtis as parental armour until he's proven otherwise to me, and to Leo.

Leo flops next to me on the sofa, knocking my laptop off my knees.

'Watch what you're doing.'

'It wasn't me.'

'Yes, it was, don't be silly. You need to be careful.'

He stands and walks to the window. 'I won't be careful,'

he says deliberately and stares at me, his chin forward and his eyes narrowed.

Leo, like his father before him, is a sensitive soul. Friends – and sometimes strangers – comment on his easy access to his emotions, the fact that he can be so open and demonstrative. They see the sunny Leo, the bright side of that inhibition – what they don't see is his frustration. When things go wrong for him – and they go wrong just as often as they would for anyone else – that same easiness that makes him such a great person to live with, that allows him to experience every happiness up close and personal, can turn into a rage he doesn't have the skills to control.

Richard, who didn't have an extra chromosome, felt his own and other people's pain every bit as keenly, even before he was ill. Things that would make me sad for a moment or encourage me to drop an extra donation in a collecting tin would make Richard out of sorts for days until he could think of something, however tiny, that he could do to help. He would trudge door to door with leaflets that took hours to make in the days before home computers and printers; he would stand in the High Street – however bad the weather – and campaign against losing a tree or closing a leisure centre. It drove me crackers.

I can feel the rolling thunder of one of Leo's meltdowns from across the room.

'Where's your book? Shall we carry on reading where we were yesterday? Remember the Turkish Delight that Edmund wants to eat?'

Leo doesn't say anything but his hands tap worriedly against his thighs, a drumbeat working up to a crescendo.

In our old flat, walking away sometimes worked, but I don't know this place well enough: I don't know how safe the windows are, whether one might burst open if Leo barrelled into it. We are three floors up. I look at Gog and Magog silhouetted behind Leo, staring out towards the garden. They might challenge any incomers but they wouldn't catch my son in full storm.

Leo is looking at his feet, a rumbling noise starting in his throat.

'What's the matter? What can I do to make this better?' But this is the thing he won't know: by the time his exasperation has reached this point, he will have forgotten what was at the root of it – if he ever knew.

'I want to go to and see Curtis.'

'Right, come on then.' There is nothing I can do but give in.

Leo cheers up the second we leave the house and start across the lawns. Araminta is striding in front of the pond, her arms full of what look like bulrushes. We are too close to her to avoid eye contact.

'Gosh, do you do everything round here?' I ask her, gesturing to the wispy stems.

'There are volunteers who come and cut the grass, do most of the gardening in fact. These are for a table display in the hallway. We have a coach party in tomorrow.'

'It's a lot of work,' I say and attempt a smile.

She doesn't smile back but her voice is a little less cold. 'In Colonel Hugo's day there were six full-time gardeners.' She looks up the field towards the trees in the distance. The grass has been cut in a wide stripe to encourage walkers but either side of it meadow grasses are waist high and dotted with yellow flowers.

'I'm going to see Curtis, Mrs Minta,' says Leo. 'He said I can help him.'

'That's a very good idea, Leo. We always need help in the garden. But Curtis will have left, I think. The museum will close soon.' She looks at her watch.

'Ah, about that: I wondered how that works. Once it's closed, I mean.' I tell myself that there is no reason to be afraid of Araminta; after all, the lady in the shop likes her. I remind myself of parents at my school, angry and indignant people who I'd stood up to in the classroom in the face of all sorts of threats, threats I dismissed without breaking a sweat. 'Are we allowed into the garden in the evenings?'

'It isn't really a case of being "allowed",' Araminta says. 'Leo is the heir here, it's more about what's practical. The gardens are locked at the perimeter gates, although I will get you a key cut so you can come and go as you please, but we are already inside so there is no reason you shouldn't enjoy the gardens after – or before – hours.'

Her use of the word 'we' is the main reason I feel uncomfortable about enjoying the gardens at all.

'I see you've met Hippomenes and Atalanta,' she says, directly to Leo and ignoring me. 'Aren't they beautiful?'

'They're very . . . shiny.' Leo pauses for a second over the adjective, trying to find the right one. Shiny is good, it's exactly what they are. He seems to have forgotten about Curtis for the moment.

'These two are from an ancient Greek story. Atalanta, that's the lady, she decided she would only marry a man who could beat her in a running race.'

'I can run really fast,' says Leo.

Araminta smiles, it is a tight smile using muscles she lost control of a long time ago. 'Hold on,' she says and puts the bunch of bulrushes on the ground. Tiny flower fairies drift from their cottonwool tops and lift on the warm air. 'Atalanta could run faster than any of the boys – and she knew it. She didn't want to get married at all.'

'I want to get married,' Leo explains to her. 'I had two girlfriends in London, but I didn't want to marry them. They weren't the right one.'

'It's good to be choosy,' I say, forcing Araminta to attest to my continued presence with a small nod of her head.

'Hippomenes, that's the boy, couldn't run faster than Atalanta either,' she says. She is warming to her subject. 'So he asked Aphrodite, the goddess of love, for some help and she gave him three golden apples.'

Araminta's voice has completely changed, it has peaks and troughs and inflection. Gone is the hard sibilance she saves for me.

'Hippomenes ran as fast as he could, but that wasn't fast enough. But, as he ran, he threw the apples, shining and perfect, and made of pure – but delicious – gold. Atalanta stopped to pick them up and eat them. Because of that he managed to run past her – just. Atalanta was so impressed by his efforts that she fell in love with him and married him.'

'What a fabulous story,' I say, feeling that we may have reached some kind of common ground at last.

She shoots me a look. 'It isn't finished yet.' Her hands brush down the front of her skirt, as if my words are irritating bits of grass that have stuck to her. 'What happened next is the good bit,' she says to Leo. 'And why they're here with us.'

Leo nods at her, his eyes wide with excitement.

'Hippomenes forgot to say thank you to the goddess Aphrodite for her help. That was a terrible thing for the Greek gods – to not say thank you. As a punishment, and there are lots of versions of this bit – this is an ancient story and it wasn't written down – but I'll tell you our version . . .' She squints into the sun and I can see the tiniest wrinkles in her powdered skin.

'Aphrodite was so angry that she turned both of them into lions.'

'Like me,' Leo shouts. 'Leo means lion.' He claps his hands on his thighs with excitement.

'Back in the olden days,' Araminta continues as if he hasn't spoken. 'People believed that lions could only mate . . .' She looks at me for confirmation of using the right word for Leo, and I nod: a tiny bridge between her and me. ' . . . Lions could only mate with leopards. Not each other. So what Aphrodite had done was punish them by making sure they could never be together.'

'Never be married,' Leo says, his voice quiet.

'Exactly. But now we know they were wrong. Male lions and female lions may not look the same, but that doesn't mean they're different species. They're exactly the same animal – they just look different.'

Leo lets out a loud, 'Phew.' He is clearly relieved that Hippomenes and Atalanta will mate after all.

'And that's why they belong here and why they – and the lion – are the emblems of Colonel Hugo's collection. Your great grandfather put these statues here and he told all the people this story. Then he took the people into the museum and showed them the lion, the lioness, and the leopard. He explained the different species to people who couldn't have found out otherwise.'

'That's very cool,' Leo says. 'I like lions.'

'The small back door by the kitchen,' Araminta says directly to me, 'it isn't linked to the museum alarm. You may use that – we call it the scullery door – at any time of the day or night. The key is with the set you got from the solicitor.'

She bends down and scoops up the bulrushes. 'Oh, of course. You lost those.'

It is the evenings that are going to be the worst here. In the evenings, there is nothing to explore, nothing to discover.

In the evenings, there is only the long empty silence of the past, rolling around the quiet of my bedroom.

I start to write to Simon but I'm not sure what to say. I want to tell him about the ledger in the chapel, about how worried I am that my entry would read *'Cate Morris, redundant at fifty. Did very little after that.'* And part of me wants to tell him about Araminta, that her loneliness is so palpable and that I am starting to wonder if the prickle of those spines is just protection, evidence of how long she's been alone, how hard it is to share with other people. Does she know that pain, whatever causes it, is easier to bear when you can hand half of it to someone else?

Sitting by myself makes the past swell up – it is a tide that returns whenever my mind is still. When Leo was ten, Simon was with us for his longest period. It was shortly before we lost our beautiful house: back when we had enough bedrooms for him to easily camp out with us, whenever his research projects would let him. Back when our lives didn't involve strangers and bitter old women intent on picking at the scars left when my happiness was removed.

Simon spent a lot of time writing up research papers late into the night so that he could be available to take Leo to school or to talk to Richard while I went to work.

Richard had withdrawn, hidden inside himself like a hermit crab. We had a community nurse visiting, a social worker, everyone who could help tried so hard but it was never enough. Richard spoke a different language to us – for him, we were all part of the problem, every dialogue we had about him moved us against him, was meant to harm him.

Richard had been proud of our en suite bathroom. He built it himself from a chunk of our over-sized bedroom. There was no room for a window so his engineer's mind had solved the problem by making one wall entirely out of glass bricks. It shone like a lantern, like a glowing heart in the corner of the room, whenever we went in it in the dark. We loved it.

I knew something was wrong when Richard wouldn't answer – I'd gone through the house calling out, looking for him, and the white-tiled bathroom was the last place I looked.

He was standing at the sink, leaning in towards the mirror. At first, I thought the tiny speckles all over the porcelain of the basin were ants. Then I saw the blood, the speckles and drips, the scarlet beads everywhere across Richard's face.

'What are you doing?' I screamed it, at the top of my voice. I couldn't immediately work out what was going on but I knew Richard was hurting himself and that he must stop.

'I don't know.' Richard's voice was a sob. 'I don't know.' He raised his hand to his face again and it made sense. In his fingers were my sharp blue tweezers, the ones that made my eyes water when I neatened my brows. The uniform ants across the basin were Richard's beard hairs. He was methodically pulling out his stubble, follicle by follicle. His face looked like meat, the raw pinkness of it, the blurring of skin and blood.

I pulled the tweezers from his hand and he sank to the floor, his face pressed against the pedestal of the basin, his blood leaking and smearing everywhere on the white.

I screamed and screamed for Simon, my arms round Richard's sunken body, trying to hold him to me, to the moment, to his life.

We went with Richard to the hospital, watched him bandaged and medicated, saw the pain leave his eyes when he was sedated into a merciful sleep. We left at the same time, Simon and I, and – together – collected Leo from his after-school club. For all the world like an odd little family when, really, the spine of our unit, the man who joined us all together, was lying in a hospital bed, unable to do anything more than face the wall and stare.

I have never revealed, to anyone, the manner in which Richard took his own life: and I never will. Apart from dedicated medical intervention, what kept my generous, humble, husband alive for longer than he might otherwise have been was his concern for the person who would find his body. I know because he told me: sometimes in those tiny discussions in the dark; often in an incongruous situation – one where we should be safe – pushing Leo on a swing in the park or basting a chicken hot from the oven. It was a strange way to live but it kept him from dying.

And then he worked it out, the way. The way to avoid a dog-walker finding his body on the beach, to save a child from seeing a corpse in the woods, a train driver, all the people he did not want to burden. His greatest fear was that it would be me, that I would find him and – alone – have to call the police, make statements, tell Leo.

The minutiae of his death kept him alive. And his being alive stopped me from realising how angry I would be when he had gone.

He had the logic left to examine the process – both the method and the aftermath – but, as he explained to me so many times in that level ordinary voice, with no hysteria or panic, he couldn't find the heart to stay alive.

One day, his fine engineering mind worked it out. The foolproof way that hurt no one. And then we knew it was a countdown.

So I never tell. Simon knows parts of it – as do the coroner and the police officers who were involved, as they must be, with a suicide – but we never talk about it, never share it. We hope that the same conundrum is keeping someone else alive. There is one part that no one knows but me.

We watched him, Simon and I, almost round the clock for the first months once we knew his death was inevitable. We would put Leo to bed, Simon or me alongside Richard – never him alone, just in case. Then we, in turns, would spend the rest of the evening with Richard. Sometimes we all sat together in our cosy kitchen, drinking wine, talking late into the night. Other times it was a chore, a real back-breaking task, to sit with him while he was delusional and frightened or cold and deliberate.

There are so many good times, wrapped inside that sad dried cocoon, time that should be out and aired, open to the sunshine. Sometimes the happy memories are so muffled in my anger at being abandoned that they almost choke. I think of Araminta and her bulrushes, of the lady in the shop and her sense of belonging, of community. I think of Leo and the long line of family that stretches out before him here.

For the first time in four years something has managed to creak open and start to fight its way back out.

I pull my dressing gown on over my pyjamas and go downstairs. Araminta is in the wide hall at the bottom of the stairs, putting the finishing touches to an incredible flower arrangement. The bulrushes reach up from the centre, their white tufts clinging on to the stems, like fireworks midway through an explosion. Below them and twining through their stalks are red-hot pokers and the acid yellow stems of a plant I don't know. The effect is extraordinary, and is the perfect elegant touch needed to bring this room to life.

I cough gently so as not to startle her. 'That's truly beautiful,' I say, and before she can say anything unpleasant I add, 'I came down to ask you if I could help you tomorrow, with the coach party.'

'Yes,' she says, looking at the flowers. And then, more gently, and in response to my offer, 'Yes.'

Where We Belong

From: Simon Henderson

To: Cate Morris

Subject: Godfatherly Duties . . .

Mail: Hello? More words than I've had in months, then a brief desperate note – that I responded to, I might add. Now – nothing.

I feel I would be failing the responsibility heaped upon me by that very peculiar (yet rather moving) service (that none of us thought we believed in/cared for until it happened and then we were a collective lump of jelly) if I didn't check you and Leo were still alive before I went to bed.

Those lions are dramatically lifelike – it would be the easiest thing in the world for a real one to sneak into the display, stand stock-still until breakfast, and then leap out as you made your morning rounds. Nothing more scrumptious for a morning snack than Leo in pyjamas.

Seriously, are you both okay?

Sx

From: Cate Morris

To: Simon Henderson

Subject: 'But I don't want to go among mad people,' Alice remarked.

'Oh, you can't help that,' said the Cat: 'we're all mad here. I'm mad. You're mad.'

'How do you know I'm mad?' said Alice.

'You must be,' said the Cat, 'or you wouldn't have come here.'

Mail: I didn't write last night because I don't know whether I'm coming or going. Which made me read Alice in Wonderland to Leo, or at least try to but Leo is now a local chav – long story involving hero worship of a boy in a hoodie – and didn't want to hear it. I read it to myself anyway. And then I thought I'd made a massive breakthrough and perhaps Hatters originally had an apostrophe and is named after THE MAD HATTER but then calmed down when I realised it's quite a lot older than the book. Maybe Lewis Carroll came here and thought, if he was going to write about mad people, he couldn't do better than to start here.

The level of hysteria in that paragraph (I have just reread it) has slightly abated since I went exploring in the grounds. I found the chapel and had five minutes' peace. Have you seen it? The whole family is buried there. Except Richard, obviously.

So I've finished googling and I can't find any information about his father. To the point where it's missing, rather than forgotten. Everyone else has elaborate death notices from The Times (except Richard, obviously, because we didn't do that – didn't know we were supposed to) but his father's notice is a few quiet lines in the local paper. Maybe they were broken-hearted.

The chapel was proper solace, every time I stand still in the house or garden that awful Araminta glides up behind me. It's like a haunting. Only twice as scary. Maybe she can't get over the chapel threshold without a smell of smouldering . . .

Even if I don't see her as I walk around, I can feel that she's been there – there'll be a curtain still flapping or a waft of old lady scent. And an eerie silence – that's her favourite. Her superpower, Leo would say.

Later, alive for now,

Xxx

Chapter Eight

It's a bright warm day. The trees that bend softly over the drive are vivid with summer and move slightly in the breeze. It is a good time to visit any English garden, to be welcomed by bold colours and long golden grasses. From behind the house, I can hear the squawk of the peacock, indignant that so many people have come to share his domain.

Leo was thrilled when I told him he could help Curtis all morning. I did my best to talk about the drugs issue while we made a picnic lunch for the two of them.

'Look, if Curtis starts smoking drugs . . .'

'Smoking drugs is stupid. You heard Curtis say that.' He does not pause in the rhythm of buttering bread, yellow against white, the colours of summer.

'But if he changes his mind and . . .'

'I will come home. It will get on my hair and my clothes and I don't want to smell like that.'

I should have had more faith in Leo's vanity: looking –
and smelling – good is everything to him.

When we get out to the kitchen garden Curtis is already
working. Leo is wearing board shorts and a sky-blue T-
shirt: Curtis is still wearing jeans and his hoodie. He must
be roasting.

I look back at them as I leave the kitchen garden.
Araminta was right: Curtis is a hard worker. In the time it's
taken me to cross the garden, he's shown Leo how to dig and
they're both getting stuck in to the job.

A couple of women I don't recognise wave to me from
the open doorway as I walk towards the front of the house
and the ticket booth. They obviously know who I am and
I wonder if word has filtered through the village that the
Lyons-Morris family are back.

The doorway is edged in bunting, pastel-coloured tri-
angles that transport the whole scene back to the 1950s, and
a smaller one of Araminta's flower arrangements sits on the
desk of the ticket office.

'You really have an artistic eye,' I say and Araminta smiles
at the compliment.

'We've got a very full house.' She takes two clipboards
from the desk. She swallows slightly. 'And I'm grateful for
your help.'

And that is it: the truce. So simple, so quietly delivered.
A white flag flies between us and the relief is instant. It
took only a few words to undo all the difficulty, all the

unpleasantness. It took one small gesture from me to open up the negotiations.

'Are you ready?' Araminta says and points to the open doorway. Framed by the bunting, two large white coaches drive slowly onto the gravel of the car park. 'This is typical Malcolm,' she says shrugging her shoulders. 'He only booked one coachload in.'

I am wearing an ironed linen skirt and a button-through blouse. I have a short string of fake pearls around my neck and simple, silver, earrings: I don't look much like me but I do, I hope, look like a member of the Lyons-Morris dynasty. 'Shall we take one each?' I ask, feeling less confident than I sound.

Araminta nods.

It takes about fifteen minutes to get them all in and paid for. They are a mix of French and English, all of retirement age, and very much looking forward to their visit.

The entrance hall is awash with noise, the chatter is light and happy. There is lots of laughter and I can hear English, French, and a considerable amount of Franglais between the jostling visitors.

'I've put all your names on your clipboard,' Araminta calls to me over the hubbub. 'Come over here and I'll assign your party to you.'

She beckons me over towards the postcard display and I understand why such a concentration of visitors has gathered in this small space. Two red-faced and very smiley old men are standing behind a wallpaper-pasting table. In minutes, they have arranged a sea of paper cups, and – in boxes underneath the table – I can see they have enough wine to fill them.

'You must be Cate,' one of them says and gestures towards me with a paper cup brimming with red wine.

I'm obviously supposed to take it. 'Driving, I'm afraid. And taking a tour group round the collection.' And it's half past ten in the morning, I add silently.

'Everything goes better with a drop of this,' he says, still waving the paper cup at me. 'I'm Malcolm. I run the Twinning Association. And this is Thierry. He brings this wonderful stuff over with him.'

'It's the only reason they ask us back,' says Thierry in accented-but-perfect English.

'I'm very pleased to meet you both.'

'I hope none of that wine is going into the galleries, Malcolm.' Araminta is standing in front of him with her clipboard. 'Please make sure no one leaves the foyer with their cup, except to go outside.'

'Absolutely, Araminta. I wouldn't dream of it.' He winks at her and drinks from the cup he was offering me. 'Waste not, want not.'

Araminta sighs, passes me a printed piece of paper, and pushes through the crowd to the corridor that leads to the galleries.

'You have to know how to handle her,' Malcolm says and laughs at his own joke. Behind him Thierry is filling more cups.

'I don't know how you dare.' I look away from him and check the names on the list. There seem to be a lot of them.

'I've known her forever. We were at school together, Minnie Buchan and me. Not allowed to call her that any more though.'

Two things make my jaw drop. The first is the image of the neat, quiet, Araminta as a 'Minnie'. I can't begin to process it. But the second is Malcolm's age. He's far older than Araminta, at least, far older than I'd assumed she was. I would put Malcolm in his seventies – Araminta can't possibly be anything like that. Perhaps it's his party lifestyle, maybe red wine's not as good for you as I'd thought.

'Did she live here then?' I don't miss my chance.

'All her life. Her mother worked here too and they lived in the red house over at the back.'

I move towards the museum entrance, to where Araminta is standing with her clipboard, running her finger along the lines of text and looking very organised.

'Group two, over here please.' Araminta looks at her notes. I wonder how many people each of those vast coaches holds. Half of them are going to be in my charge and half of that half speak a language I've barely used since my O levels.

Araminta carries on calling across their heads. I'd say the majority of them have been sampling the wine the exchange group brought with them. They are in remarkably high spirits for a group of retired people being shown round a country house and collection.

'Mrs Lyons-Morris, would you take group one?'

'Cate Morris,' I say to my group, at least those that are listening, and try to look as if I mean business.

Araminta waves her clipboard, everything below her wrist has disappeared into the throng of noisy visitors. 'I suggest you start . . .' she shouts across the din.

But I see it coming, and I say it as she does: '. . . in Gallery One.' I know how things are done around here. It makes me smile.

Gallery One is actually a great place to start. It's been designed this way to get the maximum reaction from the guests as they slip round that first corner, funnelled in by the corridor, and all see the glass cases at the same time.

'Gets me every time, this place.' Malcolm is standing behind me, his hand flat across his chest, resting over his heart. 'I've been coming here man and boy, but it never pales. I love showing it to new people.'

'How do you know so much?' I'm shaking my head and smiling: Malcolm is humanising this cold place as he speaks.

'The Colonel used to show me round. When I was a nipper.'

'You knew the Colonel?' I'm trying to stay next to Malcolm as he gathers the other visitors round him, sharing his enthusiasm.

'He was an old man by the time I met him, but we used to come up with school. From the village.' He points to the back of the glass case, his other arm is round Thierry's shoulders. 'Look at the giraffe.' He points, Thierry and I follow his gaze. 'It's half-mounted and half painted. See? It doesn't have a body, that bit's painted in 3D.'

'Trompe l'oeil,' Thierry says. 'All the best things are French.'

The giraffe isn't real. I've stared at this case, trying to count the animals, work out exactly what's there. Leo and I have gone through it together, pointing at all the creatures we weren't sure of and looking them up on the board in front of the case. And we never noticed that most of the giraffe isn't real. His head and majestic neck are real enough, his mournful eyes the same haunting glass marbles as the rest of the menagerie, but his body – now that I can make it out amongst the cloth leaves and the paper-wrapped trunks – is painted onto the wall. It's an incredible job, the long brown patches that spot his legs, the bones and sinew that jut from his chest beneath the fur. I could have looked in here a hundred times and never have noticed.

It's only now Malcolm's pointed it out that I really look at the artwork behind the animals. Dusty plains stretch into the distance, the sun catching on rocks and glinting from the speckled gold sand. In the next case along, there are hints of ice in the crags and crevices of the rocks, tufts of green-blue lichen clinging to the vertical surfaces, and water dripping slowly down boulders, leaving a slick of minerals in its wake.

Malcolm has finished his lecture, the group are moving slowly through the galleries towards the vast domed library.

'Well, I'm glad I finally got them here,' he says to me as the last of the visitors file out of Gallery One. 'I've been telling the Twinning Association that they need to visit this place ever since it started.'

'Why wouldn't they?'

Malcolm shrugs. 'It's probably me. I'm not very good at telling people what I mean, getting my enthusiasm into actual ideas.'

'I think you're a natural tour leader.'

'It's all different now they've seen it. They love it now. But before it was all, "Oh, no, not stuffed animals," or, "I don't like taxidermy."'

I approach the rest of the tour with more enthusiasm. I hear myself take on a new energy when we reach the African collection. I explain how the invasion of the Europeans is reflected in the jewellery that Hugo's party bartered and traded: brass bullet casings threaded onto necklaces, Bakelite beads used in ornate headdresses despite previously being mundane radio knobs or light switches.

There are other visitors now, occasionally gliding past us and pausing to hear what I'm talking about. They are too young to be from Malcolm's party and I assume, or at least hope, that the coaches and the buzz around them in the village have attracted other visitors to the museum. There is a group of young mums with pushchairs, their toddlers running up and down the gallery corridors. It gives me hope: if I'd lived near this place when Leo was little, I'd have been here all the time – picnicking in the gardens or showing him the animals. It's so sad that we missed it.

At the very front of the African gallery, Gallery Three to give it its proper name, there is an exhibit that enchanted me as soon as I saw it, that set me wondering about stories and histories and what we should tell our children even before I saw the ledger in the chapel.

I don't know any more than what's on the card in the front of the case – should the group peer down and read it – but I deliver it with a surety that no one questions.

The little tray of stones is one of the quieter exhibits. Its value is hidden. They are pretty enough: a shallow wooden tray containing a heap of coloured stones, almost gems from the way they've been softened and smoothed, and the size of small marbles. When you read the card, they reveal themselves: you need the key to understand.

'These are Kudu mouth stones. Girls, who . . .' I choose my words carefully for my audience, 'when they come of age, choose a stone and put it under their tongue. And there it stays, for their whole life: while they're asleep, when they're ill, when they have children. Every day.'

'How come they don't swallow them?' an elegant woman in a powder blue suit asks.

I shrug. 'They just don't – as far as I know. It's part of their culture to pass on the ways of how to do it. And then – and this is my favourite part – when your mother dies, or maybe your grandmother – you take her stone and you put it into your mouth with your own and hold it there.' I love this idea. I imagine every word my mother ever said washed across a stone, smoothing its edges, leaving the tracks of its passage like an invisible gramophone ridge. Then I think of my words: words of kindness, love; words of loss and sadness; words of wonder at all the crazy and beautiful things the world has given me. It would be lovely to know I still had them all here.

'But how did Colonel Hugo get them? Surely these are someone's stones? Someone's heritage.' Another woman is bending forward, peering through the glass at the little heap of smoothed stones. She is wearing flat sensible lace-ups, halfway between sneakers and shoes, and the white of the laces reflects in the glass in front of her. She looks up at me with genuine concern.

I've read this; the bigger picture of Colonel Hugo's ethos is explained in the foyer. 'These were stones without a home, from lines that had died out or from girls who took their mother-in-law's stone, which happened in families with no daughters.'

I deliberately stand in front of the case to say the next bit – as if I know the details off by heart and they're not in tiny script behind my legs. 'Colonel Hugo bartered with a village elder to get them. Every human-related item in this museum has been paid for – in various forms – and the transactions are all documented in Colonel Hugo's accounts from the time. They're available for you to look at in the central library.'

It's an amazing legacy: a one-hundred-year-old register of Fair Trade, of an old-school explorer recognising that the people he was meeting had as much right to the property and heritage as he did to his. Maybe this should have been the thing Malcolm tried to sell to his group as a reason to visit the museum. Maybe I could try with future visitors. There is the collective gasp I expect as the group walk into the centre of the library room. The books stand sentinel in their neat rows, challenging anyone to know more about Art, or Medicine, or Geography than they do.

In this room, the books are the stars. The shelves reach up and up, the only way to see the top shelves is to tip your head back as if you were looking at the sky. Even then, you wouldn't immediately notice the rail that runs around the inner edge of the cupola, and the spidery ladders that disguise themselves with the spines of the books that lead to it. The books line the sides like the cells of a beehive, a honeycomb of leather, and paper, and words.

The spider-eye lens of glass leaks in light at all angles. It is a bubble of pure blue today – a perfect view of a cloudless August sky. The gilt lettering on the spines dances in the reflected sun, glitters up and down the walls.

'How many books are in here?' It is Thierry, Malcolm's friend. He is staring upwards and moving backwards in tiny circles to take it all in, a bewitched waltzer in an enchanted ballroom.

'I honestly don't know. And I can't begin to imagine what they're worth – what might be here. They're mostly non-fiction, but they come from all over the world. Malcolm, do you know any more than me?'

Malcolm shakes his head. 'To be honest, I never came in here much. It's impressive and all, but the animals, the history, the real things – they're more me than the books.' He points a finger towards the vast shelves. 'I think that's why he did it.'

'Did what?'

'I think all the other rooms, all the collections and the travels, I think they're all the pictures of what these words describe. We're a rural community. People travel now, get away and see bits of the world – my late wife and I went to India three times. But that was unthinkable in my parents' time. For someone like me to see anything outside the country, outside the county even.' His eyes are misty and I wonder how many of those glasses of wine he emptied. 'But my parents came here. They wouldn't have read the books – they would have thought they were too precious – but they got a great idea of the world from seeing the way it had been laid out for them. Wonderful, really.'

'Did you know Richard?' Suddenly it is the question I most want to ask Malcolm, the first person here who has freely given up information.

'Bless him. Not well, of course – he was a lot younger than me. But I knew him when he was little.' He takes hold of my hand for the shortest moment. 'I'm so sorry about what happened to him.'

I give a little smile of thanks. 'Was he here when you used to visit?'

119

Malcolm laughs. 'I used to see him when I came up to call for Minnie. I had a bit of a crush on her, between you and me, but she wasn't interested. She doted on Richard when he was a little boy.'

Chapter Nine

To: Cate Morris

From: Simon Henderson

Subject: Before I Go

Mail: Phew, that sounds a bit more like you – try and keep that up.

Sorry to say, I'm going to abandon you as well in a sec – two-week field trip to find fossils. I know, I know, but I like them. And we need the past to understand the future. Fact.

My team are picking everyone up on the way and I live on the mountain side of the city so I'm last onto the charabanc. I'm looking forward to it in that same way that I never stopped enjoying rugby tours . . . Big kid.

Thanks for the photo of Leo in his hat, I've sent it on to my mum – she does like to be kept informed of her great-godson's progress. She says she's going to find some old ones of Rich and me and scan them in on her iPad. Ninety-two years old and scanning on her iPad: I'm proud of her!

Hope all is good and getting better.

Sx

I can trace the pivot of our lives to a Christmas. Not our last Christmas together, it would turn out, but the last one in our beautiful home. In unopened letters that Richard kept from me and in muttered phone calls he passed off as interviews with mental health professionals, the fabric of our lives was being eaten away as surely as if termites were gnawing at the footings of our house, multiplying in the damp darkness, turning their blind eyes upwards to stare through the floor.

The Christmas tree always stood in the same place in our old sitting room. Richard had been painstaking in his attention to detail when he renovated what had been the Edwardian parlour. Its high ceilings and original features were part of what had attracted us to the house from the off. When we'd seen it that first time, almost derelict and empty but for curled carpet and a smell of cats, he'd hugged me with an electric current of joy, imagining those Christmases with our clutch of children: two or four or however many we were lucky enough to have. Our eventual reality, our one perfect boy, lived up to every pulse of that wishing.

The tree was always real, tall and bent at the top to get its whole length into the room. I loved the way I would forget it was there until I opened the sitting room door and was engulfed in that scent, the oily resin that leaked into the air from its needles. The elegant tree of my imaginings had morphed, over the years of Leo's little life, into a multi-coloured mishmash of crepe-paper bows and playschool paintings, cluttered mementos of happiness, of achievements. My one concession to style was the lights, always white, winding their way from the very top – squashed against the ceiling – down and down and down to the wide prickly lower branches. Richard would moan, an exaggerated wail of despair – and say that that many plugs in so many gang sockets would blow the house up or double the electric bill, or anything else he could think of. And then we would stand back, admire the tree, and feel the warmth of our home, our lives together.

For the whole of that last year in the house, Simon had been in Mexico on a research project. It had made Richard's Christmas to know that he'd be home and with us for the celebrations, lifted him from a rigorous gloom that had followed him for weeks.

Leo had gone to bed wide-eyed with wonder, his rosebud lips in a permanent smile at the tree, the lights, the promise of presents. We tucked him in with his stocking on top of his bed covers, and told him how the big sock would rustle in the morning, over-stuffed and heavy on his legs.

I was in my element. My three favourite people on the planet under my roof, the downstairs hearths lit – the chimneys finally lined and swept and ready for a real old-style

Christmas after years of work. The house was almost finished bar two bedrooms on the top floor that we could pretend weren't there. In the end, it was a whole Christmas of pretending.

'Are you cold?' I asked Simon as soon as he got in. 'Is it still warm in Mexico?'

'Not where we were. It was bloody freezing in the mountains. But we had good tequila.' He put his rucksack on the kitchen table and dug around in it. 'Like this actually. Not for export.' He pulled out a brown glass bottle, wrapped in an old T-shirt. 'All the way from deepest darkest Mexico to this little corner of London. And I've got some bits for Leo – one from my mum and a couple from me. Hers is wrapped but, you know ...' He grinned at me and I passed him the coloured paper on its roll and the kitchen scissors.

Richard poured tiny glasses of tequila, and they sat in a row on the table. We were being careful with alcohol, trying to drink enough to make our celebrations feel like their usual selves but not enough to tip Richard's delicate stability.

'Cheers,' said Richard and he smiled like he meant it at last. He was more animated than I'd seen him in a while. Even getting the glasses out without being asked was a small victory, more like his real self. 'How long are you staying, Si? It's so great to have you here. To have you home.'

'I've got to see my mum a bit, and I fly back on the third. But maybe – if you guys can bear it – I'll stay for a few days with her after Boxing Day and come back to you for New Year?'

'Perfect,' said Richard. 'We can go up to Ally Pally like the old days.' We used to watch the fireworks from Alexandra Palace before we had Leo, the three of us huddled together in the cold, drinking from the same bottle or – in another century – sharing cigarettes from the same packet. 'Leo's old enough to enjoy fireworks now.'

Later, while Richard stacked the dishwasher, Simon and I took a tour of the house and the more recent renovations. Out of his earshot we were able to be honest.

'Thank you for coming back,' I half-whispered in the glass bathroom. 'It's done him the world of good, seeing you.'

'He's not as bad as I thought he'd be. Not as bad as last time I was here. I'm pleased. He's almost the real him, fragile, but very nearly himself.'

Simon's visit had been the result of furtive emails between us, discussing Richard's condition, his prognosis, whether Simon could help. It wasn't the spontaneous trip back to the UK Richard believed: there were so many secrets slipping in and out of our house that winter.

I knew that Simon had hoped for the boisterous Richard, the booming laugh of his party persona, his boundless energy for life. I had accepted the change, mourned the part of him that was lost but I'd had time, had seen him quietly shrink.

'Are all the fireplaces finished?' Simon asked, trying to talk about solid life, rather than the fear we were all carrying. 'Does this one work?'

We were in our bedroom. It had started to look like

something from an architect's brochure. The perfect cornice, restored and whitened, the sash windows tightened against the winter rain and slightly misted with condensation from the en suite bathroom. Simon leaned down and put his hand to the chimney inside the fireplace. 'Is this one open too?' he asked and swiped his hand in the space to check. There was a rustling noise. 'What's this?'

Simon held an envelope in his hand. Behind him, I could see the corner of another one, brown paper, and slightly above that, more white. I stepped across to the fireplace.

When I put my hand into the chimney, I could feel the crush of paper, the jumbled and tightly packed letters – all unopened. Each one was addressed to Richard. Occasionally they had my name on too. I pulled and pulled. They tumbled down from the chimney. Not Santa Claus, not gifts, not the magical reindeer and the jingling bells that Leo was dreaming of.

Simon and I sat on the bed, the huge stack of bills – because we could see that was what they were – between us.

'I've never heard of half these companies,' I said. 'I don't even know why they're writing to us. We certainly don't owe them anything.'

But we did. One by one we opened the envelopes, we did half of them upstairs and then – once we knew how awful the situation really was – we took the rest downstairs, to Richard, to read together in the kitchen.

The repossession notice was near the bottom of the pile, close enough to the nightmare being over that I thought we might have got away with it. Then I read that there had been a hearing: our creditors had been present and, when we looked at the letter more carefully, we were in a house that now – already – belonged to the bank. They had only not got round to evicting us because of the festive season.

I thought of my son asleep in his perfect bedroom, of my huge and tasteful Christmas tree, my glass bathroom. I thought of all of the secrets and all of the lies. The last letter, the repossession one, had been signed for. Richard had taken delivery of it from a bailiff, signed to say that was so, then hid it up the chimney.

Richard was silent, his face told me nothing – not that there was anything left to explain.

I screamed at him, livid. 'How? How could you have let this happen? This is our fucking home.' I sobbed into my hands, unable to look at him.

He stood, without a word, pushed his chair neatly under the table, and went to bed.

'I'll cancel my flight,' Simon said.

I check my phone occasionally during the tour, but no word from Leo. I arrange it so that Malcolm and friends can spill out into the garden and I can go and find him.

At first, I think they've gone. But when I walk right into the kitchen garden, I find them with their backs to the low brick wall of the orangery. They are tearing tiny pieces off their sandwiches and throwing them to the glossy black crow who hops around collecting the crumbs.

'Is that the same crow from the other day?' I ask.

'He's Curtis's friend,' Leo says.

'Crows can remember human faces.' Curtis says – his voice barely audible – but then sinks back into the anonymity of his hoodie.

Outside the kitchen garden wall, I can hear the coach party: inside it is quiet enough to pick up the tap-tapping of the matt black beak as the bird pecks the ground. The tangled honeysuckle that has entirely taken over the cold frame and the flowerbed next to it sweetens the air and makes everything balmy. The turned-over earth that Curtis and Leo have dug is a fresh brown against the summer colours all around it and the damp cold earth looks like respite from the summer heat.

'You've done so much.' There isn't a weed or a clod to be seen in the perfect soil. 'Have you had enough, Leo? You must both be exhausted.'

'I'm in the middle of helping.' Leo looks away from me to emphasise his point. 'I'm not finished.'

'We're dead-heading next,' Curtis says quietly. 'That's not very hard work.'

I wish we hadn't got off on the wrong foot, that I'd never seen him smoking the cannabis. There's no sign of it now: this house is starting to feel like it might all be about second chances, about new beginnings.

'Enjoy the dead heads,' I say to them. 'And text me if you can't find me, Leo. I'll be somewhere in the house.'

*

I walk back in through the double doors that lead into the Japanese collection on the far side of the library. The room is ornate and oriental. Sideboards and panels of intricate marquetry line the walls, and vases as tall as me stand by the windows.

The French doors I've walked in through are part of a long window that runs all the way, floor to ceiling, down one side of the room. If I hadn't just come in from a classic English garden, I could believe I was on the veranda of a long low bungalow in the Japan or China of a hundred years ago.

The walls are papered with exquisite silk fabric, threads of silver and gold run through it and the tiny embroidered stitches that make up its pattern are incredible. The scenes in each piece are as detailed as a fine drawing; the petals of tiny flowers, light falling on water, shadows of tall trees – all picked out in sparkling silks. Two huge jade dogs, as high as my waist, guard either side of the fireplace. The information board on the wall tells me that 'Colonel Hugo started his own collection with a trip to Japan on his eighteenth birthday. Before that, his father had been an amateur collector of anthropological material. When Hugo went to fight in the First World War shortly before his nineteenth birthday, his parents started building the museum as we see it today, in the hopes that he would return in one piece: he did come back, decorated for heroism, and determined to acquaint his fellow countrymen with animals and cultures from all the corners of the world that they would never see. He was also, by Armistice Day, the youngest ever Colonel in the British Military.'

Everything I learn about Hugo, the military career, the gifts to the community, this whole extraordinary museum, makes it seem stranger and stranger that Richard didn't speak to him. He sounds like an amazing man, he sounds like a kind man.

There is an alcove at the end of the room, underneath a smaller archway. And as I walk towards it I realise, for the first time, that I'm not alone.

The man turns round and sees me at the same moment that I notice him.

'I'm sorry,' we both say, though there is no need to be. There is something intimate about the silence in this opulent room. I feel as if I've broken in, invaded his privacy. His flushed face shows he feels exactly the same.

On the back wall of this ante-room is a cabinet made of sculpted red lacquer, each shelf holding a tiny carved object. 'Netsuke – pronounced nets-gay' reads the card. 'Carved ivory and boxwood, Japan, 17th century.' The tiny sculptures are a few inches long, polished smooth and as translucent as boiled sweets. Each one is more intricate than the last: a tiny rat with perfect fur; a miniature sailing ship packed with drowning sailors, their anguished faces perfectly gouged out of the bone. There is a cart on its way to market, piled high with bamboo chicken cages, and so tiny it would fit easily inside my closed fist. They are exquisite.

The man has a sketchbook in his hand. 'I was drawing the netsuke,' he says.

'May I?' I put my hand out towards the paper and he turns it round to show me.

The netsuke the man has chosen to draw is a tiny fox, his white-tipped tail waving skyward with vigour. It is perfect.

'That's so beautiful.'

'Thank you.'

And then a memory, the trace of someone else's words. 'Are you the artist who's moved in to Pear Tree Cottage?'

Chapter Ten

Malcolm calls across the Japanese drawing room before the artist has time to answer me.

'Cate, we're all about to leave. My lot would love to say goodbye.' He smiles broadly. 'And thank you, of course.'

'Excuse me,' I say and make full eye contact with the artist for the first time. His eyes are a piercing blue, the colour of the sky outside this afternoon, of the sea when the very edges have frozen in a wild winter.

'I'm Patch,' he says to my retreating back, 'Patch Samson.'

I am blushing too much to turn back and respond. A part of me I thought had died struggles to the surface of my skin and my cheeks boil red with heat. I need to be outside.

I'm back by the ticket office, seeing Malcolm's party to their coaches, when the alarm goes off.

Araminta comes – almost running – into the foyer. Her face is pale.

'Is that our flats? The upstairs?' I instantly worry about our doors not locking, realising that our lack of privacy is so much worse than simply that: we are vulnerable.

'No, I didn't put that on. This is the museum floor.'

'Can you tell where? Is there a panel?'

She knows immediately what I mean. 'It's not that sophisticated. It's only on the doors and some of the cases.' She turns to go back towards the galleries. People are moving out onto the lawns now, convinced that this is a fire alarm. The mums with the buggies hurry past us.

'Can you organise people here?' she calls as she half-walks, half-runs, back towards Gallery One.

'No.' I follow her. 'You can't possibly go in there on your own.'

She starts to object and then gives up. I imagine she is as frightened as I am.

The animals are still, the glass intact. If they have seen anything untoward it has not bothered them and they are not going to share it with us.

Araminta and I move on through the galleries, our ghostly reflections the only thing that is moving. The animals watch us with those round glass eyes, following our every movement, in every corner of the rooms.

The alarm has been triggered in the library. An oak door underneath one of the huge mounted heads – the bison – has been pushed open. Whoever did this has moved round behind the desk, past the red rope cordons, past the sign that says 'PRIVATE' in upper case red letters.

Whoever did this may well still be in the unlit room behind the doorway.

'What's in there?' I ask Araminta. I hadn't realised that there were doors behind the desks. When I glance round, I see three more closed doors, one on each wall.

'Books? More objects from the collection that aren't on display? I couldn't know without checking the inventory. All these storerooms are packed with cases, floor to ceiling.' She moves into the doorway of the tiny room and I have no choice but to stand behind her – just in case.

'There's no one here.' She gives a slight shiver. We can both imagine what could have happened if there had been.

The noise of the alarm shrieks round the library. We have been too frightened to hear it. It only comes back into focus now, now that we are breathing again.

'We can only turn it off at the desk,' says Araminta, and she closes the opened door behind her.

It is six o'clock before we've got all the visitors out and Leo back in. He is exhausted by his day but tanned and happy.

'Shall we have a drink in the garden before you go and have a bath?' I ask him.

'A very good idea,' he says. 'And with Mrs Minta.'

He is absolutely right: we need to capitalise on the truce while we can, embed the idea that Araminta can talk to me without scowling – even if it is only when we are hunting down intruders in our house. 'Absolutely. I'll get the drinks, you go and find Araminta.'

'And crisps,' Leo reminds me as he leaves the kitchen.

I've put two wine glasses on a tray for Araminta and me, and a beer for Leo. He prefers drinking straight from the bottle. I couldn't find a wine cooler so I've used a glass jug filled with cold water. The wine bottle is perched in it at an angle. The jug is bulbous and carved with a geometric pattern – I'm fairly certain it's crystal but we're supposed to use these elaborate and valuable heirlooms as everyday items. The water that comes out of the old kitchen taps is incredibly cold, already chilled: I try not to think about the lengths of lead piping that probably deliver it.

I settle the tray on a picnic bench near the pond and sit down. It's been a long day: we will all sleep well tonight. I run one foot against the other in order to kick off the pumps that I chose because they were so plain and, hope-fully, formal.

'You forgot the crisps.' Leo is annoyed.

I put my head in my hands. 'I'm sorry.' I move to get up and fetch them: I'm too tired for an argument.

'Why don't you get them, Leo?' Araminta sits down opposite me.

Without a word, Leo starts back across the lawn.

'And then we can have a chat.' Araminta waves her hand at her glass when I've only half-filled it. It makes me a bit more cautious with my own. 'We need to talk about what happened today. I'm sure it hasn't escaped your notice that we really don't have much in the way of security.'

'It's a worry . . .'

'And that the more people we have in, the worse a situation that becomes. I've checked the upstairs rooms – ours, and the other ones that are unlocked. I hope you don't mind that I looked in yours. Just to be sure.'

It had crossed my mind that someone could be hiding in our apartments. I was putting off checking them for as long as I could: everything of mine worth stealing is in boxes – even I couldn't find it easily. 'You should have waited for me: what if there had been someone up there?'

The peacock is parading by the pond, Atalanta and Hippomenes continue their motionless glide towards us with hope on their faces and the sun on their golden hair. It's hard to believe that anything bad could happen here.

'We're trapped between a rock and a hard place.' Araminta takes a sip of her drink, her fingers are tiny against the glass and her knuckle bones stick out from her skin. She may be brave and spiky, but she is fragile.

'If we don't get visitors in, we close. If we do, something will – eventually – get stolen.'

'Exactly,' she says. 'And there is no money to pay for a more sophisticated alarm system – or security guards. I think we can both agree that whoever opened the door was speculating about what they might find.'

'Unless it was one of the toddlers.'

She arches her eyebrow at me to show what she thinks of that idea. Leo returns with a bowl of crisps; the crumbs down his T-shirt explain why he took so long.

'Are they nice, those crisps?' I ask him.

'I don't know,' he says. 'Let me check. I'm very hungry from digging.' He takes the biggest crisp from the top of the bowl and makes a big show of holding it up. Translucent sunlight shines through it, every bit as gold as the two statues. 'I think today was my best day ever,' he says. 'I love living here.'

It is the impetus I need. 'We have to carry on.' The statues stare at me, willing me to say more, willing me to mean it. 'Everyone in the village seems so happy to have the family back.' I think about Richard before I say the next bit, but he does nothing to stop me. 'To have the Lyons-Morris family here once more. Back where they belong.'

'And when you return to London, after the summer?' Araminta is a step ahead of me. Her face is set in the grimace I'm more used to.

I take a big swallow of my wine. The oak tree to our left and the crazy monkey puzzle zigzagging its way skyward nod their leaves in encouragement. 'Maybe we won't go back. Maybe we can put more work into attracting visitors all the time, not solely for special occasions. That way, we could afford to take on staff to help us.'

'It had the potential to be a great day and we took a lot of money in tickets.' She pauses and stares at me, clearly thinking her words through before she speaks. 'I am willing to compromise.' In the distance a cockerel crows, announcing the end of his working day. 'We take one more try at a big day, an event. If that fails, we go back to how we were. For however long that lasts.' She raises her glass to her lips. 'I do want this to work, you know,' she says and emphasises the word 'want' to make me believe her.

It is a small step forward, but it's something. We can make this work, I know we can. I can make it work for my own sake, for Leo: even – I am surprised to find I care – for Araminta.

We fall into a companionable silence of sorts. Leo is humming and occasionally talking about his gardening. Araminta is as deep in thought as I am. I'm thinking about social media and avatars when I remember the artist from Pear Tree Cottage.

'Have you met Patch Samson? He's an artist.'

'I have.' Her face gives nothing away: I cannot tell if those vivid blue eyes left her blushing too or if she is judging me for asking questions about a handsome stranger. 'But not in the capacity of artist. He's here often – he brings his students to paint in the museum.'

'He's a teacher?' There was something primal, wordless, in the way he and I looked at each other. An instant and real connection. Perhaps it was simply that – he is a teacher and that made him, somehow, familiar to me, somehow recognisable.

'He took over the art group down at the community centre a couple of months ago. I did wonder if Leo might want to join. They're a lovely group, all around his age.'

Two things really please me: the thought that I have a reason to meet Patch Samson again – it makes my cheeks flush and I press my wine glass against them to cool my skin. More responsibly, I am immensely touched by the idea of Leo attending a class in the centre paid for by the grandfather he never met. It seems so very right.

I have three glasses of wine all in all. Two sociably with Araminta, and a third – more maudlin – on the lawn by myself when she'd gone to bed and Leo was in the bath.

Now that I'm back upstairs, in the flat that's not as interesting – or hopeful – as the rest of the day has been, things feel less perfect. I had forgotten, when I said that perhaps we'll stay, that we have a piece of thick green fabric for a front door and that, however much things have softened with Araminta, we have to share a kitchen.

From: Cate Morris

To: Simon Henderson

Subject: Where Was I?

Mail: I know you can't hear me up in the wilds, but I'm affirming my own positive thoughts by writing them down. One step forward, two steps back, but at least I'm not in the 'same' place. How's that for spin?

I used to write to Richard, after he'd died. Long emails and then send them to his address – and then open them myself because he was gone. I know you did it too because I saw them (why mention it now? Hashtag: BlameWine) but I didn't open yours – it seemed wrong. They weren't meant for me.

I gave myself permission to believe that because the words turned into something intangible while they crossed the ether, maybe he could decipher them. I know it's a myth, but it's one that suited me in the first couple of years.

I wish you were here. I wish he was here. That would make me glad I was here.

xxx

My anger towards Richard, stoked and fuelled by the wine, bubbles up – one of the moments where I wonder how he ever could have wanted to do this to us, to leave Leo and me responsible for each other, for everything.

As ever, the second the anger rises, the guilt pulses in behind it. The two tussle for a while, jostle for superiority, but always – and rightly – it is the guilt that wins.

I lie on my bed, tearful now that Leo has gone to bed and it is safe to be honest with myself. The top drawer of my bedside cabinet, the one I brought from home with all its contents intact is at my eye level. I know that I will find the photograph there, right at the bottom, buried under other – more honest – memories.

We'd gone to the seaside for the day: Simon was staying with us for a few weeks to give me respite care for Richard, and his mum had come down for the day. We'd gone to a garish coastal town, one with arcades and air hockey, and fish and chips for Simon's mum.

We're lined up on the concrete sea defence: Richard on

the left. I tell myself you wouldn't know, that you couldn't see how ill he was at that point – but you could. Even the other people walking past would have had an idea that something was wrong. It's in his tense muscles, his pursed worried mouth. It's written across the furrows of his face. He is sitting next to Leo but he doesn't have his arm round him. Instead, Richard sits awkwardly on both his hands. I know that was the only way he could keep from tugging at the skin around his nails, rubbing and pulling them until they were red and painful. Not one atom of him is at peace. He picked at the fish and chips, lining flakes of white cod up on his plate and refusing to eat anything that had touched the batter: he asked the waitress for a second plate that he used to pile the crisp orange batter on and tiny pools of oil leaked onto the white china.

Leo in the picture is untroubled. By that stage, maintaining the illusion of a normal happy life for him was my main concern. That day he had eaten candy floss and doughnuts from a booth by the end of the pier. His grin in the photograph is wide and guileless, smeared all round with dust that has stuck to the leftover sugar. He is wearing a red sweater and a large round badge that says, 'I am 11'.

Simon is next to him. It is typical Simon – happy, open, ruggedly healthy. He had a year-round tan long before he moved to New Zealand. He is snuggled up close to Leo, leaning in to his shoulder and grinning to the camera.

I am at the other end to Richard, bookending these two men who were the most important in his life. His son and his best friend: two of his three greatest achievements, he used to say.

You can see the worry in my face too: it's more than ten years ago but I look worn, exhausted – older than I do today.

The present-day me involuntarily touches my hair, it probably needed a cut then even more than it does now. I was thinner then too, but not in a good way. In a way that says I was constantly worried about making sure my husband was eating, that my son was happy, in a way that evidences there was very little of me left for me.

Between Simon and me – and you wouldn't see if you didn't know to look – his hand and mine are locked together, fingers knitted and thumbs wrapped under, his large palm over the back of my hand. You can just see the crimped edge of our blended hands squashed, almost out of sight, between my right thigh and his left leg.

Our knuckles are white.

Chapter Eleven

I wake full of strange feelings: it takes a while to recognise optimism and hope. We have been strangers for too long.

I make a list. It's always been my first port of call: long after lists stopped helping, when having any kind of order was impossible, I still wrote them – little pieces of flotsam, wishes awash on a tide of real life, reduced in value to less than the paper they were written on.

I write this, more positive, list in bed. The first item on the list is 'Art Club' and I am pretending to myself that it's for Leo. In reality, it would be great to have a friend, a real person – nearby – who understands my life and its complications. Perhaps Patch could be that: I'm not sure I could cope with anything more than friendship, however comforting the idea might be. I long for someone to talk to properly, to unload onto.

A brief search on my phone shows that there is an art session this morning and it's open to drop-ins. The next item to be dealt with, although I'm too embarrassed and ashamed to write it down, is 'what to wear': I don't want to look like Lady Lyons-Morris today with my string of fake pearls – nor do I want to look like I haven't really unpacked or hung up any of my nice clothes, although that's the truth.

Leo is next door, wandering about: trying to convince him that Art Club is a better idea than his 'best day ever' is going to be a big job. There's always something, I think, and the self-pity I'm more used to climbs back into bed with me.

I toss the notepad back down on the bed, the pen after it. The pen slips sideways off my bent knees and settles in a dip of the duvet cover. Black ink pools through the fabric like a flower blossoming. 'Oh, fuck it,' I say and put the pen back on the bedside table.

In the end, Leo plays right into my hands.

'I'm a bit tired and my neck aches.' He rubs the back of his neck and pulls a face far more twisted than required. 'I did a lot of work yesterday. I might take today off.' He stretches out his arms in a pretend yawn, perfect white teeth underneath rosebud lips.

'Oh, I was going to suggest we did something else today anyway. How do you fancy a painting club?'

He picks up his favourite dog-tooth-check trilby and puts it on his head: he's going out. And that's it: it doesn't eventake any cajoling or negotiating on my part.

When we get to the centre, the first thing we see is a tiny brass plaque on the wall commemorating the gift of the centre to the village. I'm explaining that to Leo when Patch comes out through the main door.

Patch speaks to Leo before he speaks to me. He accompanies his words with Makaton signing, he does it effortlessly – as if he talks like that all the time. His arms are muscled in a way that suggests serious exercise but he is slow and gentle.

'I'm Patch, I teach the art class. Have you come to join us?'

'I'm Leo but I don't know if I'll stay.' Leo is suddenly shy. 'I have a lot to do back at our house – a lot of work. But I thought I'd have a look and see if I like this.'

'Absolutely.' Patch smiles at him, and then at me. 'It's a drop-in class, no commitment. And you're Leo's mum? Well, well, well . . .' Patch stretches his bear-paw of a hand out to me.

When my hand disappears inside his and he squeezes it tightly, a ball of energy clenches in my stomach, an electricity I haven't felt in a very long time. It is a moment of light flooding in, like turning over a brick or a stone in the garden that has been in place for years. Daylight pours in over bleached roots and scuttling beetles. Worms dive for cover and spiders stretch their cramped legs. Soft virgin soil dries in the warmth after decades of damp darkness.

There is more to this than wanting to be Patch's friend. So much more.

Patch walks into the centre talking to Leo. I walk behind and try to get a grip. I am acting like a teenager. Patch is obviously years younger than me and his clothes are trendy

and cool – worn sneakers, shorts and a long-sleeved shirt.
His shirt is marked with paint and is tight across his broad
shoulders. I feel like a fifty-something frump.

He walks Leo to an office doorway where a beautiful
young woman with blue hair and lots of face jewellery
takes over.

'Poppy will help Leo with the forms,' Patch says as he
walks back over to me. 'This is a coincidence: shall I show
you round?' He stresses the 'is' in the sentence and I wonder
whether he knows that it's no coincidence at all and I've only
enrolled my son in this class so I can find out more about
the teacher.

'You didn't tell me your name.'

Of course not: the alarm, my embarrassment. I blush
more. 'I'm Cate Morris.'

'So you're something to do with the museum? That place,
it's incredible.' His cheeks plump up when he smiles, they
are faintly rosy under his tan.

'It's my late . . .' I can't say the words, not to him. 'Colonel
Hugo is Leo's great-grandfather.'

'You're so lucky,' he says. 'Leo, come into the common
room and meet some of the other people before we go
through to the studio.'

Leo follows him without a second's hesitation or
self-consciousness.

The common room, when I come in behind Leo, is
exactly as one might expect: posters, flapping paper notices
pinned to overcrowded boards, and three old and stained

sofas in the middle of the room. Four or five young people mill about, all – as Araminta said – about his age. They are sitting and standing around, drinking coffee, chatting.

A tall slender girl turns round to see who's come in.

She has wavy dark hair and an intense gaze. She wears the barest trace of shiny lipstick and a touch of it has coloured the corner of one of her front teeth. When she speaks to Leo, I see his hands drop to his thighs, tapping so gently and quietly against the legs of his shorts, palms flat and fingers splayed.

'Hello. I'm Sophie,' she says and the 's' is blurred by a lisp.

And just like that, despite an age gap of more than thirty years, my nineteen-year-old son and I find ourselves on the same unexpected page of life. Both smitten, blindsided, by people we barely know, people who just appeared out of nowhere and filled our imaginations.

When I get back to the museum, Araminta is pulling weeds from the gravel in the drive. She is wearing her customary tweed skirt and tights, her delicate gold wristwatch catches the sun as it peeks from her gardening gloves.

'Don't you ever stop?' I ask.

She looks round at me and smiles. 'This never stops.' She gestures up at the front of the house. It is an impossible task for one person: it is an impossible task for three – even if Leo and I added our efforts every minute of every day, we can't keep it under control.

'We need more volunteers, don't we? For the time being,

I mean. Until we start taking some money.' I'm trying to keep my voice encouraging, build on the optimism of the day. 'What about Malcolm? He seems keen?'

'Malcolm used to volunteer regularly. He and his wife worked in the garden before she became ill but then they both had to stop. Polly had early onset dementia, she died last year.'

'Oh, how sad.' I think about Malcolm's enthusiasm, his loud laugh as he and Thierry polished off the extra glasses of wine they'd poured before the tour. Malcolm wears his sadness lightly. I should think more about doing the same.

'I'm sure he'll be back by next season. He enjoys it.' Araminta puts single daisy heads and tangles of dandelions in the trug beside her. Her fingers dig into the gravel.

'Let me help you. Are there any more gloves?'

'There's another pair under the ticket booth counter. 'Second shelf down.' She looks up at me. 'Thank you.'

I don't have any pockets in the skirt I chose this morning so I leave my car keys and phone on the shelf I took the gloves from. There's a little lean-on kneepad there too that I take outside to stop my bare legs from hurting on the gravel.

We dig and pull in silence for a few moments before Araminta speaks. Her thin neck bones whiten and her pearl necklace tightens, the beads rising away from her skin. 'I do need to talk to you, about the alarm, about getting more people in . . .'

I stay quiet: I can hear the scraping of the gravel against my fingers.

Araminta exhales, a long slow breath. She turns back towards me. 'It's still true what I said, before you came. There is a very real threat hanging over us from the Board of Trustees. We are on a knife edge.'

She clears her throat. 'We have always had these glitches, these phases. There have always been quiet times, periods when the museum is out of favour, out of fashion and – in the past – we've been able to weather them. But there's no money left at all. No money to do things like this ...' She points at the edge we've weeded. 'No money to empty the bins in the car park or buy lavatory paper for the visitors. It's not quite as simple as filling the museum for a day or two.'

'Leo needs this flat. It's all we've got. All he's got. And we need to know that it's our home now.' There's so much more I want to say. That I found that sad book of loss in the chapel. That I was awake half the night after yesterday, brimming with ideas. I have opened the Pandora's Box of this discussion, I need to see it through.

'There is a Board of Trustees who oversee the financial affairs of the museum – as you already know.' She is still holding her trowel; there is not a single speck of dirt, dot of earth, on her skirt.

I look down at my knees, scuffed brown within minutes.

'It is made up of a collection of second cousins and distant relatives, all people Richard would have known of, I'm sure, or at least could have put a face to. Each and every one of them would like to see this museum closed, the artefacts put up for auction, and the remains of the estate sold off.

149

They wouldn't inherit as much as they imagine by the time it was all split up between them, but inherit they certainly would: Leo too.'

'Leo would inherit?'

Araminta nods. 'A significant amount.'

I take the gloves off and lay them on the drive. I am hot all over, my palms are sweating. 'Enough to secure his future?'

She nods again. 'But even then, even with what it might buy him, I have to fight to keep this place together. I'm sorry.'

A whirl of thoughts spins in my head: the worries we've had about money; the unopened bills, unanswered calls; the fear. And now, on the day that we have decided to stay, to be part of this, this cat lands among the pigeons.

Araminta sits back on her heels with surprising agility. 'Colonel Hugo's project, his life's work, was for the people, for the public. He didn't do it to have it sold to oligarchs and collectors, to have it hidden away in private collections.' Her face is rigid and puce, her lips narrowed and stressed. 'I promised the Colonel that his collection would be safe under my care: I gave him my word.' She gets up and walks back into the museum.

I want to tell her not to worry, that we'll fight the sale whatever it takes, but I can't – hand on heart – say that's what I really feel. The whole collection – the antique beds we sleep on, the exquisite china we use as everyday crockery, the elephants, the giraffe: it must be worth millions. For every parent of a child with a learning disability – especially single parents – there is an almost constant quiet babble of 'what happens when I die?' running as internal commentary. Simon is Leo's testamentary guardian if anything happens to me but, beyond that and my miserable teacher's pension, his future is far from settled.

I look up at the front of the house. Leo couldn't run this alone, either but – surely – the future is more valuable than the past.

It is a conundrum, like everything else in this peculiar house. From the glaring dead animals conserved in their alabaster homes, through the millions of books that no one can reach to read, right into the wet green foliage of the unmanageable woods Colonel Hugo's grandfather meticulously planted, this place contradicts itself at every turn, gives then takes away, frightens then comforts.

Araminta's promise wasn't just to Colonel Hugo – it was to the whole family: that includes Leo. That promise – despite the fact it goes against everything that makes any sense – seems the right thing, it seems to hold water.

'Tell me what to do, Richard,' I whisper to the air. 'Because I don't fucking know.'

There are nine missed calls on my phone. My first thought, as I wait for the redial to be answered, is that they're all from the same – local – number: whatever's happened at the community centre hasn't meant a trip to hospital. The ring tone runs on and on, each one adding to my panic. My second thought is how irresponsible I've been to wander away from it. I could have heard it perfectly from where I left it but I've moved much further down the drive since Araminta came back indoors. I only heard it this time because I brought the trug of weeds up to empty.

I run towards the car, pressing the redial button over and over while no one answers. It is a five-minute drive to the centre. I throw my phone onto the passenger seat, Leo's seat, and try and keep my hands from shaking on the wheel.

The empty seat fills with memories, apparitions of panic, of moments where I've needed to be calm, times when I couldn't help the natural order of events. I imagine twisting with pain in that passenger seat on the night Leo was born, and the crushing sadness of the day Richard died – Simon driving – holding everything we knew but couldn't speak about. The helplessness terrifies me, and the silence of my phone fills the car.

Chapter Twelve

There are no flashing lights in the community centre car park, no ambulances or police cordon. It is an unremarkable squat sixties building with a ramp and railing leading up to the front door. No one waits anxiously outside, no striped tape flickers round a crime scene.

'Curtis?' The first person I see in the foyer has a dark grey hoodie up round his ears and an uninviting scowl.

'We couldn't get you.' He talks to his feet.

'We?'

Before Curtis can answer, the door next to him opens and Leo comes out. His hair is wild and messy, there is a piece of blue sticky tape holding the side of his glasses together.

'I'm going now, bruv.' Curtis takes Leo's hand in a complicated gesture of grips and grasps. Leo executes it perfectly.

'Bruv? What exactly is going on? What are you doing here, Curtis? If you'd wanted to spend time with Leo, you could have done so up at the house.' My terror has been replaced by fury. I don't know what kind of a drop-in centre Patch is running here but it's obviously not doing Leo much good.

'Actually, I called Curtis.' Patch steps out from the office into the foyer. 'We were having trouble getting hold of you.'

I momentarily think of apologising to Curtis but he's gone. I have more things to think about. 'What on earth is going on? Leo, are you all right?'

He obviously isn't.

'Tell me what happened.' I am eye to eye with him but he doesn't want to look at me. Something is very wrong. I can see from his pale skin and the dark circles under his eyes that he's been crying. His eyebrows are straight and dark, knitted close together. His breath is still shallow and fast.

'Has someone hurt you?' I reach out to gather him in my arms but he turns his back to me, his strong shoulder brushing me away. 'Where's your hat?'

'Poppy's sorting your hat out, isn't she?' Patch takes up a lot of room in this foyer. He is larger than he seemed this morning. 'Unfortunately, Leo has been in a fight.'

I am open-mouthed and it takes a full second to recover from the moment. 'I don't believe it. How could you let this happen? Is this anything to do with Curtis?' I have been gone for less than three hours. The cloak of responsibility I wear throws itself heavily onto my shoulders, it gathers up closely round my throat and its weight is enough to make me stagger. 'Have you called the police?'

Patch puts his hand on my arm in a gesture intended to placate me. It's patronising and I shake it away.

'You had trouble calming down, didn't you?' he says to Leo. 'But you had the smart idea to call a friend when we couldn't get your mum. That's good – it shows really sensible thinking.' He turns to me. 'Curtis was terrific actually, a real help. He's a nice lad.'

'He's my best friend.' It's the first Leo's spoken since I got here.

'A fight . . .' I'm shaking my head. 'I thought this was an art class, an organised art class, Mr . . .' I can't call him 'Patch', can't use a stupid nickname when he's put my son in the way of this kind of danger. I stop just short of calling him 'Mr Samson'.

'My son does not have fights.' I'm wearing pomposity like armour; I can hear it but I don't know what else to say or do. Part of me enjoyed this break, the interaction with Araminta, a physical task: beginning to understand the museum and what it could bring me. And all the time, Leo was frightened, bullied, vulnerable. He needed me and I wasn't there. I didn't do any research about this man or his organisation, I didn't look for reviews: I saw a straw and I clutched it.

Patch is speaking. 'And, I'm afraid, it was very much Leo's fight. He started it and he finished it.'

'Leo has never had a fight in his life.' I look at the dishevelled young man in front of me.

He looks hard at the floor. Whatever has happened, Leo doesn't want to talk about it.

'I want to go home now,' he says.

'We haven't had a fight here before, Cate, I assure you.' Patch is smiling slightly, his face is solemn but his eyes crinkled at the edges. He is clearly not taking the matter seriously but is stopping short of any measure where I could chime in with righteous indignation.

'How on earth was this allowed to happen? Who was this fight with?'

Poppy – who turns out to be the blue-haired young woman we signed in with – comes out into the foyer to join us. 'Here's your hat, mate. Pretty much back to how it was.' She hands Leo his chequered hat and he turns it round and round in his hands, assessing the damage.

He nods. 'It's all right. We can go home now.'

Patch puts a hand up, stopping Leo from moving towards the door. 'I think you have some apologies to make, Leo. Some hands to shake.'

'There must be some mistake.' I can't believe my gentle son could suddenly, at the age of nineteen, develop a vicious side. 'Leo has literally never been involved in anything like this in his life.' I use the word 'literally' for emphasis, as if I am a teenager. It makes me wince.

'I think he may never have been in quite these circumstances before.' Now Patch is definitely smiling. 'Never had quite this provocation?'

A penny drops. 'Sophie?'

'And Martin, one of our students.' Patch says the name quietly, clearly wary of the effect it will have on Leo. 'To be fair, Martin could try the patience of a saint. Often does,' he says, and points at Poppy.

Leo sits down hard on the orange plastic chairs lined up against the wall. The signs and posters on the board behind him flutter and flap in the breeze of his umbrage. 'Martin isn't Sophie's boyfriend. Sophie told me.' He bangs his hands hard on his thighs, over and over, the hitting a spiky rhythm on his jeans. 'You can't say someone is your girlfriend if they don't want to be. Curtis says so.'

He looks up at me, his eyes are full of heartbreak. 'Sophie doesn't want to be Martin's girlfriend. But he said she does. And she doesn't.'

'So Leo, unfortunately, felt he needed to defend her honour.' Patch is his keeping his smile from Leo but it's there in his voice, in the curve of his mouth, in the way he holds his wide shoulders.

'Martin is a twat.'

'Leo! You can't say that.'

'I can. Curtis said it too.' His chin is dipping into his chest, his voice and pride muffled. He stands up, waving his arms in fury. 'Sophie doesn't want to be Martin's girlfriend and Martin said she did and so I punched him. Right here.' He folds his own fists into his stomach.

Patch steps forward. He puts one arm round Leo's shoulder and Leo lets him. 'We've been through this enough, I think. Why don't we try and look at some of the positive things we've done today? Are you ready to show your mum the start of your project?'

Before I have a chance to object he says, 'And we'll have a proper chat about what happened, look at the incident in the day log and so on, before you go. Is that okay . . . Cate?' He hesitates before he uses my first name and his eyes are positively sparkling now.

I'm too flummoxed to do anything other than follow the sulking Leo into the art room.

Atalanta and Hippomenes stand on every surface. They lean against table legs and hang from window frames. They drape on chair backs and squat on the floor. There are golden figures everywhere: some recognisable only in comparison to the hundreds of others crowded round them, some almost perfect in their accuracy. Nearest me, and as fragile as gossamer, is a totem pole version of them. It is made of staggered cereal boxes sprayed, almost all over, with gold paint. The brand names shine through the metallic glaze but the set of the loo roll arms and wrapping-paper-tube legs couldn't be anything other than the two skating figures.

The Greek lovers are clay, they are papier mâché. They wriggle in the sunshine as wire dancers hanging from mobiles, they are huge shapes cut from coloured plastic and pasted across the windows themselves.

Leo takes me to a painting, clipped onto an easel by a black bulldog clip. It has clouds of blowing grasses across the front of the scene and single yellow daisies dotted like jewels in the grass. The sky behind is dominated by a setting orange sun sending streaks of colour into the otherwise

158

bright blue sky. In the middle is a white circle, the two figures sketched – holding hands and facing the viewer – ready
to paint. It's quite beautiful.

'I can't believe you got all this done today. It's amazing.'

Leo's stance improves slightly; he can't resist telling me
how proud he is of the painting.

It's nothing to how proud I am of it.

'It's the view from my bedroom, isn't it?'

'It's for your birthday,' he says. 'But you can't really see it
till then. I'll have to finish it when you're at home.'

I'm suddenly moved that the museum was the place I
thought of in my panic, the place I would run to in order
get Leo out of this horrible situation, out of danger. The
museum is a place of safety and the gardens are the home of
the beautiful sculptures that have inspired such creativity. I
am on the same page as Araminta.

'Poppy helped me.' Leo points to the sketching in the
middle. 'I'm not good at people.'

'Sometimes it's about the ideas,' says Poppy. 'It's the ideas
that matter, the imagination.' She's probably not far off Leo's
age and I wonder if she's Patch's daughter.

'I'm doing an Art Therapy degree,' she tells me – as if she
can read my mind. 'And I have a placement here twice a
week. It's the best part of my course.'

'The standard is amazing.' I look around the room at the
packed benches, the busy tables.

'It's the enthusiasm,' Poppy says. 'You can do anything if
you've got that.'

I'm so glad Leo came here – despite his upset. I would never have thought this possible, this huge project that has obviously taken thousands of hours of other people's time.

'What you do here is extraordinary.' I nod my head at Patch, try to backtrack a little on my anger.

'Thanks.' He smiles at me. 'Now, we have to clear up the last bit of bad feeling, don't we, Leo? You have to apologise to Martin.'

I steel myself for the meltdown; out of habit I look at Leo's hands, waiting for the nervous tapping to start on his thighs. Nothing happens.

Instead he nods. 'Is he in the coffee room?'

'Yep,' says Patch. 'Go on through.'

Leo leaves the door open behind him and I step closer to the doorway so I can watch him.

Martin is tall and angular, and a little older than Leo. His arms hang from his shoulders like the cereal box sculpture and his trousers are too short for his long thin legs.

'I've come to apologise.' Leo holds his hand out. 'I didn't mean to hit you. It was wrong.'

'You're quite right it was wrong, especially as you've only just come here and I don't know you and you don't know me and you could have really hurt me. This is my favourite art club and you could have made me feel really insecure and vulnerable here and I wouldn't like it and it would be your fault. All your fault.' Martin speaks very rapidly and with a certain entitlement. I already get why Leo doesn't like him – I don't either.

Patch is watching from the doorway too. 'When someone apologises in these circumstances, Martin, the correct thing to do is shake their hand and accept.'

'I don't see why I should – I'm still very upset and that might have lots of ongoing effects for me because I am very sensitive to any kind of upset like this. I might not be able to come back to group and that would mean that all my Thursdays have to be different because I can't come here and that would not be good for my self-esteem or my balance.' Martin takes a long breath, clearly anticipating another long speech, but Patch cuts him off.

'You'll be fine, as long as you let Leo apologise. Otherwise you might not be able to come back to group because your name will be in the incident book too. You are not entirely blameless here.'

Martin reluctantly shakes Leo's hand: he doesn't make eye contact while he does it but I don't know if that's deliberate.

'Right, that's it – forgotten. You don't have to be friends, gentlemen, but if you want to carry on at Art Club, you have to be civilised adults. And that means no thumping people and . . .' He looks from Leo to Martin. 'No making things up about other people.'

'Can I finish my painting now?' Leo is subdued.

'It's home time anyway,' says Patch, his voice deliberately buoyant to head off any protests. 'Cate, I will need to get you to sign a couple of incident reports when Poppy and I have written them up. Could I bring them up with me when I'm next drawing in the gardens?'

I didn't know he'd been doing that, but it makes sense. All these startling sculptures and pictures have come from somewhere. I try to focus on the wall behind him and see if that keeps the blood from rushing up my cheeks. 'That's fine. I mean, please do.' I'm not certain if my burning cheeks are teenaged angst or a hot flush. I am stumbling over my words. 'But we don't have a doorbell. We live right up on the top floor. Can I give you my mobile number?' It sounds awful, like some sort of come-on. 'To let me know when you get there, I mean.'

And he nods and gets a pen as if it had never occurred to him that it could be anything else.

I want the ground to swallow me.

Leo is quiet in the car. I can't get him to engage in conversation. In the end, I let him choose a track from his phone and play it as loud as it will go through the car stereo. It's hideous making my way home to the thrashing Death Metal track, but it makes me smile that someone walking past might look up and see a middle-aged woman driving a very ordinary family car instead of the weed-smoking boy-racer they'd expected. Weed-smoking boy-racers make me think of Curtis. I wonder if I should send him a text via Leo's phone to say sorry. Maybe all the bigger people today are the ones who know how to apologise.

Our evening is a subdued one. Leo doesn't want to cook and, after we've eaten, stays in his room for most of the time. I can judge most of his feelings by the tracks that he's playing – there is no chance I can miss them at this volume but I haven't the heart to ask him to turn it down.

I try and email a few old friends but I don't know what to tell them. That my nineteen-year-old son is caught in his first love triangle? That I have a crush on a total stranger that would make a nun blush? It is sheer fantasy and I've been ridiculous to let it go this far.

I don't deserve to be happy. I've had two chances at love: been in love – I think – with two people. Each time, something has crept in from left field and stolen it away. Why would I think this Patch would be any different?

Simon stayed with Richard and me for a year. We moved into the rented flat that became home. It was hard and sad but it was a roof over our heads, safety. As Richard became more and more distant, Simon moved in closer, propping me up when I felt I really couldn't carry on.

It was lonely, watching the man I loved fade and grow hazy, muted inside a facsimile of his physical self – a self that grew ever thinner and more angular.

Richard spent more and more time inside his own head: physically with us but with thoughts that were far away, the light in his eyes dialled down to almost nothing. We nursed him, took him out for walks, talked to him. We helped him with his medication, explained to him – at great length – why he had to take it on those darker days when he would have rather given up.

If we had got him safely to bed, Simon and I would sit

together – mostly in silence – exhausted by another day's worry, another day's fear. When we did speak, it was in low voices, discussing Richard's treatment, Leo's school days. Occasionally, we would reminisce about what things had been, the good times, hoping with every heartbeat that we would all have that again.

I leant on Simon heavily in those days, and him me. And it was probably inevitable that our feelings would get clouded, that the edges of our friendship would blur into something else. From this distance, and in an attempt to forgive myself, I see the innocence in it, the way we confused closeness with comfort – but that changes nothing.

One night, after a particularly difficult day where Richard had not wanted to be near Leo but couldn't verbalise his feelings or find any logic for them, Simon and I sat close together in the sitting room, perched on the very edge of the sofa, knowing either or both of us could be called upstairs at any moment. Simon leant forward, his head in his hands and his elbows on his knees: I wasn't sure whether he was crying or not. It didn't matter. There were no words that could cover what we were feeling: the freefall of dread we were living with. I put my head against his, my chin resting on his shoulder.

The lights were out, both of us simply too exhausted to get up and switch on the tasteful standard lamps in each corner of the room. The light came in like a wedge from the hallway and sucked the colour from us.

Simon turned, his face close to mine, I could feel the

human warmth of him. There was a silent moment that stretched between us, expanding and contracting with the power of a black hole. It dwarfed us. Our breath mingled and our bodies stayed as still as statues. The silence was huge between us.

And then we kissed. I kissed Simon. Simon kissed me. We betrayed Richard at his – our – very darkest hour. We gave in to the fears that haunted him at night, let the terror that stalked our hallways become flesh: we kissed like people about to die. The taste of him was like the taste of life, sparks jumped inside my hollow drained heart. I felt the warmth of his face under my palms, the strength of his firm body as I slid my hands down over his shoulders.

And then, slowly, I opened my eyes.

Richard stood silhouetted in the doorway, his hair wild and his clothes limp on his emaciated frame, the light coming through him from behind like a ghost.

Simon left the next day and, within a week, Richard was dead. We killed my husband, Simon and I, as surely as if we had put a bullet through his chest.

Chapter Thirteen

Leo is wearing his 'party' glasses. They have square black frames made of plastic, and the bits over his nose and behind his ears are shiny silver. They have the name of the designer down each arm, running from his eyebrows to his ears, and that's why he bought them: no matter that they are ridiculous. I insisted that the other pair of the 'buy one get one free' deal be more suitable for everyday wear but those are now held together with a piece of blue sticking plaster.

'Those will get broken if you wear them all the time,' I say to him – motherspeak for 'I cannot abide your taste or fashion.'

'I can't wear the other ones. Martin broke them.'

I'm not getting into a discussion about blame right now – it's too early – though I'm well aware that's a coward's way out.

The opticians can fit Leo in at lunchtime: it's a good

way to get him into town to help me put up posters for the weekend. I am being proactive: I am setting up next Saturday as a 'relaunch' of the museum and gardens. My logic is that if people have never been, they won't complain about the lack of change. Araminta has grudgingly agreed to go along with the – what could be called – deception.

Leo and I are walking along the outside of the sweeping wall that lines the gardens. The wall is old and the bricks slightly crumbled in places but it's still a magnificent thing. Leo trails his fingers along it.

'You'll get a splinter,' I warn him. 'Or whatever the brick equivalent is.'

He doesn't look round at me. 'I don't like Martin.'

I'm surprised that he's opened the dialogue but I don't let that show. 'But you still want to do Art Club?'

'Yes. All my friends are there. And I left my picture.' He turns slightly towards me, keeping his fingers on the wall as we walk. 'It's not finished.'

'No, I remember. It's very good though. Did Poppy help you with it?'

'No.' He flakes a shard of red brick off the wall, turns it round and round in his fingers, concentrating hard. He is terrible at making eye contact when he's lying.

'And Martin. What about next time you see him?'

'Sophie isn't his girlfriend.'

'So you said. What does Sophie say about it?'

He breaks the little red shard in half and drops the two fragments on the pavement in lieu of answering. He walks with his chin held exaggeratedly high, facing forward and willing me to go away.

'She must have said something.'

Leo starts to hum. He pats his thigh with one palm in rhythm to his – barely recognisable – tune. 'I'm singing,' he says in a pause between lines. 'I can't talk about this at the moment.'

We have left the long wall now and are walking down the main road towards the town. In the distance, the silver sea glitters: more romantic at this distance than the brownish grey it will be, close to. On the verges of the road, the grass is short and yellowed by this long hot summer; patches of dusty brown show through, here and there, where footsteps have scuffed up the turf.

'Shall we have a look in the charity shops after the opticians?' I need more tools in my arsenal if I'm to get anywhere with Leo. He is firmly locked down on the subject of Martin: prising anything out of him will require bribery and corruption. Looking in charity shops for clothes and records is one of his favourite things.

Leo points to his mouth and sings louder. He raises his eyebrows slightly to show me that interrupting his singing is rude, and his ridiculous glasses wobble up and down on his nose.

'And I wondered if you might like to invite Curtis to supper. You could cook for him.' I had, genuinely, wondered this – in fact, I thought about it quite a lot during a long worried night with little sleep. Curtis may not be the ally I would choose but he seems to be genuinely fond of Leo and he was there when Leo needed him which, unfortunately, is more than can be said for me.

We send the text in the optician's waiting room and Curtis's reply comes back almost instantly. 'Okay. What do you want me to bring?'

I'm still marvelling at this unexpected dinner party etiquette when Leo tells me to help him text back.

'Red Warning 4 and Tank Tour Commando.'

Leo is doing baked potatoes and chilli, one of his favourites and a dish that he needs no help with. I've said they can eat in the sitting room – their plates on the coffee table and Red Warning 4 at full volume on the games console.

I'm debating trying to get more out of him – anything out of him – about the Martin debacle when my phone pings a text. It's Patch.

Am combining my evening walk with bringing the accident form up to you. Is now a good time?
Patch Samson

I look around the chaos of the kitchen. My son is opening a second can of kidney beans, tongue between his teeth for concentration. His friend with the criminal record and the neck tattoos will be here to eat with us any second.

There is a crash as Leo's elbow shoots out and knocks a jug from the side. The jug breaks into four neat pieces, opening like a flower to show me its smooth white interior. I don't have to touch it to see the delicacy of the porcelain, the faint translucent blue of its broken edges. I can see a number written on the upturned base. It is – was – significant enough to have its own identity in the firing.

'Sorry, Mum,' says Leo and pours the beans into a colander to drain: sludgy purple water splashes onto the shards of china on the floor.

'Now's great,' I text back. And then I add, because I realise it's the truth: 'It's as good a time as any.'

'I brought wine.' Patch holds out the wine bottle and smiles. 'It seemed like a good idea.'

He is wearing shorts, and a faded blue linen jacket over a band T-shirt. He has a light paisley scarf wrapped, just once, round his neck: one end of it falls forward over his lapel. On anyone else, this outfit would look ridiculous. On Patch, with his dirty blond hair and tan suede desert boots, it looks like effortless charm. His eyes are bluer than I remember.

'It's such a good idea.' I smile at him and my stomach flips.

I lead the way through to the kitchen. Leo is serving up his masterpiece, grating cheese over the heaped plates. Curtis leans with his back against the enamel work surface, his hood pushed down and the blue bloom around his neck more visible. I think it's a word but the edges are blurred and his chin, as usual, is folded down towards his chest so I can't make out what it says.

'You met Curtis, Patch.'

'How's it going?' Curtis speaks more loudly than I've heard him before. Patch leans forward to shake hands with both young men. Leo has to wipe his hands down his apron before he can take the large hand that Patch offers.

'We're taking these upstairs. I already took the drinks up.' Leo fusses around the plates, wiping the edges clean with a tea towel while the floor and walls where he's cooked are coated with a fine film of spattered orange fat. He and Curtis organise cutlery, salt and pepper, and – with the careless disregard for mess that only a teenaged boy can muster – they are gone.

'And I thought he made a mess when he painted,' Patch says.

'He didn't, did he?'

'Of course not. I'm joking. No more than anyone else.'

I look at the floor: bits of chopped onion, the brown papery skins that came off them, twigs of thyme and oregano that we brought in from the garden, and – worst of all – the shattered porcelain.

Patch bends and picks up the pieces of the jug. 'Ouch, this looks valuable. Looked valuable.'

'I told Araminta something like this would happen. She insisted we use the antique dinner service. I've got boxes of stuff upstairs that wouldn't matter.'

'I bet it's ugly.' Patch holds the bits of jug together in a vaguely jug-shape. 'The stuff upstairs. I bet it's functional and plain and doesn't add anything to life.'

'I like it actually.' I squat down near his feet with the

brush and dustpan, gesture for him to step out of the way. 'And it doesn't matter when it breaks.'

He has lifted a plate from the dresser; it's from the same set as the jug. Patch examines the stamp and the number on the back before placing it delicately back on the shelf. 'This stuff's beautiful. Don't you feel more alive eating a boiled egg from one of these ...' He holds up an egg cup so thin I imagine I can see light through it. Its gold and green pattern reflects the window. '... than some generic old bit of plain white china that probably costs a pound a plate?'

I sigh, long and loud. 'No. I feel sick using it. I know it's all going to get broken. I don't want the responsibility. It's two hundred years old.'

'But it's crockery.' Patch has picked up a sponge from the sink and is wiping debris from the work surface with one hand, scooping it into the other. He lifts his hand towards me in a gesture that asks where to put the detritus and I point to the compost bin on the side. 'If you put all this away in a locked-up cupboard somewhere, is it even crockery anymore? Isn't crockery something we eat off? Beautiful crockery adds to our life experience while we do something as functional as eating.' He showers the crumbs into the compost bin. 'Or cleaning up the kitchen.'

'I'm not sure I can be as philosophical as you about plates.' I empty the dustpan into the kitchen bin. When I turn round, Patch has taken off his crumpled jacket and is standing by the sink.

'I think that best thing we can do — in the

circumstances – is clean up in here then take that wine out into the garden.' He turns the tap on. 'Leo's happily shooting zombies and there's hours of daylight left yet.'

My immediate instinct is to say no. But it's followed, before I have a chance to speak, by an overwhelming desire to do something just for me. Leo is a grown man: he has cooked a fabulous dinner for his friend and they're together, enjoying themselves. And it's been longer than I care to remember since I've sat, drinking wine and chatting, with a man as good-looking as Patch. I'm not sure I ever have – I whisper a silent apology to Richard who was very handsome, but in a slightly less film star kind of way.

'Do you want to wash, or dry?' Patch asks.

And it's as simple as that. It's that easy to let someone into your heart. I wish I'd known earlier.

It was Patch's idea to take the wine out on to the grass near Atalanta and Hippomenes. I checked with Leo that he was happy for us to go – he can see us from my bedroom window if he wants to. He traded up the bottle of Diet Coke he and Curtis had been going to share for a couple of beers. 'We've got that Friday feeling,' he said when I told him I was going out to have a glass of wine in the garden. He knows it's Wednesday and he makes me laugh.

The way I feel right now, he could have asked for more than one beer each. He's missed a trick.

We've left the kitchen sparkling and ready for Araminta's eagle-eyed inspection. Patch chose the glasses, taking great care with the selection in the dresser, holding each one up by the stem and turning it in the light. His hands looked huge against the fragile stems. He pinged one with his fingernail and listened to the noise it made. 'Uhuh,' he'd said. 'Two of these.'

He hooked the glasses upside down into one hand, the stems safe between the grooves of his balled fist, and took the wine in the other. 'Corkscrew? Posh stuff this, you know.'

I pulled open the drawer – the last few weeks have given me cause to know exactly where the corkscrew is – most nights.

'I'm only kidding,' he said as he stood back to let me through the doorway in front of him. 'This wine was barely north of a fiver.'

'Is it cold and wet?' I asked.

'Oh, yes.'

'Then it's exactly what I need.'

Chapter Fourteen

It is an evening from a storybook. The peacock is strutting around nearby. He is waggling his tail-feathers in an effort to attract one of the three peahens who are pecking on the lawn, but none of them so much as glances up. The sun, though it is nowhere near setting, has turned golden and sends threads of light through the trees and dancing, dappled, across the top of the pond.

We choose to sit on the grass, despite the benches dotted around this part of the park. I don't think I could sit right beside Patch without making a fool of myself; at least here on the lawn I can pick at daisies, keep my nervous fingers occupied.

'Cheers,' says Patch and leans in towards me. He touches the edge of his glass – so gently – against mine and the antique glass rings round the flat lawn like a bell. 'To being here,' he says, and drinks.

The wine is cold, crisp. Tiny beads of condensation

smudge under my fingers as I hold the glass: they sparkle in the reflection of the evening sun.

'There are worse lives, I guess,' I say. Immediately, I remember all the other stuff, all the reasons I'm sitting here on the grass – even if this moment is idyllic.

'Someone walk over your grave?' Patch asks.

I shake my head, smile slightly. 'Sorry, I was weighing it all up. Remembering why I'm here.' That sounds awful. 'I don't mean I don't want to be here.' I'm getting myself in a mess. 'By here, I mean this house, the museum, not you.' I have gone scarlet with embarrassment. 'Sorry: I sound ridiculous.'

'Of course you don't. It must have been a wrench. Leo told me you were in London before.'

I nod again. 'Islington.'

'He said his dad died.'

My chest feels tight with Richard's presence and I have to exhale to dislodge the memory of him that blocks the top of my throat. I nod. 'Four years ago.'

'Oh, I thought it was more recent.' And then Patch sits upright, almost spilling his drink. 'God, sorry, I didn't mean that to sound flippant.'

'It didn't. I know exactly what you mean. Leo isn't very clear on the timescale when he talks about his dad.' The weight of thinking about Richard here, on this perfect evening, has shifted, settled comfortably in my centre where it belongs. 'He tends to run it all into "now" – Richard was dead then and he still is. When it happened doesn't really affect his feelings towards it. Does that sound odd?'

'Not at all. I have a bit of experience in that field. Not in losing my dad ... I mean in talking to people who see things in slightly different ways.' He screws his eyes up against the sun. 'I'm making a right hash of this.'

I sip the wine. I don't feel uncomfortable here, talking about Richard. It feels okay. It feels normal.

'What I mean is, I assumed there was a direct link between your husband's death and you moving here. That you came here because he'd died.'

I pick a daisy from the grass. With my thumbnail I make a tiny slit through its stem. I pick a second daisy to thread through the hole. 'We came here because he lived, I suppose, because it's his family inheritance. I think he even lived here himself when he was young.' I make my daisy chain longer by three, then four, flowers. 'What about you? How did you get here?'

Patch reaches over to top up my glass. His forearms are thick and muscular and the blond hairs on them catch the light. He seems to be choosing words, putting them into order before he speaks.

'I was at a bit of a loose end. A bit rootless. I'd moved back to England – I'd been living abroad for a bit. And then this job came up so I moved to Crouch-on-Sea.'

I need to know. I am slipping out of control with this man. If he has a wife, a girlfriend, I need to know now and to compartmentalise him along with the other things

I can't have and that aren't for me. 'Did you come here on your own? Is there a Mrs Patch?' It's clunky and crass. I blush again.

He looks right at me as he answers, makes sure he has full eye contact with me. 'No. I live alone. I'm divorced, have been for a long time.'

'Oh, I wondered if Poppy and you . . .'

'Poppy?' He laughs and moves closer to me. He smiles as he looks at me and I know I'm supposed to notice that he's moved closer. 'Poppy is young enough to be my daughter.' He taps my hand with his outstretched fingers and a shiver runs through me.

'Anyway . . .' He tops up my glass again, though I've barely drunk from it. 'Poppy's not my type.' This time his smile is a grin. He takes the tiny daisy chain from my hand, turns it round and round looking at how it's made.

I have to keep the conversation going, to focus, but it's getting harder and harder. The white and yellow flowers look minuscule in his large hand and yet, at the same time, so safe. He presses his fingernail into the stem of the daisy. 'Pass me another one,' he says.

I pick a daisy and pass it to him. There are only a few inches between us now.

'Do you have kids?' I ask, trying to level things, trying to make this an ordinary moment between two ordinary people. There is the barest fragment of silence, one extra beat in the air.

'I had a baby son but he died.'

It is like a punch. My face contorts and my words are sucked away.

'It was a long time ago. He'd be twenty-five now.'

I sit up straight. 'I'm so sorry.'

Patch shrugs. 'My wife and I hadn't been together long before she got pregnant, and then – well – we didn't stay together that long after he'd died. Didn't make it.'

I am speechless: me, the person who has talked endlessly of death and loss, spent four long years thinking of little else. Now I can't think of anything to say at all.

'And then I sort of went off on one. Travelled – ran away. Started painting. Ran away some more – swore I'd never paint again. Rinse and repeat.'

I think of my warm solid son upstairs, of his vivid presence, his passion. I put my hand over Patch's, squeeze his fingers together. 'What was his name?'

'James. James Patrick Samson.'

I want to hug him, but I daren't. I am punch-drunk, pounded; completely humbled by the pain he must carry.

'I'm Patrick too.' He's moving the subject away, bringing back the warm sun, the peace of the summer, the setting. 'My brother couldn't say it when I was born and so I've been Patch since I was a child. But I'm Patrick really. I went full-time Patch when I was an art student and I've never gone back.' He smiles. 'I'm a big poser.'

He has threaded more flowers onto the daisy chain. 'How do you tie it up?' he asks me.

I push the first flower through the stem of the last one

leaving a stalk sticking out. 'Like this,' I say and pinch a daisy head between my thumb and fingers. I push the bare stalk into the base of the flower to cap it off.

Patch holds the crown of flowers in his hands and places it on my head. 'Beautiful,' he says.

I cannot feel the weight of the daisy coronet but I know it's there.

'"If we could read the secret history of our enemies, we should find in each man's life sorrow and suffering enough to disarm all hostility."' Patch half-whispers it, bringing the huge lawns and wide sky down to the single point somewhere between our mouths.

'That's beautiful.' I can barely breathe.

'It's Longfellow.'

I shake my head. 'You quote poetry in random situations?'

'Cheating.' The grin is back. 'A bloke I worked with in Oz had a tattoo of it. Right down his arm, and I stared at it every day over a factory conveyor belt.' He rolls onto his back, laughing, and all the sadness dissipates. It is carried away across the lake, catching for a moment in the petals of the water-lilies as it goes. 'It's true though, isn't it? We none of us get out alive and none of us get out without some pain. I've spent a long time and covered a lot of miles learning that.'

'Have you stopped running away now?' I ask him, a tension in my chest like the skin of a drum.

'I hope so,' he says. He sits up, still leaning back on one arm, and he moves the last inches towards me. His lips meet mine and we are frozen in time, each holding a wine glass in one hand, not daring to put them down or to make any sudden movement that will change this reality.

When we move apart, I have put a barrier, a marker, between Richard and me. I have moved to a new place.

The sun drops a halo round the edges of Patch's hair, lighting his thick eyebrows and throwing his eyes into shade. I am so close to him that I can see the day's stubble across his chin. I take a deep breath to still the sickening disturbance inside me.

Instinctively, I look up, convinced I'll see Leo's shocked face at my bedroom window or Araminta's shocked disapproval at hers. There is no one there.

'Now what?' Patch is grinning at me. His hand has moved to my waist, my knees are touching his as we sit on the grass.

I am dazzled, wrong-footed. I hadn't written off this part of my life, hadn't ever consciously decided to live celibately for the rest of my days: I'm only fifty-four. The idea of being as alone as Araminta – especially once Leo leaves home – is one that haunts me in those cold waking hours when all one's worries dance around in the dark. I imagined I might meet someone one day, somewhere. But not here, not so soon. Four years concertina into moments, seconds: those four years have – suddenly – been so very short.

I can't look up again in case I see Richard standing there, silhouetted against the window of my bedroom, looking down at me with eyes I can't see but that I know are a fathomless sad brown. I don't want Richard to wave good-bye to me, I'm not ready.

Patch leans in, kisses my cheek gently. He waits, his fore-head resting on my shoulder, for me to speak.

The birds are gathering in the long grass and behind the wall in the kitchen garden, ready to perform their evensong. The wine bottle, almost half full, stands at a slight angle on the grass. The barest tufts of white cloud, stripe the horizon without the energy to climb any higher.

I could not have anticipated this when we walked out here. And that can't be more than half an hour ago. My world has turned upside down.

'You're very quiet.' Patch traces my cheek with his finger. 'Are you regretting it?'

'I just, well, I don't know what to do, what I feel.'

'It's okay to be happy,' says Patch, and kisses me again.

Eventually, Patch and I peel ourselves apart and go inside. The peacock trots behind us as we walk towards the kitchen door, bobbing his head and looking for food.

'He wants the stale bread from the kitchen. Leo gives it to him in the mornings.'

'I could eat some stale bread.' Patch catches me round the waist as I go to walk through the door in front of him, almost knocking the wine bottle out of my hand. He squeezes me tight into him, a proper hug. My nose reaches the shoulder of his T-shirt and I take in his smell: paint and washing powder and faint sweat. I need the hug.

'How much chilli did Leo make?' he asks me. 'I am starving – really.'

'He made a ton but, you know, young men eat a lot.' And I fall silent. My boy has lived to become a young man, his did not.

He is sensitive enough to pick up my silence. And kind enough to dispel it. 'Half the people I work with are young men. The other half are young women. I know exactly how much they all eat.' He takes my hand. 'Cross your fingers, I don't suppose we'll get a takeaway delivered out here and we've both been drinking so we can't go and get one.'

The pan of chilli that was cooling down on the range is still there. Leo and Curtis have obviously been down for more, the orange oily tideline has changed dramatically, but there is enough left for us. I know Leo well enough to make me check the long white larder fridge. Two more beers are gone. I put what's left of our wine in the rack in the fridge door.

'I need to check on Leo.' Reality bites. 'Do you want to come and see the apartment?' My momentary thrill at taking him to see our flat, my bedroom, dissipates quickly. 'But we have to be careful. Leo doesn't read body language particularly but that Curtis is a savvy one.'

'I can't promise,' says Patch but his smile is wide and open.

Patch and I walk the same corridors that I first walked through only a month ago. They seem to have opened up: what once felt like dark panelling crushing the air out from around me, feels safe and comforting, an extra layer to protect me from the outside. The hop-pickers' hessian sacks that line the walls on the upper floors are suddenly interesting, have history in the hundreds of years of use. Patch stops by each and every painting that hangs in the dark hallways.

'This place is incredible. I thought I knew so much about it. I only know the very surface.' He trails his fingers along the picture rails in the hall, his arms so long that he can easily reach both sides. 'It's so much better up here.'

'It used to scare me.'

He reaches forward, grabs my hand. 'It's such a world of history, it's amazing. Think of all the people who've walked through here, touched these walls. What were they doing? Where were they going?'

'They were mostly staff, up here. The family would have been on the next floor down, their bedrooms aren't open to the public.' Every now and then, we pass a window; sunlight streams across the hallway and dust dances from the carpet with the vibration of our footsteps.

'It's amazing. Like a secret world. I'd love to do some drawing up here.' He's peering at a dark face in an old portrait, cocking his head from side to side to try and get the evening light to complement the dull bulbs along this corridor. 'There's a look of Leo about this one,' he says. 'Who is it?'

I stand next to him to look, leaning in towards him, breathing him in. He's right, the portrait has the same very dark hair, the coal-black eyes. It could be Richard but that it's a good hundred years too old. 'All the men in the family look like that.' I test my voice. 'Richard did.'

The walls don't crash down on me. There is no lightning,

no fanfare of trumpets announcing the traitor walking through the house. Just Patch, resting his hands on my shoulders and squeezing very gently, letting me know that he is there, that he heard Richard's name too and that's okay.

When we get to the sitting room, Patch having oohed and aahed his way past every window, every dusty portrait, Leo and Curtis look like boys rather than men. The only give-away is the neat row of empty beer cans on the coffee table. They've been perfectly reasonable – for young men with a freely available fridge – and only had two each. They barely look up – whatever is happening on the screen is clearly vital to the survival of something, somewhere.

Patch and I step back out of the sitting room and take the – one pace wide – hall to my bedroom. I take his hand and we step across to the window. Richard's ghost scuttles into the corner with the spiders and the dustballs, hides in the gap between the skirting and the floor. I try and pretend I didn't see him.

The sun is thinking about setting, lowering itself into a comfortable position on the horizon, letting go of the heat of the day. It is the most beautiful way to see the two sculptures on the pond, dappled with golden beads and reaching up towards us as if, for all the world, they want to join us in my room.

'Do you know they're copies?' Patch asks me.

'What do you mean?'

'The real ones are in the Louvre. I've seen them. To be

fair, they look exactly the same – same size, same colour.' He squeezes my hand. 'Very different setting though. I'll take you, one day, and you can see for yourself.'

We have gone from being strangers to talking about trips to Paris. We have shared less than a bottle of wine, we are yet to sit and eat together for the first time. It should be nonsense, preposterous: here, in my bedroom, watching the sun coat the gardens, it is exactly as things should be – one more curiosity in this eccentric, and slightly magical, house.

Patch puts his fingers on the waistband of my jeans. The very tips edge over the fabric and onto the skin of my lower back. My whole body clenches with the illicit thrill of it.

'This is worse than having your parents next door,' I whisper. I turn and face him, dare a kiss with one eye open and fixed on the doorway.

I feel his cheeks fatten as he breaks off from the kiss into one of his huge grins. 'How are we going to do this?'

We both know implicitly what 'this' is.

'I get a few sessions away from Leo a week,' I say. 'If he's not fighting. But they're with you. He's with you. We're going to have to wait.'

'I can wait,' he whispers. 'But I'd rather not wait too long.'

'This Saturday is the grand event. Re-opening a museum that's never been closed and hoping no one notices. It is, honestly, all I can think about right now. But it's all done by Sunday.'

'Sunday belongs to me,' he says.

*

Where We Belong

When Patch says goodbye to Leo and Curtis and I go downstairs to finish the clearing up, there's only me and the ghost boy Richard left. I reach down beside me for his little invisible hand and hope he can forgive me.

Chapter Fifteen

I get up at 6 a.m. on the day of the Pretend Re-opening: there is so much to do. I have been giddy for the last three days, swapping texts with Patch last thing at night and first thing in the morning. Every other moment has been spent recruiting and advertising, posting on social media and booking tours. I know Araminta disapproves, that she thinks the evils of social media leave us open to all and sundry but, frankly, that's what we need. She came to me the day before yesterday, clearly worried.

'I was talking to Rosemary in the garden . . .' She didn't make full eye contact.

'Rosemary?' I was going through the galleries, trying to find the highlights to add to our new profile pages, thinking of every last thing I could use to pull people in.

'One of the volunteers. Older lady.' That doesn't help at all: all our volunteers are at least retirement age.

'She saw a news item – about a party that someone posted

on the internet. 500 people turned up – the house was almost destroyed.'

I sighed and turned to face her. 'Kids, Araminta. Those things are always kids.' I could picture the echo chamber of the two old women, exaggerating and scare-mongering, layering on the doom of every internet rumour, every small-town fright. 'It's not the sort of thing that happens at a museum.'

I noticed the single capuchin monkey hanging upside down in the diorama behind her: an animal that Colonel Hugo discovered himself, one of quite a few species named after him. I made a note in my phone to add some details about it.

'Sorry, Araminta. I have to write these things down while I think about them.' I pointed to the monkey. 'Otherwise all memory of it will be gone in ten seconds' time.'

She pursed her lips, stared at me. 'Very well,' she said. 'But at least we've had this conversation. At least you know my thoughts.' She nodded, once, at me and returned to whatever duties she was carrying out back in the box office.

'Please succeed,' I said to the empty gallery, in an effort to feel brave. If I'd been in the library, at least I'd have had the echo to help me believe.

The email that waits on my phone when I wake up today is the last thing I expect to read, and sent with the worst of timings.

From: Simon Henderson

To: Cate Morris

Subject: A Lot of Time to Think

Mail: I'm back from a two-week expedition and there's no word from you. I hope you don't think I was ignoring you – there's no signal where I've been and clinging on to the side of Mount Cook kept my hands full.

Did you miss me? I did, actually, really miss you – and Leo, of course. Maybe it was the silence and the mind-space at the top of the mountains, but it made me yearn for home. I think it's all that vast immovable rock, the life clinging to it and the secrets trapped inside it – and the unbelievable quiet – puts things in perspective. Without wanting to get all hippyish on you, I spent four days collecting bones from creatures that were last alive 70 million years ago. That can have an effect on a boy.

It made me think about Leo and how I could be a better godfather to him if I occasionally gave him some time, it made me think about my old mum and how she will need a bit more of me as life goes on. And it made me think about you and how I ran away and why I'm even here on the other side of the planet. We have things to discuss, you and I, things that I'd like to talk through face-to-face.

So I'm coming to England to put some of these things right. I can't leave yet, I have to finish the contract,

but I'm coming. Hang on in there, I'll be back before
you know it.

S x

Six months ago, I would have known exactly what to think
about this message. Six months ago I was a completely different person: in my old job; in my old flat; in my old self. I
park Simon's email in a corner of my mind. If there are any
spaces in today's events, I will think of a way to answer him
before I go to bed. I owe him too much to leave him waiting
until tomorrow.

For the purposes of social media and the general public,
we are calling today 'The Grand Event'. It looked good
on the posters I made to put up in shops and our full-page
advert in the local newspaper. The publicity has been
eating into my redundancy money but I'm hoping it's a
worthwhile investment. I made colour photocopies of a
picture from one of the children's books in the library.
There are merry-go-rounds with lions and brightly
painted horses, tigers and ostriches with long exaggerated
legs. They're very good, if I say so myself. It gives an air of
times-gone-past and a hint of what the collection entails,
what it means – I even found a font for the details that
implies this museum is a relic from more simple times, a
love letter from the past.

Our avatar on all our social media is a sparkling gold
photograph of Atalanta and Hippomenes, taken on a

scorching blue-skied day much like this one. We couldn't have been luckier with the weather. The bunting that I ordered online and have strung across the museum drive crackles in the light breeze – a sound I thought was rain when I first woke up this morning.

Leo has spent three days helping Curtis in the garden, edging borders and cutting grass. He looks bronzed and strong: Curtis hasn't taken his hoodie off as far as I can see – despite the soaring temperatures, so I should imagine he still looks the same underneath it.

I sniff Leo's clothes every time he comes in, just in case: it's not the most thorough of protection policies but it's all I've got.

'Stop sniffing me,' he said last night. 'It's not normal.'

I moved my nose away from his shirt but didn't say anything.

'I'm not stupid so I don't smoke drugs.'

I still don't say anything. He has a point.

'And I talked to Curtis about it and now he doesn't any more either.'

I have to – gladly – take his word for it. Maybe they've been good for each other.

Araminta is waiting in the drive when we get downstairs. Leo and I are enthused with the excitement that fizzes through the air on this bright summer day: we are buzzing. It's hard to imagine the drive full of cars, the silent corridors bubbling with chatter, but we both believe they will be.

'Nothing ventured, nothing gained,' I say to Araminta in my boldest voice.

'I wish you the best of luck with it all.' Her smile is unconvincing. 'Leo, could you come and help me for a moment?'

They go upstairs behind the box office, up to where the dusty office and the storerooms are. Leo comes down first, carrying a box that's wider than him. Araminta is behind him with a smaller one.

She puts them on the floor in the space that Malcolm and Thierry used for their makeshift bar. 'I thought these might be of help,' she says, opening the first box. 'A hands-on exhibit. Something to touch.'

Leo's box contains four folded skins: a zebra, a spotted cat of some sort, a buffalo hide, and what Araminta explains – with a slight shiver – is a Colobus monkey rug. 'They're things people have dropped off here over the years: things they didn't want in their houses.'

I touch the poor sad fur of the black-and-white circular rug, run my fingers over the stitches that hold six little hides together. 'Thank you, I thought . . .'

She interrupts me. 'I do want it to work.'

In the box Araminta carried are two pieces of taxidermy on stands: a hedgehog and a magpie, his black feathers a gleaming darkest blue when you look so closely at him. 'And these are the same. They have no place here, but they'll be great for children to touch.'

'And people with visual impairments,' says Leo, pushing his glasses further onto his nose.

A dead petting zoo, I think but don't say. 'It's a brilliant idea: thank you so much.'

Leo and I move a desk out from the ticket office and lay the things out.

'And if these get stolen or broken, it's not such a big problem.' Araminta is clearly still worried. 'I've checked all the alarms and the storeroom doors. And I've locked the door next to the kitchen so no one can get up to our apartments.'

'I think that's sensible.' I pat her arm in solidarity.

My phone tings to say I have a text and I stifle a smile: I know who that will be.

Have the greatest day. Although tomorrow will be better. Looking forward to seeing you so so much. Xxx

The first car comes in at 9.45, fifteen whole minutes before the museum is supposed to open, before our posters said we would start. Leo and I grab each other in excitement as we see it approach. 'Act like we see this every day,' I say to him as the car parks up and as a second comes down the drive, halogen headlights straining against the bright sun.

Leo is tapping his thighs in anticipation.

I reach out and squeeze his hand. And then, as if our dreams had come true, just before opening time – a coach. An actual coach full of visitors, visitors who disembark as if the party had already started. From the card in the front window, I can see that it is full of Cubs and Brownies.

The noises of cars crunching up the drive, children calling to one another across the gardens, the murmur of visitors contemplating, marvelling, it's all very life-affirming. The museum is waking up.

The children stream from the coach, the uniformed Akelas and Brownie leaders trying to get them into some kind of organised crocodile, and head for the ticket office.

'We've booked,' one of the leaders calls over the heads of the restless children. 'Eighty-six children, twelve adults.' It's more people than we've had in all the time I've been here. The very first two coaches have brought more people than we had in the whole day of the French exchange trip.

I take the Brownie leader over to Araminta behind the desk. 'We need to ask people how they heard about today,' I tell her. 'So we can find out which method worked.'

'We saw the article in the local paper,' the woman says. 'So exciting to have it finally re-open.'

Araminta and I exchange glances.

When the local WI ladies arrive, en masse, they bring cakes and biscuits to sell in the foyer, promising all the takings to the museum. I am overwhelmed by their kindness. Leo and I gave a talk to them last week about Colonel Hugo's mission and our part in the legacy. Leo fielded their questions masterfully, impressing everyone – especially me – with his knowledge of the exhibits. We owe this deluge of cakes to the fact that he completely charmed them.

I position myself by the entrance of Gallery One; I pretend it's so that I can assess the impact of the social media advertising but really I want to hear those collective gasps as the visitors see it for the first time. No one lets me down, no one is immune to the wonder of it: it makes me smile every time.

The same three mums with pushchairs who were here on the day of the French exchange come in with a group of friends. They are loving being the ones who know their way around, who can point out the cutest cubs, the angriest zebra.

'I can't believe what you've done to the place in such a short time,' one of them says to me. 'It's a whole new lease of life.'

Clearly, dogmatically telling people that you've done something works. The only real changes are a weeded drive and some straight edges on the flowerbeds, although Araminta did muster some volunteers to clean the glass. I make myself look busy by walking through the museum in case my face gives it all away.

In the library, small groups stand staring upwards at the books, wondering what might be there, pointing at titles on spines, guessing at the flags on the flagpoles. Once the first man finds out about the echo across the library, it is alive with vibrato and forced tenors for the rest of the morning.

I'm directing people through the library, answering questions as best I can, when Araminta appears. 'It's astonishing. It's been a very long time since this many people came.

We've sold almost two hundred tickets.' Her cheeks are pink with pleasure: it's lovely to see her so alive, so engaged.

'We need to find a way to sustain it. I feel like I've dragged each one of these in by hand.'

A man behind me booms out a pop song across the library and it makes me jump. 'Who's on the desk?' I ask.

'One of the WI ladies kindly took over so I could have a comfort break.' She goes slightly coy at mentioning the possibility of bodily functions.

'I'll go and check on Leo. Do you need anything to eat?'

There is a sudden shout from the galleries behind me. And then a man's voice, loud, urgent. Everyone turns to stare, something is very wrong. There are a lot of people in the library's circular space, their reactions to the shout bubble and babble above our heads.

'Excuse me, excuse me.' I push my way through the bewildered people. 'I'm sure it's nothing.' But we can all hear the raised voices, the man shouting.

I sprint back through the galleries, Araminta not far behind me. It takes only seconds to cover the length of the corridor, my feet clap loudly against the polished parquet as I run. The visitors are all standing still, confused, and I knock into people's shoulders in the rush to get through.

Gallery One looks like a battle scene. Vivid scarlet drips from the glass, washes across the parquet flooring. A man holding the handle of a pushchair looks up at me, his face covered in – at first I think it's blood and then the smell of paint hits me. His expression is pure shock. Somewhere a baby screams and I realise with relief that the pushchair was empty.

The man shouting is Malcolm. 'You can't do that!' I hear as I stop running and try to take it all in.

Three men in balaclavas and camouflage jackets stand in the middle of the gallery, shouting back at him. A fourth, is painting large red letters across the glass.

'MURDER.'

Araminta speaks first. 'Stop! Just stop it! What do you think you're doing?'

'Meat is murder,' the man shouts back in her face, only his eyes visible through the slit in the black wool. 'This is a charnel house.'

I shout to Malcolm, to anyone, to call the police. 'Get out!' I yell at the top of my voice, running towards the group of men. 'Get out!' I push into the middle of them, trying to separate them, trying to make them leave.

The man nearest me upends a binbag of leaflets onto the floor and I try to catch them as they spill onto the red-painted parquet at my feet. 'And the paint ...' he shouts to one of the others. The man he shouted to hurls a can of paint across the top of the pile of paper like petrol on a bonfire. It seeps across the floor like blood. Splashes of scarlet splatter up the front of his black jeans as if flames are licking his legs.

Araminta grabs the paintbrush from the hand of the man painting onto the glass. He is halfway through his second 'MURDER' and the straight line of the 'D' trails away like a gash across the glass as she pulls the brush away.

The men nearest me snatch their backpacks from the edge of the room, hook their arms through the straps. For a moment I think they are going to swing them into the vast wall of glass, but they turn towards the doorway instead. 'Come on,' shouts the tallest to the man by Araminta. He has paint on the elbows of his black jumper, smears across the back of his balaclava.

I spin round to watch them go. At my feet, pictures of dogs in cages, bears with anguished eyes – the paper pasted scarlet – stare up at me from the swirl of red. Nothing is untouched.

I hear Araminta cry out behind me. I turn and see the man wrestle his paintbrush back out of her hand. She reaches up towards it and he bowls against her with his shoulder. She shouts as she falls, her legs sliding from under her in the paste of paint and paper.

There is a single sickening snap as her arm hits the ground before she does and then a moment of absolute silence.

In the slow seconds that follow, paint seeps down every vertical surface, the smell booms and boils to fill the whole room. The animals stare – impotent and frozen – and Araminta lies very still, red and frail and helpless.

All four men bolt for the exit.

And, as they leave, I catch the eyes of the one nearest me. His balaclava slips up from his forehead.

I know those dark narrow eyes. I recognise those heavy eyebrows.

I know that if I pulled the black wool up from his throat I would see a smudged blue tattoo.

Chapter Sixteen

After the chaos of the attack, everything seems to happen quietly and calmly. The ambulance arrives but not before all the visitors have left, terrified. A nurse from the local A&E department happened to be in the library with her family: she came running when she heard the rumble of news that someone had been attacked.

The WI ladies gather as if by instinct and do their best to shuffle people out past Gallery One without them looking in too much, but the smell of paint, the red tell-tale footsteps that march all around the corridors, blushing our parquet flooring with pink prints, gives it all away.

Something horrible has happened here. And two hundred visitors have seen its aftermath.

Araminta regains consciousness almost immediately, but the unnatural angle of her arm speaks volumes. 'I'll be fine,' she says in a voice that doesn't quite belong to her. 'We can go by car – I don't need an ambulance.'

'You do, I'm afraid.' The nurse sits beside her on the floor, sticky with paint. 'You were definitely unconscious for a few moments. That makes you a risk.'

I try to smile at Araminta. For a moment, I think about stroking her good arm but I don't dare touch her. We both know without saying it that I am, essentially, responsible for this.

Behind us, the volunteers clean down the man and the pushchair as best they can but, in the end, all they can do is take his name and address and say we'll be in touch about replacing the pram and his clothes.

'I knew this was going to go wrong.' Araminta closes her eyes. 'I should never have allowed it. I've let everyone down.'

My hands flutter around her; I don't know which piece of her to touch without it hurting. 'This is my fault. All my fault.'

Leo has arrived in the gallery. 'Bastards.' He slaps his hands on his thighs. He is spitting with anger, flecks of saliva land on the floor in front of him, a drop in the ocean of red. 'Bastards.'

He kneels down in the paint beside Araminta.

I think about his best jeans, ruined. His priorities are so different to a few months ago. When we lived in London he would have been terrified by this situation – by this mess – rather than angry. Did I miss him growing, or is this how parenting works?

'Curtis and me will get them, Mrs Minta. We will tell them, tell the police.'

We stare at the chaos: the scarlet papier mâché of leaflets

already gluing itself to the floor, the red smears tattooing themselves to the glass.

'At least it's emulsion. It'll scrub off,' says one of the volunteers. 'But you have to start on these leaflets now or they'll be impossible.'

I drop my voice, whisper. 'This was Curtis.'

'How could it possibly be Curtis? This is not the moment for petty grudges.' Araminta's voice is quiet, as frail and ghostly as her face.

'I saw him.' I hiss it through my teeth. A snake, on the floor to my left, stares at me with solidarity, glassy eyes approving through his red filter.

'Cate . . .' Her voice is cracking with pain and with emotion. She is broken in more ways than just her arm. 'You don't always know as much about people as you think you do.' She tries to get up but the nurse stops her, strokes her arm. 'He's a good boy – good for the museum.' She brushes the nurse away, tries to sit up. 'And this, what we did today, was not.'

'I'm going to get buckets. Do something practical. You've had a shock, Araminta.' How can she be returning to the old her, after all this?

'I knew this would happen,' she says and sinks back down beside the nurse who kneels in front of her. 'I have let Colonel Hugo down, broken my promise.' She starts to cry. 'This is what the Board have been waiting for. Oh, Cate . . .'

'This wasn't me!' I lose my temper. 'I didn't do this.' I

wave my arms at the visceral paint seeping down the glass, at the congealed mess on Leo's jeans, at what looks like blood on my hands. I bellow at Araminta. 'I didn't do this!'

She turns and stares at me for a second. Her face is saying, *Oh, yes, you did.*

Araminta doesn't want anyone to go with her in the ambulance: she is adamant. I make her promise to call me to collect her or to bring clothes if she has to stay in.

The police have said we can start cleaning up and the paint does come off reasonably easily, although it will sit in the tiny gaps between the glass and the dioramas' wooden frames for a long time to come.

Some of the leaflets need scraping off with a paint scraper to remove them. The noise is as brittle as the atmosphere in the gallery.

'Curtis isn't texting me back, Mummy.' Leo long since gave up washing the paint with me. He went back up to the flat saying that he was too tired to help. 'I want him to come online.'

I don't know what to say. It's all too awful.

It is late when we finish. The atmosphere in the house is as thick – and as sickening – as the smell of the paint.

I pour a glass of wine from the bottle in the fridge. My hands leave a rose mist around its cold edges and I wipe them on my trousers to try and clean them. It is no good. I run the tap into the big butler's sink and wash my hands, the soapy water foaming blood against the enamel.

I take my wine into the library. I need some open space around me but I'm still a little afraid to go outside.

The library is quiet. The paint must have rubbed off people's shoes by the time they got here and I am the only thing in the room to remind anyone of what happened. Above me the black spangled sky blinks and twinkles.

'What the fuck?' I ask the books but they stay silent, their backs turned towards me. 'How is this all my fault?' I am asking about the whole of the last four years – not just tonight. I am tired to my soul – I was tired before Richard died. I am asking about my whole life.

All these books, all these secrets, all these betrayals. The house says nothing.

I watch my face reflected in the brass light fittings at the back of the desk. I am so tired and vulnerable that it feels as if the house is pointing my own image back at me in order to accuse me. And maybe I'm guilty.

Maybe I'll be found guilty of contingency, of being contingent. The last years have been a backfire of action and reaction. I have not made a decision of my own – for me – in decades. I bend around the plans that life makes for me – with no chance to wonder whether they are the right ones. Despite the horrors of today, despite being forced into yet another corner – there is one thing I am deciding, am doing just for myself: Patch. Patch is part of the new me, the antithesis of being blown about by fate and chance. Patch is something, someone, that I am choosing.

And I'm not the only person that choosing Patch affects.

Would I ever have been fair enough – generous enough – to let Simon go if Patch hadn't come into my life?

I sit at one of the desks to write the email I have to write. I run my fingers over the worn wood. So many love letters must have been written here: so many 'sorrys'; 'congratulations'; and 'I'm so sad to inform you.' The house has seen it all before.

From: Cate Morris

To: Simon Henderson

Subject: I need to tell you something

Mail: I haven't been entirely honest with you: or with myself. Something we both know I'm good at. And I don't know how to find the words for this, I only know that I need to tell you.

I've met someone. It's been swift – an absolute avalanche. I'm so sorry. I didn't expect this to happen and I certainly didn't mean it to. I don't know what will come of it – if anything – I'm surprised to find him in my life, certainly surprised that I could feel the way I do. I feel less lonely and, potentially, as though I have something to look forward to and someone to share that with. I didn't think I would feel like that again in my lifetime and that's why I've never prepared myself – or you – for the possibility of me meeting someone else.

I love you, Simon. I have done since I was eighteen years old. I love you for who you were to Richard, who you are to Leo, and – most of all – for everything you have been to me.

I can't simply switch off the way I feel about you, you mean too much. But it's not a relationship that was ever meant to be. In another place and time, if I hadn't been Richard's wife – and now, if Patch hadn't turned up – I know we would have been a lifelong love story. There was always a little part of me that believed you would come back and we would start again: that the fairytale would come true. And I think, in no small way, that myth helped me to deal with losing Richard.

But that isn't what's happened and I'm not able to belong to you. It breaks my heart but, once again, we have slipped past each other and out of reach.

You'll always be my best friend. You'll always be Leo's godfather. Most of all, I will always love you but, for now, we can't see each other: it would be too painful.

Cxxx

When I am done with crying, at least for now, I go back to the kitchen to finish clearing up. It is late, beyond midnight, and properly dark.

I search the drawers for some kind of cloth that I can use to scrub the last of the paint from the sink. I can't use a tea towel – whatever I get this off with will have to be thrown away immediately. One of the drawers in the dresser is full of things that look suitable, I rifle through for the oldest, the most disposable. At the bottom of the drawer, there is a book.

The book is thin, the cover faded. In pale blue letters it says *Crouch-on-Sea, a History* with a picture of Hatters, pretty much as it looks today, from the outside. I take the book out of the drawer and open it. On the first page it gives the author's details – no one I recognise – and the year: 1967.

I take the book with me to the kitchen table, under the central lamp, so that I can see it better. The writer has put together a pretty decent potted history of the house: I skim it. I know most of it. What is new to me is the collection of black-and-white photos. As I read on, I realise that the photographs are greyscale copies of colour pictures and that the pictures are relatively modern, presumably taken by the author specifically for the book.

Most of the galleries are reproduced – with some degree of talent. The scale of the animal collection almost makes its way onto the page although it would need a human in the picture for perspective to properly grasp the scale. It brings me back to what it looked like today.

And then, towards the end of the section, a group shot outside the front door. Underneath it says, 'The residents of Hatters, the Lyons-Morris family.'

In the line-up is a small boy. I don't need to be told who it is, it could be Leo. The dark hair, the sturdy legs, that half-frown. This is a picture of Richard – he must be six or seven. And beside him, unmistakable, and barely changed, is Araminta.

I rush through the text, trying to find out an exact year. This picture must have been taken more than fifty years ago. I open the magnifier on my phone and hold it over the photograph: the details come into view. It is definitely Richard, and it is definitely Araminta. She is wearing the same short skirt she wears now, the same light round-necked jumper. Her hair is the exact same shape and set but possibly, if I squint, a shade or two darker than it is now.

Colonel Hugo is in the middle, the tallest person in the picture and definitely at its centre. To one side of him is a woman I assume is Harriet – the only other pictures I've seen of her are in her wedding veil, but it must be her. Richard is in front of Hugo and his two hands rest on his grandson's shoulders in a gesture of pride.

Richard looks sweet. He is wearing school uniform, long grey shorts that cast shadows over his knees, a V-necked jumper with a band of colour running round the 'V', a white shirt with its pointy collars sticking over the jumper, and a school tie. He is untroubled and easy, his face – despite its natural frown – radiant and engaged. And again, no sign of his parents. I kiss my fingers, then place them gently on his little face.

Does this house let me into its shadows whenever it wants to? Does it offer up these reminders as a comfort to me – or as a reminder to know my place? Is it trying to remind me that my son might belong here, but I don't.

I get into bed a little after 1 a.m., lonely and sad. There is a reply on my phone from Simon.

From: Simon Henderson

To: Cate Morris

Subject: Thank you

Mail: Thank you, as ever, for your startling honesty. I'm so pleased that this has worked out for you, and for Leo.

I ran away when Richard died – however kindly we dress it up. I should have stayed and taken care of you and Leo and I didn't. I took my guilt and my shame and I got as far away from what we did as I could. I know now that I was wrong – just as I know (and my mum actually wrote this in a letter to me when I left) that you take yourself with you wherever you go. I have taken you and Leo with me too – along with Richard, the best friend a man could ever have – the three of you will always be beside me.

I hope you will still let me visit when I come back. I would love to see Leo. And I will have to 'screw my courage to the sticking place' to see you and your new chap: maybe if I'd done that in the first place, everyone's lives would have gone differently.

Anstey Harris

> Whoever has the fortune to be loved by you –
> and I count myself among that lucky number – is a
> privileged man.
> Simon

When you're sad and wrong, someone being noble and kind brings its own searing pain. I cry myself back to sleep.

Chapter Seventeen

Fire overwhelms every sense the human body has but, for me, the last thing that goes is my sense of smell. It is smell that wakes me: smell that makes me dream – in the moments before that – of bonfires, winter nights, of curling up on a sofa with Richard in our old house.

I have read that smell is the sense most closely linked to memory, to our primal selves: that heroin-users smell the sweet staleness of their mother's milk before they are overcome by the whoosh of the drug.

I am awake, fully awake, and everything I rely on has gone.

The bedroom is never this dark. The moon has vanished from my window and everything is a deep yellowed grey. The starling chicks are screaming beneath the eaves, a ghostly screech of chaos as they panic and flap. The panic itself is contagious and I throw myself towards my bedroom door.

Leo. Where is Leo? I scream his name but no sound comes. It is swallowed by the noise and stench of the smoke. I stagger across the room, toward what I believe is the door. I walk straight into what can only be a chest of drawers. Even in this tiny space, I have gone the wrong way.

I have no sight; and no hearing left outside of the screaming screaming birds. My nose is clogged and choked with smoke, it coats my tongue and my searing throat. Adrenalin and fear paste white sweat across my skin.

Leo.

I drop to the floor where there is less smoke. I push my face into the ancient carpet and try to inhale through its weave of dust and worn fibres. My hands are bony spiders that crawl towards the bottom of the door. Flex and drag, stretch and pull. Every weft and weave of the carpet scores into my cheeks as I inch forward.

I wrench the door open and it is a full second before I realise my skin has stuck to the brass doorknob. I scream and scream his name.

The birds are silent.

My bath towel hangs on the back of this door. I pat blindly with my wrong hand until my palm hits the fabric. I bunch the towel up in both hands and try to turn the knob. It slips and resists and stays, stubbornly, shut. I push myself upright, my face pressed against the heat of the door, the hot paint sticking to my skin. I hit the doorknob with the towel, over and over. I am completely ineffective.

I try to shout, but there is nothing in my throat but

smoke. I must wake Leo. I must get to his bedroom. Leo sleeps like a log, he will sleep right through this until . . .

The door gives and swings towards me. The roar knocks me backwards off my feet, my throat scorches and what was my larynx silently squeezes in an effort to make the word 'Leo'.

I lie on my back and bicycle my feet against the floor. One foot hits what I hope is the door and I roll forward to shove it closed with my shoulder.

Leo is on the other side of this door. Leo is somewhere in that black bedlam.

I have shut the door and I have no idea how to open it again. On my hands and knees, I crawl back towards it. I reach up, my palms flat against the hot wood. The door is tight shut, tendrils of smoke – whiter than the greyness floating in my room and hot – leak their way in, determined to invade every inch of my space.

I bang on the door, over and over, trying to knock it down, refusing to accept that it won't open. The noise behind it is staggering, a suffocating threat daring me to open the door: taunting me that it has my son.

I move my hand to the doorknob again, squeeze it tight and scream and scream as I turn it.

There are still enough nerves left in my hand to register the cauterisation when I grab the doorknob but this will be no pain at all compared to letting the fire have my son.

My knees trip on the towel as I try to bowl myself forward out of my bedroom. I grab it and stuff it against my face. An advert, a film – some memory – tells me that I should wet the towel and I wonder whether the person who decided that has ever seen the inside, the pulsing moving belly, of a fire.

Leo's room is to the left of mine. Inches away. I scrape my face along the carpet, dragging myself forward. I can't breathe, I can't see: the fire is a monster in my ears; it is the air in my lungs; it is the food I swallow.

For the first time I truly understand Richard's illness. His actions. In all my counselling – despite all the wisdom of professionals – I never processed his terror, the overwhelming horror of what was happening inside my beautiful husband. This fire, this is what took Richard. The smoke blinded him, the stench burned night and day in his nose. The choking confusion overwhelmed him. This bedlam is all he knew in those years: of course he wanted it to end.

Now that I am robbed of my senses – the way I process the world – and only the grazing pain of the carpet under my face is real, I get it. I know why Richard couldn't live through this. I have only been its hostage for minutes, seconds, not the months and years that he had to fight for breath, to make sense of the world beyond his skin.

Now, the fire is everything and the dry ghost of vomit rises in my throat where air and water used to flow. I wonder whether burning from the outside in – or the inside out – is worst.

'I know, Richard.' I slur the words, though they are silent under the raging wind of the smoke, the vast blooming gold of the fire. 'I understand.' My lips are sealed together now, like hands in night-time prayer. I can sleep.

The mane of the lion is soft, his fur winds round my fingers, soothes my burning hands. He must have been here all the time. He must have hidden in the corners, his huge feet padding – silent – through the house at night.

He roars again and his breath is fetid on my face. I understand him, I hear his words: he is the spirit of the house, he is Richard's lion heart. He is Leo.

I kiss his golden fur.

Richard leans down and scoops me into his arms. His face is as familiar as my own, the dark eyes, the straight black hair. I had thought I would never see him again and yet he is here; solid under my fingers, strong enough to carry me.

The smoke is a stinking grey veil and Richard staggers from one side of the corridor to the other, barrelling, tripping. I turn my face towards his wide chest: I bury myself in him and know that I am home.

I have missed him so. If I had known it was so easy to summon him, I would have done so long ago. The trade of air for Richard is a simple one, one I welcome with every atom of me.

I know we are outside. The night is cold – still choking, still black and swirling – but colder now. I carry the fire with me in the palm of my hand, an amber coal, the beating heart of it, the vivid ember.

We are at a fairground and the carousel of lights spins

around, blue and red and fiery orange. People shout and I try to lift my arm to wave, to tell them that I, too, have joined the party, come to the fair. I listen for the music; sniff deeply for the smell of candy floss and doughnuts.

I remember how once there was a searing pain in my hand and I laugh out loud because it doesn't hurt any more. I turn my head to tell Richard, to show him the living coral centre of the fire held in my hand, but only my eyes move. I remember that Richard is at the fair with me, and my heart soars. He is standing next to me, his back towards me. He is as solid and corporeal as before I closed my eyes. His shoulders are broad and masculine, his stance confident and true.

He is restored.

Richard turns around to face me, the red lights shine across his hair. His almond eyes are closed tight against the smoke. He slaps his thighs rhythmically with his hands: on and on.

Behind him, animals parade across the grass. I can see people's feet, boots, mud. I can see hoses and cables and car tyres. I can see paws and hooves and claws. I can see lions and tigers and bears. Books flutter and hop like birds. They hover above the ground, loose pages dropping like pieces of spring straw onto the mud below.

Something plastic fixes over my mouth and nose. I know it is white from the edge that obscures the bottom half of my vision. I am being lifted and, as I rise higher into the air, I see the full carnival of the animals. Bison swap their plaster tundra for real grass, hippo stand confused in the English countryside, wondering where the nearest watering hole might be. Zebras pass for thoroughbreds against the rusty rail of the paddock and countless deer, unidentified and generic, swarm across the lawn and onto the gravelled drive.

Stacks of books lean against fence posts, laconic as ranch-hands. I move forward through the air and the oryx – his shoulders muscular and powerful – stares balefully as I leave, his glass eyes sparkling with electric blue. I see the hunched backs of a hyena pack and imagine the siren of their laughter as they see me off.

The lion is not here on the grass. The lion would not leave: I know he is still prowling the charred corridors, checking the singed bedrooms, guarding the burnt and broken heart of the house.

Leo. I remember in the fairground. I have lost little Leo at the carnival. He has slipped from my hand and disappeared.

Where is Leo, I ask silently, as I slide, half-blinded and hallucinating, into the cavern of the ambulance.

I remember little after that except the dreams. In my dreams I was in a hospital, not this one, with a see-through plastic cot beside me. Sometimes the baby in the cot – his eyes struggling to focus, his perfect rosebud lips drawn by instinct towards me – is Richard, sometimes he is Leo, sometimes he is a baby I do not know yet: Leo's baby. A baby whose name I must write in the book. A mouse sleeps beside the baby, curls against his body, and sometimes Simon comes and strokes the little mouse, smiles at the baby. The mouse has golden hair, a yellow tail of fire. When the baby wakes, the mouse scuttles across his skin, stands upright with its tiny paws against the edge of the crib; facing me, daring me to touch the baby.

I can't smell the baby, even in my dreams. The smell of smoke is etched into my flesh. It is a tattoo.

The light is different in my dream hospital: it is a filtered softness, slipping through slatted blinds at the windows. It spills striped shafts onto my face and I wonder if it might take me back to the sky with it.

When I wake from the dreams I am trapped, pinned to the bed by a wide white tube forced down my throat. From one of my eyes, I can see the bend of the tube as it disappears into me.

The other eye is sightless, that much I have been able to work out. One eye can see the coiled snake, ready to strike: the other only a purple softness. The shafts of light stepping heavenward; the white snake choking me; the empty violet nothing: they all fight to take me.

I can't speak. I can open one eye and signal wildly to the nurses. I can convey panic by the flaring of an iris, the flicker of an eyelash. All I say with my one eye, over and over, is, 'Where's Leo?'

The people who come and go in my hospital room are ghosts. Some are solid: they float around my bed with graceful steps and have jobs to do: they move me, they talk to me, they make things snap or pop or peel against my body. Others are proper old-fashioned ghosts, see-through and wavy. Not all these things can be real. But, I know I saw Richard too. And Simon was here in the hospital. One of them is dead, one in New Zealand, one is – where is Leo?

'Leo is safe, Cate,' the policeman standing by my bed says.

'Leo,' I say to him in a voice that is not my own.

'Leo.' My face is tight with pain. 'Leo.'

'Your son is safe with his friends. He's staying with Curtis Hogben.'

The word 'safe' swamps me, covers me. The baby in the plastic crib beside me raises his small downy head and smiles, the mouse under his chin. I try to tell the policeman that the baby isn't real, he's not here.

But my son is safe.

I open my eye and the policeman is still there. The doctor is standing next to him. The walls are pale green – celery. The colour is celery. The white slatted blind swings and rustles.

Simon.

Richard.

Leo.

It took a day – I later find out – to stabilise my reaction to the morphine they gave me for my poor burnt hand and the damage the smoke did to my lungs: time was elastic. Sometimes the lion visited me and I knew nothing was real: other times I looked beside me and saw that perfect pink baby and I hoped that I was simply back in that time, the best time.

'Is Leo okay?' It has taken this long to get these words out of me. I am desperate.

'He is with his friend Curtis. I saw them yesterday and this morning.' The policeman has the look of a family man about him: he is kind, gentle. His name, he tells me, is Andrew. 'They're all right. We'll get him in to see you today. As soon as we can.'

My skin pulls so tight across my cheek that it makes me cry, involuntarily. I have to fight to stay awake. I have to get Leo back.

The red room, the bloody gallery, fills my vision, drowns me in its portent of what came next. I see the word 'Murder' dripping down the glass.

'Curtis Hogben.' I whisper it like a curse. 'He attacked us.'

The policeman sits in the chair that Simon has only moments ago vacated. 'No, Curtis Hogben is taking care of Leo.'

'I saw him.' Speaking is sword-swallowing and pain jabs through my throat. 'With the paint. Did he start the fire?' I try to sit up. 'And my son is with him? He's dangerous.'

'There's nothing dangerous about Curtis Hogben, except perhaps for his old joy-riding habit.'

I don't understand. What is he talking about?

'His erstwhile joy-riding habit, I should say. He took his mother's car, no licence, but didn't even get out of Crouch before he was caught. But you know about that, I suppose, the community service?' The policeman, Andrew, is smiling and shaking his head, as if Curtis were no more than a naughty boy, a wayward teenager.

'I saw him.'

'You saw Floyd Hogben. Floyd Hogben threw the paint.'

I don't understand. Has Curtis been pretending all along? Is he not even called Curtis? It makes no sense. I stare at the cracks across the off-white ceiling, the stress of knowing Leo is with that boy throbs across the front of my forehead.

'We arrested the Hogben lads straight after the assault on Ms Buchan. We march them in for anything involving four young men at once. This time it was Floyd. Floyd and some misguided animal rights activists who thought they'd recruited a local. Floyd Hogben doesn't do anything for "causes". Only to make trouble.' He makes quotation marks with his fingers.

'Curtis didn't answer his phone. Leo was upset.' I thought that memory was supposed to protect you from trauma. Mine is punishing me, sharpening the detail of every word, every accusation.

'We kept Curtis in until late. Till we were sure which one of them did it. It was always going to be Floyd though.' He sighs. I can only see the left-hand side of the policeman's face, his large hairy ear.

'One more thing, Cate, we need to talk to Ms Buchan – Araminta. She discharged herself from A&E on Saturday night and hasn't been seen since. Do you have any idea where she might be?'

*

When Andrew has gone, the nurses come to peel the dressing from my eye. There will be no lasting damage, apparently. My eyelashes are scorched off and I have a graze across my cheek that I know, from my memory of before the fire, matches the exact weave of the threadbare matting in my bedroom. The palm of my hand is scorched, it will need to stay dressed while the skin underneath it does its best to heal, to knit together. I wonder if the rest of my life can recover in the same way.

Andrew assured me that Araminta wasn't in the fire: they have done a thorough search of the building and there are – thank God – no casualties. But no one has seen her in the thirty-six hours that have passed since it happened and, until she turns up, the police can't be entirely sure what her role in the whole thing is or was.

I don't really believe Araminta would hurt us. She certainly would never risk harming Leo or the house: that much I would stake my life on.

My phone is inundated with messages. None of them are from Araminta and most of them are from Patch. He says he has been at the hospital most of the time I have, but he's been given very limited information and not been allowed in to see me because he's not family. It makes my eyes water, and that in turn makes my cheek sting. No one is family, apart from Leo and me. Our vulnerability has never been so vivid. There's only the two of us, and this thing, this terrifyingly close call, makes me realise that that's not enough.

I text Patch back. I tell him that I'm coming home.

Chapter Eighteen

Real life returns quickly once the confusion ebbs. The majority of my symptoms have been caused by the side effects of the morphine and I happily trade the tight pain in my hand for a clearer vision and the ability to make my way out of here.

I try to piece together the missing hours but I can't remember much of the fire – I am too relieved by that to try harder. I do remember staring out across the lawn and seeing, as vividly as real life, all the animals from the dioramas: chimps chasing tigers away from the people; armadillos – two of them, one curled and hiding, one stretched out and brave; a giant fruit bat, supine on the grass as if it had not survived the flight from its glass case. I know that I saw hundreds and hundreds of books that had taken on the powers of the people in their pages, positioned themselves around the drive, around the house. It all goes over and over in my mind, as clear as day.

Araminta almost runs into my tiny room, she doesn't say hello. 'Where's Leo? Is he all right? Please tell me Leo's all right.' Her skin is bleached white, her eyes puffy and red-rimmed. She is out of breath and her left arm is in a sling.

'Where have you been?' She looks frail and exhausted. 'And how did you get in here?'

'Where's Leo?' she asks again as if she hasn't heard me speak.

'Leo's fine. Except that he's with Curtis.'

She sinks into the chair and I can only see this side of her. 'They wouldn't tell me where he was. Even though I told them I . . .' She stops, puts her one good hand to her mouth. 'They wouldn't tell me.' She takes out a small lace handkerchief. It has been tucked inside the foam loop of the sling. The spite has gone from her voice and she sounds like the trembling old lady she is. I can only assume the nurses thought she was a harmless – and very elderly – relative.

'The police were looking for you.'

'I know. Andrew called me an hour ago. My phone has been off.' She reaches a hand out to touch me, it is shaking. She lays her hand on the edge of my pillow and then changes her mind, pulls it back. 'I don't want to hurt you.'

For a moment I don't know what she means but, from the way she holds her trembling hand out towards me, I understand that she wants to touch me but isn't sure where would be safe, where isn't burnt.

'It's only smoke damage to my eye. It looks worse than it is,' I say and then remember the tightness, the stretching, under the dressing. 'And I burnt my hand.'

'I'm so sorry,' she says. 'So sorry. I'm so ashamed of how I've behaved.' She chooses a spot between my shoulder and my elbow and leaves her flattened palm there in a strange strained gesture.

'Where were you, Araminta? Why didn't you come back to the house?' I'm piecing the hours together by trying words and seeing if they fit.

'I had to tell the police all of this. They thought I started the fi . . .' She can't finish the sentence, can't make the word. 'I couldn't, Cate. I truly didn't.'

I move my uninjured hand over to hers. She looks so small in here, away from the museum. I realise I have never seen her outside of the grounds, away from the house. It is as if she has left her shell there, her carapace. 'I know.' My tongue is thick in my mouth. The silent words, *Then who did?* float between us like a ghost.

'Where were you?' I grasp the thought again. 'Where have you been?'

She stands up, walks towards the window. The venetian blind moves beside her and I hear its plastic clatter. 'When they let me out of the hospital, I came back to pack, to get my suitcase. I heard you crying in the kitchen and I didn't want to have to see you. I couldn't . . . I didn't know what to say.

'I took the last train to London,' she says, although I have to ask her to repeat herself and I only hear her the second time. 'And I went to see my lawyer.'

I sigh and sink into the pillow.

'Then, when I'd seen my lawyer, I met with one of the members of the Board to talk about how we go forward. Once I'd made my appointments, I let my phone go flat: I had no one to speak to.' She moves, uncomfortably, in her chair. 'I knew nothing of the fire until they told me at my meeting this morning.'

I remember the end of everything. 'Have we still got a museum? Is it still standing? The animals,' I say in a half-whisper. 'I saw the animals.'

'The animals are safe, the books too. My apartment – our apartments – are . . . Unusable.'

'Did the animals escape?' I saw them run across the lawns. I watched them file two-by-two out of the house, the kangaroos, the cheetahs, slow deliberate tortoises. Did I hear a cacophony of trumpet calls and chatter, of roaring and grunting? The house cannot have woken all the animals, woken them and freed them and saved them.

Araminta rubs my arm again: she sits back down beside me. 'We need to talk, you and I,' she says. 'There is so much to say.'

Leo has aged years in the last two days: not in a bad way – not in a way that means I have lost part of him. He is 'as well as' what he was, not instead of.

When he comes into the ward he is worried for me but also engaged, interested in what has happened. He has taken charge of himself while I have been sleeping.

He is dressed in clothes I haven't seen before: a

button-through work shirt, carefully ironed, and a round-neck jumper. He is wearing blue jeans, turned up at the bottoms. He looks older, and not entirely like himself: he looks like Richard.

'Mummy.' He leans into me, presses his face against mine. It should hurt but I am so relieved to see him – so happy that he is calm and well – I don't feel any pain at all. 'You look sore.' He frowns and chews his lip. 'Does your face hurt?'

'A little.' I can't smile widely, but I hope my voice does. 'But I'm all the better for seeing you.' I make a voice from one of the stories he liked when he was younger, but it hurts my throat.

He strokes my arm. 'Did you burn your hand?' His voice is low.

I move across the bed as far as I can. 'Come up here. Come and lie next to me. It's a scorch on my face,' I explain to him, 'from the hot smoke. That's all. It'll be all right. They'll sort it all out today and I'll be home tomorrow morning. We'll be home by tomorrow.' I say it with my voice light but I wonder if we really have a home to go to.

Leo gets onto the bed beside me and puts his head next to mine on the pillow. I hold my bandaged hand in the air between us in case one of us leans on it.

'I was very scared in the fire, Mummy. It was horrible.'

I put my arm across his chest, it's the closest I can get to hugging him.

'I went downstairs but I couldn't find you. And so then I had to go back up and that was scary. I couldn't see where

I was going.' He turns towards me, gets as near as he can. His mouth is so close to me that I can feel his breath on my cheek. 'And I thought you were dead. But you weren't.' He makes a whistling sound through his teeth. 'You couldn't get up.'

I think of Richard on the lawn, patting his thighs with his hands. I remember his broad chest, his wide shoulders, how he was strong enough to carry me. 'Did you come back for me, Leo? Through all that smoke?'

He nods and I hear the tiny noise of the stubble on his jaw line rubbing against my dressings.

'And did you carry me?'

'I carried you to the outside. To where the animals were.'

Reality tilts. It was Leo who carried me: Leo the man, the man with the strength to save a grown woman. But the animals, the animals all on the drive: I didn't imagine them. The dead animals from the glass cases, the exhibits, all set free.

'What happened to the animals? How did they get out?'

'Shhh.' Leo puts his hand to his mouth, his index finger pointing up and over his nose. 'Shhh.'

Leo stays for half an hour. He won't talk about the animals at all – no matter how hard I try. And I'm too tired to try for long.

'How did you get here? And whose clothes are you wearing?'

He is happy with these more solid questions. 'Mandy brought me. She is Curtis's mum. She's very nice. She has a tiny little dog called Candy. Can we get a dog when we get home?'

'Let's wait and see.' I close my eyes, exhausted with the relief that he is happy. 'And whose clothes are they?'

'They're Curtis's dad's clothes but he doesn't need them because he is in prison and he has to wear a uniform there. And when he gets out he can get lost – he's not going back to their house.'

The relief wavers, I am definitely going home tomorrow, no matter what the doctors say.

I need to go home. To our home. I need to find out what has really happened. To find out what we have left. I think of the boxes stacked in our apartment – of our whole lives, our whole history. Did they burn, and with them every memory, every moment, of our past?

In the morning, when I am finally discharged, Andrew offers to drive me back to the house. I hadn't thought about how I would get there – or how I would feel when I did. His car is sleek and black, the interior is spotlessly clean: it is exactly how I would imagine a policeman's car to look. As I do up my seat belt, one-handed, I realise that I am trembling all over. I am so afraid of what I will – or won't – find.

The museum is scarred. The drive itself is a mess of water and displaced gravel, weals and welts of dark brown mud snake across it. A few windows at the top are blackened, which, from a distance, makes them look like gaping holes. Each individual panel tells its own account of what happened here.

I try to get out of the car seat but my feet will not move towards the house. My legs are trembling and weak. The smell that has travelled with me to the hospital, that dominates my dreams, is nowhere near as strong as the smell here. The air itself smells of smoke. The grass, the leaves, the overgrown rose bushes in the beds along the edge of the drive: everything is curled and brown from the heat, choked by the smoke. The wisteria that has climbed the front of the house for a century is powdered with soot.

I can imagine the black crystals that bloom from the banisters and wallpaper. Even here, in the untouched end, the smell is overpowering.

Leo pulled me through that smoke.

Leo saved my life.

One end of the museum is black: the end we live in; the end where our beds are. The other, inside the galleries, is red. It's like a bizarre joke. In the middle, it is mostly untouched – serene as it ever was – as if the smoke was too tired to go any higher, too exhausted to search for us.

'Is it safe inside?' I cannot imagine being back in there again, sleeping there: at the same time, I feel like I can't abandon it, that it needs me, us.

'The fire started in a striplight, the Fire SOCO believes.' Andrew clears his throat of the imaginary smoke. 'The starters in those fluorescent bulbs, especially when they're ancient, are notorious for it.'

My mind flashes to where there are strip lights. I can't

picture the ceilings, can't remember the interiors clearly. When I imagine looking up above me, all I see is grey: just smoke.

'This one was in the cellar,' Andrew says. 'It smouldered and dropped sparks onto a tarpaulin down there, a real one.'

'A tarpaulin?' I am still certain this fire was something to do with Curtis, that he came up here for a smoke, that he left a lit cigarette – or worse – near something flammable. I have printed that truth so hard upon my mind that I can't shift it. 'Why would a tarpaulin burn?'

Andrew squints up at the house, it is mostly silhouetted by the hot summer sun which blisters, silver, around its edges. 'The clue's in the name: tar-paulin. It's why we use synthetic ones nowadays.' He has his hand on my car door, and I know he expects me to walk forward, to go back in.

'But it was in my room. Not the cellar. It was on my corridor.'

'The Fire Investigator says it's very simple: yours was the only window open in the house. Classic ventilated fire.'

I wipe my face with my bandaged hand, tears are starting to gather at the corners of my eyes and I breathe hard to suck them back in.

'Tarpaulin fires generate a lot of smoke – and very little flame. The smoke travelled up to your window from a slow burn downstairs: it had probably started before you went to bed.'

'What if it happens again?' I whisper it, wondering if we can ever go back inside.

'We've disabled any remaining fluorescent strips – taken the starters away. And the Fire Service have fitted smoke alarms on all floors – Ms Buchan is a pensioner so they were able to do it for free. You're safe now. In the short term, at least. The whole place clearly needs rewiring eventually.'

I stand up on my wobbling legs, as feeble as a new-born foal, and start to step towards the door. I can feel the pull of it, that it needs me. The house didn't try to kill us: it was asking for our help, asking us to realise how close it is to death.

Up in the corridor on the first floor, it's as if there never was a fire. The quiet – the calm – at the top is eerie: I remember the silence in my bedroom, the moment the birds stopped screeching and I flinch at the idea of their little baked bodies.

Our feet pad quietly across the patterned carpet. Araminta has had some volunteers open up three rooms on the first floor for us: the original family bedrooms. She has a small brown suitcase, presumably full of more identical tweed skirts and short-sleeved, knitted, jumpers. The clothes that cover her tiny frame would take up no room at all. I have a pair of jeans and two T-shirts that one of the nurses brought me.

The volunteers have heaved the cotton cloths off this furniture, drapes that have been in place for decades in these beautiful rooms while we 'made do' with the cramped accommodation upstairs.

We are in three rooms – all in a row: one for Araminta, one for me, and one so that Leo can come home. Each of these rooms has been empty for years, the furniture shrouded with white dust covers, but the floors and mantelpieces kept clean and polished by someone: I assume Araminta. Attached to each room is its own ancient, but fully functioning, bathroom – the fittings are far superior to the servants' quarters upstairs.

My bathroom is mainly green. Encaustic tiles of emerald and black on a cream background snake their way along the floor between the door and the rusty old bath. The walls are a textured ceramic that picks out a pattern of flowers and ivy, climbing halfway up: there is so much work, so much detail in every one. The shower is a rubber hose attached to the taps and the grouting is flaking and brown between the bath and the wall, but it is mine and mine alone. Why did Araminta punish herself for all those years living upstairs when these friendly, bright, bedrooms were empty on the floor below?

I will be sleeping in a room Richard would have used when he was a little boy. I wonder if I can summon him back like I did in the hospital: it's been wonderful having him beside me.

And then I remember Patch, how much I long to see him: the dichotomy of falling in love with him here, where Richard's faint shadow still moves around me, whispers from the walls and the window frames.

When I am sure it's going to work, at least for now, I call Leo.

'Will I have a big bed?' is his first question, 'In my new room?'

'All the beds are tall, you have to climb into them. That's how old-fashioned beds are.'

'I don't mean tall. I had a double bed at Curtis's house. Not a children's bed.'

'They're massive.' I smile into the phone. 'Can Mandy call you a taxi?'

'I don't need a taxi. I can walk.' He sounds surprised, almost indignant, that I've suggested it.

It's not far – fifteen minutes at most. 'Okay, will someone walk with you? Curtis?'

'No one's here at the moment.'

My heart is in my mouth.

'Mandy is at work this morning and Curtis is out. Candy needed to go for a walk so I said I'd do it. I love walking Candy. I take her out every day.' Something distracts him on the other end of the line and he pauses for a few seconds. 'I'll walk home when Mandy gets back from work, okay? So Candy isn't by herself.'

Leo: a man who crawled through a fire to carry a fully grown woman back out. Leo, who is as brave as the lion he is named for. 'I'll see you when you get here,' I say. 'I love you.'

'Love you too,' he says and the phone clicks off.

I collapse onto the window seat in my new room and cool the back of my head against the pane of glass, grateful for more than I had realised before. My life on the other side of the fire was different, I was passive, waiting: still in recovery from the terrible loss Leo and I have suffered. And Simon, it is Simon's loss too.

The fire has cleansed me, scorched away the paralyses, the immobility of grief. The fire has lit an ember of Richard's lion heart in me, it has given me new life. I look out of my new window across the lawns and into the woodland. Indigenous Americans cleared forests and wild lands like this, fanned flames to sweep for hundreds of miles – clearing the way for new growth, for tiny green shoots to wriggle and uncurl from the scorched earth into the open air.

I call Patch. It is time to hear his voice, to bring the memory of our brief encounter into the new, fresh, time.

'I've been worried sick. I went to the hospital but they wouldn't tell me anything.' He sounds exactly as I remember.

'It's okay. We're okay.'

'Where are you staying? Do you want to come and stay with me? It's tiny, but we'll make do.' The artist at Pear Tree Cottage.

'We have beautiful rooms. Everything's all right on the first floor. Will you come? Later on, after Leo's settled in?' I need him to come. I can't imagine sleeping here alone, I want him to be there to hold me when the clouds of smoke colour my dreams, when my nostrils fill with the choking fumes and refuse to be told that there's nothing there.

'Of course. Text me as soon as you're ready. I'll be there ten minutes later.'

The silence after the call, the comfort of knowing Patch will be here with me tonight, gives me peace. These are my first real moments to think and my head is instantly full of questions.

I am ready.

I knock gently on the door next door to mine.

'Come in.' Araminta's voice is small, diminished. It makes me think of how Richard ebbed away as he seeped out of himself, of how that change was audible.

Araminta is sitting in an armchair in the corner of her room. Her legs are crossed so that her bony knee shows white through her tights. The smell of smoke is faint here – unmistakable but a suggestion, a memory, rather than the assault it is on the way up the stairs.

'I sat in this chair for a story, every single night of my childhood,' she says patting the arm of it. 'This was Colonel Hugo's study at one time. He used to read to me every evening before I went to bed. And then I would go back to my house – in the grounds – to my mother.' She nods her head towards the shelf above the desk and I notice for the first time that it is full of children's books, their colourful spines neat and pastel. 'He was my best friend.'

Instinctively, I stay quiet.

Her mouth is slightly open, her eyes dreamy. She is going to tell me more if I can wait for it.

My head is thumping but I have nothing else to do, nothing else I want to think about right now.

'And everything I've done – mistakes I know I've made – I did for him. Because I promised him.'

I remember the thing I need to know. 'What were you doing at your solicitor's? What was so important?'

She pauses, holds the arms of the chair with her thin fingers, her fingertips press on the red leather. 'I can't tell you.'

I don't believe it. After all the ground we have made, everything we've been through together. The feet of the chair are wooden, carved lion's paws; they splay out at each corner. Araminta has a window seat, identical to mine, except that the fabric on hers is more sober, swirls of mauve and pale blues. I sit down on it despite the fact that she hasn't asked me to.

'What do you mean you "can't"? You're going to have to.'

'I'm sorry. I can't tell you what my solicitor and I spoke about.'

I take a deep breath in, steady myself. The shoes I am wearing are my summer flip-flops, silver plastic shoes that I had left in the kitchen the night of the fire. I slip one foot out and feel the edge of the rug under my toes. Our floor coverings here are far more comfortable than they were in the servants' quarters.

'We have been through a near-death experience. If you'd still been in the building you would probably have died. Any of us could have. This is not the time for secrets or . . .' It's starting to irritate me, knock at the corners of my positive attitude, as if she is attempting to deflate this bubble of hope. '. . . for playing games.'

Her jawline is solid, her chin held high. She flares her nostrils once, twice, probably completely subconsciously.

'It's not something I can talk about and, really, it's not something that matters anymore. Please leave it.' And, more quietly, with definite sadness, 'Please.'

The penny drops. 'You were trying to get rid of us. Trying to get us out.' I remember her angry words to me before the fire, her face as she lay on the gallery floor with her arm so twisted and unnatural. And then, trickling in behind that, licking and snapping at my memory, I remember the fire itself.

'Tell me.'

Her eyes fill with tears and she shakes her head, gently, slowly. She is a living picture of regret. 'I would tell you if I could. I promise you.'

'After all this.' I wave my bandaged hand at her, brush the coarse gauze across the pinprick scabs on my cheek. 'After all this.' And I leave her room.

I go upstairs and fetch my laptop and Leo's games machine. It is quiet and dark up here. The taste of smoke makes panic rise in my throat but I need to think, and I need to write to Simon.

The hop-pickers' hessian on the walls has crackled and dried. Great flakes of it have fallen off and the lathe and plaster behind them is bare. This whole floor looks so much less civilised, so much less tame. I am not sorry to leave it behind.

Back in my new room, I write Simon a long email. I write for over an hour. I tell him everything that happened and how scared I was. I tell him of Leo's bravery and my, rapidly improving, injuries. I tell him that I dreamed he was beside me as I slept.

When I hear Leo calling me from the corridor, I rush out to meet him. As I pass, I can hear Araminta crying softly in her room.

Chapter Nineteen

I cannot bear to look at Araminta when I get down into the kitchen in the morning.

There is a loaf of wholemeal bread on the breadboard but neither of us can cut it with one arm and I'd rather go without toast than offer to help her.

I can hear her teacup tottering in its saucer beside me. There is a silence as she puts it down on the side.

'It's not what you think.'

'I don't want to talk about it, Araminta.'

'If I could tell you, I would. I promise you that.'

I turn round and face her: she is less important in the light of everything I've been through and survived. There was a moment there where we could have been friends, but I am not prepared to accept her change of heart predicated on nothing more than mine and Leo's accidental survival. I simply can't.

'As soon as you're ready to explain, I'm all ears.' I put two cups of coffee on a small tray and challenge her to comment on it. Moving into the proper bedrooms of the house changes so much, makes me so bold, so family. I don't understand why we couldn't do it before, why we had to be part of Araminta's sackcloth-and-ashes lifestyle.

I invited Patch here last night on my terms: to my home. I felt no need to apologise to Araminta for it – or to ask her permission.

When he got here, when I finally saw him, I started to believe – for the first time in ten years – that everything might come right again in the end. He kissed my face, over and over, and I cried until I lost track of time.

'I want you to stay.' I said it before I could let go of him. The words were going to burst out of me, drumming and pulsing behind my eyes, swelling at the top of my nose, pushing out of my throat until my face hurt. 'I want you to stay tonight.'

'Of course.' He kissed the top of my head. 'I'm not going anywhere.'

'We have to talk to Leo.'

Patch nodded, his face serious.

'It's the same as the way he sees his dad's death: with Leo, things "are" or they aren't. The length of time it's happened for or over isn't part of his process. It wouldn't make any difference to Leo if we discussed it for months and then you stayed, or if you . . .' And I held my breath as I said it. 'If you stayed tonight.'

'Thinking in the moment is an enviable power.' Patch's hands are smooth on my back.

'I've lost count of the number of times I've thought that.'

Leo was rearranging the furniture in his room, making space for his few clothes, for his games console: making it his own. I made a note to bring his posters down for him if we can sponge the smell of smoke from them.

'Patch is going to stay the night tonight.' I said it without any fanfare. Leo didn't even pause his game to ask: 'Where will he sleep? He's too big for the sofa.'

'He's going to sleep in my bed. With me.'

Leo turned and stared at Patch, his brow wrinkled. 'Sometimes I need to get into my mum's bed in the night. If I have a nightmare or if I'm scared of something.'

Patch touched him lightly on the arm. His voice was so gentle. 'That's okay, buddy. You can still do that. Anytime.'

This is the morning after that night. The newborn day. Araminta – and whatever her plans might be or might have been – will not ruin it for me. This is a new life.

I put the tray down on the bedside table. I am learning to manage with my bandaged hand – it is certainly less trouble than sending Patch down to the kitchen when Araminta has no idea that he's here.

Patch lifts up one arm and waits for me to slide back into bed underneath it. We fit together well.

The smoke did come for me in the night, weaving and winding into my dreams, but Patch was there to blow it away, to squeeze life back into my laboured lungs.

'Now what?' I ask him. 'What do we do now?'

'We begin again,' he says. 'We put everything back together. We build on what Curtis started and we move forward.' His skin is soft against mine.

'Curtis? Looking after Leo?'

Patch reaches a long arm out to nudge the curtain from the window. The sun fills his side of the room with a bold yellow. 'I saw Leo on Monday at Art Club. He didn't seem to need much looking after. They're mates, hanging out. I mean about Curtis and the fire.'

I push myself to a sitting position, my good hand flat against the linen sheet below us. 'Sorry?' I could not bear it if I was right about Curtis all along, if my terrible cursed thoughts came true.

'What he did. Now everyone – the whole town – knows that he's not who a lot of them always assumed he was, he's not his dad.'

'I don't know what he did.' I need to make this clear. 'Did he do something good?'

Please let it be good.

'Curtis ran from house to house, all through the streets, waking everyone and getting them to the galleries. He saved the animals from the smoke. It's why nothing's irreparably damaged.'

'I don't understand. How do you know this?'

He pulls me back down again, strokes my back calmly. 'It's a small town, word travels fast.'

I think about the fairground of that night. The strange smells and shouts, the swimming swirling lights, and the people – calling, running, shouting: old men heaving huge chimpanzees between them; sturdy women staggering under the weight of a tiger, taking a leg each and co-ordinating its movements; the chain of people almost as long as the drive, passing bats and birds and trays of flightless insects one to another.

'I didn't see the people.' I whisper it into the room. 'I thought it was the house.'

'Perhaps it was,' says Patch and he means it. 'Perhaps it was.'

By the time we've finished our coffee, I know the whole story. Curtis and Leo were playing a game online – out of hours and out of bounds – when the smoke first appeared. Leo had gone offline at a crucial moment and Curtis knew it was out of character.

With no one to pay any attention to where he went or at what time, Curtis ran up to the house and saw the fire engines. He was there long enough to see that Leo was safe and then he ran, at full pelt, back through the village, banging on every door and waking everyone. It was Curtis who led a charge into the galleries, when the firemen said it wasn't going to be allowed, and Curtis who'd gone through the back of the exhibits and started pulling the animals out of their cases.

'But how did he know to do that? How did he know how to get into the cases?' I ask Patch.

Patch shrugs his shoulders. 'I don't know. I don't think anyone's asked him.'

I think back to those early hours in the hospital, to Leo with his fingers across his lips, refusing to answer questions about that night, back to Araminta's first gallery tour – so long ago. 'I think I know,' I say.

Below us, the gardens roll away from the house. Atalanta and Hippomenes point up towards us, unconcerned, unafraid. For them, nothing has changed: there are people in the house – there always have been. There are animals and books and artefacts. For them, everything is as it should be.

I only realise that we've fallen back to sleep when the chatter on the path below my window wakes me up. I have slept in for an uncharacteristically long time. In my half-asleep state, before I drifted off, I meant to ask Patch where he was, why he wasn't at Pear Tree Cottage when Curtis came screaming through the town. It is on the tip of my tongue when I wake up but I am immediately distracted by the noise.

There is a definite buzz of conversation downstairs. This floor is quiet – no whirring and clanking from Leo or Araminta's bathrooms, no thrash metal from Leo's bedroom.

I pull on my T-shirt and pants and kneel on the window seat to look down. There are people moving about in the garden – they are laughing and calling out to each other. There must be ten people there, easily. The museum hasn't reopened since the fire and, even if it had, it wouldn't open until ten. I check the time on my phone: 9.15. I don't know who these people are or why they are here.

I walk quickly down the stairs. I have done up the zip of

my borrowed jeans as I walk but the button is beyond me: I pull the edge of my T-shirt over it.

Something is going on, something is wrong. Maybe not wrong, it doesn't have that kind of feel to it – something is different.

I go through the hallway and into the kitchen. There is no one there either but, when I stand still, I can hear people; a buzz of conversation, footsteps. The heavy front door still has all its night-time ironwork in place, bolts shot securely, the big black key turned.

Sunshine blasts into my face when I open the door, the smell of summer is strong – its swansong before it gives in completely to the autumn. The conversation is a stream that ripples up the drive.

I cannot count the people outside. They look for all the world like an angry mob, come from the village to storm our castle. Except that they're all smiling: they're chattering and laughing. And they are all carrying buckets and mops and ladders and cloths in place of swords and maces and clubs.

The line marches down the drive towards me. I can see Malcolm near the front, obviously instrumental in this tide of people.

He smiles and winks. 'Open the door, then,' he says. 'Let's get on with it.'

And they walk down the drive, two-by-two, into the house. Just as the animals did before them. I stand, open-mouthed, and yet to brush my hair or my teeth, as they pour through the front door and into the building.

The ladies from the WI, as varied in size as the countless antelope inside the museum – just as bright-eyed, just as neat in their dun jackets – are at the front. An army of smaller animals, Cub Scouts and Girl Guides, carry buckets almost as big as them – nimble mountain goats with over-sized horns balancing their way through the rocky outdoors. I see giraffes and bison, zebras and secretary birds, trying to control legions of wayward monkeys – monkeys who run backwards and forwards, squealing with excitement at being part of something so huge. A pair of colourful parrots, young and in love, walk in front of two old bears who have gruff low voices and long ladders on their shoulders. They mean business. I recognise one of the parrots as Poppy from the art class, her blue hair a mascot in the sun.

The people are dogs and meerkats and tortoises and cheetahs, they are butterflies and snakes. They are crocodiles and chimps and the kind of capable octopi who will use all eight arms to make short shrift of anything.

And they march, two-by-two and two-by-two, until there are more than a hundred of them in the house. People who love the museum, people who want to help. An army of soldier ants, of worker bees: hyenas to clean up the things we don't need any more, beavers to build and repair – bags full of tools on their backs.

The WI ladies are invaluable. What they don't know about how to get rid of soot, how to chip soaked paper off parquet flooring, could be written on the back of a postage stamp. They split up and take a room each, advising all their underlings in how best to sweep, how not to rub. They have potions for portraits and poultices for curtains and the smell of smoke recedes as if it is as awestruck by their industriousness as everyone else is.

I recognise Jess from the supermarket by the ticket office. She is on her knees, polishing the front side of the wooden booth. 'How . . . ? What is this? What's going on?'

'A new broom,' she says, soot on the tip of her nose. 'We'll have you ready to open again before you know it.'

'But, why, how? You're all so kind.'

'We owe it to him,' she says, sitting back on her heels pointing at the portrait of Colonel Hugo posing with his rifle. 'He did more than his bit for this community – and now it's our chance to pay him back.' She goes back to scrubbing at the panel of the ticket office as if it were the most normal thing in the world.

When Leo comes downstairs, he seems to know far more of these visitors than I do. Many of them greet him by name and he isn't at all shy with them.

'Have you seen Sophie?' he asks me.

'From Art Club?'

'She's coming with her mum. Me and her are going to cook lunch for everyone.'

'Oh.' I'm taken aback. 'When did you organise that?'

'On Monday. I went to Art Club when you were in the

hospital.' He knits his brow. 'I didn't like thinking about you being in hospital – Curtis said it was better to think about Art Club.'

'Ask Patch, he might have seen her.' I ought to get this in perspective for him. 'There are over a hundred people here, Leo. You can't cook for all of them.' But he is gone, wandering into the crowd to look for Sophie.

By the time I have got properly dressed, and gone around thanking the volunteers, Leo and Sophie have already begun a vat of soup, tray upon tray of quiche. The WI ladies did the kitchen first of all and it shines like new: at least, parts of it still do – the rest, Leo is cooking in.

'Where did all this come from?' I ask Leo.

'We made it.' He makes it clear that was a stupid question.

I point at the bowls of salad, the baked potatoes ready to go into the range. 'I mean where did you get the ingredients?'

He points at Sophie, chopping vegetables on a board, and at himself, elbow-deep in washing up. 'We went to Mr Maitland's shop and got it.'

'But how did you carry it all?'

'We couldn't. He had to give us a lift. But he said it didn't matter that he'd shut the shop because most of the town are up here, cleaning.'

'We didn't actually have enough money,' Sophie says. 'Not for all of it. But he said that didn't matter either.'

'Hatters wants to take care of you,' the ghost Richard

whispers into my ear and I squeeze my hand tight, pretending that his is in it. There is happiness that hides here: in the commitment of the local people – our neighbours – to help us, the kindness of people who were mostly strangers until they walked down our drive today.

I try to meet all of the volunteers. I offer them cups of tea where I can and then Leo tuts at me that I'm in his way while I make it. I'm not much use to anyone with this dressing on my hand – I unwind the outer bandage: the smaller dressing stuck across my fingers leaves me much more useful.

It must be an hour since I last saw Patch. 'Look at you,' he says, a wide grin on his face. 'Quite the lady of the house.'

'I think we both know that's Araminta.'

'It's a big house,' he says. 'Maybe there's room for two. Maybe she's ready to be the dowager duchess and make way for new blood.' He takes hold of my hand, peers at the palm. 'That looks so painful.'

'It's really not. Not if I keep busy.' I carry the teas outside to the group of people I was last talking to.

Araminta is sitting in a fold-up deck-chair. Malcolm is standing next to her: he greets me warmly. Araminta is silent, looks at her feet. She has the decency to blush, pink guilt climbing her cheeks.

In front of them, there must be a hundred people dotted across the lawns and benches, eating lunch.

'Leo and Sophie can't have cooked for this many people.'

I shake my head. 'It's not possible. How is there enough food for everyone?'

Malcolm smiles, 'Loaves and fishes, Cate. Loaves and fishes.'

Everyone works for hours. I distribute water and effusive thanks as I go, it's little in exchange for their incredible efforts, but it's pretty much all I can do.

The results are incredible. The animals have been put back into the dioramas in – more or less – the same spots that they left. There is the odd baboon who won't stand up straight and a couple of mongooses who look distinctly out of place but, on the whole, it's not too bad. The untrained eye probably couldn't even tell.

I take an hour out to track down a taxidermy specialist in London who says he will come and assess the damage. I will use some more of my redundancy money if I have to: we have a duty of care to these animals. The man on the phone explains that, as they've been outside, they will need specialist treatment to get rid of any potential bugs or mites they could have picked up from the grass. It's nowhere near as bad as it would have been if they'd been choked by the smoke. It makes me think of Curtis: the only person missing from today.

I go and find Leo.

'If I call a takeaway up tonight for you, me, Patch and Sophie, do you think Curtis would come and eat with us? If I begged him and if I said how sorry I am that

I've misjudged him? How grateful I am for everything he's done?'

'I'll ask him but I don't know.' Leo stands, solemn, and takes a few steps away from me. He dials by pressing only a couple of buttons so he's obviously been talking to Curtis very recently. He walks towards the trees, the sun making a halo around his head as he waves his free hand in conversation. His voice is low and I catch nothing of the negotiations.

He turns back towards me. 'Indian?' It's clearly a vital part of the arbitration.

'Definitely. With poppadoms.'

It's not so easy when I tell Patch that we're having dinner on the lawn and he's invited. 'You have to invite Araminta,' he says.

'You are kidding me? The woman who tried to get us forced out of the house? To make Leo homeless?'

He holds my arms, makes me look right into his face. 'Firstly, you don't know that – not for certain. And secondly, she didn't. In the end she didn't. Hold on to that.' He kisses me on the mouth so that I can't voice my objections. It feels like minutes later when he lets me go and says, 'You – we – have to get on. We're all in this together and we need a happy home.'

My grazed face hurts from smiling.

Leo and I have laid up the picnic table with silverware from the kitchen drawers: the WI ladies have wiped the smoke away from each knife and fork individually.

Araminta has joined us and, although she's a bit quiet, she's chatting with Leo and Sophie: talking about the one thing we all agree on – how incredible today has been.

When Curtis arrives, he is surly but noble. He doesn't want to make eye contact with me and he doesn't want to talk about what happened.

On the end of a lead in his hand, he has the ugliest dog I have ever seen: even up against our hyenas. She is a tiny wire-furred terrier with an underbite that shows the end of her pink tongue. She wears a blue–and–white spotted 'dress' and a hair clip to match. 'Candy missed you,' he says to Leo, who is already scooping up the hideous little dog to his lap. She wags her stumpy tail and drools on him with happiness.

Sophie tickles the dog under the chin. 'Oh, it's 100 per cent true what Leo says. Not that Leo would ever tell a lie anyway. You are the most beautiful dog. You're perfect.'

Curtis wears a grunting heroism, utterly reluctant. It was born of his own sense of duty, to the museum he has loved since he was tiny, and to his dear friend, Leo. And in no small part to Araminta, an old lady who was kind to him when no one else was: I am not arrogant enough to miss that.

I hadn't noticed before how much Curtis says through body language. He is upright, confident, when he speaks to Leo, Sophie or Patch, curled in slightly at the shoulders in his interaction with Araminta, and crouched – cowed – when he responds to me. It's my fault, and it isn't going to be healed unless I make it happen.

We eat without ceremony, reaching over one another to take what we want, the two young men talking with their mouths full. The food is hot and good and, as usual, we have over-ordered: Leo and Curtis do their best to solve that problem.

Not counting the occasional awkward silence when I ask Curtis a direct question and he hesitates before answering, there is more noise and chatter than there has been here in some time. Each word, every laugh, pushes the bad things that have happened back across the grass, make them edge into the house and away from us.

'Leo and Sophie, will you come and help me see if we can get to the freezers by the shop? We can take Candy with us.' Araminta looks at me as she says it. 'I feel like ice cream after that lot and I don't think anyone would begrudge us one or two.' She makes a face, 'Although they might be a bit old. Curtis, do you have a favourite?'

'Anything chocolate.' Curtis can smile at her. He goes to get up and go with them but she shoos him back down, gestures that she, Sophie, and Leo can manage, that they're going without him.

'I'll get some more beers,' Patch says and walks towards the kitchen.

It is clever of Araminta to leave us this pause, smart of Patch to pick up on it. I wonder if they collaborated. I have to apologise properly to Curtis – it's up to him, entirely, if he chooses to accept it.

'We owe you a huge debt.' Even as I say it, I know it's too

poncey, too 'up-myself' as Richard would have said. 'Sorry. I mean, I just mean . . . I'm sorry. I've been a cow.'

A tiny flicker lights the side of his mouth, it is gone in a moment; back to the alabaster silence of his face.

'I judged you and I was suspicious of you. And you've only ever been kind to Leo.'

'Leo's my friend.'

Another mistake. I've hit a nerve. 'I didn't mean to be patronising. I mean because he didn't know anyone and you've been great for him. You've even helped him get a girlfriend.'

He shrugs. His head angles slightly upwards. 'She's not exactly his girlfriend yet. They haven't had The Chat.'

I hope that Patch and I are too old to need 'The Chat': I hope that sleeping together nails it at our age.

'She's nice, Sophie. She's good for him,' he says very quietly.

I smile. 'I completely agree. Look, everyone knows what you did – the whole town – you saved this place. You saved the animals. All of them: you saved the museum.'

Curtis curls his fingers round the frayed cuffs of his hoodie, still uncomfortable.

'I made assumptions and I was wrong. Colonel Hugo himself would be impressed by the things you've done. And I don't think Colonel Hugo would be particularly impressed with the way I've behaved either. He was all about giving people chances, trying to help them. I didn't do that.'

'It's not your fault. Everyone round here feels the same.

My brothers don't help – they're always in trouble. And my dad.' His voice is small and lost out here on the lawn.

'That's all behind you now. You're a local hero. And you're a friend to the whole Lyons-Morris family, alive and dead. I'd be so grateful if you'd think about giving me a second chance too. I'm so sorry.'

He mutters something I don't hear and I ask him to say it again, louder.

'My mum keeps calling me "Noah".' And this time he does smile and it's genuine. When he smiles, his crooked front teeth stick out and he looks so young, so defenceless.

'Well, it was incredibly brave to do what you did.' And then I tell him, I don't see why I shouldn't: 'When you brought the animals out I was still unconscious and, when I woke up on the ground, I couldn't see the people. I could only see the animals – hundreds of them – and I thought they were all alive. I thought they'd all come out by themselves.'

'I like that,' he says. 'That's cool.'

'I'd like you to come and work with us, taking care of the animals, when we're back up and running. A proper job. What do you think?' I have no idea how we will pay him – my redundancy money takes another sucker-punch – but it's one more challenge I need to meet head on.

He nods. The blue tattoo wrinkles and releases. 'Can I start tomorrow?'

'Tomorrow's tricky. We haven't got any money. I mean, at all.'

'I don't mind. I just like being here. You can pay me in ice cream,' he says as Leo and Araminta come towards us with handfuls of cornets and lollies. Patch follows her lead and comes back from the kitchen – where he has clearly been waiting behind the back door.

Despite the work to do in the building behind us and to repair our relationships with each other, we have an easy evening of stolen ice creams and too much curry.

Our first family meal for years with more than two people is a success.

Chapter Twenty

The fire turns out to have been the grand event the museum needed. We are inundated with visitors who have heard of either the attack on the gallery or the fire – or both. I am learning, the hard way, that organising a hitherto haphazard band of occasional volunteers into a group who can deal with this number of museum visitors is a full-time job in itself – before I even start to think about tours and guided visits.

To her considerable credit, Araminta is more than doing her bit, working days as long as mine. She looks tired – we both do. I'm aware that the shock of what happened to us is still there, bubbling under the surface: that we will – eventually – need to deal with it. I can't forget what she did but, mainly thanks to Patch, we have found a middle ground of courtesy. We both want what's best for the museum: although we might believe in two different ways of getting it.

Without Patch, I would never be able to keep this level of work up, not and sort Leo out too. Being one of two has made life so much easier over the last few weeks.

This morning is another early start. The first visitor is the man from the taxidermy company, the second a journalist from a major broadsheet who is going to cover the story of the restoration, the repairs to the animals. I'm hoping it will bring in some funds: cleaning all the animals is going to be an expensive business. Structural damage to the building is covered by insurance, along with some of the cosmetic damage done by the smoke, but everything inside is uninsured. Araminta assures me that all museums are the same, that the contents are simply too valuable – the very definition of priceless – and can't be insured, just as they couldn't be replaced.

I expected someone in a brightly coloured overall, carrying an elaborate system of sprays and pokers and hoses. Instead, the taxidermy specialist is a fairly elderly man in a brown suit. He takes a notebook and a monitor of some sort out of his briefcase: other than that, he is disappointingly empty-handed. 'Damp meter,' he says and shuts down any attempt at conversation.

I go back upstairs to see how Patch and Leo's attempt to start the day has gone.

Patch is dressed and sitting on the edge of – what has become – 'our' bed. Leo is sitting next to him and showing him some of the music he stores on his phone.

'Lots of people know this band in America,' I hear him

say. 'They played in England though, once, and my dad went to see them.'

Patch nods, not ready to interrupt Leo's enthusiasm. He looks up at me and mouths, 'hello' without speaking.

Patch nods as Leo talks. He is leaning back on the bed, propping himself up on his flat palms, his legs are long enough to touch the ground.

'Are you going to get dressed?' I suggest to Leo and he ambles past me towards his room.

My fingers are halfway across the duvet to curl round Patch's thigh when Leo pauses in the doorway. I jump back like a teenager caught by her parents but Leo changes his mind and goes to his room.

Patch catches my hand and circles it with his. 'It's okay. You're allowed, you know.' He leans forward and kisses me despite my having one eye on the door. 'You're allowed to be happy.'

I scramble across the bed and sit up against the pillows. I lean into him. The room is warm, the smell of pollen and blossom comes in through the open window, birds are squealing and chatting under the eaves. I once longed for this life.

'What shall we have for supper?' He pushes his shoulder against mine. The curtain waves once, gently, at us and breaths of summer fill the room.

'More than anything else,' I say, 'it's those words that sound like heaven.'

And then I push my head back onto the pillow and squeeze my eyes tight: I have a sudden desire to cry.

I know that Richard was ill, that he couldn't help the things that happened, and I appreciate with every longing atom of my soul that it wasn't what he wanted, but that only makes me feel more guilty in moments like this. Moments when I'm so angry at him for leaving us. We should be two parents, shoulder to shoulder, squeezing each other's hands as we watch our child becoming a man.

In the drawer beside me is the photograph of Simon and me edging closer to each other as we pushed Richard away. I should judge Simon less: Richard wasn't the only one who made rash decisions based on emotion. In the middle of all of this is Patch and the place he has taken up in my heart. I cannot see how to fit them all in: when they will ever snap into place together, jigsaw pieces no longer puzzled.

Patch sees that I'm trying not to cry. He puts his hand on my shoulder, reaching across me and pulling us together. 'Is it too much? Am I being too full-on? Tell me if I am – I need . . .' He drops his voice. It's so soft, almost a whisper. 'I need to get this right.'

'It's completely right. Someone walked over my grave, that's all.'

'I haven't been home in three weeks – I was worried I'd out-stayed my welcome.'

I was going to talk to him about this. 'Look, my funds are limited – as you know – once my lump sum runs out, I'm buggered for another ten years until I get my pension. We need to save every penny. It seems silly for you to shell out on Pear Tree Cottage and, to all intents and purposes, live here.' I hope I haven't gone too far. The walls of the bedroom don't pulse or shiver, saying those words out loud hasn't altered the fabric of the building.

'I couldn't agree more. But I'm in a contract – I have to buy it out if I want to leave.'

I knew it would be more complicated: that's always the problem with being an adult.

'It's only two months but, well, I'm a bit strapped too – I squandered my savings many years ago.' He shrugs. 'And I've not been in my teaching job long enough to build it back up.'

'How much can it be? Fourteen-hundred? Fifteen?'

'I can't let you pay it anyway.' He stands up and pulls me to my feet. 'We'll sort it somehow. It's only money.'

'It's only money unless you haven't got any,' I say. 'I remember the constant sick feeling of that.'

'I love us,' he laughs. 'Sitting in a gigantic stately home and not enough money between us to pay off the rent on a tiny cottage.'

'Like proper aristocracy: poor as church mice.' I put my palm on his cheek, feel the short stubble on his skin, the strength of his jawbone beneath it, until Leo comes in with arms full of T-shirts and needs us to say which one looks best.

The journalist is a nice young woman. She looks like I imagine I did when I was young and enthusiastic and lived in a vibrant city. She wears a floaty summer tea-dress, this year's style, and lace-up canvas sneakers. I was never that trendy.

I walk her through from the front door – she's here long before the ticket office is open – so she sees the museum the wrong way round.

I can see her wondering what all the fuss is about and then growing ever more fascinated as we walk through the rooms: she gasps, like they all do, when we get to the dioramas at last. I tell her the story as we walk from room to room, everything that has happened since we got here. I tell her about Patch.

I've left the book I found in the kitchen, with the old photos of Hatters, open on a desk in the library. I leave her there to look at it while I go and make us both a coffee.

When I come back, she has the book open on the same page that fascinated me: the line-up of the family in the house.

'This is fab,' she says. 'Do you think we could recreate this? With the modern-day family? With Ms Buchan and your boyfriend?'

I think about how little Araminta has aged since the original picture, how strange – mystical even – that will look. 'Sure, it's a great idea. My son will love it. How long have I got to sort them out – and put some make-up on.'

'The photographer's due in about forty minutes. Does that work?' I nod that it does and leave her there to make notes while I go round up the others.

*

Araminta is coming down the stairs as I go up. 'The journalist, Janet – she's very nice – wants to take pictures of us in front of the house. Would you mind?'

'Of you and Leo?'

'No, all of us. You.'

She shrugs and nods. 'I don't mind.'

'I found the other picture, the one in the book in the kitchen. You're in it.'

She looks away from me. 'Yes,' she says and tells me nothing.

'But why? How come? Your mother isn't in the picture.'

She runs her fingers along the smooth wood of the banister, closes them round it. 'I told you: the Colonel and Lady Harriet were very fond of me as a child. They included me in everything: every Christmas, every family outing. My mother couldn't have done anywhere near as much for me – she didn't have the money. She had a hard life, a difficult life.'

I feel guilty now for pushing her. I'm about to make a half-baked apology when she speaks again.

'There used to be a huge Christmas tree, here in the curve of the stairs, from the floor almost to the ceiling, right up past the first floor. I could put my fingers between the spindles and touch its leaves. It came from the estate, each year, the gardeners would chop it down and bring it in.'

Another part of Hatters that I took for granted in my own life. Why did Richard never tell me?

'Richard used to insist on a ridiculously big tree, every year. Always a real one.'

She dips her head, coughs slightly. 'It's the smell. Nothing like it.'

But I don't think she is thinking of the smell, imagining the scent of pine needles isn't enough to make silent tears well up the way hers have: only thinking of people you love does that.

Leo, predictably, is over the moon about being photographed. He goes straight to his room to dig for clothes in the bags that have come back from the cleaners – his original choice of T-shirt is now insufficient. I know he will wear his chequered trilby.

'I don't want to be in it.' Patch is adamant. 'I won't. Sorry.'

I'm surprised. And slightly hurt. 'But you're part of the story. Our story.'

'I have to get to work. I don't want to do it. I hate things like that. There are a million reasons.' His face is set – he is bordering on angry.

'It'll look weird without you when you're in the article.' I'm annoyed too. This is for the house.

He picks up his car keys. 'Don't keep asking me. Stop. I'm – not – going – to – do – it.'

'You're really overreacting.'

'Am I?' He pulls on his jacket. 'I'll see you tonight – with supper. Tell Leo to walk down to the centre when he's finished. I'll give him a lift home.' Patch walks – stomps – down the corridor towards the stairs, leaving me – and the wide-eyed family portraits – wondering what on earth just happened.

The photographs are sweet. Araminta, Leo and me, standing in a row by the porticoed door and squinting slightly at the sun. It is a much smaller group than the original, depleted; an echo of how hard the museum finds it to survive without Colonel Hugo at the helm.

At the end of the session, as he leaves for the art club, Leo announces that he has invited Sophie for dinner tonight: a tiny flicker of hope that – one day – our group might grow larger, that we are not the end.

I'm hardly surprised that, when he gets home, Patch is distracted and edgy. He is sitting at the huge table in the dining room drawing, hunched over his sketchpad.

Leo is trying to get us both to help him cook and there is no space for Patch and me to unravel this morning, to pour oil on the troubled waters.

'May I?' I gesture to the pile of paper.

Patch nods and I pick the first picture up. It is a close-up drawing of one of the netsuke. A tiny but perfect hare, his back legs hunched and his back rounded, long ivory fangs sticking out of his mouth. On the sheet behind him, the tiny junk – crammed with chicken cages and traders in wide hats – sails down a paper river. The third is a beautiful dragon, tearing across the page like fire, scales so lifelike I could touch them.

'Patch, these are beautiful. Amazing. You could sell these.'

'I can't sell them. That's why I live on grants. I sell barely anything. That's how being an artist works.' He puts the pencil down and the anger still in him is evident. 'They don't tell you at art school that you're going to feel like this every day of your life.'

Leo, who has been running up and down the stairs with queries and comments for the last two hours, makes a noisy entrance. 'I'm nearly ready. I'm not going to cook the pasta till Sophie gets here. But I don't know what to wear.' He's flapping and anxious, his palms are tapping on his thighs.

'You said you were going to wear what you wore this morning, for the photoshoot.' He looked dapper for the pictures: skinny black jeans, and old band T-shirt – a classic – and a blazer. He dressed like Patch. 'What was wrong with what you showed me? You looked great.'

'I had the T-shirt on and I was cooking and I got tomato on it.' He rubs his forehead with his hands, his soft black fringe falls through his fingers. 'I can't wear it.'

'I'll come and help you choose another.' I reach out towards him to take his hand.

'Uhuh,' Patch says. 'You're on your own with this, buddy. You can do it, you can choose a T-shirt. Clothes are your best thing.' He looks up at Leo for a little longer than he looked at me. 'It's your best thing, after cooking.'

I'm surprised when Leo nods and leaves the room. 'You shouldn't have said that,' I say to Patch. 'He's nervous. We need to support him.'

Patch narrows his eyes at me. 'Is that the sound of a man going off to search through his T-shirt drawer I can hear? Oh, I believe it is.' He is relaxing out of the tension. I see it leave his shoulders.

He's right, Leo is sorting himself out. Leo is coping. But I feel a loss: I want to help Leo get ready for his first proper dinner date; it's my job to help him choose what to wear; to solve his problems.

Patch stretches a hand out towards me. 'He's fine. He's sorting it. He can.'

I don't take his hand. 'I don't want him to sort it. I want to be part of it. I'm here to help him.'

Patch raises his eyebrows at me and his silence says, *But you won't always be.*

Chapter Twenty-One

Sophie is as beautiful as I remember. Her skin is smooth, brown and perfect and her cheeks, kissed with the barest of make-up, make her look timeless, as if she could drift straight into the role of lady of this house.

'Sophie and I are going to have a drink in the garden before dinner,' Leo tells me in a very formal manner. 'She likes white wine.'

Out of the kitchen window to the front I catch a glimpse of a woman walking towards a car. It can only be Sophie's mum: the long black hair and the tall narrow frame are almost exactly the same. 'Excuse me a second,' I say to Leo and Sophie. I rush back into the corridor and out of the front door.

'Hi ... hello!' I call out to her. The gravel is crunching over my trainers and she has her hand on her car door. 'Are you Sophie's mum?'

She turns and smiles. It's the same smile that Sophie has:

slow to spread but warm with it. Behind her our tall oaks bow and sweep, whispering their greetings over the rusty fence rails. 'I'm Helen,' she says and walks towards me, her hand outstretched.

'Cate. Leo's mum.'

'You look alike,' she says, her smile deepening at the corners of her mouth.

I shake my head. 'No, Leo's the image of my husband. Absolute double.' And then I add, although I wouldn't have before, in our old life, 'My late husband.'

'Oh, I'm sorry,' she says and it's done: Richard is mentioned, he passes between us – he is there and then he is gone. There is no drama, there are no tears. 'It was very kind of Leo to invite Sophie: your house looks incredible. Sophie told me about it after the clean-up: I've never been before – to my shame.'

'You're not the only one.' I smile at her. 'But we're working on that.' I look back at the porticoed front and sigh. 'Actually, I was just checking that it's okay for Sophie to have a drink. Leo's about to head out to the garden with nibbles and a bottle of wine.'

'It's very kind of you to check . . .' Her face tells me that she's not comfortable with my checking. 'Sophie's twenty-two years old, she'll let you know what she can and can't cope with. She's a very independent woman.' Helen puts her hand on her car door. 'Sophie's very firm about her decisions. To a fault sometimes.'

'Leo has very little self-control.' I make eye contact with

her and can see she isn't offended. 'But his father was exactly the same so I don't think it's a consequence of Down's.'

On the way back through the kitchen, I have a quiet word with Leo and advise him, if he wants to be on top cooking game, to stick to a beer or two rather than join Sophie with the wine.

Patch has folded up the sketchbook when I come back into the dining room, and tidied the rest of the sheets into a neat pile. He is standing by the window.

'Sorry I was snappy,' he says. 'I'm really tired.'

I'm mellowed by love's young dream in the kitchen and reach my arms out to him. 'It's all right. I should have known when to quit.'

He holds my hand and pulls me towards the window seat. 'Come on.' He pats his knee for me to sit on his lap.

'I'll squash you.'

'You will not.' When I've made myself comfortable he winds his long arms round me and holds me tight. His breath warms my face. 'I didn't want to look like an ambulance chaser. Which, probably, is what I am.'

'You wouldn't. Of course you wouldn't.' I lean my head on his shoulder. 'And you're not.'

'It made me uncomfortable: and I know it shouldn't. The idea of Richard in the first picture and then me – who doesn't belong here at all, who's just an interloper, in the second. Sorry. I shouldn't have felt like that – but I did.'

'It's okay, I get it. I feel like that sometimes too.'

'Look at them,' he says, and I uncurl slightly to look through the window at Leo and Sophie.

'Sweet, aren't they?'

'They're sweet, and they're totally preoccupied with each other and not with us. That gives us – goodness knows how long – all alone and uninterrupted.' He starts kissing my cheek with tiny butterfly breaths.

'I thought you were tired.'

'I am, but I'd rather drop from exhaustion than miss this – daring – daylight opportunity.' He moves his kisses to my mouth and he has his hands under my shirt before I open my eyes and see Leo stamping across the lawn, his hands banging his thighs in fury.

We scramble up, buttoning up shirts and tucking in tops as we go. We meet Leo thundering through the hallway, on his way upstairs.

'What on earth's the matter?'

Leo is beyond words. He's making a low, grumbling sound in his throat and his breath is coming in short rasps. He is furious.

'I'll go and find Sophie. Or do you think you should? As a woman, I mean?' Patch is standing in the corridor, his arms out at his sides, waiting for my instructions.

'You're right. I'll do that. Get Leo to come back downstairs, if you can.'

Leo is already barrelling up the stairs, tripping on the carpet runner, banging his knees and his hands on the edge of the steps. His voice is getting louder and louder but without any comprehensible words. I leave Patch to it and run down and outside to see where Sophie is.

She's still sitting by the lake, serene, smiling, and certainly not in any distress.

'Leo wants me to go home now.'

The peacocks are nibbling the grass by her feet, searching for crumbs left over from the supper. Sophie's shoes are strappy sandals, low-heeled and silver, and her toenails are a bright red: the hen peacock pauses by her big toe, wondering whether to try a bite.

'Shoo.' I say to the peacocks and they look at me with contempt before walking away, their heads bobbing together and their scratchy feet flattening the lawn. 'Did you text your mum?'

'I did. She's on her way. Or my dad. One of them will be here. My mum will come in her car: a red BMW. My dad has a white Skoda. I prefer my mum's because it has Bluetooth for music.'

I look up at the upstairs windows but there is no sign of Patch or Leo. 'Did something go wrong, Sophie?' I sit down on the picnic bench, one leg either side of the seat, and look Sophie right in the eye. 'Didn't you have a good time?'

'It was very nice, thank you. Leo is a very good cook. He makes excellent pasta and sauce.' She smiles, a little absently, and looks into the distance over my shoulder.

'And then did you argue?' I am wearing denim shorts, they don't feel grown-up enough to have this conversation.

I push my hands into the pockets then regret that and take them out again. 'Why does he want you to go home?'

'Leo asked me about Martin.' She nods her head. I think it means she's cross but I have already worked out that her body language is hard to read: her deep round eyes give nothing away. 'Martin from the art group. The one Leo had a fight with.'

'I remember.' I put my hands on the table in front of me and my stomach knots.

'And Leo thinks I want to go out with Martin, that I want him to be my boyfriend.' She is still staring over my shoulder and I look behind me to check there's no one there.

'And do you?'

She sits up straight and tucks her chin into her chest – it is a clearly readable gesture of indignation. 'It's very annoying that he keeps on talking about it. It makes me cross. I wouldn't come for dinner with Leo if I wanted to be Martin's girlfriend, would I? I would have dinner with Martin.' And then she turns her gaze to the pond and the statues as if to say, this conversation is over. Atalanta meets her gaze with her cold gold eyes: Hippomenes stares over towards the house.

The beep of a car horn carries across the still lawn and, almost simultaneously, Sophie's mobile pings to say she has a message. She reads it quietly for a second or two then stands up. 'My mum's here now. Thank you very much for having me.'

'Shall I walk you back out through the house?'

'No, thank you,' she says and brushes imaginary creases from the front of her dress. 'I'm going to go round that corner there – by the hedge – that leads to the drive, doesn't it?'

'I'll walk you round anyway.' The last thing I want is Sophie's mum thinking I've abandoned her.

Sophie walks quickly, although she doesn't seem to be particularly distressed. When we get round to the front of the house, I see her mum's red BMW, exactly as she said.

'I'm so sorry,' I start to say. 'I don't know what's gone wrong but . . .'

'Sophie can be very forthright.' Helen narrows her eyes and looks at her daughter. 'Can't you?'

'Thank you for having me, Cate.' Sophie opens the car door and gets into the passenger seat. Her movements are calm and smooth and the door shuts quietly behind her. 'I had a very nice time, thank you.'

'I'll get to the bottom of it. Has she upset Leo?' Helen's smile is kind.

'I don't know that she has – something has. But Leo is as sensitive as Sophie is forthright. It doesn't take much to get him to fly off the handle. Just the wrong thing.'

'I'll find out,' Helen says. 'And I'll give you a call if there's anything to it. But, do you know what? I doubt it very much.'

'Sorry you had to come out so much earlier than we thought. It was nice to meet you.' I wait for a moment as Helen reverses out of the parking space and half-heartedly wave at the back of the car as she leaves.

It's been a long and busy day and our tiny family has been fractious and peculiar. I let myself back in through the front door of the house and pause at the bottom of the grand staircase, holding my breath while I check for noise. I wonder for a moment if it was fair – on either of them – to leave Patch to sort out Leo, but then I remember that I'm trying to trust them both, trying to let go a little.

Richard's ancestors stare down at me from the walls as I mount the curved staircase, my feet heavy as lead. Not one of them smiles or lends encouragement and yet – around the mouth and eyes – they all clearly belong to the same tribe as Richard and Leo. At the very top of the stairs, a wide buffalo head looms over me, its tongue made of plaster and painted red, its eyes staring and unhelpful.

There's a note on my bed, written in thick marker pen on a sheet of A4 to make it noticeable. 'Gone for walk. Kitchen garden. X.' The kiss is wide and dark, its marks extravagant and firm. Down in the gardens, I can see the wall of the kitchen garden in the distance, just about make out the green of the ivy clinging to the sandy gold bricks. The peacocks have got over their sulk and are back by the picnic table, pecking up the remains of Leo's supper. I remember with a pang that Patch and I haven't eaten.

The window is open and the evening still and quiet. If Leo were in any real trouble, Patch could shout and I would hear him. It allows me a moment of peace. I sink onto the bed, imagining a glass of cold white wine in my hand and, not for the first time, regretting how far away we are from the fridge.

Patch's sketchbook is in front of me. His sketches are beautiful. Each of the netsuke is detailed, one after the other, the intricacies of them so much easier to see now that they fill a whole page.

His pictures of the individual animals in the dioramas are amazing: tigers tense, ready to devour him as he draws them; an elephant raises his foot, big enough to trample Patch as he stands in front of it armed with his keen eye and pencil. A fruit bat hangs upside down from a lichened branch, I turn the pad sideways to see if he should be the other way up.

A sheet of paper slides out, floats to the floor.

It is a drawing of me. Not the me I see, the me I understand when I look in the mirror. This is another me: flawless and glowing; peaceful and smiling. This is a version of my face I don't think I've ever really noticed, not even when I was young. This is the light inside of me – the one I have never taken time to kindle, to stoke. In this picture, I radiate. It is an incredible picture to see: an enchanted version of me; an image that must be – is, I hope – the way I exist for Patch.

My default setting is the tight ball of fear inside me: as hard as I try to accept the changes; the house; Patch's kindness; these bonkers living arrangements. No moment of armistice lasts long enough – or is convincing enough – for the ball to fully unwind. It's turned into a stone I carry in my core, it's been there for four years and I'm not sure who

I'd be without it. Would I be this woman: the bright, open, beauty that Patch has sketched? This is the me I found as I recovered from the fire, the phoenix days. I need to remember that I have this version inside myself.

I trace the lines of my own jaw on the paper, the clear strokes that make up my eyebrows, my lips. My mouth involuntarily makes the tiny, parted gap it holds in the drawing.

I lean my head back on the floral fabric of the coverlet and, despite its odd smell of horses and soil, I close my eyes.

'Get into bed, babe.' Patch is gently shaking my arm. 'Leo's all tucked up.'

My sleep was thick, foggy. 'What time is it?'

'Only nine, you haven't been asleep that long.'

I start to surface. I am still holding Patch's drawing of me. 'I'm sorry.' I feel as though I've read his diary, gone through his private things. 'This fell out of your sketchbook.'

'Do you like it?' He blushes slightly, looks down at the floor.

'It's beautiful.'

Patch kisses my forehead. 'A picture says a thousand words.' He stands up, exhales and shakes off the moment. 'Go and see Leo if you're not ready for bed. He could do with a hug.'

I sniff. There is a faint smell, familiar and from the past. 'Have you been smoking?' It makes me laugh, I'd forgotten that anyone still smoked: I certainly didn't think Patch did.

'The odd rollie from time to time. Especially on sunny evenings, ones with a bit of stress in.' He kisses me again and the taste of him brings back memories.

Leo is sitting up in bed, his headphones so loud I can hear the tinny beat from the door. His eyes are tight shut and he is dancing. Every few seconds he adds in a word or two of the song, painful and tuneless.

I tap his leg and he opens his eyes. He's obviously been crying, it's made his cheeks pink and has left wrinkled grey bags under his eyes. I put my arms around his shoulders and pull him tight into me; part-man and, in moments like this, still a boy. 'What went wrong, darling? You were having such a good time.'

He talks in short chippy sentences, almost baby talk. 'Martin. Martin's job. And getting Sophie to be my girlfriend.' He stops here, hums an unidentifiable tune, closes his eyes again and screws his face up with the stress of his thoughts.

'It's hard, making relationships. It's hard for everyone. Even for Patch and me. Even for Curtis.'

'And Araminta. She doesn't have a boyfriend. Or a mummy or daddy.'

'Exactly. Everyone struggles.' My heart aches, partly for him but – against its will – with a little sympathy for Araminta's silent life, all the people she has lost.

'I'm going to sleep now.' He closes his eyes, lowers his head to the pillow. His headphones slip sideways and away from one of his ears but he's pretending to be asleep so he resists the temptation to move it back.

'How's tricks?' asks Patch when I go back downstairs. He has put a bottle of wine and two glasses on the table: I could kiss him. 'Supper?' he says and offers me a bowl of crisps and, in the other hand, an apple.

I take the crisps. 'He's not talking. I'm still no wiser to what happened – except that mention of Martin was made.'

'Bloody Martin, honestly. He could start a fight in an empty field.' He pours the wine. 'It's something and nothing – I think Sophie was making conversation rather than making a point. But she hit a nerve.'

'The job?'

Patch sits back, leaves the keyboard for a minute and sips his wine. 'Martin's got a job at the supermarket, organising the trolleys. I mean, good for him, it's great for anyone to find employment in this political climate – let alone someone as potentially annoying as Martin. Sophie stopped by on her way here and he told her all about his duties.' He pulls a face, 'I can only imagine.' He passes me the glass. 'And now Leo feels a bit . . . you know . . .'

'Inadequate.' There is no sadness like the sadness of one's child. 'In happier news, your drawings . . .'

'I'm sorry – I hope you don't think they're intrusive. They were only for me, for a record . . .' He breaks off.

'Can I use them? I mean, the museum, can we use them?'

I'm buzzing with ideas. 'Maybe make them into prints or use them on social media?'

'If you think, well, you know ... If you like them that much, of course you can.'

'I love them. I really love them.'

'I really love you.'

Chapter Twenty-Two

I am surprised when Patch finally brings his things up from Pear Tree Cottage – after he'd been worn down by my insisting on lending him the money – at how little he really has.

'You weren't kidding about travelling light, were you?' I ask him as we take the three bags out of the car.

He shakes his head. 'At first it was sheer logistics, but then it became ... strangely liberating. My books are on my tablet, all my music as well. I never keep old paintings – I always hate them after a while. I'm not a hoarder, I suppose. In the end they're just things, and they don't matter.'

I think about the boxes of stuff we still have upstairs in the abandoned apartments: stuff I might well never unpack: textbooks and teaching notes, Richard's technical drawing stuff. I don't need it, but I haven't the heart to get rid of it. 'Each to his own,' I say, determined to hang on to my boxes of the past. 'And we've got room.'

My mobile rings in my pocket. I put the bin bag down on the steps of the house. It's the journalist who wrote my article.

'I need to clarify something with you before we go to print. I'm happy with everything else and the pictures are divine. My editor is running the one of you, Araminta and Leo as the cover of this weekend's magazine.'

'Oh, my God.' I didn't expect that. It'll do wonders for the museum. 'Amazing.'

'It's just . . . I'm not sure what to say about your husband's death. I don't know whether it's too much – for you, I mean, and for Leo – to say that he killed himself. I wanted to check with you about it.'

I sit down on the step. Beside me, Patch's bag contains the last of his clothes: the last of his things to live anywhere but inside Hatters, with me.

'You can say that he killed himself, Janet. Because that's what happened.'

When the article comes out, I hope that it will change our fortunes even further: that we will make enough to live on – enough to pay Curtis, certainly, and possibly enough to pay me.

The email pings into my inbox as soon as I end the call.

From: Roger Hamilton-Cox

To: Cate Morris

Cc: Araminta Buchan

Dear Miss Buchan and Ms Morris

I am writing to you in my capacity as Chairman of the Board of Trustees for Hatters house, museum, and gardens.

Firstly, it is my sad and solemn duty to announce the death of Myles Wright (QC) who, as I'm sure you know, filled a variety of positions on the board – most latterly as secretary. The board is grateful to Myles' service over almost four decades and, should you wish to send your condolences to his family, I will be very happy to provide you with their postal details.

Myles' death leaves us with a vacancy on the board which, coupled with your recent difficulties at the house, means that we have had to cast the net wide for a family member to fill the space created. As I'm sure you're aware, it becomes more and more difficult to find suitable candidates who have a direct connection with Colonel Hugo's bloodline and we are having to look ever further afield. We have approached two candidates – both second cousins by marriage to the late Geoffrey Lyons-Morris. Both are considering the duties that they would be required to perform.

My second reason for writing is that the trustees feel that they need to inspect the damage caused by the recent fire and, more pertinently, the efforts that have been made to repair that damage. We appreciate that it is extremely difficult for two women, alone and with

a limited budget, to hope to carry out any repairs or to
make the building safe for habitation.

The pompous tone was bad enough, but Araminta and
I being reduced to 'two women' makes my blood boil.
Whoever this man is, whatever his connection to Colonel
Hugo, he has no right to speak to either of us like that. The
irony is that he's clearly unaware that Colonel Hugo's own
great-grandson lives here too.

A shadow falls across me from the drive. Araminta is
standing on the gravel – her face set in a grimace. 'You've
got it too then,' she says in response to my shocked face.

'I'm just finishing reading it. Hang on.'

We intend to combine these two factors by calling an
extraordinary meeting of the board and coupling it
with a fact-finding visit. We will arrive at Hatters on
21 August at 2 p.m. and would be very grateful if you
could prepare some tea and sandwiches for us. We
will meet in the library and obviously require privacy
for our discussion. The two prospective candidates will
accompany us, which will bring our number to eight
(numbers advisory for your catering).

    With best regards

    Roger Hamilton-Cox

'Tea and sandwiches?' I look up at her.

'I'm afraid Roger thinks that's the primary function of

the female. Or at least one of them.' Araminta sighs and sits down on the step. She brushes the stone with her hands as she sits, a single elegant motion I'm sure I couldn't carry out. 'They're basically coming to case the joint – to see what to start selling off first. I knew this was coming, eventually. I went to see a couple of the least dangerous ones in London the day after . . .' She tails off.

Neither of us talk about that day although the suspicion of it hovers between us like a constant cloud.

She clears her throat, carries on talking. 'Unfortunately, Myles was one of the last remaining members who doesn't see the big sell-off as the way forward. Roger wants nothing else: and he will make sure that the new candidate agrees with him.'

'And we get no say? You get no say?'

'They're very old.' It seems funny coming from her. 'And they do things the way they have always done them.'

'And there's nothing we can do? Nothing at all?'

'I didn't say that . . .' says Araminta.

Araminta obviously got the email before I did. She has already had time to prepare the old billiard room as her campaign office. This is the downstairs room where broken furniture comes to die: there are stacks of dining chairs with three legs or ripped seats. An armoire lurches drunkenly to one side against the wall, balanced on the top of it is a jet-black bull's head on a wooden plinth, one of his horns snapped off and jagged, his eyes wild and staring. I ought to get Leo and Curtis to clear this room: they could make good use of the billiard table, but the furniture must have been stacked in here for decades and it will be a Herculean task.

Araminta has pulled the dust cloth off the wooden board that protects the baize and slate of the table, and covered it with papers. She has yellow Post-it Notes stuck to various bits.

'I've been doing this for a while.' She pats the top of a thick stack of paper. 'In preparation. I knew they'd come for us – the fire has given them the impetus to pick a date.'

I try to push a chest of drawers, the top one missing, up against the wall to make space to stand at the other side of the table to Araminta. It is too much for my palm, recovering under the last piece of gauze. The tattoo of that night smarts and stretches.

Araminta notices me wincing, she pulls a small stool out from behind the table. 'Here,' she says and I sit on it to look at the paperwork.

It is a maze of legalese, designed – I'm sure – to defend the secrets of the trustees, keep the Common Man or Woman from interfering with the smooth running – or dismantling – of the museum.

'There is a clause,' Araminta says and points to a piece of paper in the middle of the table, 'And it will stop them. But it will have to involve Leo talking to them.'

I don't dismiss it out of hand. I give the idea some thought, chew it over. I look around the room, and let my thoughts wander around it, check it from all sides. Everything in this room is sport-themed: the paintings are of game birds and retriever dogs; of playing fields and rugby teams. There are aged and faded photographs of cricketers, lined up in order of height and preserved forever in their clean whites and cable-knit jumpers. A wide rack of cues stretches up along the wall like weaponry.

'I don't think it's a good idea.'

I can tell from Araminta's face that she knew that would be my response. That she expected it from the moment she found the clause: I suspect she agrees with me.

'You've already said they're not nice people – the trustees, I mean. And I can see for myself how pompous Roger is. They'd eat him alive.'

Araminta picks up a piece of paper, goes to say something.

'And if we do have to leave, after everything we've done here, everything we've survived – I'd rather he heard it from me at the last possible minute, not from eight strangers intent on tripping him up. And . . .' I know Patch will be annoyed at me when I tell him about this later, but that doesn't mean it isn't the right thing to do. '. . . We are still not on a level playing field.' My hand throbs. 'The trustees know what you said to them the day after the fire – Leo and I don't. So, you're asking me to let Leo put himself on the line but you still get the right to make arrangements behind our backs.'

A grandfather clock in the corner of the room chimes four deep and sonorous notes. It punctuates the silence left behind in the wake of my statement.

'I can help you make the tea and the sandwiches: I'll even get the tables in the library ready for them,' I say to Araminta. 'But I can't help you fight the Board without your total honesty.'

She stretches her fingers across the edge of the table, her nails are short and neat. The cast on her wrist has been replaced by a short blue support that cushions the heel of her hand. The one diamond ring she wears sparkles under the low-hanging lamp that covers the billiard table. She swallows, once, twice.

I hold my breath, waiting for her answer. This time she has everything to lose: this time she has to be honest.

'If I could, Cate, I would. I want to more than anything but I simply can't. I cannot tell you what we discussed.'

When they arrive, the board members are exactly as I imagined them: to a man. They are penguin-stiff figures in black suits and, like Araminta says, they come from another age. The six current members introduce themselves with a flurry of 'Your late husband's second cousin,' and 'Third cousin once removed to dear Richard.' I'll never decipher which one's which and I don't suppose it matters.

Roger introduces himself with an oily voice, even his handshake drips with it.

The other two men with them are marginally younger: possibly only mid- to late-seventies. Roger introduces them as the new prospective candidates to fill the post of 'poor deceased Myles'.

They bluster around the museum, pointing things out and – as far as I can tell – largely talking nonsense. They certainly haven't spent the hours I have learning the routes of Colonel Hugo's expeditions or researching the status-in-the-wild of the species we have. I watch them from a respectful distance and tick off their mistakes in my head: I'd love to set them straight.

Finally, they reach the library and the arrangement of tables that I helped Araminta to set up last night. We have put four desks together – to seat ten people comfortably – in the centre of the library, directly under the sparkling dome.

'Ms Buchan,' Roger calls out to Araminta. 'Could you fetch us a tray of tea?'

Araminta stands still.

I step forward under the dome, the warmth hits the top of my head and I flush, my cheeks involuntarily pink, my palms sweaty. 'I'll get a volunteer to do it. Araminta and I need to stay for the meeting.'

'I don't think so, Mrs Morris. That is completely outside the terms of the Trust.'

I walk towards the archway that leads to the gallery. I know Malcolm is waiting, out of sight, around the corner. 'We are ready for the tea, thank you,' I tell him.

I wear my voice as armour, the voice that has taken strength from the fire. It is important to convince myself as much as them. I look back over my shoulder to make eye contact with Roger. 'Our presence is absolutely non-negotiable.'

Roger is noticeably unsettled.

'Please, gentlemen,' I say. 'Do take your seats.'

'This is highly irregular.' Roger goes as pink as me as he blusters but sits down. 'These are private negotiations, covering sensitive subjects.'

Araminta puts her hands on the table, her fingers are knitted together, her knuckles white. 'And, if I know you at all, Roger – and we have known each other for a very long time – your sensitive subject will be nothing more than how quickly can you get your hands on the museum and its contents.' She looks at me, and I nod.

'Before you begin, gentlemen, there are a couple of things you need to know. Firstly, Araminta and I have worked hard to set the museum back on track after the fire – we have had enormous support from the community and are pleased to tell you that we now have commitments from more volunteers than ever before.'

They look from one to another, rolling their eyes and being openly rude. I steel myself and continue; I'm so relieved that we didn't put Leo through this. The back of my neck is moist with sweat.

'We are about to apply for several prestigious grants that would provide new signage and ramps for wheelchair access, as well as more staff and security. The ticket revenues have reached a level where we can start to take on staff – we have one part-time gardener and two assistants in the tea hut.' I think of Curtis and wonder if he's what they see when they conjure up a picture of a part-time gardener. 'This weekend Hatters will feature on the front cover of a national broadsheet's weekend magazine. This and the social media accounts we are now operating are transforming the fortunes of Hatters. We are, at last, very much on the up.'

They cough and shuffle, feigning boredom.

'And Araminta and I went through some paperwork last night. Specifically, the terms of Colonel Hugo's trust.'

A ripple of controversy goes through the eight men. They turn to each other and whisper – as if Araminta and I weren't here. The whispers echo loudly around the library – something they obviously hadn't thought of or didn't know about.

'Absolutely outrageous', 'nonsense' and 'upstarts' rattle round the heads of the moose, the elk, and the bison. Their pointed horns don't bow or break, their eyes don't look away: they're only words, they don't hurt them.

Malcolm comes in with the tray of tea. He's done it beautifully, utterly formally. The silver teapot shines in the glow of the sun, reflects across the sugar bowl, the milk jug, the tiny delicate tongs for removing the lumps of sugar. I raise my eyebrow at him: I want to ask him where on earth he found sugar lumps – and how old they are – but I can't at the moment. Leo and I made the sandwiches earlier: ludicrously dainty oblongs of white bread with the crusts cut neatly away.

'May I be mother, gentlemen?' Malcolm asks, warming to his role.

From the faces of the eight men, I can assume that they've never been served tea by a man before.

'According to the terms laid down in Colonel Hugo's Trust, any family member – and by that, he means "direct descendant" – residing at Hatters takes an immediate 51 per cent of the Trust's votes,' Araminta says.

'There hasn't been a direct descendant here for thirty years,' Roger shouts.

'Years' and 'years' echoes round the room.

'Until now.' It is the moment we've had to pin our hopes on. Araminta wouldn't give at all and so it is just her and me here fighting for the house: just the two of us on its side.

Roger smiles, showing his teeth – and the two men either side of him cross their arms over their chests, lean back in their chairs. Their smiles are poisonous, infected.

'I'm so sorry, Mrs Lyons-Morris, but being Richard's widow doesn't qualify you for that role.' Roger rests his hands on the oak desk and it blooms where his sweat marks the varnish.

'But being Richard's son does.' Araminta has waited years to say this to the Board. 'Leo is Hugo's great-grandson. His direct descendant.'

Roger closes his palms together and points his fingers under his chin, the sweat silhouettes of his hands remain on the table, a ghost of where he's been. 'With all due respect, I believe your son has a mental impairment?'

'And nowhere in the terms of the trust does it say

anything other than "of sound mind and body" and Leo is certainly that.' I am half-standing, ready for this battle.

The man to the left of Roger speaks, his neck is too wide for his stiff collar and his throat wobbles over the top of the starched white cotton. 'It is totally impossible to put your son forward for this post. He cannot be considered. How would he ever manage? How would he know what to vote? Or follow what we were talking about?'

I open my mouth to shout him down, to put him right . . .

'I have Down's syndrome.'

I spin round. Leo, in his soft trainers, has crept into the room. I did not want him to hear any of this.

'That's all. Down's syndrome. I'm not ill and I'm not stupid. Lots of people who have Down's syndrome work. They can be shopkeepers, librarians. They can be actors. I have been looking for a job.'

The men are silent. One or two of them have the decency to be puce with embarrassment at their assumptions.

'But I already have a job.' Leo gestures around the room with his arms. 'I have my dad's job. I work in the garden, and I know what to say on tours, and I look after the visitors. My dad isn't here to look after the museum – and my mum – but I am.'

Roger makes a grunt, he is about to speak.

Leo cuts him off. 'And there are more things I can do because I have Down's syndrome. I can use sign language. I know what to do when someone has a fit. I . . .' He searches for a third thing. 'I can dislocate my shoulders.'

I hear the click and grind as he demonstrates.

He stares at Roger hard while he does it. 'We had a big fire here. I didn't see any of you when it happened, or afterwards. I didn't see any of you when we cleaned the galleries and the kitchen and the corridors.'

They look at the ground. I follow their gaze to eight identical pairs of black lace-up shoes.

'I called the Fire Brigade, 999, when there was a fire.' He looks around, his fury evident. 'Down's syndrome doesn't mean I can't do that. And I carried my mum out of the fire to outside. To the ambulance.' His hands are still on his thighs, fingers splayed, palms flat, but still and solid against his legs. 'It was my friend who saved the animals. And my friends who came and cleaned up all the smoke. That means I looked after the museum. Really looked after it.'

He pauses for a moment, inhales. 'Not looked after it like you do.' He points at them, each in turn. 'You never even come here. This is my family's museum and I look after it.'

There is an awkward pause. I am in tears: Leo stands with his hands by his sides, his feet planted solidly on his family's ground. The animal heads around the room look on with pride, their antlers and horns held high.

Araminta stands and pushes a pile of paper towards Roger. 'And if that isn't enough, gentlemen, you will find every relevant clause marked in yellow throughout this document. Good day.'

Chapter Twenty-Three

The three of us made a graceful exit at the end of Araminta's closing statement, despite the fact it was completely unrehearsed. As I told Patch later, seeing Leo do a 'high-ten' with Araminta was probably the best bit of the whole thing. It isn't the best bit, of course, the best bit is that – at least for the time being – we have money coming in and we have a sympathetic board: sympathetic because Leo now controls 51 per cent of the vote. It means Leo controls his own future.

We celebrated Leo's success long into the night, Patch, Leo and me. Araminta declined our invitation – I understand, she has worked on this for days and she must be exhausted.

I volunteered to be the one to get the papers, despite my thumping head. I need to spend some time with Ghost Richard, to talk through the events of last night. I flex my good hand, curling through his invisible fingers as I walk down to the village. This is not the boy Richard who goes down to the village with me: this is the proud father, thrilled by the story about his son.

My lips move silently as I tell him everything, describe Leo's serious and determined face, his courage and commitment. Richard and I both know, without discussion, that Leo stepped right into Colonel Hugo's boots yesterday; that he held up the family name on behalf of all of us.

'What would you think about us going back to Lyons-Morris?' I ask Richard. I will have to wait until my dreams for an answer.

I squint my eyes against the vigour of this new bright day. Even my hangover cannot quench the victory that floods through me.

'Morning, Cate,' says the girl behind the counter. She has the colour supplement open in front of her. 'I've never seen Crouch-on-Sea in the paper before.' She closes the magazine and passes it to me. As Janet promised, the cover is a picture of Leo, Araminta and me with Hatters stretching away behind us. Hollyhocks bob their bright heads in the foreground and the wisteria that climbs up behind us has recovered enough from the fire to hang long lilac blossoms all over the front of the house.

'You should frame that,' she says.

'I definitely will.' And I buy four copies, one for each of us and one to send to Simon. I don't need to buy a copy for Patch, he'll share mine.

I walk back up to the house slowly, the sun behind me on my shoulders, and savouring the peace.

Leo has stationed himself in the ticket office when I get back. Giving change is absolutely not in his skill set – this could be disastrous for the day's takings.

I can't send him outside, he is wearing a suit and tie, presumably to mark his new status – he must be boiling. The suit is one he had a couple of years ago for his school prom: I hope he doesn't need to sit down in it.

'We can expect a lot of visitors today. I mean a lot. I think you'd be better off this side of the counter – doing meet-and-greet.'

He shrugs. 'Maybe.' His eyes narrow and he looks at me, weighing his words. 'But I'm in charge of the museum now, so I can tell you where to stand. It's the other way round.'

'Do you think?' I laugh. In the drive, I can see Curtis coming towards the house – we knew we would need all hands on deck today, the day the magazine arrives on doorsteps all over the county. 'Try telling Curtis what to do – see how that goes. Or, for that matter, Araminta.'

Leo frowns, I can see him rethinking this plan already.

'Is Araminta down yet? Have you seen her?'

He shakes his head.

'In the kitchen?'

'Nope.' Leo steps out to the foyer, starts tidying the animal skins and the little plastic pith helmets that I ordered the other day for children to wear on their way around the museum. I have been keeping my receipts in the vague hope I can get some money back when we start applying for grants, but it's a very vague hope.

I set off to look for Araminta through the galleries. The glass in Gallery One is so highly polished it can't be seen at all: she must have been in here at some point this morning. The fruit bat hangs from his tree without a care in the world, the armadillo beneath him roots through the rocks and leaves looking for ants. I hear the squeak of my sandals against the parquet floor and catch the eye of a little rat looking upwards and interested from the very front edge of the diorama.

The library is silent. The moose and caribou still look mightily proud of what Leo accomplished yesterday, their chins raised, their horns held high. I will have to get Leo or Malcolm to help me move the tables back: they are still in the middle of the room, where we held the meeting. Malcolm has cleared away the sandwiches and teapot – I must remember to thank him.

I look into the kitchen and out of the back door into the gardens: there's still no sign of her. I begin to wonder if she's all right – she has been working very hard.

I go upstairs onto our landing and tap, gently, on her door. After a few moments of waiting for any noise, I knock again and then turn the handle.

Her bed is perfectly made. The pillow is plumped and absolutely perpendicular to the sides of the mattress. The top sheet has been turned down neatly over the coverlet and tucked in tightly at the sides. Araminta is not here but, on the pink satin roses of her coverlet, there is an envelope, and even from here I can see it says 'Cate' on the front.

Instinctively, my eyes flick up to the top of her wardrobe, to the sad little leather suitcase she took with her when she went to London. It is gone.

I sit down on the neatly made bed, the sheet immediately wrinkles underneath me: it will be ruined when I stand up.

The flap of the envelope has been tucked in, rather than stuck down: it reminds me of a birthday card. But I know, deep down, what this letter is going to say.

Dear Cate

    Thank you so much for all your help in securing the future of Hatters. I know that you and Leo will be very happy here and so good for the museum.

    I'm very sorry that there have been times that you and I haven't seen eye to eye and I know that my withholding the reason I wasn't here to endure that dreadful fire with you has been an issue . . . part of the reason that I think it is a good idea if I leave Hatters. Without going over old ground, we have reached a stalemate with that particular situation and I feel that it will continue to make things difficult between us – particularly in the light of Leo's incredible bravery.

    The second part of my reason is that bravery itself: I promised Colonel Hugo that I would take care of his collection and make sure it stayed out of the hands of private buyers. That future is now secured and the – noble – duty

having passed down to Leo means I can move on and away
from the house without letting the Colonel down.

Good luck and please do give Leo my very best wishes.
He will be wonderful in his new role: his father would be so
very proud of him.

Yours faithfully
Araminta Buchan

I let out a long sigh, drop backwards onto the bed, the letter still in my hands. This isn't what I wanted – to drive her away from everything she knows, has ever known. We can't let this happen, Leo and I, but I haven't got time to deal with it now. I put the letter in my pocket: I will discuss it with Patch at some point during the day. I'm not going to tell Leo yet: he'll be upset by this: he's fond of her and she's part of his team.

I sigh again: the house is back to its old tricks; whipping happiness away with its sleight of hand as soon as I think I'm winning.

I need to resolve this.

The museum is every bit as busy as I'd hoped. No one seems to notice, in the mêlée, that Araminta isn't here: at times it's so hectic I almost forget too.

We meet interesting people who've come all the way from London to check us out; fascinated locals who've never got round to seeing the collection before it appeared over the breakfast table in their favourite newspaper; best of all, we get pledges to help with the garden and the galleries – a whole new clutch of volunteers. We even have one interested visitor who specialises in grant applications: I grab her business card out of her hand and guard it with my life.

At lunchtime, when I'm doing a stint in the ticket office, Sophie arrives with Martin. I can see trouble ahead.

'Hello, Cate.' Sophie smiles. 'We've come to see Leo.'

Martin looks around at the shop. 'Your postcards are very old,' he says. 'Have you considered making new ones?'

'I'll give Leo a text, track him down.'

'It's fine, he'll be here in a minute. He said to meet him here at half twelve.'

'Leo invited you? Both of you?'

'Yes,' says Martin, still staring at the postcards. 'Although he is actually two minutes late.'

I think I am beginning to understand the over-tight suit and the awful pink tie.

Leo comes out from the gallery to meet them. Martin looks pointedly at his watch.

'Welcome to my museum,' Leo says and makes an expansive bow. 'As of today, I have taken over running it.' He looks at me cautiously. 'Although I have some help, obviously: my mum, my friends Curtis and Mrs Minta. Some other people. It's a big museum.'

'You need new postcards,' says Martin. 'And I can't stay very long because I have my job to go to this afternoon.'

'Is that your job in the supermarket car park?'

'Leo.' He knows this voice – it is my teacher voice. 'Can I have a word with you please?'

I beckon him round the corner where Sophie and Martin can't hear us. 'That is not how you speak to people. You're lucky enough to have a great-grandfather who left you this opportunity: that doesn't make you better than Martin – and it doesn't make your job any better than his.'

He looks at the floor.

'A job is a job and hard work is just that, no matter where you do it. What you said to Martin is against everything Colonel Hugo stands for. Go and apologise.'

Leo's apology is genuine and I'm relieved.

'Let me show you the animals,' he says and he ushers them both into the gallery.

The rest of the day is a warm success, a series of tasks where I glide past Patch or Leo, engaged in their own contributions to the smooth-running of the day. I don't have time to talk to either of them about Araminta.

I'm about to cash up in the ticket office when Leo comes through with Curtis, Sophie and Martin.

Leo has changed out of the suit – or maybe the trousers split – and looks far more like himself back in his shorts. 'I will see you later, Mum. I'm going for a drink with my friends and my girlfriend.' He winks at me, only it doesn't quite work and ends up being an exaggerated nod of his head.

'Girlfriend, eh?' I say to Sophie. And then I ask Leo, 'Is this to do with your new job?'

Sophie answers for him. She is indignant. 'No it isn't. It was never about a job – that was Leo's idea, not mine. I don't have a job myself because I'm doing my art course. I wasn't Leo's girlfriend before because he didn't ask me.' She reaches out and takes his hand. 'He only told me. And I don't respond to that. I was waiting for him to ask me. Properly.'

Leo couldn't have chosen a better match.

'Have you got your ID?' Curtis asks Leo, and I remember that Curtis is a year too young to get served in the pub.

I've got the coins arranged in piles on the counter when the man comes in. 'I'm sorry, we're closed now.'

'Oh, that's fine. I was actually looking for a friend of mine: Patch Samson. You must be Cate?'

He is the first of Patch's friends that I've met.

'How do you do?' I shake his hand. 'I'll call him and find out where he is. He literally could be anywhere.' I get my mobile out of my pocket. 'Sorry, what's your name?'

'Mike,' he says. 'Michael Green.'

I carry on chatting while I wait for Patch to answer. 'Does he know you're coming?'

'He doesn't. It's a surprise.' The man smiles at me and I get the impression he wants me to get on with it. I turn my back slightly as he answers the phone, but I keep one eye on Mike Green.

Mike is nonchalantly looking through the postcards, picking them up and looking at them, then sliding them back into the rack.

'Everything all right?' Patch says when he picks up my call. 'Are you finished?'

'I'm cashing up, then I'm done. You've got a friend here – in the ticket office. Michael Green.'

Patch is silent. Then, his words in a rush, 'What does he look like? Actually, don't answer that.'

'Patch?'

'I'm in the kitchen garden, down by the ice house. Can you send him out?'

'Sure. I can't leave all this money here though – I'll have to give him the map.'

Patch's voice is strange, strained and low. I wonder how much he likes Mike Green. 'Cate, was my name in the article? Did it say in the paper that I live here? Regardless of me saying I didn't want to be in it?'

I turn my back fully on Mike, half-hide behind the dark oak booth of the ticket office. I don't want to squabble in front of him. 'You said you didn't want to be in the picture. Nothing else. How was I supposed to know?'

'Send Mike out to the garden. We'll talk about it later.' He pauses. 'Sorry. And I love you, I really do.' And he ends the call.

I show Mike how to get out through the side door where the peacock waits like a tour guide, and I go back to counting the takings. Each day is getting better and better. And if we add to this with grant money – now that we have had national coverage and have a platform to apply – we are going to make it: even under the tyrannical thumb of the new majority-holding board member.

*

It's about ten minutes later when Mike comes back. He is red-faced, angry. 'Where is he? Where's Samson?'

I'm quite scared of him suddenly, this ordinary-looking man. There is something very aggressive about the way he stands, about his voice.

'I don't know. Did you find the ice house?' I'm worried for Patch – this man is not his friend.

'What car does he drive? Which one is his?' He points to the car park.

'You need to leave.' At the same time, I look past him. Patch's car has gone.

'Mike Green' swears under his breath and storms out of the foyer. I lock the door behind him and lean up against it, wondering what to do next.

I call Patch's mobile on the way up to our bedroom. It rings out, but I assume he is driving and can't answer. A tiny voice in the back of my head asks where he is driving to, but I quieten it.

The top two drawers of the chest in our bedroom are open. Shirts and pants spill out in a muddle. I wonder for a moment if Mike Green came up here, went through our stuff. But these are only Patch's drawers, mine are untouched.

I know for sure when I turn round. On the bed is the drawing of me, my face as Patch sees it. 'I love you, I really do,' he had said on the phone.

And I know that Patch is gone.

*

I sit on the bed with my head in my hands. I remember despair, my companion for so long. Despair wraps its arms around me, cradles me and welcomes me back. It whispers to me, 'How did you get here? How did this happen? You know nothing about him at all.' And it's true, I don't know where he comes from, where he grew up. I haven't any idea who his family might be, where they are. And because of that, I don't know where he might have gone.

I text him, four, five, six times in a row. I tell him that he needn't be scared of Mike Green, that Mike has gone and we can call the police. Despair asks me who I think Mike Green might be and I have to answer that I've no clues, nothing to go on at all.

There is a light knock on my door. I spring up but lose the moment of hope as Malcolm's voice says, 'Cate? Are you in there?'

I clear my throat, shake life into my legs and arms. 'Sorry, Malcolm, yes. Do you need to go?'

'Someone needs to lock up.'

I open the door and step out into the hall. Malcolm has the big set of museum keys in his hand. 'I've got my own keys but I didn't want to leave these downstairs. I can't find Araminta or Leo to give them to. Or Patch,' he says and looks puzzled.

'It's fine, Malcolm. I'll sort it and put the alarm on.' I smile at him and hope he believes the fake confidence. 'Leo's at the pub with Curtis and some mates.'

'I might well see him in there.' Malcolm hands me the keys and walks off down the corridor.

And then it's only me. I'm alone in the museum. In all these weeks, this is the first time I've been absolutely by myself here.

The curtain on the landing window ripples slightly, though the window is closed. I look at the paintings against the deep green walls of the landing: each person watching me with Richard's eyes, Leo's mouth. I am not alone here, even if I might feel it at the moment. I nod my thanks to them and walk down the stairs.

This has to be the day that the alarm plays up. I do have Araminta's mobile number but I need to know what I'm going to say to her before I make that call. It would make things worse to ring her just to say that I can't set the alarm on my own and could she pop back and do that from wherever she has decided to take herself off to: no, I need to give her a bit of space. Maybe she'll regret her decision all on her own and come back without me having to say anything at all. The only way I can do this is to walk round the museum and see which doors are open. Something must be unlocked and stopping the circuit from being completed. It gives me a little shiver when I think about the day I met Patch, the day someone opened the door marked 'private'.

But there is no one here to look but me. I whisper to Ghost Richard to come with me.

The museum seems bigger than ever now that it's completely empty. The animals stare at me as I pass by: each beady black eye following my every step. I know that if I glance back, they will be looking right at me, so I concentrate on walking calmly ahead and trusting them to stay still and silent.

The last room to check – everywhere else is exactly as it should be and, thank God, no scary open doors leading into big dark storerooms – is the Japanese gallery. I pause in the doorway to try Patch's phone again. This is the room where I met him, where I started to wonder for the first time if I could love anyone after Richard.

There isn't the same panic in the silent gallery, the same burning terror, now that Patch's phone rings out, as the day I rang Richard's and – with each ring that went unanswered – knew with more and more certainty that he was dead.

Nothing will ever be as bad as that.

I check everything: the red cordon rope around the dogs of Fo with their carved jade snarls, the maroon lacquered chairs that seated emperors long before they ended up here. I rattle the doors to the glass case that contains a glazed brick from the Great Wall of China and an explanation card that says how Colonel Hugo put it in his bag while the guide was looking the other way. Even now, under these circumstances, that makes me smile.

Everything is fine, tucked up and locked up, exactly as it should be. There is one place left to check, the alcove where I first met Patch: where he stood doing the intricate sketches of the netsuke. I remember his artist's heart: his kindness and – in spite of all his talent – his ordinariness: he will be back.

The tiny brass key that shuts the netsuke case is in the lock. The door has swung open and hangs – motionless – like an accusation.

Each walnut shelf has a line of faint marks on it: the dust ghosts of the netsuke.

Chapter Twenty-Four

I have to choose what to believe. I can call Andrew, the policeman who was so kind after the fire – his number is still in my phone, my phone is in my pocket.

The second I call Andrew this is a crime: I have to believe it is a crime. Perhaps, if it stays inside these four walls – rests here with the other secrets of Hatters – it needn't be that dramatic. Perhaps Patch's visitor – Mike Green or whatever his real name was – took these. Perhaps that's why he was here. In the back of my mind, an insistent tiny voice, an echo I can't turn off, whispers that it might not be Patch's friend who did it. That Patch is not here.

'Add it up,' whispers the voice and I 'Shhh' it loudly in the silent room.

Perhaps Araminta intends to pay for her new life with the sale of these miniature sculptures, sell off the rat and the drowning sailors and the Lilliputian chickens in their ivory cages.

The voice scoffs inside my head and I throw my hands over my eyes, hiding from the truth of this.

I check my watch. It is only 7 p.m.; Leo is likely to be in the pub for another hour or two. I conjure up the image of him and Curtis, Sophie and Martin, playing pool as doubles, pound coins stacked on the edge of the table to claim the right to be the next players. They will be laughing, eating crisps and tying the bags into tiny perfect knots. They are innocent and unaware. I wish I was there with them.

Of course, I make the call to Andrew, I have no choice. I know, because Araminta explained after the fire, that the netsuke are not insured against theft. I know, because I have run tours around this building, googled, and read up on the subject, that they are highly collectable all over the world and worth well in excess of a million pounds. They are not the kind of item that people will necessarily demand provenance for, not the serious collectors in Japan, America, China. From the basic research I've done, I know that these are incredible examples of the art: I remember the microscopic fine lines of Patch's beautiful sketches.

Andrew arrives ten minutes after I've made the call. I was cagey about what had happened, fudged round his question about whether I'd be better calling 999 than a CID sergeant who happens to live in the town.

'This is a serious crime,' Andrew says. 'I will have to ring it in. Now, not tomorrow.'

I nod my head.

'Do you want to call Leo, get him home before it all kicks off?'

As he says it, my phone pings a text. Please let it be Patch's innocence, a message that describes the terrible mix-up, explains where he's gone. It's Leo. He's upstairs in our corridor, and is wondering where I am. I call him.

'I'm in the oriental gallery. The policeman, Andrew, is here too. Do you want to come down?'

I can hear the tiredness in his voice when he speaks, the kind of tiredness two pints and lots of laughing brings on. 'I'm going to have an early night. We had chips out so I'm not hungry.' The simplicity of his world.

It's easier for me, less painful, to have this straight in my head before I try to explain it to Leo. 'I'll do my best not to wake you when I come up.' He loved Patch too.

'And Araminta?' Andrew asks. 'She might want to know before the police start crawling all over the museum.'

'She's not here. And I don't know where she is.'

Andrew smiles slightly. 'Oh, I do,' he says. 'I saw her this morning coming out of the B&B on the seafront. I did wonder.'

'I need to talk to her, Andrew, before this gets any bigger.'

He nods, gestures towards the empty case, the clear glass that I'm sure will show no fingerprints at all. 'I'll ring it in. Get things started. We'll need to speak to all of you tomorrow. Do you have any way of locking this gallery off so it doesn't accidentally get touched?'

I nod that I can, wondering how best to do it. There are lots of things I'm going to have to work out how to do – things I had never expected.

'The first twenty-four hours are the most important in finding out what's happened – and where we go from here. Our computers are probably the best way forward during the night. Samson's fingerprints will be everywhere around here and, I'd bet my career, that we don't find anything on the cabinet from our mysterious Mike Green.

'I'll get a team here as soon as possible, Cate. Can you leave your phone on overnight – they may arrive in the small hours?'

I don't know how on earth he thought I was going to turn it off.

I set my alarm for 6 a.m., but I needn't have – I don't sleep a wink. I text Patch over and over. The texts start sad and, by the time the dawn light starts to creep across the moist cobwebs of the garden, they are fully angry.

I know Araminta well enough to predict that she will have gone to bed early last evening and got up with the day, even in her B&B.

The town is still sleeping. A seagull pecks aggressively at the opening of a litter bin, bobbing and diving for yesterday's fish and chips. In the distance, ships silhouette against a perfect sky. Until yesterday I would have looked at them with envy, wondering where their journey began, where it will end: now I wonder who is on the boat, and what they are running from.

The newsagent's shop is the only sign of human life. A woman comes out to put up the sign with today's headline on, written in large upper case letters with a thick black pen. Tomorrow's headline will be us, we will be the news: today's mundane problems will seem infinitesimal.

I pass a tiny pub, its window almost as wide as the building, and a greengrocer's yet to put out this morning's coloured displays of the late strawberries, fat raspberries.

I text Araminta's phone. 'I'm outside the B&B. Please come down. We need to talk.' I add a kiss, then take it off, then add it again. I press send.

The front of the little boarding house is the best of local architecture: round black flints stud the cottage walls and a twining rose climbs and clambers in and out of the porch over the front door and up into the eaves. A sparrow hops across a hydrangea bush in the tiny front garden, skipping from blousy flower to fat green leaf. There are worse places to wait.

On the other side of the road, the sea laps quietly at the shore. Pebbles drag into the shallows with a shoosh: it is calm and slow and I try to match my breathing to it.

'Cate?' Araminta is behind me, she must have come out of the side door.

I turn round to face her. She is pale, tired. It can't have been easy for her sleeping in a strange bed: the B&B must have felt so restrictive compared to the long wide corridors of Hatters.

'I'm sorry,' I say without introduction. 'I'm sorry for everything. I'm sorry you're here, I'm sorry we're not better friends.' I take a step towards her. 'I'm sorry I killed your fox.' It's the first time I've said it.

'That was an accident. It couldn't be helped.'

'I shouldn't have lied about it.'

She thinks for a moment before she speaks. 'We have a tradition – at Hatters – of not telling the truth, not whole truths. A long tradition of secrets.'

We have turned to face the last tufts of sunrise in the east, and fallen into gentle step next to each other. We walk slowly along the front.

'I have more to tell you, I'm afraid.'

She thinks in silence for a moment and the only noise is the screeching of the wheeling gulls, momentarily drowning the rhythm of the sea. 'Maybe I should be telling you things.' Another pause. A seagull shouts through it. 'I lent Patch the money to get out of his contract at Pear Tree Cottage,' Araminta says. 'I should have told you that.'

My stomach clenches. I feel sick. 'I did too.'

She nods, almost as though she expected me to say that.

'I came to tell you something else. Something worse, I'm afraid.' Our elbows are almost touching as we walk along, I consider looping my arm through hers in support but we are not that intimate.

'The netsuke are gone.' I think of the beautiful sketches, the horror on the faces of the sailors drowning in their

316

junk, the tiny toggles holding their hats under their chins in the invisible wind.

Araminta is impassive, unreadable.

'Shall we sit, Cate?' she says, and her voice sounds so much older than it did a couple of days ago, so much more exhausted.

There is a bench facing the sea, mahogany with a small brass plaque screwed to the back of it. 'For Ken and Jess, who loved this place,' I read as we sit down. I wonder if Ken and Jess got to grow old together, sit on this bench or one like it and talk about the minutiae of their day. It's not Patch I picture when I think about it, it's Richard.

'Was it Patch?' she asks and catches me by surprise.

I nod. My mouth is open but I cannot bring myself to say yes, cannot let my mouth say what my brain won't process.

She closes her eyes slightly against the sunlight, looks out to sea. 'I had my suspicions. There are a couple of other things missing. Small things but . . .' She shrugs her shoulders slightly and her voice trails away.

I close my eyes against the warm day: I want to hide somewhere; crawl into bed and tug the covers over my head; climb down into the abandoned ice house in the dark, holding the spiders and worms responsible for keeping people away. 'Why didn't you say anything?'

Her sigh whispers away across the tops of the waves. 'I couldn't risk the small steps forward I'd made with you. My relationship with you and Leo is too important. They were small things.'

'Like what?' My heart is pulsing in my ears. I don't want to hear this and yet, at the same time, I don't doubt any of it.

'A little pendant that belonged to Harriet. A Meissen mirror frame that was in the billiard room.'

'Was the pendant in your room?'

'It was in my jewellery box.'

I look down at my feet. I'm wearing flip-flops, perfect for the beach. To anyone who walks past we must look like carefree holidaymakers – an elderly woman, conservatively dressed in a twinset, and her daughter in a sundress and flip-flops; we are anything but. 'You should have said.'

'I couldn't be sure it was him.'

'And I would have stupidly assumed it was Curtis.' I exhale. 'And gone off on one.' I put my head in my hands, my elbows on my knees. I have made a terrible mess of this: just as we were coming out of the woods. I have made stupid, delusional choices. 'Andrew, the policeman, is coming to the house this morning. That's why I've come so early, to take you back up there with me.'

She straightens her legs in front of her. Her thin tights have nylon in and it shines an arc of light across her bony shins. Beside her my calves look sturdy, my bare skin tanned from a summer outside the city. Araminta flexes her feet, toes up, toes down. 'I have other things to tell you before we talk to Andrew,' she says. 'Some of which Andrew already knows.'

A cormorant skims the surface of the sea, stops and

bobs — black in the water — in front of us. He dives for a fish and is gone.

'This isn't the first time things have been stolen from Hatters, or that there's been a thief behind the scenes,' Araminta says. 'Within the family, as it were.'

Chapter Twenty-Five

'It's going to take a lot of telling,' Araminta says. I can see the reflection of the sea in her ice-blue eyes, the sparkle of the sun on the horizon. I can't tell whether the sun has made her eyes water or whether it's going to make her cry, this story from the past: she is as composed as ever.

'We could get a cup of tea?' she says. The little tea shack along the beach is starting to put out its chairs and tables, ready to catch the first of the dog walkers. She hesitates slightly as she goes to get up and I offer her my hand. She takes it without comment and gets to her feet.

The tea hut is right on the prom. A long silver rail separates the wooden tables and chairs from the pebbles. The man inside waves at us to take a seat and points to the sticky menus he has put in little wooden holders in the middle of each table.

'I'd like to sit as far away as possible,' Araminta says and we choose a table right by the edge, out of view of the village and past the end of the road. The only people going past us will be running or walking their dogs. We will be able to talk here.

'We have about an hour,' I say to Araminta once we've ordered our drinks; a pot of tea for one and a coffee. 'Then we have to get back for Andrew.'

'It won't take long,' she says and stops for a moment as the man puts the tray of drinks down in front of us. 'Which is ironic, considering the lifetime I've held on to it.' She shoos the man away and pours the first cup from the pot. 'It happened once before. Patch isn't the first person to steal from the museum and you're not the first person to trust someone in error.' She takes a sip of the hot tea. 'Love does that. It makes you blind.'

And then she is silent again, long enough that I think she might be changing her mind, holding on to Hatters' secrets after all.

'This is wrong, Cate.' Araminta sounds stronger, more definite. 'The secrets I am about to tell you belong to the house. I can't do it here.'

'I completely understand,' I say and stand up. 'My car is along by the green. Let's go home.' I leave a five-pound note on the table to cover our barely touched drinks and we walk across to the car.

We are pretty much silent on the drive back. The crunch of the gravel as we pull into the drive is familiar, comforting. You can't see from the outside that anything is different here.

'Shall we talk in the dining room?' I ask Araminta as we walk into the hall. 'Out of Leo's way?'

'No.' She shakes her head, walks towards the billiard room door. 'Follow me.' To the right of the billiard room is a smaller door, one of the many storerooms and cupboards that hide around Hatters: most of them are full of brooms and old buckets, broken furniture or paintings that have lost the chains that hang them from the picture rail. She takes a silver key from her pocket.

It isn't a cupboard. It is a room flooded with sunlight, as bright as if it has been lit with the huge lamps that hospitals use for surgery. But it's not the two sash windows that light the room, it's the glass bricks stretching the whole length of the far wall, floor to ceiling, edge to edge. It's my bathroom wall from my poor lost house, the design Richard painstakingly laid out and then built, with his own hands, brick upon brick, solid and strong even as he himself was ebbing away.

'I . . . What is this?' I am close to speechless. The gentle undulations in the bricks reflect the colours of my dress but no details, no human shape.

Araminta closes the door quietly behind us. 'It was our playroom, mine first and then Richard's. Colonel Hugo had it built so that we could be in sunlight, daylight, whatever the weather.'

There is an antique rocking horse, stationary, in one corner of the room; his painted coat is a dappled grey and his saddle, a rich black leather. Bookshelves line one wall, the bottom three shelves hold hundreds of books, the higher ones toy trains and dolls and wooden aeroplanes. There is a large leather wing-backed chair in the corner by the bookshelves, and a round rug in pastel colours directly in front of it. Leaning against the glass bricks is a small red bicycle, the size that a four- or five-year-old could ride round and round this room without ever hitting anything.

'How have I not seen this from the outside? Those bricks? The glass wall?' My head is spinning. This room speaks of such privilege, such a magical childhood. It is a part of Hatters' that Richard gave to me, brought into our house, without ever telling me where it came from.

'The big trellis with the flowering jasmine on it?'

I nod: it is a wall of flower and greenery that smells like perfume in the evenings. I have stood right up against it, inhaling its scent.

'That trellis stands about six feet away from this wall: so that it can't be seen from the outside but it doesn't impede the sun in any way.'

'Why? Why is the glass wall hidden? Why is this room locked?'

'It wasn't always,' Araminta says. She walks across to the red leather chair, sits down and rests her hands over the end of the chair's cracked, scuffed arms. The chair dwarfs her and she looks small, vulnerable.

The world is completely silent. There are no ticking clocks, no chattering starlings. There are no other people to breathe between us, no puffs of air to stir the curtains or blow tiny dust mice across the floor. The eerie light seems to usher in silence.

Something catches my eye, a glimmer in the corner. I bend down and pick up a tiny marble, a blue twist of coloured glass at its centre. I remember Leo having bags and bags of these exact same ones: I don't suppose their design has changed for a hundred years.

I look for a somewhere to sit, pull up a chair that is next to the small double desk. It is school-sized and I feel like I'm at parents' evening again, talking about Leo's progress.

'Did Richard know all the secrets of Hatters?' I ask Araminta the question without looking at her: I am peering at the tiny glass world caught inside the marble.

'He only knew one. He knew about the thefts.' She looks directly at me and I feel I have to turn my head towards her. Her eyes are rheumy with tears. 'And knowing one on its own turned out to be worse than knowing none at all. He never spoke to Colonel Hugo again.'

I am on the edge of a cliff. Below me, the secrets of this family I joined by accident – linking myself to two of them by my heart – swirl and bluster like a sea fret. Instinctively, I understand that the next words will blow me from that cliff's edge, that I will be freefalling through the family confidences and there may not be a ledge to save me. Below, the rocks are black and jagged. Perhaps Richard never wanted me to know.

Araminta takes a breath, pauses.

I can see the conflict in her mind as she forms her words.

'I told you that Colonel Hugo was my best friend.' She is cushioning her betrayal, oddly exposed in this bright room with no shadows to hide behind.

I almost miss it when she says, 'He was my grandfather too.'

I have leapt. I am flying from the cliff, sailing down and down through the air. The rocks are perilous below me.

My mind swings from fact to fact, but nothing makes sense. 'Your grandfather? Richard's grandfather?' I try to join the dots but nothing connects. 'Colonel Hugo had other children?'

She shakes her head. 'Just Geoffrey.' She leans forward in the red leather chair, dwarfed by its winged sides. She takes a deep breath. 'Geoffrey was my father.'

My words tumble out like the freefall. 'Then why do you live like this? Hand to mouth?' I can't control them. 'Why do you let all those people boss you around?'

And then, because it might have made such a difference to him to have had a sister, a sibling: 'Why didn't Richard know?'

Her sigh is long and broken-hearted: I recognise the sound of defeat. 'Because my grandfather begged me never to tell him. Made me promise that I wouldn't. I grew up knowing that I never could.'

'Why now? Why not when Richard was alive?' My voice is very loud, urgent. The marble slips from my fingers and lands on the floor with a loud crack. I hear the noise of glass against wood, over and over, as it rolls back into the corner.

'I knew this would happen. This is why I didn't want you and Leo to come – before I mean, before I met you. I knew it would all unravel.' She is whispering as a counter to my almost–yelling.

I am trying to stop myself from speaking, from shouting. I need to listen to the rest of this, to her reasons, but I don't understand how she could have let Richard be so isolated.

'But, because of the fire, the police, I had to tell the truth. Because I was in London on the night of the fire.' She sees the confusion on my face. 'I'll come to that, to all of it. But now . . . Now there will be investigations, outsiders. It is the time to give up the secrets.'

'And Richard never knew? He had no idea?'

She shakes her head. 'It was about our reputation, the family name. And Geoffrey – my father – was a risk to that. Always. My grandfather was very ashamed of him, and of everything he did except . . .' She pauses, swallows. 'Except of Richard and, privately, of me. He loved us both very much.' She gestures around the playroom: every luxury a child could want. The Edwardian dolls' house, three storeys of pristine miniature, must have been hers. Richard would have played with it too after she'd grown up, building a family inside its wooden walls without the curse that had blighted ours. Or maybe not, maybe his play family was as doomed as ours, as doomed as every family he'd ever known.

I remember the ledger, the lack of details. 'What happened to Geoffrey? Richard always said he died in a car crash.'

Now she stands, turns away from me. She puts one hand on the mane of the rocking horse and it moves quietly to and fro as she strokes her hand down the hair. 'My father killed himself in 1970. He drove straight into a wall, terribly drunk. And no one will ever know – for sure – whether he did it on purpose or not.'

There is a silence I cannot imagine how to fill.

'My grandfather never spoke his name again.'

'I'm so sorry,' I say looking more at the pen marks and carved out letters on the little school desk than at her.

'You couldn't have known.'

Real life laps at the edges of our conversation. 'We need to come back to this, Araminta. I need to understand but, right now, we have to deal with Andrew – with my part in the downfall of this poor house.'

As arranged, Andrew is waiting by the entrance to the museum. It has been easy to leave everything locked up this way, so that nothing could be interfered with. The only thing that has been moved is the door of the netsuke cupboard: I closed that carefully – and with Andrew's help so as not to smudge any fingerprints – because I couldn't put the alarm on without it. I wanted the alarm activated in case Patch came back: only one thing is certain and that's that I don't know who he is – I never actually have.

'No news, I take it?' Andrew asks.

I have had more 'news' in the past twenty-four hours than I know what to do with. 'Not from Patch,' I say. I wonder if I should call him 'Patrick' now that he has betrayed us. 'You?'

'Let's sit down and go through it all.' He's obviously used to this – to dealing with people whose lives have turned upside down. I remember that Leo will be awake soon: I'm going to have to tell him everything too. I have so many questions for Araminta: I'm far from knowing what 'every-thing' is yet.

Araminta is in the kitchen. She has put the kettle on, got cups and saucers and a teapot out for us, as if she'd never been away: at least one thing is righted.

'We have some API information from Heathrow,' Andrew says. 'Mr Samson bought a ticket there last night.'

'API?' Araminta asks.

'Advance Passenger Information, the legal requirements before you fly, passport number and so on.'

'He used to live in Australia.' My voice is quiet.

'The ticket was to Thailand,' Andrew says. 'But that doesn't necessarily mean he's gone – people do sometimes buy tickets as a decoy.'

'Doesn't a digital passport record where you go?'

'Not in the way you might think,' Andrew says. 'But we're still digging, looking into any past convictions he might have.'

'What about Mike Green – or whatever his real name is?' I sit down at the table, happy for Araminta to make the tea: my hands are shaking, I couldn't trust myself with boiling water.

Andrew nods slowly. 'We'll look at the CCTV from the Co-op in the High Street and the car park by the sea front – they both show the road – but I think we'll find he's a hired hand, a thug employed by someone who Mr Samson owed money to.'

'Do you think that's it?' I ask. 'That he owed money? I know he didn't have any money but, really, who does?' And then I remember that he borrowed the money for the cottage from Araminta as well as me: that the seeds of this deception were already in place.

Araminta puts the tea things on the table. The ancient sugar lumps that Malcolm found for the trustees are still in the bowl. 'Do you think he meant to do this, Andrew?' she asks.

'Do you mean, when he first arrived here was this his whole intention?'

She nods.

'I don't think so,' Andrew says. 'There are so many more things he could have taken if he'd been part of an organised crime operation. And he would have been more methodical.' He clears his throat. 'If I had to guess, and this is a guess – you can't hold me to it.' He half-smiles, trying to show us that he's on our side, that he's sorry to bring all this bad news to our table. 'It's not rocket science to assume that he was spooked by our friend finding him, grabbed what he could, and got out as quickly as possible.'

He nods his thanks to Araminta as she pours the tea. 'But a warrant has been issued for his arrest and, depending where he ends up, we could extradite him.'

'And the netsuke?' Araminta asks although I think we both know the answer.

'I don't think he'll hang on to them for long.'

'There's a very strong market for them, worldwide.' Araminta's cup shakes slightly in its saucer. 'They're very collectable. And they're worth at least a million pounds, depending on which ones are gone.'

'They're all gone,' I remind her.

'If you could get us as many photos of them as you can . . .' Andrew looks at us both. 'At least we'll have something to go on. And you'll have a crime number for your insurance.'

Araminta explains to him about the insurance, the lack of it. I look out of the window while she talks and wish my skin wasn't burning with embarrassment: that I'd been more cautious, more adult.

'There are some very detailed sketches,' I say. 'That Patch did.' I feel more stupid than ever.

'And there will be some photographs in some of the older guidebooks,' Araminta says.

'Why though? Why would he do it?' It's the thing I most need to know.

'Sometimes we never find out, I'm afraid. It could be drugs, gambling: we might know more when we start digging through his record. It's a universal truth, I'm afraid, can happen to anyone – every man has his price.

'And you never know . . .' Andrew continues '. . . what that price might be.'

'You couldn't have known, Cate,' Araminta says. 'You

heard what Andrew said. Probably Patch himself didn't know he was going to do it.'

And then it is 10 a.m. on Sunday – the time we have to open the museum. We can't abandon all the progress we've made by not opening on our second day after the newspaper article. Andrew asks us to keep the oriental room locked up until the fingerprint people can get there and that's it, we are left to carry on as we were before.

It reminds me of the day Richard died, of the way Leo still needed his tea and the day turned into night, the night back into the dawn of the next day. The way we had to carry on walking round, speaking, being ourselves, even though he had gone.

And then my mind cuts to an image of Simon and me, of the moment our lips met, the charged atmosphere, the electricity. Richard's face flashes like a strobe against it. Every man has his price.

Chapter Twenty-Six

If it wasn't for the questions that are burning in my mind and the big white sign we've stuck on the oriental gallery door that says 'Due to a fault with the lighting system, this gallery is closed for today' and then adds several untruths about how sorry we are and how soon we will return to normal, this would be a great Sunday. There are even more people than yesterday.

I'm suddenly suspicious, in the way that Araminta was when we first arrived, that more visitors means more opportunity for trouble. I watch them like a hawk, trying not to be too obvious as I assess their bags, their pockets, whether they 'look' like a thief or not.

'Patch is not the first person to steal from the museum,' Araminta had said to me as the sun crept into Crouch-on-Sea this morning. As soon as these visitors go, she can tell me the rest of her story. Maybe my heart will ache a little less for Richard, a little less for her, when I hear the whole thing.

Leo is meeting-and-greeting front of house. He is great at persuading the most recalcitrant teen to wear an explorers' hat as they look around the galleries. There is no time at all to talk to him about Patch and Leo doesn't seem to have noticed that he's gone.

At about 4 p.m., when the stream of visitors that hasn't abated since 10 a.m. has reduced to a trickle, most of them now wandering towards the gardens or back out to their cars, Leo comes to hand me what's left of the stack of plastic pith helmets.

'What do I want with these? I'm stuck in the box office – there's no room for them in here.' There's barely room for one human in the tiny booth.

'We're going to the beach, Sophie and me. And Curtis later. We're going to have a picnic tea. Maybe a barbecue.'

'We've got two hours left until the museum closes.' I want to remind him that he has responsibilities.

He chews his lip, pats his thighs lightly with his palms. 'I promised though.' He puts his head on one side and gives me what he clearly believes is a disarming smile: it's a comedy smile but it does the job. 'Go then, shirk your duties. Hang out in the sun with your mates.' I'm smiling but I add, silently, 'Because the rest of life, from here on in, gets so fucking complicated it's almost unbearable.' And then I think of Richard, and of 'complicated' and how life really was unbearable for him: completely unbearable.

'Have a good time,' I say, and I mean it.

*

I need to stop. I need space to think, to take stock of everything that has happened, is happening. When the last visitors are definitely gone and I have locked the huge museum door from the inside with the old iron key, walked through to our end – via the off-limits oriental room – and set the alarm, I am fit for nothing. By the time I was making small talk with the last people, I was barely talking in sentences, unable to hold the string of one thought long enough for it to link up with the next. The empty silence is exactly what I need.

There is an open bottle of white wine in the fridge door. I pour myself a glass and stare into it as if it holds all the answers, as it if were a crystal ball. I have so many questions, but I'm afraid of the answers.

I go through to the dining room, where I can open the big French windows and feel less hemmed in, but still in the house – to take care of it in the way I've failed to so far.

I stretch my legs out in front of me, flex my toes. The rug underneath them, which stretches almost to the edges of the mahogany floorboards, is faded but still patterned with the geometry of the East. I follow the pattern, the gold, the ruby-red threads, from one corner to the next, sticking to the angles and the loops, forcing myself to breathe deeply, to order my thoughts.

Next to the big portrait of Colonel Hugo is a much smaller one of Harriet. I don't know why I couldn't see it before, the oval jaw, the high temples. The outline of hers and Araminta's faces is exactly the same. Araminta looks like Harriet.

'Cate?' Araminta interrupts my thoughts. 'Room for another?' She is holding an empty wine glass and what is left of the bottle.

'Of course,' I say and, as she sits down in front of the portrait, 'You look so like your grandmother.'

'I know. She always said so.' She smiles up at the picture. 'Today was amazing, wasn't it? So many visitors.'

It's kind of her to stress the positive rather than the fact we've lost a million pounds' worth of exhibit. 'We have a lot to discuss.' I take a sip of my wine, steady my nerves.

'Let me start at the beginning,' she says. 'It's the only way I can get it all straight, protect everyone.'

'You don't have to pro—' I start to say but she interrupts.

'Explain, that's a better word. The only way to explain properly.'

I nod at her to continue.

'The thefts first. The other thief, if you like. The other thief was my father, Geoffrey. Geoffrey got into trouble – anywhere he could. He was expelled from school, sent down from university. He was a troubled boy who grew up into a troubled man. His affair with my mother was a terrible scandal: he was married, she – my mother – was only eighteen.' Her voice fades, becomes misty with the past.

'And eventually, he got into trouble with money: gambling debts. He was a compulsive man – an addict, we would call him today. And he stole from the museum to support his habit.

'It took my grandfather a long time to realise it was

Geoffrey. Colonel Hugo wasn't the easiest person either: he was prone to terrible rages. He accused the staff, the locals, anyone he could. It never occurred to him that it could be his own son.'

I can barely breathe: I sit stock-still.

'And then my grandfather caught him in the act and it was irrefutable. He called the police, pressed charges. He cut Geoffrey out of the will and banished him from the estate, told him never to come back.' She looks across at me. 'And he didn't: he didn't come back to see Richard or me ever again. Richard had been living here for a long time by then: his mother was no more capable than our father. I was lucky, really, with my mum.' She smiles then. 'I lived with my mum, had a loving home to go back to when things got rough up here at the house. A luxury my brother didn't have.'

Hearing her call him 'my brother' is almost unbearable. I reach out and hold her hand.

'And then, one day, my grandfather called us both to his office and told us that Geoffrey was dead. No details at that time. We hadn't seen him for years: hadn't been allowed to see him, we found out later. The jasmine wall against the glass side of the playroom? That was part of my grandfather's defence against what he saw as Geoffrey's terrible influence, in case he came to Hatters to see us.' She sniffs a little and reaches into the waistband of her tweed skirt for a tiny cotton handkerchief. It is perfectly white. 'The night Geoffrey died was the only time I ever saw my grandfather cry.'

I give her a hug; my sister-in-law, this pressure cooker of family secrets. An unimaginable burden was placed on her and I wonder where her fury is, how she keeps it so carefully under control.

'I was old enough to go to his funeral, and eventually to know the truth of how he died. My grandfather decided that Richard wasn't: people accepted what they were told in those days.'

'Except for Richard.' I can imagine my crazy, interested, husband with his lifelong love of questions. The not-knowing must have driven him to distraction.

'He was younger, of a different generation. Of a different background too, despite us sharing a parent.' She clears her throat and continues. Outside, the clock on the back of the house chimes and its clear note floats out and up and into the trees.

'I don't know much of the circumstances of Geoffrey's death but he had hit rock bottom. He'd been disowned and cut off from his family, he was in terrible debt and he had nowhere to turn. I don't think he was a bad man – not at all, but he had terrible demons.' She dabs her face with the handkerchief.

'My grandfather blamed himself, of course, and no one – not the employees, the family, the villagers – no one ever mentioned my father's name again. People around here adored my grandfather, you see. He was very kind to them and they couldn't bear to see him so sad. The only person who ever brought it up again was Richard.'

'When he was twenty-one?'

She nods, dabs at the corner of her mouth with the handkerchief. A tiny gold lion embroidered on its corner flashes in the light from the window. 'There was a terrible row. Richard had come back from university: he'd finished his studies and was staying here for the summer before he went to London. I don't know what had driven him, maybe another argument with his mother or something, but he blamed our grandfather for Geoffrey's absence from our lives. Geoffrey had stopped seeing us long before my grandfather banned him from Hatters, but Richard would never believe that. He didn't remember it all as clearly as I did.'

There is little noise around the house. The trees above us dip and whisper in the gentle breeze, birds sing in the distance. Apart from the faint but constant smell of old smoke, of bonfires, it is bucolic, idyllic. If you close your eyes, you can convince yourself that the smell is just an autumn bonfire: that we are clearing the garden of the summer's vines, getting ready for the season's change, for the shorter evenings.

'I wasn't part of it: I remember my grandfather smashing the study door shut. Making sure it was only Richard and him in there, that no one down the corridors or in the offices could hear them: everybody in the building heard them of course, every single person.' She sighs. 'Richard asked me too, but I couldn't tell him anything: I wasn't allowed.' She grinds her shoe against the floorboards, tips the toe of it onto the rug. The black leather is dusty grey with what is left of summer. 'I wondered for years whether I should have told the truth. And then, when Richard . . . You know.'

I have no idea what to say next. I am a dumb beast and my body has been replaced with the mounted frame of one of the animals. My eyes are glass and staring, my mouth is full of plaster teeth, solid pink stone tongue.

The house has claimed me as its own.

I try to remember that this loss belongs to her too – the loss of the brother she loved and hadn't been able to see for years – but there isn't room in my hurt heart for other people's problems.

'And that's it?' I am reeling. One stupid conversation, one banal argument. One single moment that ricocheted through my family for years: that cast a shadow over my whole marriage. 'That's the whole reason he never spoke to his grandfather again? Ever? Just a family secret?'

'Family secrets can be huge, Cate.' She gestures at herself. 'They destroy those who know them and they torture those who are outside them.'

I shake my head. The pain caused by Colonel Hugo's decisions whispers through the leaves outside, drifts in through the French windows.

'My grandfather was a deeply principled man.' Araminta's voice is controlled, measured, and I hear some of the old her in it. 'His overriding sense was one of duty. We were his family and he loved us but this . . .' She means the house, its secret playroom, the soot stains rising up under the eaves and choking the gargoyles, its stolen treasures. 'This was his duty and he did everything he could to protect its legacy, our heritage. That's what drove him. He owed it to his parents, his grandparents. He owed it to his children and their children.'

I almost speak, but I can't find the words.

'My responsibility towards this house, this line, is everything to me. And I think it runs through Leo completely naturally.' She takes hold of my hand again. 'I think you have it too, Cate. I think you feel the house in you. You are part of its story now.'

Now that Araminta has started, she cannot stop. She is completely disarmed by these memories: I am paralysed by her revelations.

'My grandfather was not a cruel man. He was kind and loving and generous.'

I almost interrupt, this is so far from my truth, from what I can see of her story, of Richard's.

'Hugo was an officer in the First World War. Part of his instructions were to supervise the execution of men who had deserted: he went through unimaginable horror. My grandfather had nightmares about "Those boys," about what happened to them. He woke up screaming, every night, for the rest of his life. He had been a boy too, of course, but one from a different social background.' She is pleading for his memory, for me to forgive him. 'But when he was young, he was desensitised, frozen by his experiences. He couldn't understand what Geoffrey did. Couldn't forget.'

I reach forward to top her wine glass up but she waves her hand across the top of it. I fill mine.

'My father was so reckless: a gambler; a drunk; a woman-iser – my mother was far from his only affair. Geoffrey rebelled in every way he could and he and Hugo spent a lifetime at loggerheads. I have spent decades trying to put my father's mistakes right, trying to do the best by my grandfather. It hasn't helped anyone.'

'Leo is your nephew.' It is like a birth, the realisation that I am not Leo's only living relative.

'I cannot tell you how much he brings to my life.'

I have to get out of the house. I have to put some space between me and these seething, overwhelming, ghosts.

'Are you up to a walk?' I ask her. 'I need some fresh air.'

I check on Leo on my way out. He texts back quite quickly, still on the beach, still blissfully unaware.

I hook my arm through Araminta's as we walk the gravel path at the side of the woodland. 'How do you live with this sadness? Doesn't it break your heart?'

Araminta smiles. 'When I was young it made me sad. I was eleven when Richard was born and, oh my goodness, how I loved him. But although I knew – I knew he was my brother, I mean – I also knew that no one must find out. My mother imagined the difficult days would be the feast days: birthdays, Christmas.' She stops for a moment as we round the corner of the house, as the emerald lawns open up in front of us. 'But the difficult days were the ordinary ones. The days when my grandfather would read me a story and then I'd get my wellington boots on to go home – in my nightie and dressing gown – while Richard went to the nursery, stayed here in the house.'

My heart aches for the little girl she was. The gravel crunching under our feet as we walk is the same path she would have taken back to the cottages in the dark, her mind full of witches and dragons, ponies and explorers.

'Didn't you think it was horribly unfair? It's so unkind.'

'Not at all. Our father was at boarding school by the time he was six, our grandfather even younger. We thought we were lucky, Richard and me.'

The peacock sweeps past us, shaking his tail in disdain. None of these revelations have made him better tempered. Araminta points up and I see two of his hens on the flat roof of the stable block to my right.

'So Richard was happy here?'

'Enormously. We both were. Our father was hardly ever here and Richard's mother, well, I assume you know her – knew her.'

I nod. 'They weren't close.'

Araminta weighs it up. 'She wasn't the simplest of women but then, her life – and her marriage – wasn't always easy either. And Richard was fine – he had our grandfather – Hugo – and he had me.'

We walk the boundary of the garden in silence. There have been so many words already. They all click through my thoughts in turn: Richard; Hugo; Geoffrey; Patch.

Back to the holes left by each of them. The hole left by Patch is shrinking with each minute: it's Richard I long to talk to.

Araminta makes her customary hot milk when we get back to the house. I choose another glass of wine.

'Did you hear that?' Either my ears are playing tricks on me or there is something outside the back door.

Araminta shakes her head, listens, and shakes it again. 'Hear what?'

It comes again. It is a scratching, and – faintly – a sort of mew.

I go down the corridor and open the back door. Three fat round fox cubs dart away from the movement. They wait, at a safe distance, and watch me. Their fur is glossy and red, their eyes alive and black. I close the door gently.

'Araminta.' I open the fridge, take out ham and cheese. 'I think you have visitors.'

Chapter Twenty-Seven

Leo is sad that Patch is gone. We sit out at the table by the lake to talk and the two gold statues make my heart ache for what might have been. I pick at a patch of green lichen on the table to keep from looking up at them.

Leo is rubbing his head. 'I don't feel very well today.'

'Did you have a good time last night? Did you drink beer at the beach?'

'Yes.' He fails to see the connection. 'Martin came too. We had a laugh. He'll never be my best friend though. That will always be Curtis. I thought Patch was my friend too, but he's not.'

I don't elaborate, not yet. I will wait and see how much the loss of Patch bothers him before I go deeper into it with him. It may never be necessary.

He takes the news of Araminta's family connection in his stride too, barely bats an eyelid. 'I can't call her Mrs Minta now,' he says. 'I have to call her auntie or aunt.'

'That would be lovely. She said that your dad, her brother, used to call her Min. Shall we call her Aunt Min?'

'Like Minnie Mouse,' he says and seems happy with that.

Andrew's fingerprint people finally finish in the Japanese gallery. They have had to have full access to our rooms upstairs too: to poor Araminta's jewellery box.

'There is always a chance Mr Samson is still in the UK,' he explains. 'And, of course, he might always change his mind if he has gone, try to come home.'

Although I want Patch to be punished for the way he has treated Leo, the house in general, I have no desire to ever see him again. I have shut the trapdoor of that relationship as fast as it once opened.

'He bought his ticket at the airport – that wasn't planned.' He shrugs as if the fact that Patch hadn't made advance plans to leave will make things better: perhaps it will in time.

'I don't know why I'm surprised,' I say to Araminta after Andrew has gone. 'Every man I've ever loved has run away.' I stare down at the grey cobwebs clinging to the legs of the bench outside. Araminta is snipping at the unruly grass with a pair of kitchen scissors.

'Suicide, archaeological digs, fucking Thailand or wherever. It's all the same. Do all men run away?' It's a rhetorical question and I don't expect her to answer.

'My grandfather suffered because he didn't run away,' she

says quietly. 'He stayed and did everything he thought was expected of him. That didn't help anyone either.'

And then she hugs me. Bends her small frame – small like Richard and Leo, I see now – and curls her thin arms around me. I press my face against her jumper, stretch my hands up to hug her back. I am not alone and nor is she – anymore.

Leo is over at the pond, trailing his fingers in the green water. The orange back of a fish swells to the surface, a flash, a gift.

'What did you talk to your solicitor about?' I need to know. We cannot pretend that it didn't happen.

'I have a trust fund: a stipend that pays out from my grandfather's estate. I wanted to see if it could be cashed in: if we could use it as a lump sum to keep the museum going for longer.'

So simple. 'Why didn't you tell me?'

'Because I promised him.' It's the tiny sad answer to so much.

My heart aches for what she has sacrificed on the altar of familial duty.

'If I'd told you, you would start to unravel the family connection, inevitably. I went to see Myles too – the trustee who died – he was the only one to know who I am. My grandfather trusted him implicitly.'

There is so much time we need to make up.

Leo looks back at me from the edge of the pond. 'Not all men run away, Mummy.'

'What?'

'What you said to Mrs Minta, to Aunt Min, I mean. About Daddy and Simon. And fucking Thailand.'

I am stunned into silence, overwhelmed by guilt. These men left me, not Leo. This is not his axe to grind: he is, literally, the collateral damage in a world that hurtles past without sympathy and he was never supposed to hear me say that.

'I didn't run away. I never have, and I'm a man. I didn't run away in the fire and I'll never run away when I'm married to Sophie.' And then he adds, quickly, 'When I'm older, when we want to get married.' He bangs his hands onto his thighs, just once, loud in the still air. 'But I didn't run away so you're not right.'

I have never been so glad to be wrong.

Later, when I am sitting in my room processing all of this information: reframing my place in the house, in the family, there is the familiar gentle knock on my door – too soft to be Leo, it can only be Araminta.

'Come in,' I call.

She turns the door knob slowly and seeps into the room like a ghost. 'Can I talk to you?' She gives me a half-smile.

'More?' I smile as I say it. My privacy – my contemplation – has lasted little more than an hour but I don't mind.

'There is more, but I want you to be certain of the context. Sure that you understand that no one meant any of this, especially not my grandparents.'

She sits on the windowseat, her hands on her knees.

There is a diamond ring on the ring finger of her right hand, her wedding finger is bare. 'My father loved Richard and me,' she says. 'And he adored Colonel Hugo. But some things are bigger than rational thought, than what we want. What Geoffrey did was terrible, absolutely broke his father's heart, but he was in over his head. As Andrew said, every man has his price.'

And then I remember the white envelopes fluttering from the chimney, the bailiffs at the door, the horror of watching the postman walk up the path with more and more bills and last chances.

'Richard spent all our money. That's how we lost our house.' It is my turn to whisper. 'He took out loans, a few thousand here, some hundred there. I never knew what he did with the money. I suppose it was a genetic trait.' Gambling was the most likely thing Simon and I had decided at the time. Online gambling was starting to be recognised as the pernicious danger it is, and we could only conclude that the long hours Richard spent on the computer, locked away, were evidence of another – secret – part of him, a part he couldn't share with either of us. A part that consumed him.

Araminta is that suspicious calm again, the face she does so well: drained of animation and unreadable. Her cheekbones stand out and her jaw is a firm line of bone. The woman in the painting behind her holds her face the same way.

'Richard wasn't a gambler,' she says.

I don't want to make her think ill of her brother. It doesn't matter now whether he was or he wasn't: it's in the past and the consequences of it are all unchangeable. 'It's gone, Araminta. It doesn't make him a bad person. Like your father, he was eaten up with demons.'

'You don't understand,' she says. 'Richard didn't gamble with that money. At least, not in any conventional sense. I didn't know where it had come from – he was completely estranged from our grandfather by then.'

And the bombshell lands, launched from her to me across my bedroom.

'I had letters, over the years, from Richard,' she says.

'He wrote to you?' It's a complete surprise to me. A wave of frustration swells in me and I wonder if Richard was still writing to Araminta during those years when he found it almost impossible to communicate with me or with Simon. When he couldn't talk to his counsellor or the psychiatrists, the legions of professionals who tried to help him. I will feel betrayed if he was. I will be more angry, more cheated, than I already am.

'Each one of those envelopes contained a cheque. It kept us going. I assumed he'd done as well in life as we'd always believed he would, that he could afford it.'

A flicker of light opens in the back of my mind, glows and turns amber, licks at and catches the crinkled edges of my understanding. The explosion of realisation is colossal. Memories and conversations and suspicions and arguments stream through my head in a sudden wall of sound: the soft persistent noise of Richard crying; the gurgles of an infant Leo; the rumbling growl of the lion who came to me on the upstairs landing when I thought I was going to die.

Araminta walks the few steps across the room. She stands beside me, looking concerned. I want to laugh.

'He couldn't afford it. No.'

'Richard sent cheques every few months. No card, no address, just a few lines and a cheque. Until the last one.'

My lost house, my stolen bricks and mortar, is here. All the lunatic loans that Richard took out, all the stupid risks, the dangerous secrets: they made their way here; they propped up the apes and the elephants and the ocelots; they cut the grass and mended fences and cleaned the wide glass fronts of the dioramas.

I learnt not to care about the money a long time ago: I only resented the secrets. I say the same thing I've said about Richard so many times: 'Why didn't he tell me?'

But even as I say it, I know Richard didn't tell me lots of things about being ill. He didn't tell me what tortured his dreams and made him scream out in the night.

He kept so much to himself: the demons; the debts; the despairs.

'The last one, no cheque – just a letter – came a week or so before he died.'

'Araminta, Min. Can we take this downstairs? Get a cup of tea?' If secrets are going to spill out, if there are going to be hard words and difficult confessions, I don't want them to be in here, to be in my bedroom. This space is not yet recovered from the loss of Patch: I need it to be clear and happy – my sanctuary and home to the tiny lightning-quick bats who roost in the spaces above the window. It cannot be a place where dark thoughts can creep about in the night, shuffle and twist under my bed.

Araminta has brought the envelopes downstairs with her. They are in her hand, I know she is going to ask me to look at them but I don't know that I can. She closes her eyes and I sense she is imagining him, summoning him up. I do the same.

Behind her closed eyes she is far away: elsewhere, else-when, but the Richard she sees will not be the grey-faced man I saw at the end, the broken man who couldn't take another day of the torture his life had become.

She hunts for the handkerchief again, this time it is in her sleeve. She blows her nose elegantly: I hadn't known that was possible.

'He told me, in the letter, that he was going away. And he talked about you. He talked about things that didn't really make much sense – at least, not before he died. He talked about the nature of exploration, of moving on to new experiences. I didn't know what he meant by that then. I could have stopped him.'

I am crying now too. I can feel Richard here in the room, the pale quiet breath of the ghost boy. I imagine that I can reach down and take his little hand in mine, that he leans his small soft body against my leg.

'And he said his marriage had been a wonder. "As much as I could have ever hoped for, Min, and then some more," were his exact words.' She unfolds the paper in her hand although she obviously knows it off-by-heart. 'And I was so very pleased for him, so glad that it had worked out that way for one of us. He said that he wasn't afraid to leave you because he had the best friend in the whole world and that he could trust Simon to take care of you when he was gone.' She chokes on the word 'gone', gulps in air after it as if saying it threatened to suffocate her.

I wipe my eyes again. 'You couldn't have stopped him. No one could. Except perhaps me.'

She offers me the handkerchief but I shake my head and wipe my nose on my sleeve instead.

'He said it was time for him to go: he was excited – it had taken a long time to get things into place with you and Simon and Leo, apparently, and it hadn't been easy. But now he'd got all his ducks in a row and could rest easy.

'And then he was gone,' she says. 'What if I could have saved him and I didn't?'

Those last days were liminal. Richard slipped between waking and sleep – there was little difference between the two states of being. When he was awake, his eyes focused on objects that weren't there, when he was asleep he cried, softly and quietly.

The flat was dark in the day and light at night. I kept a routine for Leo, took him to school, cooked his tea, but my own life was beyond fixable: I had taken a leave of absence from school – compassionate leave that I knew, in my heart, was the countdown to Richard's death.

Death waited for us like a friend. We asked it to leave

when Leo came home from school, hid it in the cupboards – shoved in and ready to pour out when we forgot it was there and opened the door. We disguised it under piles of coats, tried to put it out with the rubbish, asked it – over and over – to leave. Death outstayed its welcome and it was all we could do to keep it from Leo's door, from introducing itself with that sickly breath, those thin red lips, to our son. We shuddered at the thought of death's long bony hand clasping Leo's, walking him along the road and out of sight. We did not trust death.

And then, one morning, Richard woke up. The real Richard. The man I married, the man who held me up, who made me laugh. The man I trusted above all others.

'Stay here,' I begged him. 'Stay the same while I take Leo to school.' I just wanted to talk to him, to grip him to me. I wanted to spend real time with him.

The real Richard ate breakfast with Leo. He was slow and croaky, but he was him again. There was a light in his eye that had blown out before: I could see the spark wavering and glowing, ebbing and flowing as he breathed.

The real Richard was hidden inside the body of the ill Richard. His arms and legs were emaciated. What had once been a muscled barrel chest was pale and slack, his skin too big for his ribs, but the real Richard was here and he was shining out of the dim dull body.

When I got back from taking Leo to school I was breathless and sweaty. I had run home through the leafy streets, past our old house – the scar of a journey that Leo and I had to make every day. I burst into the flat, threw my coat off and looked for Richard. I had imagined a hundred conversations on the way back. I had seen him enter and leave these phases so many times. I had not believed he would come back from the last one – it had gone on for months.

The unwashed dark smell of madness still hung around the flat. It wasn't something that could be banished in a day. You can't open the windows and blow that kind of illness out, empty your world of germs and right it instantly. There is no amount of hot yellow lemon drinks or vibrant orange juice, no bright luminescent colours you can swallow, that can relight the person you have lost to depression. But, if you are lucky, they will occasionally swim to the surface, gasp at the air there like a dying man, and maybe float awhile.

Richard was in our bedroom. He was sitting on the edge of the bed, and facing away from me. The room smelled like a damp wool coat – that is the smell of death as it hovers nearby: damp wool, and daffodils that have been in a vase too long, that have turned sweet and rotten. I would know that smell anywhere.

Richard's back was a knobbly xylophone. His vertebrae shone inside his skin and his ribs were dark stripes whipped into his sides. He was wearing tracksuit bottoms that had once stretched against his runner's legs, but now hung from him, emphasising his weakness.

He patted the bed and I lay down next to him. I turned and kissed his cheek.

'I can't do it anymore, darling.' His voice was calm, controlled. 'I can't go back there.'

I nodded. Even if I could have found words, they would have been platitudes, hollow promises. I understood exactly what he meant.

'As soon as I'm ill again . . .' He put one arm around me. His fingers traced the shape of my shoulder. 'As soon as I'm ill again I'll lose the motivation. It's not that I want to live, Cate, it's that I can't move myself to die once I'm trapped in that Hell.'

The words were painful. But listening to him weep while he slept, hearing him call out to hallucinations of demons and dread, that was worse.

'If I was an animal, my darling, you'd let me die. You'd help me.'

And I nodded again, nodded my assertion that, yes, I would help him, I would set him free.

I moved over in the bed and death rolled into my place.

'And so I helped him,' I whisper to Araminta. 'We were careful that I didn't break the law – Leo would only have one parent as it is – we couldn't risk anything. But I helped him: I facilitated his death. And then I waited to be told about it, that it was done.'

She says nothing.

'So you couldn't have saved him: I would have been there to stop you.'

She reaches down into her bunch of letters. Richard's

writing looks up at me, a real piece of him, here in his house.

'He sent me this with that last letter. He said I would know when to give it to you.'

And there it is. An everyday white oblong envelope: and at the same time the thing I had dreamed of. One more message from Richard. I reach out with trembling hands and take it from her.

Chapter Twenty-Eight

'*To Cate, when she gets home*' it says on the envelope. It says it in Richard's writing.

I know that where I open this letter matters. I will only read it for the first time once. I cannot imagine what Richard has left to say. The benefit of knowing exactly when someone is going to die is the hours of crying together, the holding each other tight, the words of love that are all you have left. Richard and I have said it all.

I walk away from Araminta in silence, and through the quiet of the museum. We are closed today and there is no danger of being interrupted.

When I get to Gallery One, I switch on the light. The lighting shudders and flickers, before peeling into brightness like the first dawn. Around me, sleeping bears and startled chimps stare wide-eyed, not even the sudden light making them blink.

I look at the back of the envelope where it has been stuck

down. Four years ago, Richard licked the line of glue on this, ran his fingerprint along its fold to make it stick. He is in the DNA of this paper, and his words are inside.

It opens easily, the glue was never designed to stay closed this long. I unfold the single sheet and, with the silent lions, the sombre elephant, the wide-winged stork watching over me, I start to read.

My darling Cate,

What do you think? What do you make of my grandfather's crazy world? Have you realised yet that the black dog that has devoured me ate up every man in my family, generation by generation? I assume so – and if not, ask Araminta. Tell her to tell you everything she knows, tell her I want you to.

I know Araminta well – she has been like a sister to me my whole life and I love her dearly – but she's a cantankerous old sod and, if you're reading this, then the two of you must have reached some kind of peace. It is peace that I want for you, my darling, and that is why I sent you to Hatters. For all its oddness, it is a beautiful place with so much happiness lying unnoticed beneath its silence and its secrets. Find the happiness, my darling Cate, for you and Leo – let Hatters take care of you. I was very happy there once upon a time.

I hope that Simon is there beside you – he has been the best friend a man could have. He has been in love with you since the moment we both set eyes on you, but I was the lucky one, I was the one you chose. Thank you for every moment.

I'm so sorry for how things worked out, that the curse of my family followed me however far away I got from the house. I could never explain how relieved I was that Leo had an extra chromosome, that he was not a carbon copy of my grandfather, my father, and me.

Even after everything you've done for me and we both know how much that is – I will always be, have always been, in your debt – I need you to do one more thing for me. Will you bring me home, Cate? To my grandfather who I punished with the pomposity of youth: by the time I was old enough to understand, it was too late – he'd died, lonely and without me. To my father who I didn't know how to forgive – or that forgiving him might have saved me. To Min, who has always adored me. To my magnificent son, the best thing I ever did. And to you, Cate, who gave me everything. Bring me home where I belong.

All my love, my darling. Be happy.

Richard

From: Cate Morris

To: Simon Henderson

Subject:

Mail:

The email sits, open but unwritten, on my laptop. I can't imagine what to put next. Part of me wants him to come immediately. But another part of me knows that I've changed. I'm not the person I was when Richard died, or directly afterwards: I need different things now and so does Leo. Leo's life and mine, at the same time as becoming ever more entwined, have diverged into our own independence.

I was sort of in love with Simon once, I know that. But that doesn't necessarily mean I still am. I know that if Richard walked back into my life, my heart would jump in my chest, thud with longing, and I would be in his arms before I'd drawn a breath. But Simon isn't Richard.

I have to ask Simon here – if we are to carry out Richard's last wish, Simon needs to be here too. Richard wanted Simon to be standing beside me.

I don't miss Patch like I miss Simon. I can't miss someone who never really existed, whose character was merely one more of his beautiful creations, a veil that he had invented, painted with all the shades I thought I needed. I know deep down that there was more to him, but that's something I can't share with anyone. We are all a product of our lives, and something in Patch had broken, stoppered up.

Andrew doesn't believe Patch will ever return to the UK – why would he, he has no one to return for. He has been charged, in his absence, with burglary and theft. His passport will not let him across UK borders without arrest or into any of the countries we have extradition treaties with. He is gone.

*

We have two major events today. We have prepared for them both, frantically, over the last four weeks.

The 30th of September is Colonel Hugo's birthday. He would be 125 years old today. He was born and died in this house, saw the orchard of apple trees, heavy with fruit now and gnarled with age, grow up past his head and celebrate each spring with clouds of blossom. He would have seen generations of peacocks, perching vainly in the trees, turning themselves in the sun to make the most of their iridescent feathers.

When Colonel Hugo first looked out of the nursery window, the bedroom that is now Leo's, there would have been wide waterlilies blooming pink under Atalanta and Hippomenes, and gardeners bustling and busying, making the most of every corner of the garden.

We may yet get back to that. We have a commitment from the local Horticultural Society to get the kitchen garden back in shape. The fruits of the labours will be shared between the local schools and the food bank: grown for the town, by the town. That turns out to be very much how things are done around here, how they have been done for centuries.

Leo decided that his time as an artist was over: Sophie was always the biggest draw of the class and now he sees plenty of her without having to go. He gave his picture of our two gold statues to me: the two figures that he was going to paint in remain people-shaped spaces: white and anonymous, skating across the pond. I like that they could be anyone, might be anyone, one day. It hangs, framed, in my bedroom, echoing the view to one side of it, the view of the real thing.

Today is the 'official' launch of our new – sparkling clean – museum. We have opened more rooms, let the sun into the dusty sadness, removed covers and polished furniture. We haven't had time to make signage that explains the rooms but we have volunteers dotted around all over the place – new and enthusiastic – who will tell visitors what they know. Malcolm and Araminta are jointly in charge of the volunteers and are spending a lot of time together 'planning' and pottering in the kitchen garden.

I've worked closely with Poppy on today. She is running the art class now, fitting it around her studies and doing an amazing job. Today will publicise the work she does as much as the museum. Each day more and more visitors come, as the ones who've been the day before tell their friends how crazy it is, how very much worth seeing.

Poppy and I have only mentioned Patch once. 'I'm sorry about Patch,' she said, when I first went to her with the plan.

I shook my head. 'It doesn't matter.' I was surprised to find it was true.

She and I have worked like Trojans on this. Last night we were up till 2 a.m., praying to the gods of fine weather, and fixing and sorting the last tiny details.

Our prayers have been answered. The gardens are kissed with sunshine today, the wind has dropped away to a complete calm, it is as if every power, every wish or thought or spirit, is on our side.

The exhibition starts at the French windows in the Japanese room. We have moved the red cordon ropes so that we funnel the public through the side of the room and out into the garden.

There the magic begins.

Atalanta and Hippomenes dance in every shade of gold, every glowing incarnation. They point and run and balance, stretching their lithe legs and their long arms out towards the sky. They run from the danger of Aphrodite, away from her wrath, and – here and there – they appear as lions in papier mâché and clay and silver foil and every media under the sun, where she has caught them.

It is an astonishing display. Mobiles hang and spin from trees, totem pole figures of cereal boxes and glittering spray paint rise up from the lawn, paintings perch on easels – placed in the exact spot they represent. There are hundreds of versions of the lovers, each one made in Poppy's classroom, each one an achievement.

We are so proud to be displaying them today.

I check my watch. It is time to walk round to the front of the house. I walk slowly, trying to gather my thoughts, trying to stay calm.

The familiar sound of tyres on the gravel reminds me of my first day here, of how little I knew and how much I assumed. The slam of a car door makes me look up.

Simon hasn't changed. There is more grey in his beard and his tan is darker, but the way he opens his arms to me, the tightness of the way he holds me: that is all as it was. The awkwardness I had expected doesn't appear – it is safely stored away with our memories, with our younger selves.

'Thank you for coming,' I whisper into the fabric of his shirt.

'I'm here for good now,' he says, 'should you need a friend.'

I hug him back. It feels great to be able to do that again.

The chapel is cool and quiet. The visitors, and there were record-breaking numbers today, have gone home.

We changed out of our working clothes when we finished for the day. Everything was carefully timed so that we had an empty house, empty gardens, but time to walk down to the chapel together.

Everyone here loved Richard – except for Sophie, and she loves Richard's son. The local vicar, whose father baptised Richard as a tiny baby, has come out to say a few words and to make this the solemn occasion it needs to be.

I went to London to collect Richard's ashes earlier this week. I took Leo with me and, while we were there, we dropped into his old day centre: we saw Eric and Ollie and Sadie and Dean, just as he'd begged me when we first arrived at Hatters.

Everyone greeted him like a film star: lots of hugs and hand-shaking, lots of 'welcome back'.

'It's different now, Mum,' he said when we left. 'I love my old friends but I'm different now. My new friends are my now-friends. They know who I am.' He waved goodbye to his old classmates as we got in the car.

I understand him completely. Leo and I have been through so much together this summer. We have risen, phoenix-like, with the house and there is a special bond between those of us who really know how it all happened: the restoration applies to all of us who were there.

Exactly as he asked, I have brought Richard home. His ashes, left with the funeral director for four years while I thought about what to do with them, are in a strange black plastic urn.

I took it to the chapel when I got back and he will be there today, waiting for us, when we go in.

I stayed in that cool quiet when I took the urn in. I wanted to be alone with him for a few more minutes. I wanted to thank him, for everything.

'You would be so proud of Leo,' I whispered. 'Of who he is, of his bravery. And I hope you're proud of me: I've done my best.'

I smile through my tears. 'And thank you for sending Simon, I need a friend. I love that he loves Leo, I love that he loved you: but I'm not in love with him – I never was. We both know that, you and I.' I kiss the top of the urn before I leave him there. 'It will always be you, Richard. Always.'

*

We sit in one row of the chapel, all squashed on to one dark wooden pew. Sophie and Leo, Araminta, then me, Simon on the end.

The vicar is sensitive to our lack of organised religion. He talks, very briefly about Richard and about the family. He mentions, as I've asked him to, Geoffrey and Hugo. He talks about Harriet and the family.

He reads their names from the ledger, his hands wide on the gold edges of the lectern. We have had a calligrapher add 'Araminta Mary Buchan. 5th June 1952. Daughter of Geoffrey and Mary, sister to Richard.' She is the first woman to be recorded in the book. I am confident now that she will not be the last.

As we whisper our farewells to Richard, Simon squeezes my hand. Our fingers interweave, the crimped edge they made once before. It is good to have a friend.

On the other side, I hold Araminta's hand. It is good to have family.

The vicar lodges Richard's ashes in a cubby hole near the altar. Tomorrow, a stonemason will come to seal them in and, in time, a tablet will be laid over the top of it. A stone that will proclaim, in strong carved letters, who he was and that he lived here. A stone that will say the words we have chosen: that he was 'Richard Lyons-Morris, son of Geoffrey and father to Leo. Much loved father, husband, brother and friend.'

We are quiet as we walk back. The fox cubs skitter amongst the new statues, batting at dangling details with their paws, looking towards the back door for Araminta to bring them their tea. The sun is setting over the tops of the trees and sparkles of light dance in the leaves.

These are the gardens laid out by Richard's great-grandfather, a man who was part of my family. These are the lawns my husband and my sister-in-law played on as children. This is the place where, one day, a man will go down on one bended knee, tapping his thighs only once with nervousness, to ask his raven-haired solemn girl to marry him.

These are the lawns outside my house.

This is where we belong.

Acknowledgements

As usual, there is a whole village behind the writing and making of this book, even beyond my amazing teams at Simon & Schuster and Touchstone/Gallery.

In no particular order (because every piece of help and support is vital) ...

Thanks to Phil McIntyre, as usual, for his insightful comments and eye for a story. To the Inked Fingerlings for their support as friends and writers: good at both. To Fionnuala Kearney for reading it about 100 times and Jacqueline Ward for always being at the end of a phone line. Thanks to Susan Johnson for unerring support and museum tours: without you this story really couldn't have been written.

I'd like to thank Jess and Chloe Overton for giving me a space to start this story, and Dilys Hall for feeding a starving author. Thanks to Moniack Mhor: to the staff for my retreat week and the incredible care you show your writers, and to my MMU MM lot for being great – year in, year out.

Thanks to Nicola Martin and Deborah Michaelis for being a voice for Leo before it turned out that he had his own. Thanks to Max Richards for the game and Zachary

Frith for the hat. Thanks to Cate Benjamin and Patch Friend for the loan of your names and to Ben Fielding for fixing a stubborn technical problem.

Enormous gratitude goes to the Deal Bookshop, to Charn, Gemma, Ali, and Adam, for being so amazing. Best bookshop in the world: fact. And to Clare Baker, Janet Lewis, Hattie Douch, Jess Ryn, Fay Franklin and Bex Rechter for reading and making helpful suggestions. Thanks to Simon Nicholls for the mental health advice you gave me for another book that's ended up in this one.

I owe an enormous debt to the East Bridgford Support Squad Girls, without whom I would not have got through this year. I have found it so difficult not knowing where Jane is, but she is here – between each one of these pages, in every one of these words.

My amazing teams at Simon & Schuster and at Gallery books have been beyond fabulous and put together such a gorgeous package of a finished product: Jo Dickinson, Louise Davies, Clare Hey, Maggie Loughran and Lauren McKenna; Judith, Pip, Bec, Jess, Polly, Laurie, Rich, Gen; and all the sales team, especially S-J Virtue.

Thanks to Sarah Hornsley, best agent in the world, and to Colin for years of love and support.

Most of all, thanks to everyone who supported Grace: readers; bloggers; reviewers. You are the people who put the wind beneath my wings so that I could write a second novel. Thank you, I hoped you've enjoyed it.

THE
TRUTHS
AND
TRIUMPHS
OF
GRACE
ATHERTON

Grace Atherton, a talented cellist, is in love with David. Her life is about to fall apart in the most shocking of ways.

Nadia is seventeen and furious. She knows that love will only let her down: if she is going to succeed it will be on her own terms.

At eighty-six Maurice Williams has discovered a lot about love in his long life, and even more about people. And yet he keeps secrets.

Sometimes you have to hit the bottom in order to find a way back. And sometimes you need a friend, or two, by your side when you triumph.

AVAILABLE NOW IN PAPERBACK, EBOOK AND AUDIO

**SIMON &
SCHUSTER**

NEWS & EVENTS | BOOKS | FEATURES | COMPETITIONS

Follow us online to be the first to hear from
your favourite authors

booksandthecity.co.uk **@TeamBATC**

Join our mailing list for the latest news, events and
exclusive competitions

Sign up at
booksandthecity.co.uk